THE CUBIT

THE 2012 TRILOGY I

Fate or Coincidence...
It is your choice
to decide.

Chuck & Joanne :- My new friends from
Barclay Cottage
7-28-11

PETER GALARNEAU, JR.

ISBN: 978-0-9825129-0-6
978-159858-550-6 (Hardcover)

Text set in Times New Roman

This book is printed on acid-free paper.

Printed in the United States of America

Published by:

www.PTWilliam.com

DEDICATED TO:

Nelda, Forrest and Bobbi
For providing support for it all

The Drunken Sausage
For providing a place from it all

Arah Edgel Galarneau Cox Maloney
Who finally found Paradise

INTRODUCTION

I Was There...
And So Were You

It was near midnight on December 31, 1999. I'll never forget it. Beyond thinking about Prince and how he wanted to "Party Like It's 1999," I could not assure myself that all of the lights would not go out, that all of the computers would not shut down, that Mankind would not, in the next five minutes, find itself without the electronic means to support itself. The Computers would finally win. And my poor ass, along with thousands of others, standing dazed on, or near, the Roberto Clemente Bridge in Pittsburgh, would become nothing more than statistics. In all of my well-reasoned, left-brained conglomerations of experiences, I still imagined, on that starry night, that life was going to change in some dramatic way that made all of the idiotic soothsayers... intelligent.

Didn't we all?

If the clock turning "00" would have been the end of the world, then all of us—me, my wife, my brother-in-law, everyone I cared about (which suddenly included a couple of thousand people standing on a bridge)—would have met a collective, untimely death, one that had been invented by man, accelerated by man and promulgated by the information channels that man had crafted.

And that got me thinking...about End Times, about all the End Times that had already ended. You know, like the ones said to be predicted by Revelation. Names such as Joseph Smith, William Miller, The Watchtower Society, Herbert W. Armstrong, Jim Jones, Pat Robertson, Osho, David Koresh, Marshall Applewhite (the list really is very long) surfaced. Of course, so many of these "prophets" took with them too many innocent lives. These "prophets" were the antitheses of what prophets were really meant to be. For every Good there is Evil. For every real prophet there is a false prophet and in many cases, it's hard to tell them apart.

Taking the idea one step further, I started wondering why good people turn bad, why that wonderful mother who leads PTA meetings and takes SUV loads of kids to soccer practices ends up throwing her own children into a lake. What gets into people? What makes them turn? What nests inside us waiting to be released and what is the "thing" that induces such darkness to surface? Something ancient? Certainly, something not created by man. Something like…the Cubit, an antithesis in its own right.

I have always believed that the very best way to scare someone is to base a selected fear on truths rooted to reality. I started thinking about Revelation, rereading it for the umpteenth time, and how rote the idea was since, if you follow the scholarly theologians' way of thinking, Revelation is nothing more than a sign of its own time. But that's not how most of us think about the final book of the Bible. We think like fundamentalists. It's more exciting this way. We get to ask ourselves a whole slew of What If questions that can never, really, truly have answers, not unless you ally those answers to first-century Rome, and what fun is that?

Unfortunately (for me anyway), there are as many interpretations of Revelation as there are those who believe in it. And that can be quite daunting to wrap one's head around. So, in my search for an End Time that we could all believe in and that provided for me and my readers lots of possible twists and turns in plot, I chose an End Time rooted in reality—one that is just around the corner and was created by no one who has been alive for about a thousand years.

The ancient Mayans had their Gods but their calendar was not based on belief and therefore their End Date is not up for interpretation. The ancient Mayans used the Earth and the Sun and the planets and the stars as ultimate predictors and who can argue with such celestial magnates? Unlike the Bible that never really dates anything, for me, the Mayan calendar dated everything, beginning 26,000 years ago. How could such a primitive culture know of the precession of the Earth? How could such a primitive culture know that at the culmination of a 26,000 year cycle, the Earth and Sun would align on the Galactic Center? While Europe debated the flatness of Earth and how our planet was the center of the universe, the Mayans were documenting facts that would have proven these European thinkers wrong. And that primitive culture nailed down a date that would have, today, scientists and faith-mongers alike promoting ideas that *will* happen on December 21, 2012. What if this will be the end of the world…or, at least, the end of the world as we've lived it?

It's a human necessity to think about What If? The world that we know can't work correctly without a big, heaping helping of the unknown. What if everything had shut down on December 31, 1999? We will never know because, of course, Y2K was only as important as a calendar day clicking forward. The year 2000 came, nobody died on that beautifully yellow (they call it gold in Pittsburgh) bridge, and we all drank something to commemorate our continued, ignorant control of this planet.

Earth…

Time…

Humanity…

No wonder there continues to be a quagmire of confusion that ultimately culminates in masses of people wandering aimlessly on yellow bridges in big American cities waiting for The End.

Computer "geeks" told me I was going to be changed (and perhaps die) one second after December 31, 1999. I didn't believe them, only after I found that, since nobody threw me over the yellow bridge, I remained standing and everyone else looked depressed.

It was the first day of the new millennium: a day I had always looked forward to, more in regret of getting older than of the scant significance of the date (still, I did collect bottles of water and cans of green beans). But it was also a time for looking forward to the next End Date scenario. That is when The 2012 Trilogy was born.

You see, I AM only human and I will always drive myself crazy thinking about how people die (particularly me). How much better is it to die not alone, but with everyone else on the planet? That is why, I think, we hold onto these extinction scenarios. We live as social creatures and we should, therefore, die as social creatures. As one. Together.

So what does The 2012 Trilogy have to do with all of this opportunistic End Days' forecasting, the unending sagas presented by the rich exclamations of past fears, present ideals, and future ramifications emboldened by electromagnetic mind feeds?

It has nothing to do with them at all! It has to do with you and me and perceptions. Because, like all dates, December 21, 2012, will come and pass. Either humanity will continue to live by such Gregorian time capsules afterward, or some other planet will witness the bright light of a distant primitive culture as it quits.

But...sorry...there I go again.

Prophesying.

PART I

ENDANGERED

SUMMER 2007

Lenny's mother had warned him about the dangers of hitchhiking.

"I said, LET ME OUT OF THIS CAR!"

The driver's fist struck Lenny's left eye. The driver growled, "And I said, shut 'yer goddamn mouth!"

The station wagon fishtailed around the sharp corner at Pickett's Crossing and accelerated, sending a box, the size of a small coffin, to the back of the cargo bay and into the rear hatch. Behind them in close pursuit fishtailed two Kansas State Police cruisers. The lead cruiser lost its slide, hit the gravel shoulder and scraped the guardrail with a metal-to-metal screech that easily overpowered its siren.

The old man began mumbling again, talking to the steering wheel, slamming his large fists against its hard plastic. He looked in the rearview mirror and then abruptly at Lenny.

"See! I told you they were chasing me. Christ, they're gonna kill us both."

The old man whimpered. His eyes drooped; wrinkles rippled from the horrified brown marbles in sagging circular waves. He'd not slept in a long time—at least, that's the story he'd given Lenny when he'd picked him up that afternoon.

Lenny had been waiting for an hour at a 76 station near I-70 when the dusty 1984 Oldsmobile Custom station wagon had pulled in.

"Where you headed?" the old man had asked while topping off his tank.

"Pickett's Crossing, Kansas."

"Kansas!" The old man had scratched his gray stubby chin. "Yeah," he'd said. "Kansas. They'll never think of that."

"Excuse me?" Standing on the other side of the pump, Lenny had not heard the old man's mumble.

"Oh, nothing. Forgive an old man and his blabbering. I've not slept in several days."

He'd replaced the pump, had plucked a twenty from a thick wad of bills and had shoved it at the station attendant who'd walked from the garage to stare precariously when the old man had pulled in. "Come on, son. We got miles to cross."

Just a lonely soul out for a relaxing weekend drive, Lenny had thought—a simple farmer who'd suddenly decided that Pickett's Crossing, Kansas, would make a wonderful destination even if it was five hundred miles out of his way.

And the wad of money? His life's savings? Or, more realistically, blood money picked from a dead convenience store clerk, bank teller, or gas station attendant.

Lenny should have known. He should have listened to his mother.

It wasn't until they'd crossed the Missouri line into Kansas that Lenny had become concerned. The old man had become increasingly jittery, keeping his eyes more on the falling sun than on the road. He'd stopped talking about his lovely wife who'd died a few years back, about his grandkids (one of which had died recently), and about the beautiful state of Missouri and all the good years he'd lived there. Then, when the sun had disappeared and night had grown dense, the old man had clammed up altogether. He'd stared at length in his rearview mirror, often weaving across the four-lane interstate and onto the grass median or rocky shoulder like a blindfolded drunk driver.

That's when Lenny had noticed the box. Turning out of curiosity to see what attracted so much of the old man's attention, Lenny had seen it in the cargo area shoved tightly against the back side of the rear seat.

A wooden box the size of a small coffin.

Lenny had remembered their earlier conversation—the recent tragic death of the old man's three-year-old grandson—and Lenny had wondered. The box seemed to be just about the right size for...

"Shit!" the old man grumbled as one of the police cruisers rammed the tail of the station wagon. The old man hit the brakes, the cruiser collided with the tail bumper, glass from the rear hatch imploded, and the coffin rushed backward then forward, crashing into the back side of the rear seat as splinters of window stabbed Lenny's head and neck. The crumpled front end of the police cruiser sped up alongside the station wagon and veered into the rear door behind the old man. The squelch of the police cruiser's PA startled Lenny.

"Pull the fuck over, Professor Cower! You ain't got no escape this time! We'll make sure of that!"

Lenny saw two uniformed outlines in the front seat of the cruiser. The passenger raised his revolver and fired. Lenny flinched as the bullet webbed the front windshield, having missed his nose by the smallest inch.

"I'm gonna blow your goddamn head off," the officer warned, "if you don't stop this shit right now!"

The second cruiser came up from behind and smacked the tail of the station wagon as the lead cruiser continued to press the car from the left. Suddenly, the professor jerked the steering wheel hard to the right. Lenny saw the rushing guardrail as it snaked by his door at sixty miles an hour. He lowered his head and clutched the seat, readying himself for impact.

But none came.

The professor had found a side road, had abruptly turned onto it. Lenny raised his head in time to see the fiery inferno as the police cruisers collided, flipped, split the guardrail, and disappeared in a tumbling blaze down a steep embankment on the far side of the road.

The professor sat rigid. His foot seemed glued to the accelerator pedal. Stalks of corn a month from harvest sped by on either side of the station wagon, slapped the headlights and windshield as if trying to prevent passage. "Okay, kid. Where to now?" he grumbled.

The voice seemed far away. Lenny's mind was too busy sorting out the terror of being kidnapped and shot at. Hell, the cop's bullet had almost taken his head off. He stared at the windshield, his left eye swelling, and imagined his brains scattered across the dashboard, blood pasted in sticky masses to the webbed glass. Absently, he groped his face with his fingertips, assuring himself that his head was still there.

Kid, someone was saying. God, how he hated that name. His stepfather had always called him that. The wife-beating alcoholic had once threatened to blow Lenny's brains out, had placed a .44 magnum handgun right to his temple and had pulled back the hammer. "Okay, *Kid*," he'd slurred. "Tell me who the fuck your mama's been whoring around with."

Of course, his mother had never "whored" around with anyone. The accusation was his stepfather's Jim Beam delusion and Lenny had told him so. That's when his stepfather had pulled the trigger on an empty weapon. Click! And Lenny had seen his brains and blood scattered throughout his bedroom in much the same colorful way as he now saw them stuck to the windshield. The fear of death in 3-D Technicolor. It had made him sick then as it did now.

"Goddammit, kid! You're from around here. How do I get back to the main road?" The professor pulled a gun from under the seat and pointed it at him. "I said, how do we get the fu…?"

Lenny puked in a thin stream onto the dashboard, then turned and continued spraying across the gun and the professor's lap.

"Shit!" the professor yelled and stomped the brake pedal. The station wagon quickly jumped off the dirt road into the corn field, sliced through green stalks, and settled in a cloud of heavy dust. The professor quickly opened his door and rolled out. "Shit, shit, shit," he growled as he scoured his lap with dirt and crumpled stalks.

Lenny had the opportunity to run but his stomach was in control of the situation. He hiccupped a tiny amount of bile and rolled out of the car. The crisp smell of broken corn stalks deodorized the acidic stench of vomit. He took a deep breath, removed his shirt and wiped his mouth and chin, then spit the remaining taste.

The professor crossed in front of the station wagon's headlights and Lenny turned to run. "Wait!" the professor demanded. Lenny stood still, believing the gun was pointed at his spine. "Please. I need your help."

"You might as well shoot," Lenny said, "I'm not aiding and abetting any criminal."

"Ease up. I don't have the gun. And even if I did, I wouldn't shoot you." Lenny heard the shuffle of the professor's feet, felt him at his back. "Turn around, for God's sake."

Lenny thrashed out as he turned, throwing a kick to the groin and a backhand to the face. But the professor was quick—too quick for someone who looked to be nearly sixty years-old. He kicked Lenny's leg out from under him while grabbing his wrist in the same motion, then tossed Lenny aside as if batting away an annoying insect.

"Listen!" The professor knelt. "I haven't enough time for this. You're just going to have to trust me." The professor stared into the broken cornfield. His eyes were wild, intense. His nose flared, sucking in deep breaths. His hands played nervously with broken corn stalks. "They won't stop until they retrieve the Cubit," he whispered to the summer breeze, his voice quivering, acknowledging some fact that apparently scared the living hell out of him.

"The Cubit?" Lenny said.

The professor grabbed Lenny's upper arm and pulled as he rose. "Sorry about all of this. I shouldn't have involved you. It's just that...I needed some help. I'm getting tired. They won't let me sleep. The last time I had a solid meal was in Philly and that was two days ago."

"I thought you said you were from Missouri," Lenny said, backing a step from the professor's wrinkled stare.

"I lied."

"And your wife—your grandkids?"

"Dead as I've said. Murdered in their sleep the night I took off."

Murdered, Lenny thought. Now that made more sense than any of the lies the professor had told so far. Of course they'd been murdered—by the good professor no doubt. The police chase, the gun under his seat, his crazy mood swings and occasional unleashed anger, each a checkmark in the "yes" column for Lenny's description of a psychotic killer on the run.

"Hey kid—listen to me." The professor grabbed Lenny's shoulders and Lenny flinched. "I'm not going to hurt you. You got that?" Lenny's tears dropped and the professor shoved him away. His eyebrows drew tight with anger. The folds around his eyes deepened. "You think I killed them, don't you. DON'T YOU!" Lenny nodded. "It wasn't me, dammit." He slammed a fist against his thigh. "It wasn't me."

Suddenly, the professor stiffened. He looked around like a bloodhound on the scent. The station wagon had traveled twenty yards from the dirt road into the cornfield. The engine had died but the lights were still on. The rear hatch had opened and lying in the trampled stalks halfway between the station wagon and the road was the box. It lay askew on a tiny ridge of plowed earth and glowed red from the taillights.

Lenny stared at it, thought that a three-year-old could easily fit inside, that maybe a wife—if chopped finely enough—could have been stuffed inside as well.

The box shifted on the mound of earth as if something alive was inside. And then a knock—knuckles on wood. Something inside the box wanted out. The rapping of knuckles turned into the thrashing of fists as the trapped beat feverishly from within the box.

"Let—them—out," came a voice, seemingly from within the box. The pronunciation was slow, disoriented, sounding like a cassette tape running at half speed. "Let—them—out—now."

Standing on the dirt road, a shadow highlighted in pink, was one of the state troopers.

"Can't—you see—they—want out—pro—fes—sor..." the trooper said while raising his revolver.

"Tough shit," the professor responded, standing near the opened passenger door, eyeing the gun that lay in a puddle of puke on the front seat.

The trooper fired and the professor jerked backward. Lenny dropped to his knees as the professor dove through the shattered rear passenger door window, flipped into the car, and grabbed the gun. The trooper ran into the plowed lane created by the station wagon as the professor brought his gun out and steadied it on the roof of the car.

Bang!

The trooper lifted off the ground and fell flat on his back ten feet from the box.

Lenny crouched at the professor's heels wondering what to do. Everything was moving too fast. There was too much information and too little time to sort it out. Murders, gunfights, psycho killers—Come on! He was just hitchhiking home to see his mother for Christ's sake. *Let them out*, the trooper had said. Let who out? Of what? Shouldn't his demand have been, *Halt, you crazy murderous scumbag or I'll blow your damned head off.* Didn't anyone watch T.V. around here?

Stop thinking, Lenny, and act.

Save your ass.

Get the gun from the professor.

Lenny dove at the back of the professor's legs, yanked them up and away and the professor went down. He grabbed the gun and pointed it at the professor's head. "Enough of this shit! You hear me?" The gun shook in his hands. His voice trembled. His body quivered. This was much different than in the movies. Real guns, real blood—*really* a matter of life or death. "You...You stay there or I'll blow your—" *Go ahead. Say it. Or I'll blow your goddamn head off. Clint Eastwood would say it. Hell, he'd do it; he loved blowing holes in things.* But Lenny couldn't say it, couldn't do it; he just wanted to go home and get this nightmare over with.

Fortunately for Lenny's cowardice, the professor was in no shape to go anywhere. The trooper had shot him in the right breast and his stomach was gashed open from the shards of window glass that he'd dove through to get the gun. His mouth worked as if he were chewing gum and Lenny moved closer, pointing the gun haphazardly at the bullet hole in the professor's chest.

"Watch out," the professor gasped and slid an arm through the crumpled corn stalks with his index finger pointed in the direction of the felled trooper. Lenny jerked, thinking the professor was stretching for some hidden weapon.

"You killed him, man," Lenny said now steadying the gun with both hands. "There's nothing to watch out for except you." That's what Clint Eastwood would say, he thought.

"No. Not dead. Never dead. Watch out." Blood trickled from the corner of the professor's mouth and red bubbles escaped as he coughed up more.

In the distance, a gun fired and Lenny felt the buzz of a giant insect nip his left ear. He turned. The trooper advanced with his revolver raised. Lenny dropped as the trooper fired another round.

"Hey!" Lenny yelled. "I'm innocent! I'm one of the good guys!"

"Don't let him get the Cubit," the professor moaned. "Trust me." He closed his eyes and exhaled.

"The Cubit? What?"

The trooper had acquired the box and was now carrying it back toward the road. "Hey, professor. He's got the Cubit. Professor?" His hands shook. He wasn't Clint Eastwood. In fact, his actions resembled those of Clint Eastwood's victims. Men too big for their britches. Men too scared to draw and shoot straight. Men who were kids.

What are ya gonna do, kid? Draw or whistle Dixie?

The state trooper turned and fired again. The bullet missed his head by fractions of an inch; he heard it buzzing, like a fly stuck in his ear. Was he actually going to shoot a cop?

You gotta start livin' or you gotta start dyin'—

"Yes, Clint. I know," Lenny yelled out then squinted and fired two rounds. The trooper flinched and returned fire as Lenny dropped face first near the rear bumper of the station wagon. Something stung his shoulder; glass shattered in the distance. His right arm went numb and, lying face down in the cornfield, he transferred the gun to his left hand.

This was it. He was going to die. He should have known better than to ignore his mother. He should not have hitchhiked. Hitchhiking was the same as stealing, she'd say, and stealing was against God's Commandments. He could see her crooked finger slashing the sign of the cross in a cumulative gesture of accusation and forgiveness.

The crunch of snapping corn stalks assaulted his ears and a scorched black shoe appeared in front of his nose. The trooper's pant leg was burned away and in the red taillight luminance, a bare, bubbled calf and shin offered Lenny the nauseating odor of burned flesh. A shoe heel prodded Lenny's spine. A toe poked his ribs. Lenny gasped.

The trooper's breath became deep and excited, sounding like a mad scientist who'd just seen the first jerky signs of life from his monster masterpiece.

And then—

Click!

It was his stepfather again, pointing and firing an empty .44 at his head. Again, the visions of brains and blood in his bedroom—across the dashboard. His stomach churned.

Not this time, coward, Clint had the nerve to remind him. *You keep that puke to yourself.*

Click! Click! Click!

Lenny quickly rolled and lifted his gun with a wavering left hand, leveled it at—

But, it couldn't be alive—the trooper—this thing. It stood naked. Bone poked through brittle black skin across the length of its body. Its genitals, dangling directly in Lenny's line of sight, resembled an unattended weenie roast at a Boy Scout camp. The pin from the trooper's badge punctured its left breast and dangled from abused, blackened tissue. The badge had a bullet hole through its center. The flesh around the things lips, nose and eyes was totally burned away leaving a grin full of teeth, a white stare, and a broken jaw. It struggled to breathe, sucking air through dime-sized holes just above the charred gum line as it gawked with two lidless eyeballs down the barrel of Lenny's gun.

But this was a human being, wasn't it? Lenny thought. What if the guy was just burned real bad—maybe the fire had gotten to his brain and had burned some part of his logical center. He could be just whacked out, disabled, not knowing what the hell he was doing. Yeah—that had to be it. Lenny couldn't shoot someone who wasn't responsible for their own actions. Besides, it was against God's Commandments to murder.

Shoot the Mother Fucker! Clint demanded.

The thing that had been a Kansas state trooper kicked the gun from Lenny's hand. Its black shoe tore loose and followed the gun into the cornstalks. Lenny's body wanted to roll away as the thing leapt at him but his mind was too busy listening to advice from his mother and Clint. Bony fingers wrapped around his throat, tightened their grip. A gritty trail of brittle flesh broke from the things flexing hand and fell underneath his shirt. Its bulging eyeballs, gnashing teeth, and whistled gasps floated within a black mask above Lenny's face.

Lenny beat and shoved with his left arm as his throat was strangled but this only broke away more burnt pieces of the thing's body. Soot came out of its nose and fell into Lenny's gasping mouth. The trooper's white teeth hovered over his lips as if it wanted a kiss and this took Lenny over the edge. His mind shut down. His vision dulled.

Before blacking out, Lenny saw the white glimmer of what he thought was the holy light.

Heaven was dark red and it kind of smelled like Kansas. Lenny opened his eyes, believing himself dead. The pain had eased in his shoulder but his right arm remained mostly functionless. He rose with the intent of propping himself with his left elbow but hit his head on the rear bumper of the station wagon. It was still night. He was still in the cornfield. He wasn't dead, this wasn't heaven and worse: all of it—the professor, the gun fight, the burnt thing—had not been a dream.

Lenny kicked himself from under the car and wearily stood. First, he examined his shoulder, bending toward the red glow of the station wagon's taillights for assistance. The bullet had passed cleanly through the meat near his collarbone. What little blood he'd lost was drying in a splotchy half-moon above his breast. Then, he gave the station wagon a troubled stare. Somehow, the box that the professor had called a Cubit had jumped back into the cargo area, had closed the rear hatch and had turned off the engine. Finally, he noticed that the professor and trooper were gone.

Lenny slipped around to the front of the station wagon, looking back across his injured shoulder. Corn rustled in the dim red taillights. An arm rose from the cover of the stalks, revealing a wrist and five fingers that were tightly wrapped around a knife. Down went the wrist, stabbing what hid in the cornstalks, then back up to reveal wrist, fist and knife. Something screeched, sounding, to Lenny, like the villain Scorpio when Eastwood shot him in *Dirty Harry*.

Then…silence. The professor stood.

Lenny looked for the gun and found it sitting atop the Cubit in the back of the station wagon. He ran for it as the professor yelled, "No!"

As Lenny fingered the steel of the pistol's barrel a small blue spark grabbed his left pinky. There was a gentle tug that lasted for the slightest moment, an electrical tingle not unlike the static touch of hand on metal. The blue spark changed to red so quickly that Lenny was not sure the vision had occurred at all. And then the gun was in his hand. He turned it toward the approaching professor though his eyes remained where the blue-red spark no longer existed. He leveled the gun.

"The Cubit," the professor said. "You touched it."

"No. You're wrong. Stand back or I'll…"

Lenny then noticed the knife in the professor's hand. Its blade was quite long and it appeared to glow in the station wagon's taillights.

"Put it down," the professor demanded with a bit of exasperation and a lot of fatigue. "The gun's empty."

Lenny fired. Fired again. Click. Click.

The professor snatched the empty gun and flung it into the back of the station wagon. "Let's get out of here," he said, then added something before he collapsed that Lenny thought was quite strange. "You've got to protect me. Help…please."

◻ ...

The drive would take less than fifteen minutes. Lenny sat on thin remnants of the vomit he had swiped from the car seat before climbing in. His right shoulder ached and he could lift it only enough to manage the steering wheel. The professor's injury looked more serious. A large red spot soaked his plaid shirt on the same side as Lenny's injury but his was a few inches lower, more centered around the upper breast than the collarbone. In the dashboard's dim light, Lenny saw a drop of blood trickle from the professor's mouth. The injured man no longer gazed apprehensively into the rearview or side view mirrors which meant that he was either satisfied they were no longer being chased or that he was much too tired to care.

Lenny turned onto a dirt road that led to the Bender's farm. A newspaper protruded from his mother's mailbox and Lenny stopped to fetch it. As he exited the car, he suddenly felt that he'd made a grave mistake. He suddenly realized that he had now placed his mother in great danger, not from the professor so much as from those that were hunting him. He suddenly realized his own selfishness, how getting home and climbing into bed with a warm, home-cooked meal in his tummy was all that had been on his mind. As he snatched the large Sunday edition of the *Topeka Capital Journal* from rusted steel, he gazed hopelessly in all directions, into the middle-of-the-night solitude. The smell of corn rustled his nostril hairs as a thin wave of wind rolled across the darkness. He imagined a legion of burnt, ashen state troopers converging on his mother's house. He imagined Clint Eastwood leading the charge. Clint was no longer big, tough and good-looking. He was now bubbly, torched, and grotesque. He could not see them now but he felt that they were on their way. Somewhere beyond the corn. Somewhere, stalking.

When Lenny climbed back into the station wagon the professor was looking at him with a silent stare that acknowledged understanding. Now you know, the stare said.

Two miles down the front road, between a hundred acres of unplanted farmland (barren due to the neglect of his stepfather) sat the Bender barn and farmhouse. Two years ago, before his father's death, the Benders had made a pretty good living on cotton and corn. Today, Lenny's mother survived as a self-employed seamstress for the Pickett's Crossing community. Her new husband, Albert, had sold nearly all of the farm animals, including several dozen head of cattle, horses, and a pair of prize-winning Labrador Retrievers that had brought substantial added income to the Bender household, not to mention notoriety. Cash from this 'liquidation' had gone to feed Albert's alcohol and gambling addictions. It would not be long before the land itself would be traded for booze, cards and craps. It all depended on how lucky Albert remained at the Vegas tables. It all depended on whether cheating would one day get the best of him. How Lenny prayed that his stepfather's card-counting would one day summon some large man named Vito to a hotel suite on the outskirts of Las Vegas with a gun in hand and bullets marked for cheatin' Albert Stine. Perhaps Lenny would return home for good, help his mother get the farm back on its feet, help his mother get her life back together. Right now it was impossible. Lenny was afraid of Albert. Lenny had very little courage. Lenny could not protect a fly from a spider with a can of Raid in hand. The puke at his feet was a reminder of his cowardice, a summation of his life, a putrid digestion of lost chances, lack of responsibility and selfishness. A tear emerged and dropped to the red stain encircling his right collarbone. Crying was not a manly thing to do either.

He figured it was somewhere close to two in the morning since the Sunday paper was already in the mailbox. Paper delivery was very efficient in Pickett's Crossing. The paper's circulation depended on early delivery to early-rising farm folk.

He doubted his mother would be awake, doubted even more that she'd appreciate being intruded upon on the Lord's day of rest, and was certain that a stranger at her doorstep would not sit well. She trusted few people outside of the Crossing's community. Her extreme reclusion had started after his father's tragic death and had only become worse since Albert's continuing yard sale of all that she and her husband had built together.

As she'd promised Lenny in a letter he'd received a week ago, Albert would be in Vegas. It would be "safe" for him to come home and see his mother. He could help her clean up the barn and do a few field chores. He could share a little love that had become so elusive between them.

Albert's car was not in the yard. His mother's F150 was. As he turned to park beside the truck, the headlights revealed the Ford's rusty shade of white paint. When he switched off the station wagon the professor sighed, closed his eyes and propped his head against the car door window. A circular pattern of breath-fog emerged against the window at the point where lips touched glass. And then he said something that made Lenny think he was dreaming again.

"You need to kill yourself," he said with shallow breaths. "When it comes out, and it will, you need to kill…" His eyes fluttered as if he were about to pass out. "…to kill you."

Lenny's gaze shifted to the wooden box then back toward the professor.

"The Cubit," the professor said. "Yes. And it won't be long."

Lenny remembered the tiny blue-red spark of electricity no stronger than that of a static charge. He remembered his arm tingling. He remembered that the moment had lasted much longer than the split second it took for the tingle to subside. He rubbed his left hand, studied it, turned it in the palm of his right hand which still did not work well with the bullet hole through his collarbone. When he looked up again, the knife was in the professor's hand. Lenny flinched.

"Take it," he said. "It's the only way."

Lenny immediately reached forward but paused just inches from the blade. It glistened as if containing a light source of its own. To take it would involve him further. He would become a murderer of children and wives. He would get his own little box and…

The professor shoved the haft of the knife into Lenny's motionless hand. And as Lenny began to study the weapon which looked more like a dagger with a long thin blade, three things happened simultaneously. The professor passed out, the porch light came on, and his mother emerged with shotgun in hand. She chambered a shot and pointed it at the trespassing car.

Lenny didn't want to emerge from the station wagon with a weapon at two o'clock in the morning while his mother pointed a loaded shotgun at his head, so he quickly tossed the dagger in the glove box.

"Mom," he yelled as he opened the car door. "It's me…Lenny."

⌑ …

Janine Bender would not lower the shotgun until she was absolutely sure that the man in the car was really her son. Albert's latest acquaintances made her untrusting of all strange cars, especially those that appeared on her doorstep in the middle of the night.

She moved across the porch to her right, avoided a pair of wicker chairs that she'd refinished last week, and poked the barrel of the shotgun across the hood of her pickup to the two men sitting in the front seat of an old station wagon.

The porch light reflection bouncing off the car's windshield made it difficult to see. The passenger appeared motionless, head to window. Something stained his shirt but she couldn't tell what it was. The driver was her son; she could see him clearly as he stood from the car. His thin brown hair cropped above the ears outlined the small face of a boy who'd moved another six months toward manhood since she'd last seen him. His shirt was also stained in about the same location as the passenger's. She looked past him, following the gray outline of the front road beyond the barn, until she was satisfied that nothing else was out there.

"Mom," Lenny repeated. "Please. Don't shoot."

It was then that Janine realized she had the shotgun pointed at her son's head and immediately lowered it. "What in Moses' name are you doin' out here in the middle of the night, Lenny?" Janine gazed at the man beside Lenny as her son emerged from the station wagon. "And who's that? You know me and strangers."

"He's hurt real bad." Lenny walked around his mother's truck and ascended the five wooden steps to the porch. "He gave me a lift but then we had a little..."

"And you?" She grabbed his shoulder, lightly. Lenny flinched. "Are *you* hurt real bad?" She pulled him closer to her with one arm while setting the gun on the wicker table with the other.

"Oww," he yelped and pulled away like a little boy whose mother had just touched his little boo-boo.

"Gun shot," Janine said, surprised. "Who in Moses' name has been shooting you?" She turned him to look at the hole in his shirt where the bullet had exited.

"Long story," Lenny said, exasperated. "The professor—he's worse off. Probably needs a doctor."

Janine held her son gently by the sides of his head, looked into his brown eyes for answers that she was certain would not be revealed until much later, if at all. "Doctor!" she said. "You know me and doctors." She didn't wait for an answer; she could see that Lenny was concerned. She didn't like strangers and she didn't like doctors but she couldn't turn away an injured man, especially on the Holy day. She'd have to repent for months. "Come on. Let's get him inside."

◻ ...

His mother was much grayer than when he'd last seen her. She looked as old as the professor though Lenny was certain she was at least ten years younger. Her eyes were grayer as well having shifted from azure shortly after his father's death. It had been a strange transformation: blue eyes to gray. He'd never heard of a person's eyes changing color in the middle of adulthood. It had started with little gray flecks here and there. Now the pupils' were completely gray. They walked together to the passenger's side door of the station wagon.

"He doesn't look well," his mother said. "Lost a lot of blood."

Lenny opened the door slowly and the professor's body slide sideways. He was awake but terribly weak. Lenny helped him into a sitting position.

"We're going to move you inside," Lenny said. The professor responded but Lenny could not understand. He slurred as if drunk. "We're gonna need your help. Okay?"

Lenny reached under the professor's left thigh and arm and scooted him toward the edge of the seat. The professor helped, but not much. When Lenny looked around for his mother he saw her standing motionless and staring into the cargo bay of the station wagon.

"Mom. A little help. Please?"

She remained motionless.

"Mom—"

Lenny was about to loose his balance. His thin frame could not withstand the professor's weight much longer.

"Ka-yaa-buut," the professor moaned. "No Tuuchh."

It took Lenny less than a second to realize what the professor was saying since, simultaneous with this understanding, Lenny watched as his mother leaned into the glass-shattered rear window, her right arm stretched toward the Cubit.

❐ ...

It was the feeling associated with knowing something no one else knew. It was the feeling that she'd seen it somewhere before but was uncertain if it had been something real or something that had been a part of a dream. It felt like desire and fear and helplessness wrapped together into one extremely unwanted emotion. She could not control herself. She had to touch it. Every fiber of her Christian being screamed for resistance, and this caused her arm and hand to shake as she reached into the station wagon.

"No! Mom! No!"

Its smooth wooden surface was a foot away. She hesitated.

"Don't touch it!"

A little red star was buried in the wood at its top edge, centered, as if serving the function of a hasp but it had no latch. It winked at her, or so she thought. She smiled. Giggled. She hadn't giggled in years. The pads of her fingers wanted to gently caress it...its electricity...and in one quick motion, she was suddenly jerked forcefully backwards.

"Mom!" Lenny screamed.

She glared at the box, at Lenny, at the man who now lay on the gravel driveway after Lenny had let him fall. The man attempted to roll onto a knee, pushing himself upward with his good arm, before falling back onto the gravel.

"Come on, Mom," Lenny said, exhausted. "Let's get the professor inside."

The man whom her son had called the professor had only enough strength to allow the limited combined efforts of herself and Lenny to guide him into the house and onto the couch. His blood quickly marred the green and white fabric and Janine thought, briefly, how terribly difficult it was going to be to remove those stains. The professor eased onto his back without aid from either of them, blinked a few quick times while studying the ceiling, then closed his eyes. A few driveway pebbles were stuck in his short, matted gray and white beard and Janine brushed them away.

"Go to the bathroom and get me a couple of washcloths," she said to Lenny. "And bring me a small pan of cool water."

Lenny exited the living room and disappeared into a hallway that led to the bathroom as Janine unbuttoned the professor's shirt and peeled it from sticky skin. She rolled the right half of the shirt to fully uncover the bullet wound. Blood still oozed from it, creating a darker pattern in the center that resembled a red star.

And she was suddenly back outside, dazed and confused, wanting to caress the smooth wood surface of the box in the station wagon. The red glistening star. The desire. The fear. Uncontrollable.

"Here ya go." Lenny's voice broke the spell. "Is it bad?"

She grabbed both washcloths from her son's hand, dipped one into the plastic mixing bowl that Lenny had filled with water, then folded it lengthwise and draped it across the professor's forehead. She wetted the second washcloth and began mopping up the sticky mess of blood from the skin surrounding the wound. She rinsed the washcloth several times until the bowl of water turned crimson.

"He'll live for now but I'm afraid the bullet is still inside him," she said over her shoulder, not looking at Lenny. "I'm afraid he's going to need a hospital. Don't know what the bullet's done to him inside but he needs to have it removed."

The professor suddenly snapped his eyes open and started to rise but was gently forced down by Janine's hand.

"No," he demanded without shouting. "No doctors. No hospitals. No policemen. They'll find me if you do. They'll find the Cubit. You can't let that happen." He grasped Janine's hand and searched her gray eyes. "*You* can't let that happen."

She immediately connected the word 'Cubit' with the wooden box outside. Again, there was that feeling of knowing something but not remembering just how you knew it.

"You'll die without help," Janine demanded and reached forward to flip the wet washcloth on the professor's forehead.

"The dagger," he moaned. "Use the dagger." Then he closed his eyes and became silent. His breathing came in short spurts. A tiny runner of blood emerged from the right corner of his mouth. Janine guessed that he had little life left.

"What about this dagger?" she asked Lenny. "You know what he's talking about?"

"Yeah. It's out in the car. But I don't understand how it's gonna help matters." Janine rose from the professor's side and turned to her son. "I mean, he used it to kill a cop."

She could have asked him to explain in more detail and probably would later. Right now she believed that the man on the couch would soon die. She didn't know what the dagger was nor how it could possibly help the situation but the professor's last words had been: *Use the dagger.*

"Please get it for me," she said and reached forward to pull the collar of Lenny's T-shirt away from his neck. "Once we take care of him, I'll dress you up."

□ …

Lenny's first thoughts were those planted by Stephen King's *Children of the Corn*. His mother had never allowed him to watch that movie while growing up in a cornfield. Those images were not conducive to a healthy, young Kansas mind. And Lenny had found this assumption to be true when he'd finally seen it in his University of Texas dorm room just last week. His roommate had rented it. It had not been Lenny's choice.

Now, as he stood on the porch, he wondered where "he who walks among the corn" might be. Had the professor really killed him? Or was the dead state trooper out there still? Was *he* walking among the rows just beyond the porch, waiting for cowardly Lenny Bender? His imagination coalesced into a fear that had him looking in every direction. He stepped from the porch and scampered to the back of the pickup, brushing the bumper with his blue-jeaned thigh hard enough to embed a rust red streak into the fibers. By the time he reached the passenger-side door of the station wagon, he'd freaked himself out so badly that a Sunday morning crow, looking for an early meal, made him squeal when it flew a few feet above his head. He gasped in much the same way as he'd done while watching *Children of the Corn*.

Once inside the station wagon, he slammed the door, breathing hard, trying to regain composure though the puke-encrusted seat was a gentle reminder of his cowardice. He snapped open the glove box, thinking as he did so that a blue-red spark might shoot from its black depths and abruptly cause Lenny to abandon his effort. Cautiously, he stuck his hand in; the dagger's blade was quite sharp; he was not interested in the pain that it might cause. He was a coward, a paranoid and scared little boy who should have never gone hitchhiking.

His hand shuffled across a folded piece of paper, a small book and the haft of the dagger. He grabbed all three items and set them in his lap. The folded paper was a map that charted southwestern highways through Texas, New Mexico and Arizona. The professor had highlighted in yellow Interstate 40 as it ran through the top half of the three states. In Arizona, the highlighting continued south from Interstate 40 through Flagstaff and ended in the city of Sedona. The professor had drawn a yellow circle around Sedona and Lenny guessed that this was his intended destination.

The book was about an inch thick and a bit smaller in width and height than a regular sheet of notebook paper. The cover was worn and felt like cloth. There was no title. When he tried to open the book, all of the pages seemed stuck together except for the center spread. Strange symbols were written on one of the two center pages. He closed the book to reveal an image of a dagger embossed in gold on the back cover. A star, much like the one on the Cubit, was etched in the dagger's haft. He rubbed his thumb across the star's edges; it felt warm.

His attention shifted to the dagger in his lap. It, too, had a star embedded into the haft just above the blade. It, too, felt warm in his left hand. He moved the dagger into his right hand and a pulse of energy moved up his arm and into his shoulder where the bullet wound still throbbed. A tingling sensation massaged his collarbone; it kind of tickled. He shoved the book and map into the glove box, closed it, then rubbed his shoulder; the throb decreased. The pain was subsiding. He still could not lift it easily without accompanied pain but there was no denying that it felt better.

When he exited the station wagon and ran to the house, he didn't notice that the red star centered at the top edge of the Cubit was glowing and that lying on the ground behind the station wagon, encircled by the star's red light, was the crow which had frightened him just minutes before. It writhed in the red glow until Lenny entered the house, then became stiff and still as the red star on the Cubit also died.

◻ …

Janine finished cleaning the blood from the professor's chest and moved his legs and arms into a comfortable position on the couch. The bullet hole still oozed and she quickly mopped stray dribbles with the washcloth.

"This thing just might do the trick," Lenny said in the doorway. "It has some…" Lenny struggled for the right word. "It has some kind of electricity in it. It helped my shoulder."

"What are you talking about?" Janine rose from the professor's side and studied the dagger in her son's hand.

"I don't know. I felt a kind of electric tingle that went all the way up to my shoulder. Look, my arm moves a lot better now." Lenny raised and lowered it twice. "It is still painful but at least it moves."

Janine pulled back the collar of his T-shirt. Had she blinked, she would have missed it. And even after some of the flesh at the edge of Lenny's wound seemed to magically stitch itself back together, Janine could not believe it. She rubbed her eyes.

"Let me see that," she asked, stepping back. When Lenny gave the dagger to her she studied the haft's smooth, white surface. The top and bottom of the haft were fatter than the middle and were capped in gold. It was chiseled in such a way that it had five sides. A star embellished one of the sides just above the blade which curved seven inches in length to its very thin point; glistening in the living room's lamplight, it revealed no imperfections. Janine cupped the dagger in her hand but felt none of what Lenny had described as electricity. She waved it through the air a few times, first overhand then underhand not knowing why she did so.

"Mom." Lenny pointed at the professor whose face had become pale. "Give it to him."

She placed the dagger in the professor's unconscious right hand but she could not get his fingers to wrap around the haft. The red jewel in the star started to glow. She snatched it back, and felt its warmth and electricity.

"Do you hear that?" she asked Lenny.

"What?"

"That noise—that hum."

"No," Lenny said. "No hum."

But Janine heard it.

Mmmmmmm...

The dagger's glow began to pulse with the sound.

Mmm...Mmm...Mmm...

And then Janine, for reasons she would never understand, moved over the professor's chest and positioned the point of the dagger above the bullet wound. How shoving a sharp object into this man's flesh was going to save him, she didn't know. But it seemed to make sense. Slowly, she inserted the blade a quarter of an inch into the bloody wound. Lenny gasped and rushed forward, but was propelled backward by his mother's left arm.

"Not now Lenny," she urged.

"But you're…"

"Shhh!!" She turned to her son. "Do you want me to kill this man?" She didn't wait for an answer, "Then be quiet."

A full inch of the blade disappeared into the professor's chest. The farther the blade went, the brighter the star jewel glowed. Janine wondered how close the blade was to the man's lung; she wondered if she was cutting away vital arteries or veins. She was schooled in first aid but not surgery. Down the blade went through flesh that presented only minor resistance. The red jewel grew brighter.

And then the dagger met an obstacle that Janine was afraid to push through. The blade was in at least four inches and filled the bullet wound at the skin's surface completely. She believed she had struck bone since only the slightest nudge of the dagger met with staunch resistance. The jewel blazed red. Her arm trembled. The professor stirred, said something unintelligible, a mumble with no meaning.

Janine began to draw the dagger out of the wound but as she did so, she felt a gentle tug as if the man's body did not want the blade to be removed. She lifted with more force.

One inch emerged—two inches—like a medieval sword from a fleshy stone.

Three inches—four.

Both Janine and Lenny gasped simultaneously. Clinging as if magnetized to the point of the dagger was a half-inch, misshapen piece of metal. The bullet was coated in blood and was blunted from its impact with the professor's body. With the blade and bullet out of the professor, the jewel in the dagger's haft faded and the bullet dropped onto the professor's shoulder where it rolled, creating a narrow trail of blood toward the center of his chest.

Janine snatched the bullet, rolled it between thumb and index finger, then dropped it into the plastic bowl of red water. She wiped the professor's chest, rinsed the washcloth several times, then wrapped the blade of the dagger with the washcloth.

"I don't know, Lenny," she said, expecting questions. "I just don't know. It is a miracle. In the name of Moses it is a miracle." She turned to face him. "I'm going to guess that your friend here will recover, but he's going to need some rest. He's lost a lot of blood and I don't think even this has the power to replenish it."

After dumping bloody water into the bathroom sink, and placing the bullet next to the sink's faucet, Janine retrieved a blanket from the hall closet and draped it over the professor. The color was returning in his face and this satisfied her belief that he would recover. She took her son by the hand, placed the dagger in the pocket of her housecoat, and headed for her special room, the one she kept under the house.

❒ ...

Janine and Michael had agreed on the internal basement shelter the day after a Category 3 tornado had destroyed the north end of Pickett's

Crossing. It had missed their farm by just a few miles. Had the tornado taken a different track, one to the south of town, much of their crops and perhaps even their home would have disappeared into the late June summer afternoon.

The only discussion they'd had was not if they needed a shelter but where it would be located. Most storm shelters were external but Janine had seen in an issue of *Family Circle* how internal storm shelters were economical, safe, and could double as an added room when not being used to protect the family from imminent harm. If the Benders were to decide on an internal shelter, they would have to build an addition onto the house. The cost, with the addition, would be nearly double that of an external shelter. And this is where their discussion—which was never an argument but a "discussion"—had heated by the smallest degree. Janine and her husband never fought but the added investment which would essentially add two rooms to their house was one of those rare moments when discussion neared the intensity of an argument.

Could they afford it with a ten-year-old child whose complex move into adolescence was just around the corner? Certainly, the weather could never be predicted. Tornadoes aside, drought could hit and decimate their crops. Or perhaps their crops would become infested by some of the diseases or insects that Michael had read about in *Agricultural Digest*. They needed the extra $10,000 as an investment that would always be available for such "just in case" circumstances.

Janine had always wanted an addition. The house seemed just a bit too small, especially with Lenny requiring more and more privacy as he grew older. She had discussed the prospect with Michael on several occasions and Michael had always told her, as he did when the idea of a storm shelter arose, that they needed to be frugal, watch their expenditures. Disaster could strike anytime and they had to be ready for it.

But the Bender farm had been prosperous for five straight years. Their newest venture—that of raising AKC registered black Labradors— was starting to show a profit. It was time to stop thinking about all the bad that could happen and do something for themselves.

This is where Janine's side of the "discussion" had won out. They had waited so long for something bad to happen that they were not enjoying the good while they could.

Had Janine known that within the next ten years, her husband would be dead and much of the Bender assets would be sold, she would have put the money that an external shelter would have saved them into an account that, today, would be of great use. Some amount of savings would have helped her run from this collection of bad memories and move some place special, a place she often thought of as paradise. A place with sandy beaches and ocean waves where small-town friendly people knew you by name. A place far from here that was, just like in the *Wizard of Oz*, somewhere over the rainbow.

Janine gazed at the snapshot photo of a scene from the *Wizard of Oz*. The professor and Lenny were both fast asleep upstairs. It was just a little before dawn and she could not get back to sleep. Her mind was preoccupied with the picture. Dorothy was leaning against Auntie Em's wooden wagon wheel singing about rainbows, pretty little bluebirds, and why oh why can't I. Janine sympathized with Dorothy. Why oh why couldn't they? Dorothy was stuck in a world of grown-ups and rules. Janine was stuck in a world of alcoholic control. And just like in the *Wizard of Oz*, along came a professor to offer them both the hope of miracles. She didn't know what the professor's name was upstairs but doubted very seriously it was anything close to Marvel. The man upstairs, however, had something even the Wizard did not, a magic dagger. One that could draw bullets from bodies. One that, by its simple touch, could heal and certainly kill. The professor's dagger was as marvelous as anything in the world of Oz and perhaps, just perhaps, it could help Janine fly from here, just like pretty little bluebirds, to her own Oz—to her own paradise.

The storm shelter, which doubled as Janine's private room, was adorned with several pictures in frames that depicted images of what she believed to be paradise. Along with the movie scene from the *Wizard of Oz*, there were pictures of sunny warms places, each showing sandy beaches and crashing tidewaters. One was a shot from a beach just outside of Cancun, Mexico. Another depicted a shoreline along the African Mediterranean coast. A third was a beach along the southern end of Australia. All totaled, there were nearly a dozen framed "Janine paradises" all of which she knew were unattainable beyond a miracle.

On the other walls of her room hung an array of biblical renderings, artifacts and icons. Most referenced Moses and the exodus from Egypt. There was a swatch of Hebrew cloth, stone recreations of the Ten Commandments, a picture of Moses standing before the split Red Sea, the words "Let My People Go" scribbled on a tapestry that covered no window, an autographed picture of Charlton Heston, and many dime store novelty items that had some part of the scripture from Exodus inscribed on them.

Against the wall adjoining the paradise picture collage and opposite the narrow set of steps that led up to the storm shelter's floor-framed door was a three-drawer wooden dresser that she had refinished back when things were good. Atop the dresser was a tall mirror framed in the same dark-stained oak as the dresser, a small lamp with a shade that was printed with a repeating pattern of angels, and three framed pictures: one of Michael, one of Lenny and one of the three of them together with their prize-winning, and most beloved Labrador, Betty.

Janine rose from her bed, a double-sized mattress that took up two-thirds of the space in the room, and stepped to the dresser. She grabbed the picture of her family, ran a finger across the outline of her husband, tickled the chin of Betty, rubbed the shoulder of her son. The Janine in the picture was not the Janine she now stared at in the mirror. Though it had been only five years since the picture had been taken, the changes in her face were three times in age. She would be forty-two in three months but the lines under her eyes, the crinkled forehead and a full head of gray hair made her look much, much older. Physically and mentally she was forty-two but her appearance was frail. Her aged look was one of the reasons why she had become reclusive. Albert was the other.

She gazed over at the miracle dagger lying on the mattress at the foot of the bed and thought about Albert, about escape, about paradise. It could be used to cure but could it also be used to kill? Better yet, would it recognize Albert for the scumbag alcoholic he was and somehow fling itself into the demon's heart? She could not do it herself. She was a Christian lady.

Thou shall not kill, the picture of Moses seemed to say to her.

But was wishing for death the same as committing the act? Was it right to free oneself by killing others? Moses had, hadn't he? He'd slain an Egyptian slavemaster who was beating a frail Hebrew worker. He'd killed all of the Egyptian first born. He'd directed Pharaoh's army into the Red Sea and drowned them. Not to mention all of the people his Israelite army massacred on the way to the Promised Land. In his Exodus, Moses had killed many.

So it was right, then, to kill for freedom. With her Bible as rationale, she would not rot in Hell—instead she would be free to find Heaven. Still, she could not, by her own hand, thrust the dagger into any person. Even if Albert was asleep (which was the only time she felt that it might be possible to kill him) she could not. Even if she found out that it had been Albert who had killed her husband, she could not. Even if Albert threatened her once again, with wife-beating ramifications to her threats of leaving him, she could not.

She stared into the mirror, searching her own slate gray eyes for an answer. She looked at her hands, already spotted and wrinkled well beyond her age. Were these the hands of a killer? Were these the eyes that could forever withhold the truth about the murderer she would become? Further, how many times had she stood in this exact spot, gazing at her reflection and wondering *What If*? She'd never done it. She never could do it.

But then there was the dagger. And again there was that feeling of knowing without knowing how you knew. The dagger was the key to her salvation.

She stepped to the edge of the bed, grabbed the weapon, unwrapped the washcloth. She moved the haft from hand to hand, caressing its smooth surface, thumbing its fine craftsmanship, gazing at the golden star that was jeweled in red in only one of the five points.

A knock on the storm shelter's door above her, broke her from the trance.

"Yes?" she said.

"Mom." Lenny's voice was a whisper above the heavy wooden door. "I can't sleep. You mind if I come down?"

Janine wrapped the washcloth around the blade of the dagger and set it on her dresser. She, again, stared into her gray, sad eyes—searching. Perhaps Lenny could tell her more about this dagger, about the red stars. Perhaps with his help she would be able to do it.

"OK," she said. "Come down."

The first thing Janine did when her son reached the foot of the steps was pull him close to her. With a gentle hug she asked him about his shoulder. Lenny had changed shirts into one which pictured Gravedigger, the monster truck he'd raved over through his teen years. This jerked a tear from the corner of her eye. It was the same T-shirt he was wearing in the family picture on her dresser.

"My shoulder is still sore, but I'll live," Lenny said.

Janine pulled the collar of his shirt forward to reveal red inflammation underneath a large band-aid. She peeled back the band-aid, was satisfied that the bullet wound was not infected and replaced it. "How's your friend?" she said.

"Well, I wouldn't exactly call him my friend..." Lenny stepped back from his mother's embrace. "He's still sleeping. He was mumbling something before I came down. Probably just dreaming, I guess."

"Come over and sit down. We haven't talked in a good while. You don't write or call much." Janine stopped short of sounding confrontational as she and Lenny sat at the foot of the bed. "Anyway, it's really good to see you."

"I dropped out of school." Lenny stared at his socked feet.

Janine was not surprised, but she felt his withholding of information up until now added another degree of detachment between them.

"Agricultural science just isn't my thing," he continued. "Besides, without Dad…" He looked up and into his mother's eyes. "I mean it was him who wanted me to follow in his footsteps, to take over the farm some day." Though he tried, Lenny could not fight back the welling tears.

"I know." Janine caressed her son's hand between both of hers. She was upset with her son's decision to leave college but knew that he was right. After all, there was not much left of the farm for him to follow in the footsteps of the man who had built it. "If it is the will of the Lord then so be it. How long has it been?"

"Dropped out before the beginning of last spring semester. It was hard to study and work and stay interested in agriculture all at the same time."

"What are you doing now?" Janine remained supportive.

"Doing now?" Lenny looked confused, tired.

"In San Antonio—you working?"

Lenny hunched forward and stared at his feet as if trying to think of something to say. Janine was beginning to feel that a change of subject was necessary.

"I, uh—well I was just laid off from this construction company." His feet dangled an inch off the floor and he shuffled them back-and-forth as he spoke. "They were good people but the work just dried up."

"What happened tonight?" Janine said, squeezing and pulling his hand as to nudge him into looking at her. He turned. A slight tremble emerged in the corner of his mouth.

"I had a really horrible dream," he said.

"No. I mean with the professor and all."

"That's what *I* mean. Before I came down here I was dreaming about it. At least parts of it…the really bad parts. Stuff that didn't even happen. At least I don't think it happened—I mean—oh hell. I don't know what I mean." He looked up at the walls where Moses' picture stared down at him. "Sorry. I didn't mean to say hell."

Janine pulled him as close to her as his body language would allow. "Tell me. What did you dream?

Lenny's eyebrows curled inward, helplessly. His lip trembled more briskly as he said, "I have to kill myself."

Inwardly, Janine gasped but she didn't want to show such shocking emotion in her son's time of need. "You know this from your dream?" she said.

"From the professor."

"The professor told you to kill yourself?"

"Yeah, I know. Why would he do that? Hell..." He looked up at Moses and the split water walls of the Red Sea behind him. "Heck, we saved his life. He saved my life. That thing was dead but it was alive. He killed it after that dead thing shot us. And the Cubit. I didn't touch it, I swear. But he said I did. And now I have to kill myself. I have to kill myself with that dagger."

"Whoa. Hold on." Janine double-clutched his hand. "Let's take this one step at a time."

Lenny's eyes suddenly boiled with intensity, fear and shock. He stared straight through her. "I saw *Me*, mom. I saw *Me* in my dream and I was dead. I looked just like me but it wasn't me. It was a dead Lenny trying to kill me. An anti-Lenny. An evil Lenny." He clutched his mother's elbow with his right arm while his left hand remained clasped within hers. "That was the dream part. The dead trooper was real. But they are connected. They are both a part of that—Cubit. Whatever you do, don't touch it." He squeezed her arm tight enough to constrict the blood flow. "Stay as far away as you can. It's evil, mom. It wants to destroy the world."

Lenny collapsed onto his mother's lap. She caressed his temple and forehead as his eyes fluttered in a fight between consciousness and sleep. The revelations he'd unleashed in the past couple of minutes were too much for her to even try and comprehend. All she knew was that her son needed her. Something traumatic had taken his mind and had ripped it apart and now his dreams were keeping him awake. And they had to be dreams. Dead people didn't shoot guns.

She eased Lenny onto the bed and snuck a pillow under his head. He'd finally fallen asleep. She stretched out beside him and draped one arm across his chest, felt his racing heartbeat that seemed to skip a beat or two. Her own eyes blinked with exhaustion. Her mind raced with scattered pieces of information. Dead people. Lenny committing suicide. A magic dagger. Paradise. The Cubit.

Lying beside her son, Janine fell asleep thinking about the small wooden box in the back of the professor's station wagon, the red star on its top edge, and how it had drawn her to it—how it had wanted her to touch it.

❑ ...

Albert Stine was pissed off. He could not believe that he'd been caught cheating. How dare they accuse him of doing something like that? How could they know he was counting cards? They couldn't read his mind. They were going purely on the word of the dealer. And how the hell could she know? The stupid whore was just tired of losing, that's all. If he ever saw her outside he'd teach her a lesson or two about treating men with respect. Damn bitch!

Albert swilled from a pint of Jim Beam then quickly chased it with a swallow of Diet Coke. His foot had mashed the accelerator with the thought of the casino blackjack dealer and he eased it up, looking into his rearview mirror for cops as he did so.

He'd get her, he thought again. No fucking woman was going to get the best of Albert Stine.

Kansas State Route 22 was nearly deserted of traffic. Occasionally, a sedan or van packed with Sunday-dressed families would buzz by in the opposite direction and Albert would giggle. Church was as useless to a man's soul as were women. Both wanted to save you. Both wanted to turn you into something you weren't. Both wanted to meddle in your life, ask too many questions, then leave you feeling guilty about being a man.

He thought of the casino dealer and his foot reacted against the gas peddle. How dare she meddle in his life? How could she have known? The technique was sound. Jimmy Jacks had guaranteed him that no casino in the country would ever know. Jacks had gotten away with counting cards at the blackjack table forever. There's no way *that* casino bitch could have known. And now he was banned for life from gambling at the Sandbox and it wouldn't be long before the word on Albert Stine spread.

"Shit!" he grumbled, swilled whiskey, chased it. He pounded his fist against the steering wheel of his blue Monte Carlo and half a shot of Beam spilled onto his lap. He ignored it.

He snapped on the radio, having pawned all of his CDs to get enough chips to play that one last hand of blackjack. Nothing but gospel and sermons. Angrily, he snapped it back off.

Being mad was not uncommon for Albert. And the more he drank the more pissed off he became. By the time he reached the Bender farm access road, he'd finished the pint and had worked himself up into such a furious frenzy that a mere infraction on his patience by anyone would set him off. He was going to sell the farm; that much he'd already decided. With the cash he would buy his way back into Vegas. Tons of rich farm land meant tons of cash. Perhaps even six figures. He could live well on that kind of dough—more dough than that bitch dealer would make in a lifetime.

And Janine? He'd take her with him. She'd often talked about paradise. Vegas was the perfect paradise. She'd have much to do. If she wanted to continue fixing people's clothes she could do that. There were plenty of people in Vegas who'd lost some portion or all of the shirt off their backs. If she got tired of that, she could become a dealer. She'd be popular. Players would love a kind, naive country girl, one that didn't accuse them of cheating, one that would treat men with respect.

It was close to noon when Albert stopped his car along the Bender's front road short of the house. He tapped his fingers on the steering wheel, anger welling, wishing for another bottle of booze. His breaths became an anxious imitation of an animal ready to fight.

Parked alongside Janine's truck was a station wagon that Albert had never seen before and he immediately jumped to the conclusion that Janine was seeing another man. Made sense too. Every time he left for Vegas, she never said one word to him. She never asked him why he spent so much time there, never asked him to stay home with his wife, and, quite frankly, seemed to urge him to leave by helping him pack and opening the front door as he left the house. She never called him in Vegas or tried to keep tabs on him in any way. Didn't all women do that? Didn't all women question where you were going and what you were doing and how long you'd be gone? Yeah, all women except those that were whoring around on you. The last thing those women wanted was you anywhere around them. Guy was probably from out of town. Probably someone wanting to romance the farm from under her. Probably that Markson character. He'd offered Albert a criminally low price for the farm the last time he'd thought of selling it. But Markson drove an Explorer not a station wagon. Still, covert actions required covert camouflage and this Markson was pretty sneaky.

Albert backed his Monte Carlo along the access road to a point behind the barn so it could not be seen from the house. He would not need a weapon. His courage came straight from the bottle. Besides, he'd already eclipsed the point of level-headed reasoning and this gave him the strength of ten Alberts. He felt he could chew bullets and spit nails even if those bullets were being shot at him.

Slowly, he moved to the barn, hunching a bit as to make his 240-pound frame a bit less revealing. He slid his back across flaking red paint as he stealthily moved from beyond the south wall of the barn and out into the open. The sun blazed his forehead and sent bumper metal reflections from the station wagon and truck into his eyes. He wiped away sweat, shielded his face with the palm of a hand and shuffled, still hunched, to the station wagon where he squatted by the driver's door. He peered through the window for evidence of its occupant, certain that he would find something to finger Markson as the adulterer. What he found was more confusing.

Blood, shattered glass, and something that looked like dried puke smeared the front seat in a macabre mosaic that pulled a small squirt of Jim Beam from Albert's stomach into his throat. Suddenly, the front door of the house opened and Albert dropped immediately. Breaths intensified. Sweat rolled down his forehead and into his eyes. He heard a man's voice then the door closed.

This verified his assumption that his wife was an adulterer. His anger became immense. He gripped rock from the drive path so intensely that when he released his grip and rose to his feet, several pebbles remained stuck to the pads of his fingers.

He sidestepped to the back of the station wagon. His adrenaline pumped energy that he did not know he had. He rose, planted his feet, eyed the five porch steps that he would easily leap over and chose a spot next to the door handle where he would plant his shoulder. He would catch them by surprise.

Out of the corner of his eye Albert saw what he thought was a laser beam, the kind that centers a target in a scope. It painted the side of his face with a red dot that pulsed across his cheek.

Markson had a rifle?

Wondering if he'd be shot as he did so, Albert slowly rose and looked for the source of the light. In the back of the station wagon he saw a wooden box. At the top edge of the box a small, bright, red star glowed.

◻ …

Janine awoke to the sound of shattering glass. She quickly rolled from the bed and onto her feet. Lenny was up a few seconds later. Although his eyes appeared rested they remained shadowed by disquiet and bewilderment. He immediately went for the dagger lying on her dresser.

"He's coming," Lenny said, unwrapping the washcloth from the dagger's blade. "I knew he would. Just like the professor said."

"Who's coming?" Janine knew his answer before he said it.

"Me."

The boards in the roof of the storm shelter squeaked as heavy footfalls walked through the kitchen above them. Quickly, both climbed the stairs, Janine in the lead. She slid the floor door's latch and raised it only far enough to see into the kitchen. Broken glass scattered the vinyl floor in front of the refrigerator. She continued out of the storm shelter and laid the floor door back on its hinged legs. Lenny was quickly out behind her.

"Good morning!"

Janine and Lenny turned simultaneously to the voice behind them.

"Sorry about the glass. I can't find a broom anywhere." The professor sat on the couch with a glass of milk in his right hand and a chocolate chip cookie in the other. He'd wrapped the blanket around his shoulders and his bare chest revealed the red circular bullet wound which looked like it had nearly healed. "These are really very good." He waved the half-eaten cookie in front of him. "I was very hungry so I took the liberty. I hope you don't mind."

Lenny had unconsciously raised the dagger when he'd turned. He lowered it to his side, finding that his right arm functioned quite well.

"Ah, I see you found my dagger." The professor took another bite of cookie, laid the rest on one knee, shifted the glass of milk from his right hand to his left and took half the contents down in one drink.

"You gave it to me last night," Lenny said, shifting the point of the dagger downward in a less offensive position. "You don't remember?"

The professor returned the milk to his right hand. White froth remained on his gray-peppered mustache. "Lot's of things I don't remember and many I would love to forget."

"I heard that," Lenny said while moving toward the professor. "Your arm still not quite right?"

"Very sore. Can't move it for nothin'." He attempted a simple arm raise and lifted it two inches off his thigh before it collapsed. The half glass of milk splashed but did not spill. He looked from the milk to Janine. "But I'm alive," he said to her.

"It saved your life," Janine said. "Fixed Lenny's shoulder too."

"The dagger—Yes, I know."

"But how?"

"Lots of questions. And I have many answers. But first, the cookie and milk." The professor took another bite of cookie, dropped a large chip onto his bare chest, grabbed the stray piece and plopped it into his mouth. "I wanted to thank you for saving my life," he said, finishing off the cookie and milk in succession. "Janine is it?"

Janine moved closer to her son. "Who are you?"

"Cower. Christopher Cower." The blanket had shifted from his shoulders; he pulled it up and back into position. "Do you have a shirt I can borrow?"

"Lenny," Janine said. "Could you grab a shirt for Professor Cower?"

"Preferably a button-up," Cower interjected. "Easier to get my arm in." He grinned.

Lenny set the dagger on the small end table near the head of the couch. "I believe this is yours."

"Keep it, Lenny…" *You'll need it.* He didn't say it but it was implied in the way his voice trailed off. The knowledge was exchanged in the two men's stares. Lenny left the dagger on the table and went to fetch Cower a shirt.

Janine bent forward to inspect Cower's bullet wound. "It's healing nicely," she said. "Lord works in mysterious ways."

"Funny you should say that." Cower stared sternly but kindly. Their eyes were a foot apart.

Janine looked away and toward the dagger, the red star. "What is it…I mean what does it mean?"

"The dagger?" Cower picked up the dagger and set his empty glass in its place. He twirled the dagger like a baton between the fingers of his left hand. The long blade sliced close to his wrist as he expertly maneuvered it.

"The red star," Janine corrected.

Lenny returned with a plaid shirt that was a bit too heavy for June weather. Cower accepted it gratefully, dropped the blanket from his shoulders, then easily placed his left arm into the shirt. Lenny came around the back of the couch to help him with the other arm. Cower winced as Lenny manipulated the shirt onto his back. He left it unbuttoned.

"And I want to know why you wanted me to kill myself," Lenny said.

"I think you know the answer to that," he said to Lenny then added to both of them, "You know much about the Bible?" Lenny stared at the dagger on the table, the blade, how it shimmered in the light from a window behind the couch, a light that grew brighter as the rising midday sun erased barn shadows.

"Old Testament, mostly," Janine said.

"Good." Cower sat back into the couch. "Then you know what I mean when I talk about the five books at the beginning of it?"

"The Pentateuch," Janine said. Lenny looked bewildered.

"Please, sit down. This might take a while."

Lenny went to the kitchen for a couple of chairs and returned. Both mother and son sat. Cower cleared his throat and seemed quite calm for a man on the run. "Genesis, Exodus, Leviticus, Deuteronomy and..." he began.

"Numbers," Janine finished. "So the star represents the Pentateuch. Each of the points of the star represents one of these books." She said it as a matter of fact and not a question.

"Something like that," Cower said. "The five books. The five ages of creation. The five signs of the Apocalypse."

Lenny interrupted, "I thought there were seven signs of the Apocalypse."

"In some Bibles," Cower answered as if correcting one of his students.

"There's only one Bible." Janine said in a tone that was hinted with accusation of blasphemy.

"What makes you say that?" Cower leaned forward. "Because someone told you so?

"Who are you?" Janine huffed. "A professor? A professor of what? Ancient history?"

"The Torah and Qur'an are bibles are they not? They just give a different account of what is considered to be right and what is considered to be wrong. Now if we're talkin' Christianity then..." Janine sat stiff. Lenny shuffled his feet. "Then I gotta say that there are more versions of that Bible than any Qur'an or Torah. Isn't that what organized religion is all about in this country? Different interpretations of the Book?"

"So what Bible have you been reading?" Janine said, knowing that whatever he said would be dismissed by her own knowledge of the facts.

"One that would give another account of what really happened in those early days of man's ascent into God's own image." Cower suddenly shot a left hand forward and grabbed Janine's left, clammy wrist. "I know that faith is the strongest force on this Earth. I don't mean to even attempt to persuade yours differently. What I give you is knowledge. You want to know about the star, the dagger and, no doubt, the Cubit. What I have to offer is an explanation that will not make sense to someone unable or unwilling to accept possibility."

Janine said nothing.

Cower continued, "What would you say if I told you the world was created in five ages rather than seven days?"

"That's not how I know it," Janine said.

"Exactly!" Cower released her hand as gently as he'd grasped it. "Five ages to create life. Five ages to kill it. Depends on what you believe."

"Is that the Bible you're talkin' about?" Lenny said while pointing at the front door. "That book I found in your glove box? It had a picture of *that* on the back cover." Lenny moved his hand from pointing at the door to pointing at the dagger that was still clutched in Cower's left hand.

Cower nodded. "A Bible perhaps few have ever even heard of," he said.

"It explains all of this?" Janine asked.

"Only if you believe," Cower said, again as a teacher talking to a pupil. He shifted slightly on the couch, revealing a small splotch of bloodstain on the couch's middle cushion. "Genesis was about the creation of life but it was also about the creation of death. Exodus introduced us to a great savior but it also introduced the antichrist. With every Good there exists an equal and opposite Evil."

"The Cubit," Lenny said. "How does that fit in?"

"Arc of the Covenant," Cower quickly responded as if in anticipation. "For every Good there exists an equal and opposite Evil."

"So there's another Arc?" Lenny scratched his wounded shoulder.

"Perhaps I should fetch the book. It'll explain everything."

"I'll get it," Lenny offered.

"I need the fresh air," Cower countered, pushing himself up gingerly from the couch. Lenny snatched the dagger from Cower's left hand and helped him to his feet. "I'll be right back."

Professor Cower stretched then slowly shuffled to the front door. The sun's rays, shining through the living room window, reached the couch, signaling that it was close to noon.

◻ ...

Janine had lost track of time in the interim between Cower's departure and the scream that now brought both her and Lenny to their feet. She'd been thinking about the many sermons that Pastor Kindle had used to post his own interpretation of the Good Book. She'd been questioning all that she'd come to know as right, according to the Book, and Pastor Kindle. *For every good there is an equal and opposite bad.* Isn't that what Cower had said? Did this mean that whatever Pastor Kindle had said was only half truth? She'd never seen anything in the pastor's performance that equaled the magic in the dagger that Cower had introduced into their household. Janine knew a lot about the Bible, at least the one that was generally considered as the documented truth. But she wondered: Was there another story?

The initial reason why she bolted upward to snatch the loaded shotgun leaning near the front door was that she wanted some answers and she needed Cower to answer them. Ancillary to this was a concern for Cower.

"Holy shh..." Lenny looked at his mother. "What was that?"

Neither knew. Neither questioned. Both headed out of the house, Lenny clutching the dagger in his left hand, Janine clutching the shotgun in both.

Outside, the sun blazed with a strength that immediately fostered sweat on Janine's forehead. She hunkered down not really knowing why she did so. The shotgun felt safe in her hands. Lenny crouched, similarly, behind her. He held the dagger by the haft, underhanded, blade curled upward, as if he were going to a rumble.

Janine peered across the drive, the access road, the acres of uncultivated, top-grade farmland. She did not see Cower anywhere. She did see that one of the barn doors was wide open. Footsteps littered the ground in a path from the back of the station wagon, through the rocky parking area, across a small stretch of access road, through an area that had been used a few years ago to feed chickens, and into the barn.

The Cubit, Janine thought. *The anti-Arc of the Covenant.* But why would the professor take the Cubit to the barn?

To hide it, of course.

And what about the scream?

Cautiously, mother and son stepped from the porch to the Ford and toward the back of the station wagon. The Cubit, as she expected, was gone.

Lenny continued along the footstep path while Janine stopped for a moment to inspect the car. She poked her head into the cargo bay, saw pebbles of shattered glass and a few drops of what looked like blood and she remembered how the Cubit had beckoned her.

A little of that memory flooded into her vision and she jerked backward, knocking the barrel of the shotgun against the tailgate with such force that she nearly pulled the trigger on a gun pointed at her chin.

The glowing red star. She could see it as plainly as if she'd been suddenly transported ten hours back in time. It had pulled her toward it with inescapable energy.

Janine shook her head but the image of the star did not rescind. And by coincidence or pure mystic luck, lying by her feet near the left rear car tire was a book turned face down; a magic dagger was etched in the center of its back cover.

She knelt, released her hand from the barrel of the shotgun and snatched at the book, stumbling forward as she did so. She dropped the shotgun as she lost her balance and fell onto all fours. Tiny rock edges dug into her palms and knees and she quickly rolled onto her butt.

"Mom. You all right?" Lenny said, standing a few dozen feet from the open barn door near a small blackened crater created by one of Janine's recent dynamite tree-stumping efforts.

She grabbed the book and shotgun and rose from the gravel in one swift motion that was much too easy for a woman that looked her age. She shoved the book into her housecoat pocket and ran to catch up with her son not knowing that, when she'd fallen, she'd ripped her housecoat pocket. The book fell from the hole without her knowledge.

Sweat rolled a salty sting into her eyes and she absently looked down, her vision blurred, into the tree-stumped crater. An empty, pint bottle of Jim Beam was lying in the hole. Alerts sounded in her head. She'd dynamited this tree stump just a few days ago, which meant that someone had put the bottle in the crater since then. And she knew only one man that preferred his Beam in a small bottle that he could easily integrate into the take-a-shot-and-chase-it-with-Coke cocktails *he* preferred.

"Albert's here," she whispered, pointing at the empty bottle.

Lenny shook his head as if he did not believe what he'd just heard. "What?"

"Bottle of Beam. Has to be his."

"But I don't see his car."

Both walked toward the open barn door, a little added caution in each step. Forget that his car was nowhere in sight; what if Albert had come home early? What if he'd lost so much in this excursion to Vegas that he'd had to pawn his car and had gotten a bus ride back? What if by chance, he'd shown up right when Cower had gone out the door to fetch his Bible? What if Albert had been drinking, had believed this man was sweet on Janine and had decided to take matters into his own hands? What if *that* was the scream they'd heard?

Lenny led his mother through the open door and into the barn. His grip was death-tight on the dagger. Janine had raised shotgun to her shoulder; her finger touched the trigger.

The barn was of average size. You could get a couple of tractors in and still have plenty of room to work and move around. Inside, stalls long empty sat unattended along the far wall. Old bales of sour hay were stacked ten feet high to the right. An old John Deere that was missing much of its engine occupied most of the left side of the floor. Beyond the tractor and at the back wall was an area where all of the hand tools were kept.

As Janine entered the barn's shadows she did not see the man lying in the rotten hay as quickly as did Lenny. Lenny ran toward the stall at the back of the barn. In that same instant, Janine saw motion in her periphery to the left. She also realized that the professor's footsteps swooped around the open barn door and disappeared behind the engine-gutted tractor also to her left. She tiptoed the path, looking ahead while keeping an eye on Lenny and the man lying in the back of the barn.

Behind the tractor was the Cubit. It rested among a scattering of tools. A shovel and hoe were propped against it. On the floor in front of the Cubit was Albert. He was quite dead. A pitchfork had been planted through his neck, the tines of the pitchfork secured in the dirt floor under him. Into one eye socket a stick of dynamite had been jammed three inches deep. There was plenty of blood, both on the dead man and on the thing that kneeled over him, which now looked up with what looked like flesh in its mouth. Janine leveled the shotgun.

It was Albert. But it couldn't be. Albert was skewered and dead on the ground. The thing that looked like Albert dropped what it had been gnawing and Janine saw what looked like a pinky fall onto the still corpse of the real Albert.

"Janee," it said. "Whoring on me, Janee?" Its voice was much deeper than the real Albert's. Its red eyes possessed an intelligence greater than Albert's. It plucked the pitchfork easily out of the ground, shook it a few times to get real Albert's neck off of its tines then pointed it at Janine. "Whoring on me?" it repeated.

It lifted the pitchfork in the air as if it were about to throw it and Janine pulled the trigger.

◻ …

The light from the barn door illuminated only the first third of the barn's interior. Small slivers of sun sliced down through unsealed cracks in the barn's roofing boards, creating a dancing montage of thick shadow interspersed by sunshine spotlights. Lenny was under one of these spotlights as he knelt down to find Cower struggling with shallow breaths. He turned the professor gingerly onto his left side. Cower's face was a mess, looked like it was broken in many more places than just his nose. He was not conscious. He was pretty close to dead, Lenny thought. And that's when he saw Albert eating Albert.

It seemed like a very long time but the numbness that locked him into place lasted only seconds. In a fraction of that moment, his body had decided that it was no longer time to run from trouble. It was time to face up to his responsibilities. His mother was somewhere over there for crying out loud. He had to at least save her.

But he couldn't move. Even when the thing dropped its food and called his mother's name, his knees remained locked. Even when the limp head of the real Albert dropped from the pitchfork's tines to a dirt floor mired in blood, his body said No!

It took the blast from the shotgun to get Lenny moving. The Albert beast suddenly lifted and flew backward into the Cubit where it bounced off one sharp wooden edge. As it rose, Lenny rose. As it moved again toward his mother, Lenny stepped away from the professor. Lenny bolted forward with the intention of thrusting the dagger through Albert's face but was held back by a hand that darted from shadows.

"No," Cower groaned. "You can't win one-on-one. You don't have the skill. You gotta surprise it." He pulled Lenny's denim pant leg, urged him to calm down. He could barely move from his fetal position. "The dagger. Into the…into the neck. It is the only way." A bit of bloody spit oozed from his mouth.

His mother screamed then appeared from behind the tractor, her hand on the barrel of the shotgun as she ran out of the barn. Behind her rushed the thing that looked like Albert, moving but not quite running, with a smile large and cunning spread wide on its face. Lenny shook his leg to break free from Cower's grip.

"Please, Lenny—" Cower moaned then went silent. He released Lenny's pant leg.

Albert exited the barn and Lenny gripped the dagger tight, took two giant steps toward the barn door with as much courage as he'd ever known, then froze in his tracks. The Cubit glowed red from behind the tractor. It filled the barn with maroon shadows. It emitted a soft hum that became inaudible when a shotgun blast echoed outside the barn.

The star on the Cubit blazed in dark red before the wooden top started to rise.

Crimson, darker than the red in the star, escaped from the Cubit's top edge. The crimson grew wider and deeper as the top panel of the Cubit rose as if hinged. It radiated an energy that drew Lenny to it.

What had Cower told him? This thing was the anti-Arc of the Covenant?

From within the Cubit rose—something. It used its hands to hoist itself through the open top. It then crawled out as a shadowy crimson outline before the Cubit slammed shut. The blaze from the Cubit's red star blinded Lenny and he lost sight of whatever had crawled out and into the shadows. Lenny shuffled back several steps, swiped the dagger out in front and around himself, sliced haphazardly at nothing he could see. The light from the red star on the Cubit died out. The barn returned to a mixture of dark shadow and sunshine spotlights.

Lenny continued fumbling backward, hoping like hell there was nothing behind him. And then movement through a few sunlight strokes that disappeared, reappeared, and disappeared too quickly for Lenny to understand. The barn grew brighter, at least in Lenny's vicinity, as he neared the rectangular patch of light that fell onto the dirt floor from the open barn door. Suddenly, something smelled very bad. And then a voice.

"Ya haf to keel ya'self," it said.

Lenny was fully immersed in the sunshine that fell through the door and his irises contracted. The barn's interior turned black. But instead of running, he waited. He knew what he would see. He was brave but afraid. He wanted to run but he stood right there.

And then the face of the beast from the box poked itself into sunshine. Something that looked like Lenny was within arm's reach and Lenny yelped like a little girl.

"S'prise," Lenny said to himself, then two hands shot into the sunshine and yanked the real Lenny into darkness.

❏ …

Janine was in panic as she raced from the barn, tripped over the tree-stumped hole, dropped the shotgun which fired on impact with the ground, ran to the house without it, closed and locked the door behind her, and headed for the storm shelter bedroom. Instead of entering the shelter, she closed the floor door and hid in the kitchen.

Right behind her came Albert. He easily kicked in the front door and headed straight for the storm shelter.

"Ya down dere?" Albert grumbled, lifting the door back onto its hinged legs. He cackled two brash belts of laughter then started down the steps.

A second or two elapsed.

"Where you? We talk. We move on to Vegas. Me, Cubit, you, dead."

Janine slammed the floor door closed then raced to the couch and began sliding it the twenty feet it would take to reach the door. The couch was sturdy and heavy. She only hoped she'd have enough time.

Four steps from the storm shelter, the floor door cracked open. Janine saw Albert's bloody eyes within; when Albert saw her he grinned in recognition. She dropped the couch and leapt as far up and as far forward as she could, landing squarely on the floor door. She heard his body tumble down the steps and she rushed back to the couch, sliding two legs across the door just as his fists beat from underneath. The couch jumped from the pounding; Janine doubted it would be enough. The only other heavy piece of furniture in the room was a cherry wood china cupboard her mother had given her years ago. Without concern for the plates and cups that toppled and broke against each other, she pushed the cupboard across the wooden floor, scratching wax as she went, to a place on the floor door next to the couch. The added weight appeared to silence his efforts.

"You die, bitch," the beast Albert hissed and punched the door. A board in the floor door rattled, loosened. "You and pain, guarantee."

Janine ran from the house. She knew what she had to do and she had to do it quickly.

She retrieved her shotgun from the yard where she'd dropped it, expelled the empty cartridges and loaded two more from her housecoat pocket. She slid, SWAT-like around the open barn door, shotgun held ready for anything.

"Lenny?" She questioned the darkness.

No answer.

"Lenny. Are you okay?"

She couldn't see much but she heard something that sounded kind of—squishy.

"Lenny—that you?"

At the far edge of the rectangular patch of sunlight that fell from the barn door onto the dirt floor was the dagger. Its haft lay in shadow but its blade glistened blue steel in the sunlight. Without hesitation, she rushed to it, retrieved it, then slipped into the darkness. It took her eyes a moment to adjust. She blinked then squinted. Lenny was at the back of the barn near one of the center stalls. Cower's body was lying in a fetal ball two stalls to the right.

"Come on Lenny!" she yelled. "You gotta help me. We gotta blow that damned Cubit back to hell, while we have a chance. I don't know how long that thing in the storm shelter's gonna stay there."

She lowered the shotgun and walked briskly toward her son. Lenny was bent down, his back to her. "Lenny?" she said, stepping more cautiously the closer she came to him. Lenny turned.

But it wasn't Lenny. As much as that thing in her room was not Albert, the thing that now faced her was not her son. It wiped something from its face with the sleeve of its Gravedigger T-shirt. Beyond it and inside the stall was what looked like a slaughtered animal.

"Mommy," the not real Lenny said.

Janine took a half step toward her son, almost hypnotically, then changed direction and ran quickly behind the tractor where the Cubit and the dynamite she used for tree-stumping were located.

"No Mommy," the Lenny-thing said. "Come here!"

Janine hunkered behind the front end of the tractor. She saw Lenny moving through shadow, walking briskly and confident toward her vantage. Her one hand gripped the dagger tighter; the finger of the other tickled the shotgun trigger.

To her left and just ten feet ahead was the Cubit. Behind the Cubit was the tool shed. In the tool shed was the dynamite.

From the right, Lenny sauntered into full view, apparently not knowing or not caring that she was there. She unloaded both shotgun shells into it.

At first, she felt the joy that is often accompanied by victory. When she saw her son's arm blow off of the right shoulder she could not believe she had just murdered her son. The second shotgun blast hit Lenny in the same location, serving only to decimate the flesh that used to be its arm. The combined blast sent Lenny to the ground and Janine bolted forward, dagger held haft up and blade down.

But it was her son. How could she drive this dagger into her son? She hesitated.

The Lenny thing turned to look up at her. It had crazy looking red eyes that were flecked with silver, as if the mind behind them belonged solely to someone or something else. Some of the shotgun pellets dotted its cheek and only part of the ear remained. Then its face turned down into barn hay.

This was not her son. Lenny was that slaughtered animal she'd seen it eating. This was everything that Lenny wasn't, all packaged in something that looked just like him. This horrific resemblance needed killing...

Janine thrust the dagger through the back of its neck. The star in the haft blazed as she thrust again and again, not realizing that with each strike, the thing that was once Lenny was aging rapidly, turning to old flesh and bone in concert with her efforts. Then, as if all the moisture had been removed from its body, the Lenny thing's chest imploded, turning to dust. She stepped back. The star in the dagger blazed so bright that most of the interior of the barn turned some shade of red. Within seconds, her son turned completely into a misshapen pile of bones.

She quickly raced to the tool shed, snatched up ten sticks of dynamite, a bag of caps and a plunger. She moved in front of the Cubit, did not look at it but only the ground beneath it, then began jamming sticks of dynamite in every soft place she could jam them. She jimmied the final stick into a spot behind the Cubit, being careful as she'd done with all the other sticks not to touch its wood surface with her hand. That's when Albert stepped through the barn door. She quickly hid behind the tractor.

"Real slow," the Albert thing said. No weapon was visible. "Gonna kill 'ya real, real slow."

She took one step forward, revealing herself from the safety of the tractor. Albert was next to the professor's body, toeing it for life signs. It saw her and immediately reacted.

"JANINE!"

It was the creepiest and most insane sound she'd ever heard. It was yelled and screeched and slurred in rage all at the same time. Albert was three times as large as Lenny. Even if she could retrieve the dagger before the Albert thing caught up to her, she knew that there was little chance in easily dashing the anti-Albert aside with a few quick dagger thrusts as she'd done with anti-Lenny. She stepped back behind the tractor and began wiring up the dynamite sticks. There was only one way out of the barn and she planned to take everything and everyone with her.

"Mind me," anti-Albert said. "Get ready. We got good lovin' ta do."

Anti-Albert was a few feet from the tractor when Janine finished wiring what would be one mighty explosion. She closed her eyes and plunged the dynamite. But nothing happened. She'd been squinting so hard, thinking that her body was about to be blown into small fragments, that opening them was painful. She looked from anti-Albert, who now turned and started after her, to the one wire she'd forgotten to attach.

She was out of luck. Out of distance. Out of hope. The entire evening had flown by so fast. There was no time for wondering about life. It was a time for dying. She attached the last wire.

And then, just as quickly as it had taken her to write her life away, the professor suddenly leapt from the shadows to her right. Cower wailed, "RUN!" as he and the anti-Albert thing fell together into the bone pile that had once been an evil incarnation of her son.

Janine ran, the shotgun forgotten behind her, her son now convincingly dead in her mind, her new husband hopefully dying between the hands of Cower. Once in the house, she stood before the decimation of the couch and china cupboard, and a storm shelter door that was ripped into pieces.

Why she jumped into the shelter, she didn't know. If she hadn't, she would have surely been ripped apart by the blast that swept from the barn and through the house. From Janine's vantage on her back at the bottom of the staircase, her head throbbing from the impact with one or more of the steps, she saw what she believed would be the last thing this reality had for her.

A vision of everything that had been hers and Michael's and Lenny's blew past her in a destructive wave of fire and rubble.

PART II

PARADISE LOST

SUNDAY, SUMMER 2008

Much has been said about the small island town of Port Aransas. Tales too tall to believe are common. As with most stories that are passed on through generations, facts are changed as dozens of storytellers add personal nuance. Like the story of what many in the town refer to as the "great white summer." Fishermen will argue that *Jaws* was much more than a blockbuster movie in the 70s. Most will argue that Peter Benchley based his story on actual events that took place right here, along the beaches of Mustang Island more than a dozen years before the construction of the Corpus Christi shipping channel.

And then there's the most popular tale of pirate Jean LaFitte's treasure. As he did in so many coastal towns along the Caribbean Sea, LaFitte left a mark on Port Aransas that is so powerfully convincing that it goes beyond legend. It is a part of Port A's history, so much so that the story accompanies many of the town's tourism brochures. The legend provides for much marketing hype that has brought more than just a few to the island in search of immediate wealth. Somewhere buried in the thirty-mile stretch of beach sand, LaFitte is said to have stashed a great wealth, plundered by he and his crew throughout the infant days of the United States.

More recently, there is the not-so-tall tale of corporate and political corruption—nothing that had been proven so far, but the evidence was so apparent a blind man could see it. Onshore table gambling had never been allowed in Texas, but the powers that be were pushing for a new casino on the island. Their argument was simple. Legalized offshore gambling thrived in Gulf States like Louisiana and Mississippi. Port Aransas was an island therefore it was "offshore." Port Aransas was also a major summer vacation spot and a popular winter retreat. And to help move the tall, illogical argument forward, Port Aransas was now run by a bunch of bumpkins who would let anyone do anything as long as *they*, not the island, could profit from it. This new political structure had already usurped the power once held by the island conservationists by allowing new construction on protected marine life habitats. How would the town grow if the damned sandhuggers always got in the way, they'd argued.

And just as it was with any policy or procedure or law, once you gave special interest latitude, the road to social change was already mud on the boot—or in the case of Port Aransas, sand in the toes. Once wealthy island residents began raking in the cash, progress and backhoes would be forever linked. And tearing up a small part of the beach for a casino would seem like necessary evolution. All you needed was money, influence and a few toughs who could happily offer the choice of blackmail or bribery or something much, much worse.

Billy Jo Presser believed Chancey Lett came to Port A to ruin his island by using such corruption as a tool and he was going to prove it. However, unknown to Billy or anyone else on the island, Lett's arrival and the accompanying controversy had nothing to do with the building of a casino. It had everything to do with myth, legend and lore.

It had taken him only a few minutes to place his robotic starfish inside the canister tube of the drive thru at the Port A branch of the Big Texas Bank. He now sat in his vintage 1963 VW Bus, a hundred yards from the bank, manipulating the joysticks on a computer console that, hopefully, would move Shoe up the tube and into the bank.

Shoe's video eyeball revealed a plastic tunnel of dull sunshine capped by darkness, but the drive-thru tube schematics pinned to a corkboard above the computer monitor showed that at the tube's apex, a ninety-degree turn would enable Shoe's entry into the teller window. Moving Shoe beyond that point would require Billy's accurate memory of the bank's interior.

In his periphery, Billy saw the city police cruiser before it pulled into the parking lot of the Treasure Trove Inn. He remained in the back of the VW Bus and calmly watched the cruiser as it passed a full lot of June vacationers' vehicles. Billy's VW was parked at the rear of the lot nearest the bank and as the cruiser passed, it slowed. Officer Keadle knew the vehicle. Billy knew Officer Keadle. And even though Officer Keadle looked right at him, Billy knew that the sun's reflection off the VW's windshield effectively hid all occupants within. It was not unusual to find Billy Jo Presser's classic VW parked anywhere within Port A's city limits. He owned and operated one of the town's best seafood restaurants and was renowned for some of the best catering this side of Texas. Officer Keadle would suppose, incorrectly, that Billy was inside the Trove conducting business. The cruiser passed without suspicion.

Billy returned his attention to the computer monitor. Shoe had already halved the distance to the top of the tube. Apparently, the adjustments he'd made to the robotic starfish's five feet where working better than he'd anticipated. He studied the schematics that he'd obtained rather effortlessly from the manufacturer's web site and coupled them with his memory, a skill he'd honed from his two years at MIT. He was superb at memorization. The talent had saved him both academically and socially more times than he could recall.

He'd gone into the bank pretending that he was interested in some long term investments that went beyond his restaurant. Just as the Big

Texas Bank slogan promoted, "Meet the friendliest people in Texas," Billy was quick to find the helpful services of the bank's executive assistant, Stephanie Drake.

For three days Billy visited the bank with questions about investments he'd supposedly heard about from restaurant clientele or from Internet research he'd conducted. Each day his mind's memory machine logged as much of the apparent distances to points beyond Stephanie's desk. Last Thursday he'd been fortunate enough to witness the changing of the tellers and had seen the interior of the teller window through the open door. It was pretty much what he'd anticipated. It looked very similar to the pictures of teller windows he'd found at the drive-thru tube manufacturer's web site: a chair where the teller sat, a waist-high shelf that ran the width of the window, and most importantly, the plastic, not wire, version of Drive-Thru Tube's Model #DT9000. The wire version would have made it next to impossible for Shoe to crawl down once inside the bank. The plastic version, unlike the wire version was totally encased, making the crawl within a solid tube much more manageable than along four stainless steel cage wires.

The way Billy had figured it, Shoe could breach the exterior of the bank through the tube then crawl down the interior section of it and onto the teller shelf. He'd have to take the chance that no obstacles would be lying on the counter shelving which would impede Shoe's movement to the wall. Once down the wall and onto the floor, Shoe would have to crawl under the teller door. Billy had the approximate height of the opening in mind from his visit Thursday but until Shoe tried it, he'd be unsure. Then it was onto Shoe's destination: Stephanie Drake's desk.

Not only did Drake's desk sit pretty much in the middle of all the action, the surface was covered by an assortment of sea creature ornaments in celebration of Port A's "Sea Life Month." Beyond the conventional selection of real sand dollars and seashells and the kind of fake seaweed you can get at Wal-Mart, there was a SpongeBob Squarepants plush toy and several of his cartoon plush friends sitting around the plastic seaweed as if they were talking to each other. More importantly, several of Drake's ornaments were starfish and were anchored to the wooden sides and legs of the desk. Thanks to Port A's celebration of the sea and Drake's creativity, one more starfish ornament would not make a difference. The starfish motif made perfect camouflage.

Shoe scaled the tube, crawled through the dark transition between outside tube and inside tube, then crept downward and onto the teller's counter. The progress lasted more than thirty minutes, during which Billy did not move his eyes from the computer monitor.

As Shoe settled onto the teller counter and squirm-crawled in a clockwise direction, a coin tray became visible in Shoe's video eyeball and on Billy's computer monitor. There were no coins in it, of course. Still, the coin holder could prove immovable. Shoe's delicate construction could nudge a few ounces and no more. Billy had already wasted too many hours trying to increase tension strength in the robot's five starry legs but repeatedly found that anything heavier than a half a can of Budweiser only served to pop the water vessels that served as the lifeblood and mechanical motion for the starfish.

Billy thumbed the joystick forward, gently, as the first orange-yellow bands of Texas dusk pierced the VW's interior. Glare made the video monitor hard to see, revealing dusk specks that he had not wiped clean in some time. His hair twinkled in a banded blonde array that fell to his shoulders. A bead of sweat rolled into one eye.

One starfish arm nudged at the coin tray. Graphic bars in a pop-up window on the computer monitor rose into the yellow as tensile pressure rose against Shoe's extremities.

Billy pressed the joystick further. Graphic bars rose from yellow to red. The coin tray didn't move.

Orange sunshine wrested beads of sweat from the nape of his neck and they collected in a half moon of dampness above the Pat McGee's Surf Shop logo on the back of his T-shirt.

Just a little more, he thought. He'd reengineered Shoe just for this possibility. If the robot was going to break, it would have already done so. *Just a little more.*

He pressed the joystick ever so lightly. The pressure bars lifted, bright red and maxed out. And then, suddenly, the coin tray flew off the counter making an audible cling-thud as it hit the carpet below. Shoe scooted quickly forward as the pressure bars returned to normal. Billy released the joystick. On the counter where the coin tray had rested was a circular imprint left by what Billy guessed was a can or glass of Coke. The syrupy residue had anchored the coin tray until Shoe's last desperate push forward had freed it from the sticky connection.

Billy wiped sweat from his neck, moved Shoe to the teller room wall and started the robot down, keeping in nearly perfect sync with the sun as it dropped toward the Texas horizon. As the sun's glare left the VW's windshield, Billy maneuvered Shoe to the floor. The computer monitor now showed the gap at the bottom of the teller room door. There was about an inch of clearance. Shoe would fit, but just barely.

The interior of the bank was still visible but would not be for long. Billy guessed that he'd have about forty-five minutes before all dusk turned to black. He would not be able to maneuver the robot in darkness. Fortunately the path to Stephanie Drake's desk was a straight line, about twenty feet ahead. The loop pile carpeted floor would provide good traction for the starfish's tiny tube feet and as Billy had calculated the night before, the trip to the desk would take about twenty minutes to traverse and another ten would be needed to climb to a position on the side of the desk. That left about ten minutes of "wiggle room."

The view on the monitor was like a scene from the movie "Land of the Giants." The castor of a chair was a black spherical rock. Trees of finely carved chair legs towered on four corners. Twenty feet seemed like twenty miles in this video world of Giants.

Shoe reached Stephanie Drake's desk in a little under twenty minutes and started its ascent to an undecorated spot that would provide a great view of the bank vault, Mitchell Bone's office, and a cluster of three chairs where those waiting to speak to the bank manager would sit. If evidence was to be gathered, this would be the most likely place to record it. The evidence Billy hoped to gather would tag Mitchell Bone, in collusion with Chancey Lett, as a liar, a cheat and someone who didn't give a damn about the small island community. He and his bank had emblazoned "Meet the Friendliest People in Texas" all over billboards, newspaper inserts, the town's trolley and the trolley stop benches, and the island ferries, but the truth of the matter was that Bone didn't give a damn. His "friendliness" began with a crooked grin and a small hand that he used to welcome people and their money into his bank. His eyes were peevishly small and his toupee was horribly fashioned giving his entire "friendly" appearance a childish indignation that most people could not see through.

Except Billy.

He knew what Mitchell Bone really meant to do. Gambling in Port A would not place it on the map as the "Southern Las Vegas." Gambling in Port A would destroy a hometown atmosphere that made it a beach laden vacation haven unlike any other. It would destroy the island's marine sanctuary and change one of the Gulf's best fishing locations in ways Billy and many deceived fishermen could not imagine.

A door opened and voices murmured outside of the VW, breaking Billy's concentration. Two doors slammed shut and he watched the back end of a Chevy pickup roll away from the parking spot next to his. The

Chevy's headlights snapped on as the truck left the parking lot and Billy turned back to the monitor. Darkness veiled much of the bank's interior.

He punched a set of commands on the computer keyboard to place Shoe in a standby record mode that would fire up once light returned to the office the following day. Tomorrow, he would check the collected evidence that Shoe was programmed to transmit to his apartment atop the restaurant.

Mitchell Bone had little time left in Port A. The residents would run him out of town once they saw what Billy knew he'd find: connections to crime syndicates, bribery of local officials and other flavors of coercion.

Billy took the usual detour on his way home. Even though night had fallen, activity on the beach, especially in mid-June, would have only slightly diminished. Weekenders from Corpus would have already taken their tanned bodies back to the city but locals and those from Rockport and Aransas Pass across the channel were rarely done by nine-thirty. There was an ambiance to the surf after dusk that was more enticing than the hot Texas sun on sandy brown beaches, especially for those who lived their lives under it. Vacation pamphlets never touted this as one of the island's great treasures and Billy was grateful for this ignorance.

He drove Alister Street to Avenue G where Pat McGee's remained brightly lit. Inside, several people roamed about, shuffling through a large selection of shirts, shorts, shells and shoes that each hoped would make the perfect souvenir. As he turned onto Avenue G toward the beach, he saw Coolie and Sweets outside, talking and pointing at a selection of boards. Billy slowed to a stop.

"BJ," Sweets yelled. "Coolie wants a new ride but he ain't got the cash for it." Sweets pointed at a freerider that sparkled fluorescent green under the surf shop's canopy.

"Ugly," Billy acknowledged. "Girls'll run away when they see his skinny legs on that thing." He grinned. Coolie was always looking for a new surfboard. "Besides, since when did you find three hundred bucks?"

"Just lookin' and dreamin', man," Coolie countered. "Sides, I got into some cash just the other night."

"Yeah," Billy said. "And what bank did you rob?" He couldn't help glancing back at the computer monitor where minutes before he'd used it to commit a felony.

"No, man. It's not like that. Yo' mamma paid me good for some good lovin'."

"A dollar won't even do a down payment," Billy said.

All three of the surfers laughed. Sweets walked toward Billy but traffic behind pushed the VW onward.

"You two still comin' to the luau Tuesday night?" Billy said.

"Hell yes," Sweets said. "We'll be there a couple of hours before it starts if the swells they're predicting show up." He stopped at the curb as Billy's VW moved slowly forward. Someone hit their horn behind the VW. "Up it, Eastcoaster," Sweets added and threw both arms in the air.

"See you tomorrow," Billy said.

"Right on," Sweets agreed.

"Later," Coolie yelled and turned back toward the fluorescent board to dream.

The coastal dunes showed in silhouette under the waxing moon that was three-quarters dark. A salty breeze ruffled his hair as a coyote howled somewhere close by. Drifts of clouds interrupted sparse moonlight, shifting silhouette to darkness in intermittent spurts. Between the dunes, Avenue G split the natural barriers and Billy saw the comforting froth of white surf. The car that had honked behind him shot by in the no-passing lane and the driver, an apparent male tourist and his female companion, scowled at him. Billy paid no attention. Off-islanders always seemed to want to get places much more quickly than the locals. Billy was used to it. Besides, he was already aware of Officer Keadle's police cruiser which sat just beyond the last dune in wait for those who didn't have patience. Keadle's blue and red rollers lit the quiet night and the guy that had passed him, which Billy now realized was the same Chevy pickup that had been parked beside him in the Treasure Trove's parking lot, came to a stop a few hundred feet from the beach. Billy waved at Keadle as he passed.

Several cars slowly roamed the wide beach in opposite directions. Many more were parked closer to the shoreline but would soon have to move as high tide crept inland. Several tents stood along the beach but they, too, would soon move since county ordinance prohibited camping overnight in all but the state park campground a few miles to the south. Up ahead was the Horace Caldwell Pier. Billy passed it, slowed to dodge a group of fishermen, then parked on the north side of the pier where many of the local surfers gathered. The surf was lame this Sunday evening and no one was out.

The sound of crashing waves pulled him from the VW to the surf and he stepped into it knee-deep. Moonlight glittered atop shallow breaks. There was a magnetic pull to it all that only surfers understood. Riding waves was the only place left on the planet that one could find complete solace. Man and nature together as one. And Mitchell Bone wanted to destroy it all. If Bone's plans went through, the surf culture in Port A would die. Plans were to build the casino on the south side of the pier where some of the better surfing on the island could only be found. He'd spent the last two years in Port A, on the beach, at the pier, and now it was all about to change. Unless he could find evidence at the bank, Coolie, Sweets, Bottlenose, CrabMan and he, BJ, would have nowhere to surf. And Billy could not let that happen. None of the local surfers could let that happen. It was the reason why they were having the luau: to protest and hopefully convince voters that a casino was wrong. Even Officer Keadle had promised to show up. He was one of the few officials that Bone and his bank had not coerced. Keadle had lived his life in Port A and Billy knew he was not about to let any amount of money change his native community.

At the end of the pier to his right, several silhouetted fishermen stood two hundred yards from the shoreline, casting and reeling against a blacker ocean background. Tiny poles in tiny hands fought against fish and surf. To Billy, they looked like statues in a black and white cartoon made by animators stuck back in the 30s. Simple up and down motions. An occasional shift from one point on the pier to another. Just a bunch of easily drawn frames, repetitious, and not difficult to create even for a child. Almost mechanical. As fishing, to Billy, seemed to be.

Far off to his left, the south jetty of the channel that serviced Corpus Christi Bay was hidden except for the marker lights at the head of the jetty and several fishermen's lanterns that pockmarked the length of the rocky passage. Joel Canton stood near one of those lanterns, Billy suspected. He'd be reeling in tonight's catch of speckled trout and redfish that he'd want to sell to Billy at his restaurant the following morning. And Billy would buy whatever he had to offer. He always did, regardless of the health of the fish. Joel needed the money. Fishing is all that he did. Fishing is all that he knew. He was poor because of it. Half the time, Billy would chuck the fish in the trash but he would always buy, for prices that easily exceeded what he spent for larger quantities from the local companies.

And that's how it was in this little island town. People helping people. People taking their time to get from one place to another. People dreaming about things they would never afford. People unlike Mitchell Bone and his greedy desire to destroy it all.

Before returning to his VW, Billy noticed that one of the jetty lantern lights, just a starry dot against the night, abruptly turned black.

☐ …

Joel's hands were much older than he. They'd pulled in enough Texas Gulf sea life to feed a small country. Scars from hooks and sharks teeth and fillet knives and bar fights riddled the valleys between the veins. They were strong and weak at the same time. They could reel in a fourteen-foot Marlin or snap a man's arm who'd looked at him the wrong way after he'd pounded an assortment of Jack Daniels and Stroh's, but they could never caress the soft check of a woman or hold the nimble hand of a child.

Both his bar fighting days and marriage were over. He'd never had any children. Women and kids had always been second to fishing. Nothing to him had ever been more important than fishing. And every time he threw out a line he regretted his selfish history. Tonight was no exception.

He jerked his fishing pole and the line snapped, toppling him against his lantern which rolled, broke, and died immediately. There were no curse words left in his vocabulary—really wasn't a need for any anymore—so he sat on the jetty rocks wondering how he was going to afford another reel of fishing line and, more importantly, another lantern. He had a dozen fish in his basket—not enough to buy a new lantern. He exhaled against the Gulf breeze which tossed his unwashed breath back in his face. Slowly, he collected his gear and his catch and made his way from the jetty toward the shoreline. He'd walked it a thousand times and remembered the rocky uneven path as a blind man remembered his own home's interior. Tonight that memory would be quite valuable since it was almost impossible to see his footsteps without the lantern. He slipped a couple of times but nowhere as many as he'd slipped up in life.

PART II

EVIDENCE

Stephanie Drake was a consummate depressant on Monday. It was the job that made her so. Even in a "beach town" it was hard to relegate the weekend as a memory for what would dictate the rest of the next five-day span. And to her that's what life now was. Weekends and the five-day span. And the catalyst to the depression was always Monday.

"Sea Life Month" lay spread across her desk. She'd taken a little pride in most of the adornments since more than half of the objects had been dictated. Even in creativity, she'd been shackled. She didn't like sharks, but there one was, doubling as a stapler. Chomp...chomp... here's the report you wanted Mr. Bone. Chomp...chomp...here's your loan application Mr. and Mrs. Jones. The stapler never worked right—it always took two chomps (and sometimes three depending on the number of pages) to get the Jaws-like stapler to do what it was supposed to do.

But she had SpongeBob. His cheery, plastic face always made her smile.

She fell back into her chair, a hard, wooden, decorative piece of furniture that was more show than function. Her ass went numb during the day as did her mind, especially on Monday.

Carol stood behind her as if appearing from nowhere. She dropped a stack of papers on the desk that the Jaws stapler couldn't handle. "Bone's got some heavy investors coming in this morning," she said.

"What time?" Stephanie said. Stephanie and Carol had not liked each other since the day young Steph arrived.

"I don't know for sure," Carol said. Stephanie spun in her uncomfortable chair to look at Carol who had chosen a complimentary wardrobe of sea life patterns on her skirt and blouse. "You're the exec. assistant."

Stephanie mustered a smile, the same one she used each time that a natural smile could not surface. "This morning is what Bone told me." The surname was absent but she had not meant to sound so reproachable, especially to Carol, the bank's most senior employee and holder of numerous "Employees of the Month."

"Just be ready," Carol said. Stephanie thought Carol treated her like an unruly child that often needed a swift kick since the "real world" was still only concept.

"Got it covered," Stephanie said, holding back a dictionary of words that begged for release. "I just wanted to know if he'd given you any..." She struggled for patience. "I just wanted insight into the arrival time."

"You're the exec. assistant," Carol reminded her. "*You* should have all the information."

Carol's emphasis on "You" meant that it was *you*, a young pretty thing fresh out of college that got the job of executive assistant instead of *me*, a dedicated employee who *deserved* the title—and raise.

Carol was another of the reasons that made Monday and the four days that came after it so hard to deal with. The woman turned and stepped quickly toward her post, one she'd occupied for twenty-five years, behind the teller's counter. Stephanie ignored her and riffled through her preparation of the day's clientele.

Not all of the bank's employees were as hateful as Carol. Many, in fact, were quite friendly. It was easy for most of them to serve the bank's mantra as the "Friendliest People in Texas." For Carol, it was all fiction.

"Good morning, Stephanie," said Barbara Wallace as she spun the dials on the bank vault to open it. Her smile was genuine.

"Good morning," Stephanie acknowledged and returned the smile.

Chester Kalimaris, one of the bank's loan officers, came up from behind her and gently patted her shoulder. "How was the weekend?" he asked, smiled, and continued toward his office next to Mitchell Bone's.

"Fine, fine," Stephanie said, trying to sound appreciative. "Lots of sun and sand."

"Never any shortage of that around here," Chester said. "You all settled into the apartment now?"

"Just a couple of scattered boxes, but mostly, yes." Barbara walked over to her as Chester entered his office.

"That offer is still open you know," Barbara said. "Anytime you want to do a girls-night-out just say so. Corpus has a great night life."

Stephanie appreciated her, and Chester's, kindness. They understood how Carol got under peoples' nerves, especially those that Carol believed had stolen her promotion.

As the rest of the bank's employees shuffled in, Stephanie sat at her "Sea Life" desk and began thumbing through the stack of papers that Carol had dropped in front of her. All of them dealt with the acquisition of funding by Mitchell Bone's greatest new customer and friend, Chancey Lett. There were documents of collateral security originating from Las Vegas, several pages of reports from the three major credit bureaus, a list of real estate interests in Sedona, Arizona, and much more. All tolled, Chancey Lett was worth more than a hundred million dollars according to the net worth total revealed in summary on the last page of the stack. No wonder Mr. Bone had been in such a pleasant mood these past few weeks. His bank was about to open its largest account in history. The proposed Mayan Casino would make this branch of the Big Texas Bank much richer and Bone would rise in whatever circles bank managers rose into.

It was shortly after nine o'clock when the day's first customer, a local lady who owned a small coffee shop on Alister Street, strolled in and toward Carol who remained busy at her window and did not look up. Mrs. Black, owner of Black's Café, moved to Barbara's window instead and Stephanie saw Carol almost grin. Seniority kept her in the job. Friendliness certainly did not.

Stephanie fired up her computer and began going through the daily routine of account checks and balances but her mind soon wandered and the columns of dollar signs became apparitions. She typed methodically while the cast of SpongeBob characters on her desk beckoned for attention. Patrick the starfish, Gary the snail, Mr. Krabs and, of course, SpongeBob were lined up along the left corner of her desk. They were *her* addition to the sea life motif.

Who lives in pineapple under the sea...

The dollar signs and decimals blurred. Her typing slowed.

SpongeBob Square Pants.

She stared at SpongeBob's bucktoothed grin and couldn't help smiling.

Absorbent and porous and yellow is he...

The theme song took control of her thoughts.

SpongeBob Square Pants.

If nautical nonsense be somethin' ya wish...

"SpongeBob Square Pants," she murmured.

Then drop on the deck and...

"Flop like a fish," she said a bit louder.

"Miss Drake!"

Her mind was suddenly wrenched from daydream. Mr. Bone was standing in front of her. He smiled but only because of the two other men that were standing beside him.

"The SpongeBob song," the man with the greasy hair said. "I love that show." He plucked the SpongeBob toy from Stephanie's desk. "Aye, Captain," he said to it.

"Miss Drake," Mr. Bone said, the tension across his forehead tentatively easing. "This is Chancey Lett." He pointed at the man who held SpongeBob. "And this is his..."

Stephanie stood and shook Lett's free hand.

"This is Mr. Lett's head of security," Mr. Bone continued.

Stephanie turned her body to acknowledge the large man beside Lett but he offered no hand as greeting, did not smile and only looked cautiously around the bank. His face was pockmarked with scars, some tiny, some long and hard. He carried a satchel that was brimming with papers. He gazed at Stephanie without emotion.

"Don't mind him," Lett said. "He always looks like that. It's his job." He returned SpongeBob to his lifeless companions on Stephanie's desk, leaned forward and placed a hand to the side of his mouth. "A job I could never do. I smile too much," he added, thumbing toward his bodyguard and producing a wider grin that was strangely comforting.

Mr. Bone returned the conversation to business. "Miss Drake. Would you please gather Mr. Lett's documents together and bring them to my office?"

"Mitch," Lett said. Stephanie had never heard anyone call Mitchell Bone that. "You are too much business sometimes."

"Sorry Mr. Lett. I just thought that…well you have a flight out in just a few hours."

"Chancey, my man. Please. Mr. Lett sounds too formal."

"Ah, yes, Mr. Chanc…" Stephanie had never seen Mitchell Bone squirm before either. "Yes, Chancey."

"Nice meeting you Miss Drake." Lett was used to being in control. It was obvious by the ease of his conversation and the sweat that suddenly appeared below Mr. Bone's toupee forehead. "What is your first name, dear? Miss Drake is quite amorous if not mysterious but I prefer first names."

"Stephanie."

"Wonderful," Lett said, his smile never faltering. "Stephanie Drake. Well it's good to meet you Stephanie Drake."

Mitchell Bone swayed impatiently. His smile, having been a part of his face for the entire introduction, must have been agonizing to maintain.

"This way, Mr.—Chancey," he said.

Lett and his bodyguard followed Bone to his office. Stephanie collected the papers that Carol had given her and followed the trio inside. She didn't look behind her but could feel Carol's cold stare.

Bone sat behind his red mahogany desk, the trophy from a long horn steer positioned on the wall directly above him. Stephanie set the documents on his desk and turned to exit.

"Miss Drake," Bone said. "Would you mind helping Chancey's…"

"Assistant," Lett interjected. "He's my bodyguard, assistant, and encyclopedia of self-defense knowledge. But Assistant will do just fine."

Bone's cordial smile returned. "Would you mind assisting Chancey's assistant with an addition to our vault?"

"Of course."

"Thank you," Lett said as she and his bodyguard turned in unison. "If all of Port Aransas is as charming as you then I know my investment will come back to me tenfold."

Stephanie left the office, waited for Lett's bodyguard to follow, then closed the office door behind him.

"How can I help you?" she said.

"Outside," the bodyguard said, pointing. His voice was exactly how Stephanie expected it to be. Man of few words. Matter-of-fact. Deep and without inflection. The long scar etched above his lip and deep into his cheek seemed to damper any hope of a smile. He led her out of the bank's entry without offering the door.

Outside, the bodyguard opened the rear hatch of a black Hummer that was parked in front of the bank doors, pulled out a hand dolly, then muscled a wooden crate that was about the size of a large television set. The bodyguard's thick arms stretched wide to wrap his hands around the width of the crate as he hunched into the rear of the Hummer. Slowly he slid it out, teetered it on the Hummer's tailgate, then, very gently, lowered it onto the dolly. He didn't grunt even though the box seemed heavy and was awkward to handle. He didn't sweat even though the Port A sun had already warmed the island to ninety degrees. He didn't say a word even when Stephanie asked him what was in the crate. He did smell, however— body odor and Aqua Velva.

The bodyguard dollied the crate toward the bank and Stephanie shuffled forward to hold the doors open. Once inside, he rolled the crate directly into the vault without her help, as if he'd worked inside banks and vaults all of his life. Safety deposit boxes lined most of the vault walls but there was a small space toward the back about the size of a large coat closet that the bodyguard set the crate into.

"Yes. That will do just fine," Stephanie said, knowing that it would be useless to ask the bodyguard to move it. He followed her out of the vault and stood there as if protecting the crate, both hands clasped together in front of him, his concentrated stare passing over Stephanie and toward the front of the bank.

The door to Bone's office cracked open slightly but the two men remained just beyond. Stephanie heard the muffled end of their conversation.

"Well it's coming up for a vote on Saturday. I think we have the numbers," Bone said, his voice barely audible. Stephanie inadvertently craned her neck in that direction.

"I hope so," Lett responded. "There's a lot of money to be…"

"Miss Drake?" Carol interrupted her concentration on the conversation. She stood behind her.

"…up their beach," Lett continued.

Carol intentionally distracted her. She desperately wanted to put Stephanie in her place, wanted to tell all of the bank employees that Miss Drake was eavesdropping but, perhaps because of the importance of the client visiting today, she refrained.

"…a million dollars…" Lett said whose voice was again suffocated by Carol's incessant intrusion.

"Don't you think Mr. Lett's assistant might like some coffee?"

You ask him, Stephanie thought. *He's not much of a conversationalist.*

And before Carol could become any more annoying, the door to Bone's office swung wide open.

"I understand," Bone said, following Lett out of the office. "But I can assure you that I have all the vot…" He looked a bit startled when he noticed Stephanie and Carol both staring at him. "You ladies have work to do?"

Carol immediately turned and went back to her position behind the teller window. Stephanie turned her attention to her desk. Lett smiled at her.

"You have every right to be curious, dear," he whispered, bending closer as if what he said was secret. "Lots of changes coming your way." His grin widened. "Lots of changes for lots of people." His complexion was flawless, tanned, strong. "I will see you again very soon, perhaps in a much less intimidating atmosphere."

"Nice meeting you," she said.

"My pleasure." Lett walked confidently, his black Ralph Lauren suit glistening within the rays of sun that marked his exit from the bank. Bone was right on his heels. The bodyguard took up the rear.

Stephanie turned back to the open vault; her gaze landed on the crate. It looked out of place within the sterile, symmetric feel of the deposit boxes that lined the walls. It emitted an electric buzz that she'd never heard in the month since she'd started working at the bank.

She thought about Lett and his charm, his bodyguard and his smell, Mr. Bone and his greed-driven groveling, SpongeBob and his friends.

A customer entered the bank and went right to Carol's window. Carol mustered a smile and took the woman's deposit.

Stephanie tried not to think about Carol.

❐ ...

The Surf Side restaurant was actually located a couple of blocks over from the surf. It was close enough that beachcombers could easily stop in for a quick afternoon snack, and far enough from the tourist trap seafood restaurants lined up on Cotter Avenue that it was considered by the Port Aransas tourist brochure to be: "a quiet dining experience away from the busyness of fishermen, fishing boats, and overpriced dinners."

Billy Jo Presser lived atop the restaurant in a two-bedroom apartment-like space that was plenty large enough for a single guy and his robot hobby.

The place had a small bathroom with a standup shower, a center space that was both his living room and bedroom, and a third room that served as both his lab and his office—he called it his "lab-office." In the center space was his bed, one five-drawer, tall dresser with a second-hand lamp on top of it, a brown bean bag chair, and an old, white end table, the kind you buy in a box and assemble yourself. A coffee pot sat on the end table. There was no kitchen but he did have a small, dorm-sized refrigerator where he kept cold water, an occasional beer, and leftovers from the restaurant.

He'd been up since seven o'clock even though his restaurant would not open until eleven-thirty. Running a restaurant was replete with paperwork and Billy used Monday mornings to gain any early-in-the-week advantage over a chore that would otherwise overtake him by Friday. His quarterly tax statements were coming due and he needed to get his employees withholding information organized. He did not complete the tax processes; he was too impatient for this financial mandate. Besides, every time he'd attempted to do his own taxes, the idea of giving his money to the government always fired him up so much that he'd never been able to complete, accurately, all of the necessary forms. The town's only CPA handled this task for him. Still, the CPA needed organized information and Mondays were the only days when forms that started with a "W" came anywhere close to Billy's hands.

By the time he'd finished organizing Uncle Sam's needs it was nearly nine-thirty. He'd already downed a half a pot of coffee and stood from the paperwork to grab a fourth cup. The "paperwork" desk in his lab-office was small. It had been a grade-schooler's homework station before Billy had purchased it from the child's mother at a yard sale for only twenty bucks. It had two drawers that sometimes stuck and a space under the desk top that was only slightly wider than his two knees pressed together, an uncomfortable piece of furniture to say the least. Why had he purchased such an uncomfortable workspace? He loathed paperwork. Subconsciously, he had decided that buying something uncomfortable and barely usable would decrease the likelihood that he'd be spending much time using it.

Paperwork aside, the small desk did serve a much better purpose. It provided for a great assembly station when soldering his robots. His soldering iron and coil of solder, his small jewelers hand tools, and his eyepiece magnifying glass, once positioned on the desk top, left him plenty of space on his workbench to assemble one robot. Unfortunately, on several occasions, he'd forgotten to secure paperwork inside the tall file cabinet next to his small desk before working on his robots, and had burned away small corners of important documents with the soldering iron.

He shuffled the employee paperwork into its appropriate manila folder and jammed it into the top drawer of the file cabinet. A folder full of merchant receipts for supplies and food, plus the utility bills remained on the desk, but the blinking green status light on one of his computer hard drives vied for his attention. Shoe was busy recording a day in the life of the Big Texas Bank. Every time the green light blinked, more evidence against Mitchell Bone was being stored. Billy itched to watch as the evidence was received, a nearly synchronized vision of what was going on in the bank at that very moment. He took a step toward the computer then gazed back at the folder of bills to be paid, reminding himself that Mondays were for paperwork and that to allow distractions would mean that the rest of the week would be agonizing, especially since he'd be occupied with protesting and surfing and collecting evidence.

Billy refilled his coffee cup and returned to his lab-office to pay bills, review inventory and create a list of supplies and food he'd need this week at Surf Side. By eleven o'clock, much of the paperwork had been completed. He'd have to put another hour into it Tuesday morning but for now he needed to get downstairs, and prep the restaurant. "Sea Life Month" always increased activity for all businesses in Port A, especially for the seafood restaurants.

Downstairs, Jerry, from Devries Seafood Supply, was talking to Kale

Jurgenson, Billy's restaurant manager. Kale turned as Billy approached.

"How many are we serving at the Trove, Thursday?" Kale said as Billy walked up to the two men. "Jerry says the Specks are running fat and delicious right now."

"Fifty adults and a few kids," Billy said. "What do figure, Kale?"

"I'm thinkin', with the increased business inside and this catering gig… about two to three hundred pounds of Speck should get us started. But I'd like to get half now and a fresher half later in the week. Order might go up by then."

Jerry appeared quite pleased.

"And shrimp?" Billy asked.

"A hundred pounds at least," Kale said, "but we get that from Brigade's across the channel."

Jerry's face lost its happy salesman appearance. "I can give you a better price on the shrimp," he said.

"And quality?" Kale asked before Billy could do so. "We still remember that last 'deal' you gave us. Shrimp were puny compared to Brigade's."

Jerry was silent.

Kale smiled. "But the speckled trout you guys get is still some of the best on the island."

"Especially when the Surf Side fixes em' up," Jerry added. "OK, then. But promise me you'll keep us in mind. We *do* pull in some pinky-sizers to rival Brigade's. I'll add a couple of pounds to your order, no charge."

Billy left the two men dealing, and headed into the restaurant.

Kale was one-of-a-kind when it came to restaurant managers. He was always on time if not early, had a good relationship with most of the wait staff, cooks, and suppliers, and was just, generally, a nice guy. He'd come over to the island after completing a year at the restaurant management school in Corpus, but much of what Billy liked about Kale could not be taught in class. He was people-oriented, a personality trait that one could only be born and raised with, a trait that was absent from so many so-called restaurant managers. Billy was lucky to have him, and he'd told Kale this more than once.

He was also lucky to have his head chef. Unfortunately, Pedro Melindez would loose his work permit this summer unless Billy and he could find a way to meet the immigration requirements for renewal. They had already applied for his admittance into a culinary school, and if accepted this would get him another couple of years in the United States, but, as in any catch-22 situation, going to school meant providing some sort of permit or proof of citizenship, and you couldn't get a permit without showing evidence of need, such as attending school.

"Mí jefe," Pedro said from the kitchen when he saw Billy cross in front of the service counter. "Buenos días."

"And good morning to you," Billy replied. Pedro slipped through the kitchen's swinging door and stood offering his handshake while smiling a set of bright white teeth that were augmented further by his dark Mexican skin.

"We will be busy today, yes?"

Billy nodded. "Sí. And all the rest of the month." He returned Pedro's smile which always seemed to lift the spirit, even on Monday. "You ready for it?"

"Estoy…" They released hands. "Estoy preparado for sure, dude."

It didn't quite come out as surfer talk (especially with the Mexican accent) but Pedro continued to try. It was his attempt to fit in. Not only was he doing a great job at learning the English language, he'd also made great strides in matching the island culture. Both men chuckled.

"Cool beans, dude," Billy replied and shot Pedro the surfer's hang ten hand sign.

Pedro's three middle fingers curled inward but the thumb and pinky still had trouble remaining outstretched. He had to push them outward with his left hand. "You rock," he said.

"What's the lunch special today?" Billy asked. "Something smells wonderful."

"Carib…Carry-bean…" Pedro struggled with the word. "Island shrimp platter," he said instead.

"Caribbean shrimp platter?"

"Sí. Pineapple and sweet apples and Gulf shrimp. Light and…" Pedro thought for a moment… "tasty. Will not make you feel fat when you walk the beach in a bikini."

"Great advertisement! You hooked me…except for the part about wearing a bikini, but I sure don't mind looking at them."

"We are the same, mí jefe." Pedro winked then returned to the kitchen.

Alicia and Candice were busy placing the tables, sweeping the floors around the tables and changing light bulbs. The waitresses pulled up the wooden blinds on two walls of storefront windows and the interior of the restaurant came to life. Texas sunshine immediately warmed and lit the entire space. Surf Side could serve about a hundred people, if you included the stools at the small bar near the entrance. While the weekdays tended to fill only half of the restaurant, weekends needed every chair, even in months that weren't celebrating Sea Life.

Two waitresses would probably be enough until four o'clock when the early dinner crowd began, but Billy decided to remain in the restaurant just in case. He enjoyed helping prepare meals, serving dinners and chatting with diners. His volunteerism was one of the reasons why he and those who worked for him got along so well. There wasn't a thing he'd ask someone else to do that he would not do himself.

A dozen people entered when the restaurant opened. An hour later, at least thirty people were enjoying the diverse menu that the Surf Side offered, including a happy array of diners feasting on Pedro's Caribbean shrimp special. Billy served a few guests then took up a position behind the bar since Alicia and Candice were inundated with alcoholic beverage orders. Billy made a mean margarita and several requests, an unusual amount for Monday afternoon, were tended by his talented hands.

Around three o'clock, as the afternoon lunch-goers dwindled, a man whom Billy did not know entered the bar. He was much too large for the stool on which he sat. A large scar traced the flesh above his lip.

"Bar opens in an hour," Billy said to the large man.

"You're here," the stranger said, staring at the bottles of liquor behind Billy. "Jim Beam and Coke."

Billy was the consummate bartender gentleman. He welcomed all newcomers to his restaurant regardless of policy. Still, he felt that this man was trouble. Intuition was his best angel for thought. If he'd told the man to leave, he believed that the bar stool on which the man sat would quickly take flight. He turned and grabbed a bottle of Jim Beam.

"Don't mix it," the man demanded. "Shot and chaser."

Billy poured a heavy shot into one glass and filled another with Coke. He placed both on the bar in front on the man.

"There any good surf around here?" the man asked. The question caught Billy off guard, not so much that he'd never been asked it, but more so because the man asking it did not look to be the surfer type.

"Yeah," Billy said a bit too cautiously. "Down by the pier."

"You surf there?" the man said, knocking back the shot and Coke in swift succession.

Warning bells sounded in Billy's head. *The controversial casino.* Perhaps he was being paranoid but the man's demeanor and direct question were too coincidental to deny.

"Yeah," Billy answered. "I surf there a lot."

The man pushed both glasses forward in a nonverbal request for seconds. "You...*Dig* the small waves there, don't you?"

Instead of an answer, Billy replied, "You ever surfed?" He filled both glasses then pushed them toward the man.

Instead of answering, the man said, "I've always wondered what was so special about this damned island." He swallowed the Jim Beam and then the Coke. He'd been sizing up the restaurant, never giving his full attention to Billy until now. "Good fishing—that's about all. Surf, well, it sucks."

"You're not a surfer," Billy said.

The man's thin grin showed no reaction. "Says you." He wiped a drop of whiskey from the scar on his cheek. "Nothing ever breaks above five feet around here. You call that surfing?"

"Every wave is a good wave," Billy countered. "All *surfers* know that." Generally, Billy maintained his cool, especially in the restaurant, but this guy was getting under his skin. He was dissing Billy's great love. He was dissing Billy's home waves. When the man asked for another shot, Billy refused to serve him.

"That'll be eleven-fifty," Billy said and removed the glasses from the bar. He expected a right cross at that moment. Instead, a grin too wide for his face spread above the man's square chin without showing teeth. The scar above his lip lengthened diagonally across his cheek into what looked like a fleshy, bald caterpillar. The pupils of his eyes changed color, a deep crimson, perhaps—Billy wasn't sure. The stare seemed to caress his very soul. Billy blinked.

"Expensive," he said. "Too expensive for a shit-hole restaurant on a shit-hole island that couldn't attract flies even if its roads were made of shit. What this town needs is a little excitement. What you need is to find some other surf—before it's too late."

The man dropped a twenty on the bar, turned from the stool, and walked through Candice who could not grab the margarita glass that fell from her tray and crashed to the wooden floor. Billy watched the man climb into a black Hummer then pull out of the parking lot, nearly swiping a few parked cars as he left.

"Who was that asshole?" Candice said as she came around the bar to get a broom.

"An asshole," Billy acknowledged, trancelike. "I don't think he likes surfing."

"What?" Candice gazed at her boss who still had not looked at her.

"That guy. He's trouble. And he's probably brought a whole lot of it with him."

"Brought what?" Candice began sweeping up the remains of margarita glass.

Billy turned to her. "Ah...sorry. That guy's probably with the casino people."

"Definitely asshole," Candice said. She dumped the shattered glass in the trash and asked Billy to make her two Mega-Margaritas.

Billy mustered a smile. "Coming right up." Some of the dozen or so diners had turned when the glass had shattered. They now returned to their plates. A lady with a wide-brimmed, frilly hat motioned for Candice.

Billy made the margaritas as his concern increased. He should have expected that "muscle" would accompany any gambling venture. The man knew something about Billy Jo Presser, knew that he was a surfer and probably knew that he was the protest organizer.

The intimidation had begun.

⊓ ...

Lantern globes cost fifteen dollars and a reel of twenty-pound test line was another six or seven. Joel did not have twenty dollars worth of fish to sell Billy. The one fish that did survive, a nice twenty-six-inch redfish, might get him five bucks, and a generous five bucks at that. Short of begging, Joel was out of cash; his meager welfare money was spent.

And so, that is why he waited outside until the afternoon crowd at the Surf Side began to dwindle: to beg. That's what his life had really come down to after all. Joel Canton was one of the best fishermen this side of the Gulf, was renowned for helping capture the great white shark that terrorized the island back in 1972, was the hero who saved a woman's life during the floods caused by Hurricane Alicia in 1983, and was a self-proclaimed Port Aransas historian. He'd lived here all of his life, never having to ask for anything no matter how hard things got.

But, anymore, things were just too hard. His hands ached incessantly. His knees were not as flexible as they'd been just a year ago (a condition most locals would call a "hitch in the giddyup"). He was slowing down both physically and mentally. Even the fish he'd pulled in last night, a good fifty pounds worth of redfish and speckled trout, did not survive the night.

Joel sat at the curb far enough from the Surf Side that he would not be easily seen, but close enough for him to determine the number of people inside. He stood up, took one step toward the restaurant and stopped. Another customer emerged from side door. It was the same guy who'd pulled up in a black Hummer just a few minutes ago. The man was stocky with short dark hair and looked alarmingly similar to the man who'd taken his wife from him a long time ago. The man who jumped into his Hummer and haphazardly sped out of the Surf Side parking lot, nearly sideswiping a parked Monte Carlo, looked like Bert Nookle's twin.

But of course that couldn't be true. Bert Nookle was one of a kind and had died several years back. Joel had gone to the funeral. Bert Nookle had been his "best friend." They had been a part of the crew that had captured the murderous great white. Bert had been the captain (who not so coincidentally looked a whole lot like Robert Shaw who played Captain Quint in the movie *Jaws*). Joel, who looked nothing like Richard Dreyfuss, had been the first mate. Both of them had ended the Great White Summer of 1972.

The man behind the wheel of the Hummer gave Joel one quick scowl as the black vehicle sped past. It was Bert Nookle reincarnated! Or perhaps Joel's eyesight had also finally found old age. He'd never thought that fifty-five years of life labeled a person as old. It all depended on how much life had been lived in fifty-five years. In Joel's case it was at least a hundred and ten. Old—and a beggar.

Joel halved the distance between where he'd been sitting and the side entry door to the Surf Side when he realized that he was just too good for begging. He couldn't—wouldn't stoop that low. There were other ways to make a few bucks; he'd just not thought things through. He'd figure this out. Survival was his middle name.

Joel left the parking lot, rubbing his belly because he was hungry and because the scars were there—the scars from 1972—and they began to itch.

❐ ...

"Later, Mr. Presser," said the bartender. Jelanie was his real name; his surf name was Gelatin.

"Have a good evening," Billy said, smiled, shot him a hang ten, and then rushed up the stairs to his apartment. The man with the scar over his lip had invigorated his desire to see what Shoe had recorded. He tossed his keys on the bed and headed straight to the computer. He would not be able to review everything tonight; there was just too much of it. His intention was to move through the data randomly in hopes that something would quickly catch his attention.

For sight, Billy had equipped Shoe with one of the newest mini-micro cameras, the kind used by covert operators—detectives and such. He'd ordered it through the mail; he still didn't trust the security features of the internet enough to release credit card numbers into the vastness of fiber optics and hackers. The camera was programmed to snap stills every ten seconds then send the images over radio frequency to the receiver in the back of Billy's computer. Its implantation into the robot's mechanics had been easy. Shoe's ears, however, had not.

Since continuous hours of video would eat up massive storage space Billy had not only opted away from video streaming he had installed an extremely sensitive microphone, unidirectional and twice as powerful as any other listed in *Popular Mechanics*. Audio was lenient with hard drive space and a good microphone would provide all the evidence he needed. The challenge had been with feedback. For some reason, the small motors in the starfish robot's legs (all five combined) caused the mic to squeal unexpectedly. He'd had to rework the motor configuration to allow for the microphone's sensitivity. This had added another two weeks to his timetable, giving him and his island that much less of a chance to thwart the casino efforts.

As luck would have it, the added two weeks had conjoined with the arrival of Chancey Lett.

Lett, it was rumored, was a Las Vegas casino boss, very rich and very connected. How he'd become interested in fucking up Port Aransas no one knew beyond what some editorialists in the local paper had suggested: he had family in Corpus Christi (false), he and the governor where tight as oil sheiks (false); he was a greedy, self-centered bastard that would sell his mother's farm if that's what it took to remain at the top of the food chain (most likely true). He was also rumored to be a collector of fine antiquities, thus the reasoning behind the name of his new casino venture: The Mayan. But beyond all of that, Lett was perhaps best at finding greedy people and greedy governments looking to fill their pockets: all Lett asked was that they look the other way, drop an influential vote or two—but of course, this was all rumor. And that's what Chancey Lett pretty much was: a rumor.

There had been nothing beyond rumor written in any of the papers, not the island's *South Jetty* nor the city's *Corpus Christi Daily*.

Greedy people—looking the other way.

Billy's computer and monitor were crammed into the opposite corner from his "paperwork" desk; the robotics workbench separated the two. He switched on the monitor and opened up Shoe's programming interface. Status bars indicated that Shoe had begun recording at 9:01 in the morning and had ended at 6:15 in the evening, numbers that were slightly off from those Billy had set, a minor problem he'd deal with later. The robot had transmitted more than three thousand frames of video and over nine hours of audio. Billy tapped the keyboard and a window full of thumbnail images cluttered the space. He scrolled through several dozen shots that depicted little more than three chairs, an open vault and the bottom two-thirds of two office doors. Occasionally, legs that were blurred by the camera's inefficient auto zoom shuffled passed. Then, at 9:38:10: something interesting. For the next several frames, thumbnail images showed three sets of legs standing in front of Stephanie Drake's desk. Billy double-clicked the first of this sequence, synchronized the time with that of the audio feed and clicked "Play." An image filled the computer monitor, one every ten seconds, while the audio narrated the scene.

The legs belonged to Chancey Lett, Mitchell Bone and a third man whose name went unannounced. Stephanie Drake's voice was background noise but easily heard with the microphone's sensitive pickup.

Don't mind him, Chancey Lett's voice said. *He always looks like that.*

Once the formalities of introduction had ended, the three sets of legs, visible from the middle of the thigh down, disappeared, then two frames later reappeared, a few feet more distant, in front of Mitchell Bone's office door. Stephanie Drake's legs joined them. All faces were turned away and only their bodies from the neck down could be seen. One frame had them entering the office; ten seconds later, Stephanie was walking out of the office.

How can I help you? her voice asked.

Outside, was the answer. Though the person that said it remained hidden, Billy had a good idea who it was.

More than thirty video frames later Stephanie stood, once more, in front of the starfish robot. Ten seconds later, she was in the vault; standing in front of her was the man who'd accosted Billy back at the Surf Side, the thug who'd preferred his Jim Beam straight. He gripped an empty hand truck. Beside his leg was what looked like a wooden crate; Shoe's angle from the desk did not reveal any more than an inch or two of it as the edge peeked into the video frame from beyond the vault door.

Yes. That will do just fine, Stephanie's voice said. The thug remained silent.

At that moment, an office door squeaked open and Lett's voice sounded hushed through the computer's speakers. The sensitivity of Shoe's microphone had enabled the recording of his whispers to Bone beyond the doorway. The men did not appear in the time-synced video grab of a partially opened office door but their voices had been captured with clarity that made Billy smile.

Well it's coming up for a vote on Saturday. I think we have the numbers: Bone's voice.

I hope so. There's a lot of money to be lost. Remember, your cut in this could pretty much buy this island: Lett's voice.

Most of them know nothing about it. They don't know where and they don't know when: Bone.

That won't be enough. Lett.

I told you…

…now I'm telling you! We're going to stack the deck. Let's just say for now that those that vote our way won't be able to pass up a chance at a million dollars.

I'm beginning to think that…

You're not in this to think, Bone. Let me and Sedona do all of the thinking.

There was a long pause and then more dialogue as the next video frame appeared on the monitor. Bone followed Lett out of the office.

I understand, Bone said. *But I can assure you that…*

Lett ignored him, opting instead for a few pleasantries with Stephanie, then in the next minute, Lett and his bodyguard thug left the bank.

Billy slammed his fist against the computer hutch, almost nearly crushed his keyboard. The vote was no doubt the one that, by town referendum, was not supposed to take place for another month. The concerned conservationists and fishermen had been pushing for a delay and a month was all they'd been able to wrangle from a town council well stacked with profiteering business interests. What Bone and Lett were planning had to be illegal, Billy thought. He'd remained a quiet distance from everything political at MIT but common sense told him that much. In the least it was unethical. Bone, however, sat on the town council as did most of the influential residents, including the *South Jetty* publisher, Noel

Kilpatrick, which meant that information was controlled. Lett was going to "stack the deck," whatever that meant. Unfortunately, before any honest powers became wiser, the construction of the Mayan would be underway.

But not if he had anything to say about, Billy thought. And he didn't need no stinkin' newspaper. He could make flyers and distribute them all over town. He also had the luau tomorrow night, one he'd worked hard to organize in an effort to protest the casino. He'd tell the townspeople of the impending change of plans and let them burn the appropriate demigods at the stake. At least he'd get the word out about the vote so that there would be no stinkin' deck stacking of any kind.

Shoe had done its job. Billy had done his job. Perhaps he'd never be able to use the recording in a court of law (he'd committed a felony just to get it), but the information had, minimally, enabled him to delay connived plans. Still, the audio could be useful in the future. He'd been politely threatened earlier in the day. Who knew how far these men would go. Having a little bargaining chip could help.

Billy reversed the video and audio sequences back to where the three mens' legs first appeared, set the timer for twenty-five minutes and clicked record. It was ten minutes before eleven and the Surf Side would be closing down at the top of the hour. He stood with the intention of heading downstairs to help with the cleanup, but dropped back onto the metal chair; one of the video clips grabbed his attention. He paused the recording.

Mitchell Bone's legs stood along the right edge of the frame, Chancey Lett's were in the middle and the bodyguard's were to the far left. Lett held a leather satchel and something was sticking out of it. Billy drew a marquee around the satchel to zoom in on it. The top inch of two sheets of paper became visible but the zoom made what was written on them hard to understand. On the first sheet was drawn what looked to be some kind of hieroglyph: the troubled stare of a man in a mask; and beside the mask, appearing much fuzzier in the zoom, was what could have been a spear or a sword—a weapon of some kind. The hieroglyphs reminded him of some of the ancient temple drawings he'd seen on the History Channel.

The top paper partially covered a single word on the paper underneath it. Billy could not decipher the entire word; the zoom made the letters almost illegible.

A word puzzle, Billy thought. Seven words. The first letter was probably an 'L' although it could have been an 'I.' The third letter was easy: a capital 'F.' The fifth and sixth letters were the same; Billy thought they were 't's.

"L-F-tt-"

The word was written in an old style Calligraphic cursive that reminded Billy of the writing on the Declaration of Independence. Very colonial. He mentally went through every letter of the alphabet and tried them in the empty spaces but nothing worked.

It was eleven-thirty when he decided that his brain, at this time of night, was not going to decipher either the word puzzle or the hieroglyphs. He printed the zoomed image, restored the record settings and left the computer to its task. He took the printout to bed with him, studied it further, then set it next to the coffee maker before switching off the lamp light.

L-F-tt-

His brain wouldn't let it go.

PART II

NO MAYAN FOR

MY ISLAND

Though his bed was extremely comfortable (one of those adjustable types that uses a number) Billy's sleep had been restless. He'd even forgotten to set his alarm. Most days, he was up by six. The morning sunrise was his addiction.

He woke with the image of the Port Aransas public library in his mind. The word puzzle, the hieroglyphs and the library had connected in his subconscious. The idea of research had pumped its time-consuming curiosity into him once again—a feeling he'd not had since Cambridge.

It was a little after eight o'clock when he swung his feet from the bed, snatched the empty coffee pot, walked it over to the refrigerator and filled it with the water pitcher from inside. His mind raced with the to-do list in his head. He went through the coffee-making motions but paid no attention to what his arms and legs were actually doing. He realized that he spilled water while filling the coffee maker reservoir only because the water fell onto the printout he'd left there last night. He quickly mopped the water with the tail of his T-shirt before it smeared the ink.

L-F-tt-

"You won't keep your secret long," he said to the paper. "That's why man invented the public library."

Billy had no internet service to his restaurant. He'd never seen the value in such an investment. He'd known too many users who'd spent too much time with too little to show for it. Besides, if he wasn't working, he was surfing, in the Gulf, where no connection to the wired world was necessary. The public library had internet; that's all he needed.

He started the coffee and went to his lab-office. Paperwork that needed to be finished beckoned. Just one hour and it would be done.

He pushed it out of his mind, opting instead for the computer. It took him only thirty minutes to finish the flyer he would distribute around town. It read:

**Don't let big money interests destroy our Island Paradise.
VOTE NO for the Mayan
Saturday, June 22**

Simple. To the point. Nothing flashy except the eye-catching red lettering he'd used.

He printed the flyer just as the hard drive status light flashed the start of another day's worth of robotic data collection at the bank.

He opened the program interface and watched video frames as they were received every ten seconds. Again, the same three chairs, the bottom two-thirds of Bone's office door and the vault. The lights in the bank had not yet been turned on, but enough sunlight fell through the windows to see that the vault door was open but only a couple of inches, as if it had been left that way all night which, of course, could not be true. Suddenly, the lights in the bank came on and one of the bank tellers approached the vault door, swung it wide open and went inside. Her name was Carol, he thought. The video frame showed her hand on the vault wheel and one foot inside. She then disappeared but never reemerged from the vault. He watched three minutes worth of static images that did not change then decided he'd been wrong. Maybe she hadn't gone in the vault. Maybe she'd just looked inside. That was the trouble with capturing ten-second images: you always had a ninety percent chance that you'd miss something.

He turned off his computer screen, showered, then put on his normal wardrobe of surf culture: boardies, a beach shirt with Mr. Zoggs prominently displayed and sandals. His brown eyes and shoulder length blonde hair completed the stereotypical islander look. He snatched the flyer and the printout of the word and picture puzzles and headed outside.

Downstairs, Kale met him at the side entry door apparently distressed.

"No specks, man," he said, almost imitating the Cheech and Chong accent. "All of the Specks never came. Devries Seafood didn't deliver all that we asked for and the price was much more than Jerry had said it would be."

"How much?" Billy said, hoping to calm Kale down.

"Ten bucks a pound." Kale could hardly say it. "And we only got fifty pounds."

"That ain't gonna do it, is it?"

"Not with the catering gig at the Treasure Trove Friday...not even close."

Billy smiled. "That's not going to do it even without the catering." He pointed at the restaurant. "Look around—see what can be done. We'll just have to raise our prices a bit."

Kale nodded.

"Pedro inside?" Billy asked.

"Sí," Kale said. "I'll check for food in Rockport for starters."

Both men entered the restaurant. Billy turned toward the kitchen and Kale walked to the hostess podium to make a few phone calls. Billy entered the kitchen to find Pedro cleaning shrimp near the sink at the back.

"Mí jefe," Pedro said, moving his hands under the sink to rinse shrimp.

"How creative are you?" Billy said.

Pedro wiped his hands on a towel. "Creative? Yes I am very creative. Always trying out new specials."

"We might run a bit short on food this week. Cutting back a tiny bit on our very large portions might help."

Pedro dropped the towel and walked toward Billy. "Mí jefe. I can make masterpieces with very little comestibles." He opened his arms around his belly which was not very large; his thin frame looked as if it needed more nourishment. "And people will still feel very full. When you are from a town like Chiapas, you learn to estiramiento lots of things."

"Estiramiento?"

Pedro smiled. "Stretch. We stretch lots of things. Two pounds is four pounds easy with a few potatoes." He looked at Billy's hand and pointed at the papers he held at his side. "Wayeb?"

Billy lifted the paper and looked at it.

"Wayeb," Pedro repeated. "This here. Unlucky days." He stepped closer and touched the image of the face in the ceremonial mask.

"What's so unlucky about them?" Billy asked.

"Nothing stops the underworld." Pedro bent forward and whispered as if he didn't want anyone but Billy to know. "Evil can cross over."

"Serious?" Billy chuckled. "I mean…really?"

"By my father's honor." Pedro bowed slightly. "He told me. A Mayan symbol for the last five days of the year. That's Wayeb. You should stay indoors on those days."

Billy pointed at the weapon pictured next to the Wayeb. "Anything you know about this?"

Pedro studied it for a few seconds and said, "No…Not sure. And what is this?"

Pedro grabbed at the corner of the flyer and Billy let him have it. "The town vote for the casino is Saturday and I wanted everyone to come out and vote No."

"I have not heard of no vote." Pedro handed back the flyer.

"Not many people have. They've been keeping it a secret."

"I will come out and vote if you want me too, Mí Jefe. You know I'll help in any way I can." Pedro returned to his preparation of today's new 'leaner' menu.

"I wish that you could," Billy said. "You still need to get your work permit in place. It will be a few years before you're ready for citizenry."

"And I thank you for all of your help." Pedro nodded.

"No problem." Billy waved a hand and shook his head. "And I thank you for yours." He turned to leave and added over his shoulder, "What are you cooking at the luau tonight?"

"Sí," he said, grinning. "Grilled crab cakes and island-marinated vegetables...a leaner version of them."

"Island-marinated?" Billy turned around as he started through the kitchen door.

"It's a secret sweet and spicy sauce that combines a couple of old Mexican recipes." Pedro said it as if he were making an advertisement.

"Mmmm..." Billy licked his lips. "If I don't see you before, I'll see you there."

He left the restaurant with Kale still on the phone, trying to cut a deal for tuna.

Billy had gotten a lot of unexpected information from Pedro, primary research that he'd not intended to conduct. Mayan symbols? Were the papers simply a collection of decoration swatches showing interior design ideas? He'd become so critical—of everything— scrutinizing all of society much more than he used to. As was reflected on his flyer, he hated the influence that big money had on people without big money. But these were just decoration ideas, that's all. The only secrets Lett and his followers held was the vote. All they wanted was the casino. There were no other conspiracies. Right?

Billy now wondered if the contents of Lett's satchel held nothing fantastic—mere architect's sketches perhaps. The Wayeb symbol was nothing more than decoration for the new "Mayan" casino.

Outside, Billy got into his VW, but before he closed the door, Joel appeared as if from thin air.

"Billy. Hello." The old fisherman almost gasped. He looked as though he did not feel well.

"You okay?" Billy stepped back out onto the asphalt.

"I think I had some bad fish for breakfast. I've had bad trout before and got over it. I'll just have to be more careful with the catch."

"Can I get you something? Medicine?" Billy started for the restaurant but Joel grabbed him—a fisherman's grip—firm but not uncomfortable.

"Well. Yes. Yes you can." Joel burped and turned away from Billy. "Sorry." He rubbed his stomach. "It's just that I busted my lantern and I don't have the money to buy a new one. I don't have any fish to sell either."

"How much is it?" Billy reached into his pocket.

"Now you know this is only a loan," Joel said. "I will pay you back as soon as possible."

"A loan."

"Thirty dollars?"

Billy peeled off a ten and a twenty. "Here," he said. "An interest-free loan."

"I will pay you back double in fish. Thank you. I really hated to ask..."

Billy waved away the explanation. "No big deal. I know you're good for it." Joel put the money in his coveralls pocket. It was ninety-five degrees out and Joel was wearing coveralls, but Billy had rarely seen him dressed in anything else. Occasionally, he even wore a different set of coveralls. "Make sure you come out to the protest tonight. There'll be some good eating."

Joel rubbed his belly. "Hopefully, I'll be ready by then."

Billy got back into his VW Bus, waved to Joel, and drove off.

Around ten o'clock, he pulled into the empty parking lot of CopyKatz. Business appeared slow. Inside, the clerk was helping a customer at the copy machine. "Be right with you," she said.

For most of the population of Port A, everyone knew everyone else. Small towns were like that—knowing everyone else's business while maintaining what others thought of your own. But if you lived in Corpus Christi and were currently working a summer job on the island, chances were few people knew you. Billy did not know the CopyKatz clerk.

The clerk came around and behind the counter. Billy laid the flyer in front of her. "Fifty of these, please," he said, grinning cordially.

"Cool," the girl said. She wasn't tall but she was very cute. Her dark, red hair looked natural. "Full color is ten cents a copy." She read the words on the flyer. "Vote no for the Mayan. What does that mean?"

"You from the island?" Billy said, knowing the answer.

The clerk continued her chore. "Naw. Going to school in Corpus. And you?"

Billy smiled. "You are the curious type."

"Pre-law," she said. "Professors kind of instill that curiosity thing in you." She fidgeted with the copies for a few seconds as they sprang one-by-one from the copier. "You're an islander. One of the good ones. Not one of the real nasties around here. They are just plain snobs." Her lip curled and she thumbed her hand in the direction in which the rich that she talked about lived. Billy knew exactly what she meant. They often ate at his restaurant.

The copier ended its operation and the clerk plucked Billy's stack of flyers from it.

"That's five dollars and thirty cents with tax." She entered the numbers into the cash register.

Billy gave her the exact change and invited her to the protest luau. "Good eats," he said and smiled. "Hope you can make it."

"Yeah. I'll give it shot. Bye…eh…mister." The clerk shut the cash register door.

Four guys plucked all but ten of the flyers from his hands. Billy knew he'd find energetic volunteers at Pat McGee's.

"Yeah, I'm helping," local surfer J.J. White said.

"I'll hit the hotels and ranches," said CrabMan, one of the surfers that Billy regularly hung out with.

"I'm going to cover the pier," Billy told them. "I'm curious to see the fishermen's reactions."

The other two surfers that offered to help were Shana Greathouse (and some would say she had one), and Peter Jennings, spelled just like the news anchor from ABC; he got a lot of crap for having a name like that. That's probably what made him so…touchy.

"That tropical storm has turned inward, Billy. You hear about that?" The manager of the store tapped his shoulder. Bottlenose was his surf name. Nobody knew his real name, not even Billy who was his best friend.

"No." Billy turned. "I haven't been paying much attention to the news lately."

"Yeah, I figure. The luau is eatin' up your time." Bottlenose read the flyer; immediately, his face turned red. "This fuckin' blows, you know? I mean, it really blows. Makes me want to pound some politicians." Bottlenose could certainly put a pounding to anyone he chose. He was built like Charles Atlas.

"We'll pound 'em with the pen," Billy said. "And when they lose they can blow us all the way back to Vegas."

"He-he," Bottlenose replied. That was about as close to laughter as the big man ever got. He had a great sense of humor, but whenever he found anything to be funny it was always a short *He-he*.

Billy raised his voice intentionally to catch everyone's attention. "Tonight should be a good time. Starts at nightfall. A dozen local chefs have entered the cooking contest including my very own Pedro Melindez."

A short round of clapping began, then quieted.

"Come hungry. Bring a friend. A few protest signs might even be appropriate." Billy grinned while applause again rose; this time it included some of the patrons near the surfboards at the back of the store.

"And remember everyone," Billy continued in true political fashion. "Vote No to the Casino. No Mayan for my Island. No Mayan for my Island."

And that became Billy Jo Presser's rallying cry for what would hopefully become a small island protest against the intrusion of bad money and manipulation into their paradise.

After a short chant of "No Mayan for My Island" settled down, everyone departed for their designated assignments. Billy left his VW at Pat McGee's and took off on foot for the pier. It was less than a mile away and he felt that a brisk walk in the fresh Gulf air would open up his mind. Everything was getting a little crazy. Timelines had sped up. The vote was this Saturday and he grimaced at the thought of how "undercover" the whole thing had become. Trust was becoming an issue. He hated scrutinizing everything. One of the reasons why Port A appealed to him was because of the feeling of trust within a community, a kind of trust that allows car doors to be left open and a back door unlocked. You had to be careful when tourist season peaked because of off-islanders, but other than that Port A cared for itself.

And then came Mitchell Bone. The false smile. The clammy, tiny handshakes. But as much as he wanted to, Billy couldn't hang all the blame on Bone even though he was a major contributor to a change in trust that had begun when outside influences were allowed to control island interests. Some of the "rich" people that the CopyKatz clerk had talked about included many of these outside influences. These people were more into their own positive cash flow and would easily, and without guilt, leave very little to the Port A community. That's why they were down the island a few miles, out of the city limits. God help them if they ever had to pay a little bit of the tax money to help support a community which provided the vacationers who rented their time and spaces.

Billy crested the first set of barrier dunes to a wave of Gulf breeze that slapped his hair into his eyes. He inhaled deeply. The heat of the day combined with the pure salt smell of the Gulf yanked a breath from his lungs. He gasped twice more.

Second to the trust of an island community, its culture was as big a reason why he'd chosen Port A after dropping out of MIT. The beach. The sun. The waves.

He'd gotten really sick of the New England culture, especially around the campus in Cambridge. At MIT, and in much of its community, everybody acted as if they were better than you, had been more places than you, had more education than you, had more stuff than you. It was too competitive. And the competitive culture naturally created an aura of mistrust. That's how it was at MIT. He couldn't trust people. He'd experienced students plagiarizing his ideas on many occasions. Where was the trust in a culture like that? He'd even had a professor claim one of his robotic components to be his own design. That's when he'd had enough. The professor had held credentials that Billy could not litigate against.

His parents hadn't been too happy about his departure. Both his father and mother were educators. Having one of their sons drop out of college was against their academic religion. His own savings had been enough to get him started in Port A. His parents had provided nothing.

He crossed a second set of dunes and headed for the shoreline. The brown sand was Texas hot. If you weren't from Port A or didn't visit often, you probably weren't aware of just how hot it could get. That's why whenever Billy saw a beachcomber without sandals cursing, he knew that person was an off-islander.

The beach grew crowded as the sun neared its daily peak. Its width could hold many people plus a two lane sandy road of slow traffic, which made for a great weekend cruising spot. The beach roads were, most times, packed on Friday and Saturday evenings.

And that's about as much of the outside world as Billy wanted on *his* island. A casino would not only change the tradition of cruising the beach, it would change who was driving in those cruise machines. Instead of high school kids with hot rods and four-wheel drives, there would be pimps in long Cadillacs, drug dealers in slightly larger Cadillacs, and lots of people with lots of money and lots of outside influence.

Billy walked the shoreline toward the pier a few hundred yards ahead. He studied the waves as he sloshed through the soupy froth. The warm water invited him in. Breaks were uneven. The onshore winds were beating them down, dumping them in big uneven chunks. He thought about the tropical storm Bottlenose had mentioned. Storm swells could make for some superb surfing later in the week. The storm didn't need to hit the island; the best surf was when the storms remained a hundred miles out before turning north like so many of them did. The strong side of the storm whipped around some knarly waves once it was up the coast.

A couple off-islanders raced up the sand without sandals as Billy walked in from the shoreline toward the pier entrance. "Damn that's hot," the fatter man said. Billy chuckled.

The cost to get on the pier was three bucks but no one ever charged the regulars. It was just one of those "island" things. He posted a flyer at the entry to the pier and one at the bait shop.

On the pier, he talked with many people; most he knew—most didn't realize that the vote was this Saturday. He handed out all of the remaining flyers except one. This last flyer he posted on the railing at the end of the pier. All of the locals said they would be voting. Many of them said they'd attend the protest luau.

"You're gonna love my dish," said a voice from behind.

"Burgess," Billy said, acknowledging the voice. "I only wish I could be a judge. Pedro would certainly get high marks."

"What's he making?" Burgess, who worked at the Terrapin, looked like the chef from a can of Chef-Boy-Ardee. He didn't have the hat on but it was easy to imagine.

"He hasn't told me. Secret I guess," Billy teased, remembering Pedro's "island-marinated" menu. "I'm just glad that there's going to be such a great spread from some of the local best."

"My contribution will be *my* best." Burgess didn't have a French accent either, but again it was easy to imagine.

Billy left Burgess on the pier contemplating his dish for the night, waved good-bye to several people, exited the pier and continued down the shoreline toward the channel. The local newspaper was another half mile up and across the dunes. He'd originally intended to return to his VW before visiting the newspaper but the walk felt good. It gave him energy. And the energy would come in handy when he confronted Nole Kilpatrick. The *South Jetty's* responsibility was to tell its citizens of important items affecting their community. Billy wanted to find out just how much money Kilpatrick's silence cost. What was the sanctity of Port Aransas worth?

He reached the offices of the *South Jetty* a little after noon. Kilpatrick was conveniently out.

"You guys know anything about the vote on the casino proposition coming up this Saturday?" Billy said to the lady at the front desk. He didn't know her name.

"Proposition vote?" she said, still sitting. "No. I haven't heard about that."

"When's Kilpatrick get back?"

"Mr. Kilpatrick may not return the rest of the afternoon." Billy couldn't tell if she was lying or if that is exactly what Kilpatrick had told her to say. "He's a very busy man."

"I bet," he said, defensively. It was that lack-of-trust thing intruding upon him again, making him suspicious. "Can you tell me where I could find him?"

"Mr. Kilpatrick doesn't tell me where he goes, Mr...." she grabbed a pen. "And your name? I'll leave him a note that you were here."

"That's OK," Billy huffed. "I'll catch up to him later."

"Would you like to make an appointment?" The lady flipped through the appointment book.

"No," Billy said and left the building, not meaning to slam the screen door so hard.

Billy returned to Pat McGee's by walking the beach and chuckling at apparent vacationers. He tossed out to sea several broken sand dollars, wondering again if the tropical storm would create the knarly waves Port A usually lacked. He'd not caught a good one in a while. He'd told Coolie and Sweets that he might do some surfing before the luau but the way things looked now, he wouldn't get much more from this surf than a sunburn. The surf did, however, provide the white noise catalyst that calmed his mind and prompted reflection.

L-F-tt-, he thought. *A puzzle. Seven letters.*

Wayeb. Five unlucky days when Evil can cross over.

And that damned bodyguard goon son of a bitch.

The waves crashed and foamed around his feet. He stood for a moment, trying to cancel out the screaming children behind him and the parents who screamed after them.

Just what the hell had the bodyguard put inside the Big Texas Bank vault? A crate? Full of what? Valuables? Illegal secrets? Shoe could not see the vault's interior well enough to gather much of anything. Would Stephanie Drake know? All of the puzzles were driving him crazy. His analytic cogs were overloading. He needed some answers. The library would provide only so much. He would have to go back to the bank and talk with Stephanie Drake. He'd invite her to the luau. Perhaps while "unwinding" she would reveal further clues. He also needed to get into the vault and check it out—personally. The only way he could do that was to rent a security box.

On his way back to Pat McGee's, he decided to visit the bank before heading for the library. He returned to his apartment and Kale caught him at the front door as Billy shoved a meager coin collection that his father had given him into a small backpack.

"Looks like the local fishing companies are going to be doing much less business than usual," Kale said. "There's a report of dead fish in the catches."

Billy slung the backpack onto his shoulder. "What's causing it?" he said.

"Red Tide was the general consensus."

"Anyone gotten a hold of Walker?" Billy snatched his checkbook from his lab-office and met Kale at the doorway.

"Well—I'm not sure." Kale's voice was calm but it came in gasps. "I could call him."

Billy led Kale out and closed the door. Kale's expression as he watched Billy lock it was one of astonishment, but that's the way the new "suspicious Billy" had to proceed.

"I'll tell you what," Billy said, leading Kale down the steps. "I'll give Walker a call. I've been wanting to talk to him for a month now. Just keep on looking north for supplies and try not to break the bank. Whatever it is won't be around for long."

"You think it's a spill?" Kale released the rumor that had apparently been nagging him. "While talking with the fishing companies, I got the feeling that, though everyone was saying 'Red Tide,' most were thinking 'chemical spill.'"

"All I can say is, I hope not." Billy walked to his VW. "It's a slim possibility but only slim. Let's stick with a more reasonable reason. I'll call Mark. He'll know what it is." He tossed his backpack to the passenger's seat and slid under the steering wheel. "How's business?"

"Good...considering." Kale looked at the restaurant.

Billy rolled down the VW's window. "Good," he said. "Pedro got everything he needs?"

"He hasn't said otherwise."

After a quick wave, Billy drove off. Typically, he would have stayed and fixed the problem himself, but his days of micromanagement were just about done. Besides, Kale could manage. Kale would *have to* manage, at least until they closed at seven. Tonight would be an early night for Surf Side. Everyone would be at the luau.

◻ …

It was hard for Stephanie to believe it possible.

Carol had said very little all day long. It was kind of creepy, like the way you feel when you know someone's going to come up behind you and yell, "Surprise!" At any moment, Carol would do just that. She'd catch Stephanie off-guard as she studied her computer monitor. And then without warning, Carol would blurt out, "Surprise, Miss Drake! And tell me…how does it feel to have stolen my promotion?"

But Carol never surprised her. She conducted business behind her teller window and escorted people to their security boxes in the vault without grunt or grimace. Almost robotically. It was very creepy.

No one had seen Mitchell Bone. He'd not called Stephanie to reschedule several appointments all of which she had already cancelled and apologized for before lunch. Now, it was shortly after one o'clock and his next appointment was due in ten minutes.

Stephanie dialed Bone's cell number. It was at least the tenth time she'd done so. Again, all she heard was his answering service. Again, she left him a message to call her.

Carol walked passed her desk with one of the owners of the Mustang Ranch just south of town—a Mr. Farber, if Stephanie remembered correctly.

Both she and the young man entered the vault. They were in there for what Stephanie believed was a long time—ten minutes perhaps. Then she escorted the owner to the front of bank and waved good-bye.

It had been like that all day. Everyone Carol had led into the vault had remained in there with her for at least ten minutes. There must have been a dozen of them, and every one of them was an owner of some business or property that had needed financial help from Mitchell Bone. Stephanie knew all of them. Several had cancelled appointments with Bone earlier in the day. Each of them had done business with Big Texas Bank within the last month.

So what if everyone in town suddenly wanted to look inside their security boxes, she thought. Coincidence, that's all.

But Carol acting the way she did—that was different. She just wasn't right at all.

"Hello."

The voice surprised her. She jumped in her chair.

"Sorry. Miss Drake? It is Miss Drake?" Billy stood behind her. "I didn't mean to scare you."

Stephanie smiled with a small bit of embarrassment.

"Stephanie," she said. "Or Steph if you like." She thought about his name for only a moment. "Billy Jo Presser," she added.

"Just Billy," he said. "I'd like to check out one of your security boxes."

Yeah, you and a dozen other business owners, she thought. "Go ahead and have a seat," Steph said, pointing Billy toward one of the three red chairs that Billy had already seen in a hundred image snapshots.

He looked over the numerous ornaments occupying her desk then leaned far forward as if analyzing one of the starfish that decorated the sides of the desk.

"These are really nice," he said, smiling. "We all got to do our part for Sea Life Month, eh?"

Steph moved the paperwork for security box rentals in front of her. "So how's the seafood restaurant business going?" she said.

"Better than ever. Having a theme month was a brilliant idea—one of the few our council has had of late."

"And people are more into doing beach things." She knew that Billy was a local surfer. She picked up a pen. "Will that be a small or large box?"

Billy hoisted his backpack onto a knee, unzipped it and pulled out four thin blue books: the entirety of his silver dollar coin collection. "What will these fit?" he said.

"Small should do it." She checked the appropriate box on the rental agreement. "You should have a pretty good turnout at the luau tonight," she said.

"You want to join me?" He put the backpack on the floor but left the coin albums in his lap.

"I'm not much of the protester type," she said, wanting to go.

"Doesn't matter." He leaned forward. "You don't have to do any protesting. Just being there is enough. Besides, it'll be fun; a peaceful protest with lots to eat. I'll introduce you to some of my friends."

"What's your address?" she asked.

'That's OK. I'll pick you up."

"No," Steph smiled and tapped the rental form with her pen. "I mean for the rental. Your address?"

"Will you go?" He said it as if her answer was a prerequisite to him renting the security box.

"Sure," she said, perhaps too quickly. "Now let's see some identification."

Steph finished with the paperwork, handed Billy his driver's license, stood up with a hand on a set of keys that she'd pulled from her desk drawer and asked Billy to follow her into the vault; she'd not been inside since yesterday.

The crate was still where Chancey Lett's bodyguard had left it. It was about two feet wide on all six of its cubed sides. Its boards were darkened with age, appearing almost rotten in places. The top of the crate was securely attached. No seams in the crate existed that might reveal its contents. There were no hinges, screws or nails…only wood. Steph felt its *chill*, smelled its ancient dusty moisture. She walked into the vault not realizing how much distance she'd given it.

To the left of where the crate sat was a deeper room of about ten-feet squared; most of the security boxes lined these vault walls. A small stainless steel table sat in the middle of the room. Steph stuck both keys into one of the smaller box doors about halfway up the right side wall, opened it, and pulled out the drawer inside.

"Here you go," she said, handing him the drawer and one key. "I'll be outside. When you're through, just slide the box back in and lock the lock."

"This won't take long." Billy dropped the coin albums into the drawer, replaced the drawer into the security box and locked it. "All done." He clapped is hands together as if dusting them off.

"It's just that we're not supposed to be in here while the renter is going through their box. It's personal courtesy."

"You've been quite courteous already," Billy said. After a short pause, he added, "What's up with that crate? It seems a bit…"

"Out of place," Steph finished. They walked together toward the wooden cube. "The guy who's building the casino—It's his."

"Maybe some valuable artifact that they are going to use as decoration?"

Steph had not considered that. It made sense. They both gazed at the crate for another dozen seconds then Steph led him out of the vault. "Probably just decoration," she said.

Carol looked up from her teller window. Her eyes followed Steph and Billy as they walked back to her desk. She continued to stare at them as Billy pulled out his checkbook.

"The box is fifteen dollars a month." Steph said. "First and last month's rent due at the time of rental."

"I'd also like to try one of your short-term CDs," Billy said. "A thousand dollars."

"Really?" Steph was surprised. "OK. Well let me get the paperwork."

"Don't you just hate that?" he said, grinning.

"CDs?" Steph placed a form in front of her.

"Paperwork," Billy clarified. "I hate it."

Steph started writing on the form. "Unfortunately, a necessary evil," she said and looked at Carol who, still, was staring.

Billy signed two papers, and wrote a check. "I'll pick you up at...say eight-thirty-ish?" Billy stood. "Where do you live?"

"Paradise Cottages," she said. "Number 10."

As Billy left the bank, Carol went into the vault, reappearing only moments later. She glared at Steph then toward the front door of the bank. Billy disappeared around the corner.

❐ ...

Billy thought that the creepiest thing about his visit to the bank had nothing to do with the crate in the vault; it was the way that the bank teller had stared at him on his way out. It was something in her eyes, dark, almost lifeless, set in an expressionless face, as if painted on by a very unimaginative artist. She could have doubled for a mannequin except that her neck had turned as Billy had walked passed. He thought he'd heard her spine cracking. That teller had been the same woman whom Shoe had videotaped going into the vault earlier that morning.

He got into his VW and headed for the library but his concentration was not on the questions he would try to answer there. Carol the teller's stare kept intervening. It reminded him of the encounter he'd had with Lett's bodyguard at the bar the day before. He'd remembered being consumed for only a fraction of a second by the depth of the big man's lifeless eyes. And somewhere deep inside the pupils there had been fire. That's when he'd looked away. He'd felt that if he'd stared for only a second longer, the bodyguard's eyes would have swallowed him. Carol's eyes would have, too, had he been close enough to her and had he had the courage to stare into them for only a second longer.

And then there was the crate. There had been something coming from within it—something invisible—an energy that repelled and attracted erratically. He'd felt suddenly weak the moment he'd entered the vault, and the closer he'd gotten to it, the stronger the attraction and repulsion and his weakness became. Its energy again reminded him of the bodyguard. He, too, had had an invisible force about him—something that pulled Billy in toward his dark stare but also repelled him at the same time, as if some sort of spiritual battle between the man's demonic intent and Billy's soul had been played out right there in the Surf Side restaurant.

Shoe had appeared to be functioning better than expected. Billy had seen no water leaks and was pleased how well the little robot blended in with the thematic environment of sea life on Steph's desk. Billy had worked on Shoe's stealth for many weeks and this, too, was functioning better than he'd anticipated. Nothing mechanical could be heard. The water propulsion system had worked tremendously well. If only the guys back at MIT could have gotten a hold of Shoe. They'd tear the little robot apart trying to understand, again, how Billy Jo Presser had managed to pull it off. To them it was always another "breakthrough" in robotic kinesiology; to Billy it was just a hobby that constantly needed tweaking.

And then there had been Steph. She'd looked much prettier today than she had last week. Perhaps she had worn less makeup which had allowed the light skin tone of her rounded cheeks, chin and nose to pop out in natural nakedness. Perhaps it was the way she'd styled her dirty dishwater blonde hair that, instead of lying in curls on her shoulders, had been much straighter, falling behind her back just inches below her neckline. Perhaps Billy just liked the simpler look of the native islander, one who cared less for how everybody else thought a bank manager's executive secretary should look—one who had dumped the flashy business suit for a more relaxed slacks and blouse wardrobe. For whatever reason, Billy had found his heart racing just a little bit louder, his cheeks flushing just little bit brighter and his desire growing just a little bit stronger. He'd been happy that she had accepted his invitation to the luau. As he pulled into the library parking lot, he envisioned their evening together and how it might very well turn into something more romantic in the future. He could always hope.

The library was dead as was usual during weekday afternoons. Only one person strolled through the stacks at the back of the reference section and Billy supposed that it was the summer librarian. He didn't know her. Most summer librarians were college students from Corpus who'd found

Port A to be the perfect place for an internship in library and information science: They'd spend the day amongst the stacks and the evening amongst the waves and get college credit for it. What a life.

The girl, who appeared to be no older than twenty-one, looked over at Billy as he entered the reference section, pulled out the computer printout from his front pocket and sat down at a computer station. She did not offer any immediate help.

Thanks to Pedro, his first search was easy. Instead of combing through screens of information about ancient civilizations in hopes of finding a picture of the ceremonial mask, he simply typed "Wayeb" into a Google search.

Just as Pedro had said, Wayeb was a term used by the Mayans that denoted the final five days of the calendar year. Their calendar contained eighteen months of twenty days each. Each of these months was named for a seasonal or meteorological event or animal. Wayeb, however, literally meant "days without souls." Mayan culture warned that on these five days it was best to stay inside, to comb one's hair often and thoroughly so as to cleanse any evil spirits that may have hidden within the strands, and to pray that none would be born on such unforgiving days. These were the days when evil was allowed to cross into the mortal world without boundary or limit. Unsuspecting mortals who did not heed the warnings were often found to be maimed, dismembered or missing.

Billy scoured the many links that Google presented about Mayan culture. There was little else about Wayeb other than what Pedro had told him; however, he did come to understand the Mayan calendar as a whole a little better. He'd never examined anthropology or ancient peoples while at MIT therefore much of the information he now scrolled through was new to him: for example, the Mayan Calendar Round. A picture of it showed a circular piece of golden metal inscribed with many colorful symbols of ceremonial masks, animals, and nature. The Calendar Round dated a complete Mayan cycle that started more than 26,000 years ago. What Billy found to be most interesting was the calendar's end date: December 21, 2012, a day that was just around the corner.

Several links led to cheaply designed web pages full of prophetic warnings that on December 21, 2012, the world would end. Dozens of books had been written about the End Date, most calling it the alpha and the omega—the beginning and the end.

One web page read: "According to Mayan calculations, the current cycle of the world is due to end in December 2012. There is some disagreement over whether the end of the current cycle of the world will involve the end of the world itself."

Another read: "The Maya messengers, renowned for their architectural, artistic, mathematical and scientific achievements, left a calling card as a series of superhuman-sized stone monuments and pyramids with precise calendric computations. Planted with great intention, these dates were left to ensure that future generations would be alerted to the coming end point of this great 26,000 year cycle."

For this date, connections were made to Revelations in the Bible, the Muslim calendar, the birth of Buddha, North American Indian tribes, a rare astrological alignment of Earth, Sun and the Milky Way, interdimensional shifts, pole shifts, reversed magnetic fields and just about every apocalyptic catastrophe the mind could imagine. The amount of information ranged from spiritualistic nonsense and foreboding to doctoral theses on zero time and its conjunction with the year 2012. From pure nut cases to philosophical doctorates (and sometimes it was hard to tell one from the other), what was known as the Mayan Prophecies was thoroughly documented.

Not that any of this had anything to do with Chancey Lett, the crate in the Big Texas Bank vault or the building of a casino, but it was fun to read. It had been a while since Billy had become so engaged by research that time seemed to stand still. An hour had passed in the blink of an eye. His concentration was broken only by the librarian; he suddenly realized she was standing next to him. He did not know how long she'd been there.

"Strange," she said. Her voice made her sound ten years old. Billy shifted in his seat.

"Excuse me?" Billy scowled. He did not like people reading over his shoulder.

"I'm sorry," the girl squeaked. "It's just that my professor always tells us that it's very rare that two people will research the same piece of information on the same day in a public library." She smiled apologetically. "In college libraries it's common, but not in public libraries."

The scowl remained on Billy's face. He had no idea what the girl was talking about.

"Those links," she said and pointed at the computer screen. "Another guy was in here this morning searching for the same information."

The scowl left Billy's face and was replaced by a squinted question mark. "And why is that unusual beyond what your professor says?"

The girl did not answer. She turned away, her head drooping, as if she'd done something bad. Billy turned back toward the computer screen.

Interruptions greatly disrupted his research methods. After all, he did not take notes—that was not his way. He memorized much of the information but to do so accurately he had to go without interruption.

He started a new search, concentrating this time on the word puzzle: *L-F-tt-*

He entered the word, leaving spaces for the unknown letters, into Google. Results included pages by a man name Jay L. Fitt, the law offices of Lavrey, Fitt, and Fitt, a book on How to be Fit in Fifteen Days by an author named Joe Fitt, and screens filled with other useless clues. What he did come to understand is that there are a lot of people named Fitt.

But there was only one LaFitte. And there he found, on the fifteenth screen full of results, the answer to his puzzle. Jean LaFitte. He clicked the link which went to the Wikipedia online encyclopedia.

Jean LaFitte...circa 1780 to 1826. The year of death had a question mark next to it. He'd been a pirate in the early days of America, had aided troops against the British at the Battle of New Orleans, had engaged in slave trade and, though actual accounts differ, robbed ships as they came through the Gulf. He later became active along a neutral strip of lawless land from Spanish held Texas to Louisiana. He is believed to have died in the Yucatan but no one knows for sure where or when, the Wikipedia entry claimed.

As he continued to move through screens of information he found that, basically, Jean LaFitte—a.k.a. Lafette or La Fite—was a conundrum. Accounts had him being born in many different places including France, Spain, and Haiti. He worked the Mississippi delta in slave trade, which was a highly acceptable and respectable means of living back in 1809. Some would have called him a pirate—others, including himself, referred to him as a privateer, a man who understood the politics of three countries well and used that knowledge for profit. When politics changed in the Monroe years, LaFitte was hunted down by the U.S. Navy; he burnt down his own town (which was in Galveston, Texas at the time) and slipped out into the night. What happened to him from there is as much mystery as the rest of his life. Some say he moved to Charleston, South Carolina where he raised a family and moved west. Others have him disappearing to Mexico in the Yucatan, perhaps up near Cancun.

Of great interest to Billy were the *similar* accounts of LaFitte's actions during those last days of his Gulf empire. Once LaFitte had escaped the U.S. Navy, most accounts merged into one theory. He moved south and regardless of where he ended up—the U.S., Mexico or some island in between—most were certain that he'd taken his loot with him and had buried it at one or more locations throughout the Gulf. Most scholars concur that LaFitte's treasure had been worth in excess of a half a billion dollars in an 1810 economy. He would certainly have been a multibillionaire today.

And then it struck Billy suddenly, unexpectedly and rather off-guard: Treasure map?

He picked up the printout with the tops of the letters of Jean LaFitte's name now easily understood. It was only a sliver of evidence: only the top five percent of the page and not much else. It was in the calligraphic script of that time period but that style could have been duplicated easily.

So what Billy came to understand in almost three hours of memorized searching was that the two papers in the satchel carried by the bodyguard were, number one, related to the Mayan culture and number two, related to Jean LaFitte. The only connection to Port Aransas was the one account of LaFitte moving to the Yucatan in his last years. The treasure map idea was intriguing but, really, was it realistic? What Billy had uncovered was not mystery…it was easy to see. Chancey Lett was going to build a casino and name it The Mayan. He had collected information pertaining to all things "Mayan." The Wayeb symbol is Mayan. Jean LaFitte, perhaps, ended up in Mayan territory. If Shoe could have jumped off the desk and wrenched open the satchel, the robot would certainly have taken pictures of many more documents pertaining to both the interior and exterior décor of Lett's new venture. All Lett had in the satchel was a wish list of Mayan artifacts to decorate the casino. One of those artifacts was in a crate, stored in a vault of the Big Texas Bank, Port A branch. There was no conspiracy here. Mitchell Bone was doing exactly what Mitchell Bone always did: grovel and brownnose and answer yes-yes-yes if a buck was to be made in it. Lett wanted to use his vault to store what appeared to be some very valuable artifacts. One piece was in there now. More would be coming in the future. The satchel was full of the descriptions of these pieces. Lett was "renting out" space in the vault for these items.

Nothing more. Nothing less.

And the idea made Billy angry. He mashed the Exit key on the library computer keyboard and stood. He snatched the printouts from the table and headed for the door. On his way out, he saw the librarian, who spoke like a ten-year-old, hiding behind the comic book rack. He waved good-bye to her though he knew it would not help her nerves. He'd been a bit brash but that's how he was when it came to research. The librarian had been an innocent bystander.

☐ ...

At ten minutes to five, Steph got a phone call from Mitchell Bone.

Now? she thought. Minutes before it was time for her to leave the bank and prepare for the luau and, finally, Bone calls.

"I want you to pick up an investor from the airport Friday afternoon," Bone said.

She hesitated as if she was really going to say: *No! Are you out of your fucking mind!*, but instead she said, "Yes. Of course, Mr. Bone. And what should I do with today's appointments?"

After a short pause, Bone said, "Stick them in where you can and call them back. As for tomorrow, cancel them all. I'll be tied up with other interests."

Canceling his appointments for tomorrow meant that Steph would have to work after five o'clock. "Yes," she said reluctantly. "I'll cancel. The new appointments will be in the computer calendar."

Bone hung up without gratitude and this burned Steph. One part of her job responsibilities was to aide Mitchell Bone in his daily activities even if, on occasion, those activities entailed after hours work—but of all the days to have to work overtime. She took a deep breath and counted to three before calling Bone's first appointment for the following day.

By five-thirty, most of the staff had said their good-byes; some frowned in recognition of Steph having to stay late, others patted her hand in sympathy. Only she and Carol were left in the bank. Carol said nothing as she went to the vault, entered briefly then reappeared and closed the vault door. She yanked the handle and spun the cylinders on the four lock dials. She never looked at Steph. She never said good-bye to anyone. It was very programmed. She left the bank moments later, leaving Steph all alone.

☐ ...

Billy arrived at the Surf Side around five o'clock. Business was slow in the day's transition from lunch to dinner. Only one man sat at a two-seat table near the window at the back of the restaurant. He was busy with a plate of boiled king shrimp, one of Pedro's specialties. A handwritten sign on a dry erase board hung from two small hooks in the hostess station:

SURF SIDE RESTAURANT WILL CLOSE, TUESDAY, AT 7:00. JOIN US AT THE LUAU ON THE BEACH INSTEAD. PEDRO'S DISH IS FOR SURE TO BE THE BEST!

Billy chuckled. Candice's work, no doubt. She had a great way with words and people. He didn't see her immediately.

"Slow," she said, appearing suddenly behind him. "Been like this all day." She wiped her hands with a towel; she'd been washing dishes. "Pedro's getting ready—packin' up in the back." She thumbed in that direction.

"You the only one here?" Billy looked around at empty tables that were well lit by sunshine that beat down on the tinted large bay windows. The guy eating the shrimp had a large pile of casings on a plate next to a nearly equal-sized helping of fresh king shrimp. Like a machine, the man peeled, dipped and ate the shrimp then discarded the casing on the appropriate pile. He had gone through two dozen large, pinky-sized shrimp already and he showed no signs of slowing.

"I am," Candice replied. "Alicia went home around two-thirty. Lunch was weirdly slow, like, bizarro slow." She rolled her eyes then walked away from Billy toward the shrimp-eating machine. She turned and whispered as she left, "He'll eat all of today's profits with his all-you-can-eat coupon." At the table, she dropped off an additional bottle of Surf Side Cocktail Sauce, a wonderful elixir of flavor that Billy hoped he might package and sell one day. Candice was cordial and talked with the customer for several minutes before heading for the kitchen. As she passed Billy she quietly said, "I think he's full."

Billy followed her into the kitchen and immediately saw Pedro at the back of the room. He lifted up a small plastic milk crate that was full of cooking utensils and turned to a hallway that led to the rear service door. He saw Billy and looked up.

"Getting mí cooking gear packed up," he said. "This will be a good time?"

It took a moment for Billy to understand what he meant. "Sí, indeed," he said. "Great food. Great people. On the surf. Not a cloud in the sky. What a wonderful day for a protest." Candice began washing dishes to his right. "You need some help packing?"

"If we were feeding more people then yes," Pedro said. "But only one hungry shrimp eater. I think I will be OK." He hugged the crate, which didn't appear to be heavy, freed the right hand and moved his fingers and thumb into an OK sign. "I guess everyone is waiting for the big beach party to eat. Nobody hungry has been in here for today."

"Kale around?" Billy asked.

"I think he went to market up d'coast to find a supply man." Pedro entered the hallway and Billy could hear the hallow acoustic of his voice. "This is going to be fun," the voice said, fading.

Billy followed him out the back door; Pedro was loading the crate into the trunk of a small Fiesta. "You'll never get all you need into that small box on wheels," he said.

"It is a little crowded, yes?" Pedro closed the trunk gently. It barely latched.

"You can borrow my VW if you'd like. There's a lot more room."

"Really? Mí jefe!"

"However, I'll need to borrow your car to take care of some things before my date tonight."

Pedro fell silent and a smile slowly emerged from the right corner of his mouth. The left cheek remained stationary as the right corner stretched high, revealing six teeth.

"Señorita, eh?" Pedro seemed pleasantly surprised. "That will be very good for you. We all need a compañero. Is she from here?"

"From over at the bank. She's the executive secretary. Stephanie is her name."

"Esecute…esecutive?" Pedro tried to say it.

"Executive secretary," Billy corrected. "She's the manager's assistant, basically."

"Like I am your assistant, basically." The smile still captured the right side of his face.

Billy thought for a moment. "Yeah. Something like that…basically." He returned the smile though not as brightly. "Here's the key to the VW."

"Here is the keys to my little car."

Billy looked at the small Fiesta, which, for a beach car, had only a small amount of rust on it. "Cozy."

"Cozee?" Pedro said.

"Comfortable," Billy added.

"Sí. She is that. Muy cómodo."

Pedro walked toward the parking lot where Billy had left his VW. Billy was not concerned that Pedro would see his computer surveillance equipment. Pedro knew Billy's hobby was robotics. Pedro had met Shoe shortly after Billy had built the starfish and shortly before the hydraulic systems in the robot had failed for the first time. All of the digital components in the VW, should he see any, would only fascinate him. Besides, the equipment was mostly out of sight behind cabinet doors that Billy kept locked.

Billy pulled the latch on the Fiesta's trunk and set Pedro's crate of cooking utensils on the pavement beside the car. He grabbed the set of large bowls sitting in the passenger's seat and set them on top of the crate.

Pedro kept the car in good, clean shape; it was very "beachy." Traces of brown sand scattered the floorboards and the car had that sea smell: it kind of smelled fishy and salty and wet all at the same time. With the artificial sweet odor of Hawaiian Tropic suntan lotion mixed in, the car smelled very beachy. Atop the car was a surf rack that could hold two long boards. Billy had never seen Pedro surf and didn't remember seeing the surfboard car racks until now. Perhaps he'd taken up the sport and just hadn't said anything.

Billy moved the driver's seat back and climbed in. It was less cramped than he thought it would be. He started it and drove off, adjusting the rearview mirror as he did so. Looking into the mirrored reflection, he saw Pedro park the VW near the restaurant's back door and easily load the bowls and crate.

And then, suddenly, Billy felt very dizzy. A nauseous tightening of his stomach made him stop the car before leaving the parking lot. He grabbed his belly. The view of Pedro and the VW in the rearview mirror became very blurry. He placed the car in Park and just sat there, staring at the mirror, watching as the vision in it started to change.

At first he thought it was the heat, the sea smell, the Hawaiian Tropic lotion and the cramped car all working against his intestines. But the nausea wasn't in his stomach—it was in his mind.

He shook his head as all of his senses became involved in some strange altered vision.

It was suddenly dark outside. He felt that he was driving very fast. Tires screeched. In the driver's side mirror he could see two sets of headlights blazing very close to his bumper. Shots were fired and the rear window blew apart. In the back of the car, which was much too large for a Fiesta, was a wooden box…a crate.

"Pull the fuck over," someone yelled.

Billy blinked and turned toward the voice to his left.

And just like that the vision disappeared. His mind and senses jolted back into reality but still swirled with the experience of being in another place at another time. Momentarily, Billy was lost. His mind said "someone is firing a gun at me" while his eyes read "Pedro is packing my VW." The nausea subsided. His breathing eased.

It had been like a really bad nightmare, one which you awaken from screaming, or punching at the wall or falling out of bed. For an instant it had seemed so real. He'd seen something that was not a part of his memory. He'd never experienced being shot at or even driving a car much beyond a few miles over the speed limit.

But the vision had been so real.

Pedro waved at him in the rearview mirror then disappeared through the back door of the restaurant. Billy shook off the chills that raced across his spine and placed the Fiesta in Drive, then cautiously peeked back into the rearview mirror half expecting to see headlights, shattered glass, the sound of gunfire, and a crate.

A crate?

No…more like a cube. It was nearly two feet across in all dimensions. Some kind of energy from it attracted and repelled at the same time. It was something to be avoided but was also the object of much desire.

The altered vision had lasted a mere second but Billy had memorized the entire event. In the altered vision, not much of the cube had been revealed. It had hidden itself in shadow as window glass rained around it.

But it *was* the crate in the bank vault! Billy was sure of it.

Like a projector stopping on a single frame from a movie reel, Billy's mind captured the memories of the image of the crate in the altered vision and the image of the crate in the vault and made a mental comparison. Whatever the reason for the altered vision Billy didn't know, but he was pretty damned certain that the crate in the vault of the Big Texas Bank was a part of it.

Perhaps the crate had even caused his vision. He'd gotten within a foot of it. Maybe it had infected him somehow. The crate contained some kind of hallucinogen, perhaps. Maybe it infected *anyone* that came too close. Maybe Carol had been infected too—that's why the woman seemed catatonic. She'd been too close to the crate on too many occasions and was now the proud owner of one hefty helping of mind-altering drugs.

And then it hit him—Chancey Lett's box contained drugs. It made the most sense of anything he'd guessed so far. There were no Mayan artifacts or pirate artifacts or any other kind of decorative ornament for a new casino. The bank was a front for the distribution of some kind of hallucinogen.

Perhaps he couldn't "prove" a conspiracy to stack the vote but, if he could show that Chancey Lett was a drug runner, the "Mayan" would have no chance and gambling would move onto the next unsuspecting Texas town. Mitchell Bone would be ousted. The island would return to normal.

Billy turned down Avenue G, looked over at a relatively quiet Pat McGee's and headed for the surf. Officer Keadle's cruiser sat in the same spot where he'd pulled over the impatient couple the night before. Billy waved at him as he passed, but Officer Keadle did not respond. Apparently, he hadn't recognized that Billy was driving Pedro's Fiesta.

Out on the beach road Billy found traffic to be light. Many off-islanders were packing up and heading out as Billy drove by. Perhaps it was a good sign. Perhaps most people were heading home to clean up and get ready for an evening of luau entertainment and great food.

The beach side where the proposed *Mayan* casino would be erected and where some of the only good surfing in Port A could be found was slowly transforming into a small Bedouin city. Billy saw the tents and the tractor trailer flat beds near the pier in the distance. Three surfers were out trying to grab what meager waves washed in. He supposed that Sweets and Coolie were two of the surfers. A new tent suddenly sprouted among the others, its red canopy a stark contrast to the subtler beach prints around it. *Enjoy Coca-Cola* was emblazoned on its surface. By the time Billy parked near one of the flatbed trailers, all of the tents that would be needed for the luau had been erected. There were twelve tents for the cooks and another nine or ten for amusement games and refreshment.

A man on the flatbed behind Billy moved a set of speakers around a tangle of wire and set them down, one on top of the other.

"Everything going okay?" Billy asked the young roadie.

"You bet," the dark-skinned kid said. "We gonna rock this house, gonna tear the place apart."

"When's the band due?"

"Got me, man." The roadie kid stopped what he was doing and lit up a smoke that he pulled from behind his ear. "I'm supposed to have all this shit together by six."

"Need any help?"

The roadie kid inhaled deeply and blew a large cloud of smoke. "Naw. Jacksie will be back in a second." He pointed at Billy with the cigarette pinched between two fingers. He smiled and added, "But I appreciate ya askin'," then puffed and blew another large Marlboro cloud.

It appeared that everything was on schedule for a seven-thirty start. The cooks would begin at that time. By eight-thirty, all the dishes would be completed. Judging would begin shortly after that. Five locals agreed to be taste judges; however, their collected opinion would not be final. Half of the cook's score would come from a vote by the luau guests.

A country beach band would provide the entertainment. They called themselves *Knights in White Satin* however it was rare to see them in anything other than shorts and T-shirts or no shirts at all. The "White Satin" probably described the extreme bleached blonde hair of all five band members.

Billy made his way through the small tent city, shaking hands with the workers, thanking each for their volunteer efforts and donation of tent usage. Many of the volunteers, Billy knew. Most told him that they understood what they were doing was for a good cause. All of them were vehemently against gambling moving in anywhere near their great little island town.

Closer to the surf, two men and a woman were busy digging a wide, shallow hole. They looked to be in their late teens or early twenties. Beside the hole and anchored in the sand under the skinnier man's knee was one of Port A's tourist brochures. It was folded to the panel that described Jean LaFitte's legend and the treasure that was buried somewhere on the island's beaches. As Billy walked past, he gazed down into the hole. It was about three feet wide and three feet deep, a perfect size to bury a crate full of drugs from Las Vegas, he thought.

"Don't touch it, man," the skinny guy said.

"Yeah," the girl giggled. "If you do, it'll pull you in and you'll become part of it forever and ever."

Billy stopped and turned around. He was about five yards from the hole.

The other guy, who was as large as both of his friends put together, slapped the girl on her forearm. "Shut up," he groaned. "That's not part of the legend."

"Oh yeah it is," the skinny guy said. "Why you think no one's ever found it? Because they became part of it!"

The fat guy reached down into the hole. Billy saw something glisten silver in the sun under his hand. The girl pushed him and he fell headfirst into the hole. The skinny guy and the girl laughed hysterically.

"Not right, man," the fat guy said, pushing himself out of the hole. He wiped sand from his eyebrows and forehead. His frown turned into a half smile. "Just for that, I ain't sharin' the treasure." He opened his hand.

"Whoa," the skinny guy said. "Look at that."

The three friends craned their heads forward. Billy bobbed his head for a better view as well.

"Is that a nickel?" the girl said. "It kinda looks like a nickel."

"Great find, Columbo," the skinny guy added. "Don't spend it all in one place." He giggled.

"No. Wait, man," the fat guy said. "You ever seen a nickel like this?"

Billy couldn't see what the fat guy held in his hand though it was certainly shaped like a nickel.

"Yeah. My dad's got a collection of them in his attic," the skinny guy said. "It's a buffalo nickel."

"That ain't no buffalo. How can you say that's a buffalo?"

"Let me see it," the girl said and opened her hand.

"Forget you. Find your own treasure," the fat guy said.

Billy thought again how ridiculous off-islanders could be. The whole idea of buried treasure was made up—a marketing gadget—a mystery based on historical speculation. There was no treasure to be found here: not by any fat guy and his two friends and not by any visiting hoodlum from Las Vegas. How could Billy Jo Presser, MIT genius and dropout, have ever even considered that Chancey Lett was here to dig up treasure? The Nevada hood wanted to spread his illegalities to the Gulf Coast. Drugs and gambling and, most likely, prostitution is what Lett and Bone wanted to peddle. These things were their treasure.

The trio started to dig again. The tide was slowly moving in and would cover their hole in the next thirty minutes. The three looked like a pack of dogs digging for bones.

"BJ!"

The voice startled Billy. He turned to see Coolie standing behind him with the fluorescent green surfboard he'd been caressing outside of Pat McGee's two nights before.

"Surf sucks," he said. "But the board's got grab, dude. I mean it might not be the pertiest thing but it's a swell grabber sure enough."

Coolie was skinnier than the guy digging the hole. His sternum and ribs etched uneven trails under the skin of his chest. His arms had little meat to them but the muscles he did possess knew how to maneuver a surfboard. He was strangely pale for someone who spent most of his time in the Texas sun.

"How'd you afford that?" Billy asked. He walked up to Coolie and ran his hand across the tacky waxed surface of the board.

"I told you. Me and yo' mamma. She pays well." He snickered. "No really, dude. Bottlenose said to take it out for a spin. Said no one but me was lookin' at it. He's had it there since spring. Wanna' try it on for size?" Behind Coolie, Billy saw Bottlenose and Sweets roll into the shallow soup. They wiped muddy froth from their hair and face as they approached.

"What's with the corpses?" Bottlenose said, thumbing toward the three treasure hunters. "They're tearin' up the hang."

Bottlenose had his own language. "Corpses" was a term he used for off-islanders from Corpus Christi and "hang" meant a beachside surfer's hangout. In complete contrast to Coolie's thin frame, Bottlenose looked as if he'd pumped weights most of his life.

"Hey," he yelled at the corpses. "Stop diggin' on the hang. Get out of here."

"We're just looking for LaFi..." the fat guy started to say.

"Out!" Bottlenose took a step toward them and they quickly stood and began walking away. "Fill the damn hole back in. You come in to someone's house, you gotta leave it the way you found it."

The triumvirate quickly complied then rushed away toward the pier without another word.

"So what's this I hear about the fish around here?" Bottlenose said as the four surfers walked to the spot where the hole had been. His voice dropped an octave lower as he added, "Damn corpses anyway."

"I don't know," Billy said. He slipped off his sandal and wiped his bare foot through the moist, cool, loose sand where the hole had been. "What have you heard?"

"DuPont went and dropped another load of industrial cleaner into the gulf."

"Really? I haven't heard that. Do you believe it?" Billy looked into Bottlenose's turquoise eyes, wondering if the surfer was serious or simply playing around. He turned to Coolie and Sweets. "I guess not if you're out there swimming in it."

"Whoa, man." Bottlenose lifted his hands in defense. "It's only what I heard not what I believe. I mean if DuPont had gone and screwed up again, don't you think we all would know about it?"

All four surfers looked at each other knowing the answer. Billy shook his head.

"I heard it was an underwater heat vent," Coolie said, stroking the green fluorescent fin of his borrowed board.

"I heard it was a red tide," Sweets added. "I also heard that there's absolutely nothing wrong with the water and the fisheries are creating a panic to drive up the prices."

Bottlenose looked at Sweets and smiled. "Now there's a logical answer!" He clapped Sweets on the back. "Let's go catch a sulfuric acid wave." He grabbed his board and turned his head around toward Billy. "You coming? Surfin' sulfuric is the bomb, man!" He grinned.

Before Billy could answer, he heard Pedro shout to him from under one of the tents. "Mi, jefe!" Pedro waved a spatula over his head to get his attention.

"Maybe some other time, Bottlenose," Billy said. "I'll see you tonight?"

"Wouldn't miss it." Bottlenose ran into the surf and paddled out to where Coolie and Sweets had already taken the lead.

Billy took a step in the direction of Pedro's voice and something squished up through the wet sand between his first and second toe. He bent down to pick it up.

It was shiny and looked like a nickel. But that was no buffalo etched into the surface. It didn't look American at all. A wave of surprise and confusion consumed him. The design on both sides of the coin looked exactly like the symbol he'd researched earlier in the day, the same one that was on the sheet of paper carried by a Las Vegas hood in the Big Texas Bank of Port Aransas. It was the face of Wayeb.

❑ ...

Steph finally finished Mitchell Bone's appointment calendar realignment at a quarter to six. She'd made contact with fifty percent of the phone calls; she'd left messages with the others. The late afternoon sun cast shadows across half of the bank's interior. She stood into one of them.

She clicked off her computer screen and looked across the top of her desk to see that everything was mostly in order. She rotated SpongeBob a quarter turn to the left. She readjusted Mr. Crabs arms so that his claws were resting on his hips in a stance that depicted determination. Patrick she left as is, his pointed, starfish head and face smiling at her. The toy made her smile, too.

She rose and stretched and grabbed her small purse, and turned to exit the bank when a very low hum stole her attention. It came from within the vault. She turned toward the steel door unconvinced that she was hearing anything at all.

Mmmmm—it was very low and nearly inaudible, sounding much like a boy's chorus exercising their voices before a performance. If the bank wasn't so quiet, she probably wouldn't have heard it.

Mmmmm…

And then a red glow—just under the edge of the vault door. It undulated, maroon in color, the low hum accompanying its pulsing glow in perfect synchronicity.

Mmmmm…mmmm

The red, thin line from under the vault door seemed to creep slowly through the bank shadows toward her. But, of course, that could not be so. The seal of the vault door was tight. No air or water or light could enter or escape.

She stepped away from her desk while watching the red line of light that could not possibly exist. Feeling backward with one hand for the teller windows she knew she would run into, her flat rubber heels briefly slid on ceramic tile flooring and she turned toward the counter for support.

And just like that, they were gone.

The hum…the light…gone.

The bank was deathly quiet. Steph shook her head as if clearing it from dizziness. This was just her imagination, right? It had to be. The vault was airtight and blast proof. And why would there be light coming from *within* the vault?

And that strange hum.

Steph convinced herself that what she'd just seen was only imagination brought on by stress that had been agitated by Bone. She looked across her shoulder to the bank's sunlit entrance. A luau awaited her out there—and she needed it.

She reached for her purse, which she'd dropped on the teller counter during her slide across the tiles, and realized that she was standing in front of Carol's window. The counter on the other side of the glass was a mess. Dozens of papers had been left scattered in small piles. Steph knew several of the names written across what appeared to be signed security box rental agreements. All were owners of real estate and businesses within Port Aransas. Steph had just cancelled appointments with each of the names that were written on the dozen or so applications.

That was her job, not Carol's. Unless her responsibilities had been subverted, she was in charge of security box rentals. Perhaps Bone didn't want her to do anything but run errands for him any more. Perhaps Bone was circumventing her gatekeeping by going through Carol instead. Why he would do that, she didn't know. Maybe Steph was on her way out. Maybe she needed to start looking for another job. Maybe another job was in her best interests, one where creepy bosses and creepy clients and creepy employees were not standard regimen. And there was the crate, of course. She certainly needed a job where glowing, humming, creepy crates didn't drive a person's stress to the point of hallucination.

◻ …

Pedro told Billy that the *Knights in White Satin* were stranded in their broken down van just over the causeway from Corpus. The band had phoned the restaurant shortly before Pedro had left and had asked if someone could come pick them up. Billy had set the band up for the evening. He was their contact. So he agreed to pick them up. He quickly calculated that driving out and back would give him enough time to return to the restaurant, settle the evening's business and take a shower before his date with Steph at eight-thirty.

But another calculation kept rolling through his mind as he took the VW's key from Pedro, walked to his vehicle and got in. What were the mathematical laws of chance that were related to coincidence? He remembered studying something about the subject while at MIT. He remembered reading that the laws of chance predicted that coincidence would occur sooner or later. He remembered reading that without coincidence the world would be even more surprising.

So what mathematical law could explain how the Wayeb symbol on the paper from the bank had caused Billy to print that symbol out so that he could investigate it at the library, which caused Billy to have the printed paper in his hand while talking with Pedro in the restaurant that morning, which caused Pedro to recognize the symbol as being the Mayan Wayeb, which gave Billy needed information for further research, which somehow (and this could have been a separate coincidence within a coincidence) connected Mayan history to the mystery of Jean LaFitte, who supposedly buried treasure somewhere along the Gulf Coast, perhaps by the pier in what is today Port Aransas, which was being excavated by a group of "corpses" from the city in a location where Billy found a coin that had the symbol of Wayeb stamped onto its surfaces.

What were the chances?

Coincidence?

Or—and Billy (a proud scientist) had a tough time thinking of the possibility—was it metaphysical?

Something that could not be explained.

As Billy drove the VW out of town his mind tried to comprehend what it could not explain. He rolled the silvery coin between the fingers of his left hand, glancing down periodically then back out onto the straight, flat, Texas road. Dry waves of heat lifted from the asphalt, pulling his vision into them. The horizon ahead turned hazy, wavy and blurry—a Texas mirage induced by the sun.

And suddenly he was thrust into that altered reality again.

He was in another car, at night, moving very fast, was being chased and shot at, and the crate from the Big Bank of Texas was there with him. The Texas dirt around him transformed into fields of corn that slapped at his windshield. There was an explosion and a bright orange ball of fire blazed behind him.

Billy suddenly felt very ill. He grabbed at his stomach and pulled the VW to an abrupt stop on the side of road. An old Oldsmobile station wagon blasted its horn and sped by as Billy stepped from the vehicle, grabbed his knees, and gagged. Just a small amount of spittle dribbled onto the steamy asphalt. He stood, looked around to gain composure. He saw no cornfields. No one was chasing him. There were no gunshots. But the station wagon that had just passed him and was slowly fading into the hazy horizon suddenly backfired. Billy reactively ducked. But there were no bullets. It was all just another illusion…a hallucinogenic illusion brought on by casino bosses and bank vault drugs.

He'd been shot at in his illusion and a car had backfired in reality.

What mathematical law could have explained that?

It was all just coincidence.

◻ ...

Janine Bender arrived in paradise by cab an hour before nightfall. She wore the same sunglasses that she had worn back when she was living with Albert. The lenses were very dark for a reason: it provided great camouflage for black eyes and bruised cheeks delivered by open-handed slaps during drunken rages.

She'd found out about Port Aransas (or "Port A" as the brochure she held in her hand read) from a lady who'd asked her to adjust a wedding dress back in Kansas. The lady's daughter had become pregnant and the dress needed a little "letting out." The lady had lived over in Chucktown and had been good business for Janine from that wedding day on—until Albert had driven her away. Albert had driven everything away.

Except paradise.

Not even Albert could erase such longing. Not even if he was still alive.

But, of course, Janine had been the only survivor—at least that's what the doctors and nurses at the hospital had told her shortly after she'd awakened. They'd also told her that the barn had been completely destroyed and that much of the barn debris had hit the main house. Her home had been condemned.

Many of her material memories she'd left behind. Two duffel bags carried what was left, and she'd packed them lightly and tightly so that she could carry both to the bus stop. A friend in Kansas City had helped. They'd gone to high school together. Beth Blandford had been a year ahead but they'd kept in touch, even after Beth had moved to the city shortly after graduation.

As she stepped from the Corpus Christi White Cab onto Alister Street, a jolt of fear accompanied the force of a strong Gulf breeze that whipped through her grey hair; she peeled blowing strands away from the front of her face.

"Thank you," she said to the cab driver. The driver set her two canvas bags on the sidewalk.

"My pleasure, señora."

Janine handed the driver his fare plus three dollars. She didn't have a lot of money but cabbies worked for tips, right?

She stood there with two bags of life and déjà vu slamming her psyche from all angles. As the White Cab slowly disappeared down Alister

Street in the direction of Corpus Christi, that intense feeling of loneliness consumed her. She cried, briefly, then wiped away the tears.

It was when her eyes regained focus that she realized she *was* in paradise. Alister Street looked just like it did on the brochure: very quaint with a touch of—but not too much of—commercialism. It really didn't look much like a "vacation town" at all.

She'd worn shorts and a light blouse all the way from Kansas City. It had been a scorcher in the city when she'd left two days ago. Though Port Aransas was hotter, the Gulf breeze at least made it bearable.

She pulled a piece of paper from her blouse pocket and read from a small map, one that Beth had found online and had printed out for her. Her new home was a one-bedroom apartment located off of Alister Street. Appropriately, the name of the rental complex was Paradise Cottages. She quickly realized that not only was she on Alister Street but the place where the cabbie had dropped her off was Paradise Cabins. The sign in front of several one-room buildings across the street said so. The cabbie had misunderstood her. According to her map, her true destination was on the opposite end of town, and though she would have loved to walk the streets of her new home (Paradise Cottages was only a couple of miles away), her sacks were a bit too much to carry such distance. A small, brown sign with a green trolley car etched in its center was directly across the road. *Trolley Stop* the sign read.

"Can I help you? You look lost."

Janine looked over her shoulder at a tall, slender woman whose very long black hair covered much of the front of her body. "I'm new in town," Janine said, not really knowing what else to say.

"Yes," the lady said. "You don't have to be a fortune teller to see that." She smiled a perfect set of bright white teeth.

Behind and above the tall woman was a shop, presumably hers. The sign above the front door read: *Marcy Can See Your Future.*

"Marcy?" Janine asked.

"Yes. You have the gift of E.S.P.," she grinned pleasantly and turned to her shop sign. "And the gift of logical deduction."

"I am…"

"No. Don't tell me." Marcy the fortune teller whipped around dramatically to face Janine, closed her eyes and held her hands out toward Janine's shoulders. "You are a traveler looking for a place to stay." She opened her eyes with a smile.

"That obvious?" Janine returned the smile.

"I saw the taxi cab drop you off." Both women chuckled. "Would you like something to drink?" Marcy said and bent forward to grab one of Janine's bags. Her long hair touched the sidewalk behind the bag.

"Yes." Janine picked up the other bag. "Yes. That's very nice of you."

And that is how Janine made her first new friend in her long imagined paradise where a total stranger helped another, no strings attached—just a simple, friendly gesture that is common to inhabitants of paradises. Loneliness, for the moment, was forgotten.

The two women talked for more than thirty minutes but could have gone on for hours. It was Marcy who brought the conversation to a close.

"You want to catch a luau?" the fortune teller said, her hands on the end table that separated the two chairs in which the women sat.

"Well, I need to check in with my landlord. I think he's expecting me today." Janine thought the inside of Marcy's shop was just as she'd imagined a fortune teller's would be. Dark. Lots of things hanging from the ceiling and door frames. A round table in the main room covered with black silk. A deck of Tarot cards. Even a crystal ball. And in Marcy's waiting room, where the two now sat, the craft of her alchemy was advertised heavily. What Janine hadn't imagined a fortune teller's shop to contain was a fortune teller who went against all of Janine's stereotypes, and Janine had many, most of which were a product of her Christian beliefs. Marcy wasn't creepy or crazy or un-Godly in the least. She was a single mother whose daughters played soccer for the local youth group but were currently spending a summer month with their father who lived in San Antonio. She was a very active member of the community and prided herself for having attended every community council meeting since she'd moved to Port A five years ago. Her activities also included protesting the construction of a proposed casino.

"Let's give 'em a call," Marcy said. "I can take you over after the luau or if that's not good for the landlord, you can always stay in my extra bedroom upstairs."

Janine thought for only a moment. She did not want to be lonely her first night in paradise and a luau actually sounded quite exciting. What a better way for her to relax and separate herself from the past than with a beach party.

"All right. Let's do it," Janine said and patted Marcy's hand on the end table. "Sounds like fun."

◻ …

Close to sunset, Billy turned onto the beach road from Avenue G and looked over at his passenger. She was much prettier than the *Knight's* singer, though that guy was perhaps one of the "prettiest" men he'd ever seen. She smelled much better too: a peachy fruit smell that slowly consumed Billy's nostrils. The *Knights*, in contrast, had smelled like men who'd spent too much time sweating in the sun.

Steph had chosen a halter top with dolphin prints and a pair of red shorts that were invitingly snug but not too tight. From her earlobes dangled small silver dolphins that jiggled as she laughed. She wore very little makeup and Billy was glad. Beaches and cosmetics were not meant for each other. The purity of the ocean and sand made lipstick and eyeliner and rouge seem blasphemous. Her hair was pulled up into a single pigtail that fell through a hole where the strap of her ball cap connected at the back of her head. The ball cap announced that Pat McGee's was "Your Surf Shop Stop." The guy riding a shortboard above the lettering looked a lot like Bottlenose.

Beyond Steph's silhouette, the ocean's azure light continued to fade and was increasingly consumed by the red-orange hue of the Texas sun which closed in on the horizon opposite the Gulf's skyline. Scant rays of sunlight that were interrupted by shadows of distant buildings pierced the driver's side window and intertwined with Steph's smooth cheeks, strands of light and dark blonde hair and the silver dolphin earrings. Her entire face twinkled as she turned to Billy.

"What were they like?" She smiled as she had been doing ever since Billy had picked her up. "Were they…knightly?"

"Well…I would say they were more Nightly with an 'N' than Knightly with a 'K'. Not too much nobility with a group like that. I'd describe them more like dark and surreal. They've got an interesting concept on life."

"How so?" Steph shifted in the seat so that her tanned leg draped closer to Billy's hand which rested on the long stick shift.

"Freewheeling," he said. "They told me that they had even considered naming themselves the Freewheelers but some of the band members thought that would associate them with trucker music."

"Trucker music?"

"Yeah. My thought exactly. What the heck is trucker music?" Billy replied. Steph let out a quick giggle. "They don't really have a home. They call Earth their home and 'freewheel it' across the country from one 'Earth gig' to another."

"Hippies?" Steph suggested.

"Kinda. Perhaps a better term would be New Age Hippies or Millennium Hippies or something similar. They don't do drugs and don't eat processed foods although the lead singer told me that if he had a choice he'd go with the drugs since any amount of marijuana could not be compared to the chemicals the food companies use in packaging."

They laughed together. Ahead, a bon fire blazed near the surf and glowing lanterns denoted each tent farther up from the shoreline. Some of the *Knights* were atop the flatbed trailers tuning instruments. Several dozen cars and trucks were parked along the beach road and several more were headed toward the luau from the opposite direction. Another half dozen advanced in a slow line behind Billy's VW. To Billy, this was a great sign that the protest would pull more people than he had hoped. The gathering was not to officially start for another twenty minutes or so and already more than thirty vehicles appeared headed for the party.

Billy parked near the flatbed trailers in the same spot where he'd dropped the *Knights* off earlier. They'd told him that they'd save the parking place for him so that he could "be right up near his freewheelin' brothers." As he excited the VW, Richard, the band's lead singer and leader immediately recognized him and yelled out, "My brother!" The three other band members yelled out simultaneously, "Brother!" Billy and Steph approached Richard who leaned his acoustic guitar against one of the four-foot speakers and kneeled to the floor of the flatbed.

"This is Steph," Billy said.

"Excellent, man," Richard replied, extending his hand which Steph took and shook. "She's everything you said she was."

Billy had not said anything about Steph to the singer while driving them to the beach. He blushed but in the waning light it was hard to detect. "Yes. She is…uh…and more."

Steph beamed brightly. The luau bon fire which had gradually risen in height fifty yards behind them cast an angelic halo around her head. She released Richard's hand and grabbed Billy's arm. She turned him, a little flabbergasted, and together they walked toward the tents.

"Hang with ya later, brother and sister," Richard added behind them. "We're gonna rock this place into the wee a.m."

"What did you say to him?" Steph asked quietly.

"I, uh—" Billy tried to think of what he would have said to Richard had he said anything at all. "I told him that I had this really cool chick…"

"Cool chick, aye. I guess that's the language he understands the most." She grabbed his forearm with both hands and drew closer to him. "Very nice of you to say so."

"Very pretty is what I should have told him." Her ball cap had tilted askew while exiting the VW and he straightened it, positioning the brim above the fire reflections in her eyes. He placed his right hand on both of hers and felt the cool dampness of sweat.

"Mí jefe!"

Pedro approached them with open arms.

"Mí jefe and his senorita. Buenos días."

"Hey Pedro." Billy removed his right hand and Steph released his arm as if she suddenly felt that the touch was inappropriate.

"No please," Pedro pleaded. "I did not mean to intrude."

"That's OK," Billy said. "You weren't." He motioned toward Steph. "This is Stephanie Drake."

Pedro shook her hand with both of his. "Esecutive secrary," he said.

Billy swallowed hard and turned to Steph. "Yeah. Uh, I told him that you were the executive secretary at the bank."

Steph smiled, flattered. "You've said much about me."

Billy turned back to Pedro. "How's the dish?"

"Increíble." Pedro smacked his lips. "The best crab cakes in Texas."

"We'll be the judge of that," Billy teased.

Pedro led them through an aisle of tents; exhilarating smells assaulted them from all sides. There were soups and stews and skewers and slabs of meats and seafood and vegetables of great variety and spiciness. From one tent came a sugar sweet maple and pineapple aroma; from another came a pungent waft of jalapeno pepper, chili powder and garlic. Pedro's cooking tent was last on the left next to the Budweiser keg tent. Billy asked for two cups of beer as he passed and handed one to Steph who swallowed half the contents in one motion.

"Thirsty," she said, wiping the foam from her lips and burping a tiny amount of air.

"Would you like a crab cake to go with your cerveza?" Pedro offered.

"Yummy," Steph quickly replied. "I'm starved."

"An you, mí jefe?"

"Of course," Billy said. "These look a little different than the ones you make at the restaurant."

"Yes. Like I say already. It is a secret Mexican recipe mí madre give me many years ago."

Steph cut a wedge out of the round patty with a plastic fork. The piece was so moist it barely made it from the plate to her mouth without crumbling. "Oh my!" Steph savored the bite. "What is that…it tastes like…"

Billy forked a piece into his mouth. "Like honey mustard?"

"Well, yeah. Sort of."

Pedro smiled. "It is a spice that is found in the Guatemalan rain forest. It has a mustard and honey taste but it is not. It's a little peppery too, you think?"

"Amazing," Steph said while dividing an even larger chuck from the cake with her fork.

On the table skirt below the dish of crab cakes Billy noticed a piece of paper tacked to the fabric. It was a flyer that read:

NO MAYAN FOR MY ISLAND

The lettering was bold and black and centered in the middle of the white paper. As he looked back down the aisle of tables, he saw that each table skirt around each tent's table also had the same sign.

Steph finished her crab cake and followed Billy's gaze. "No Mayan for My Island. What a great slogan," she said. "Who made that up?"

"Well, Mr. Presser here did." The voice came from behind them, near the beer table. Port Aransas police officer Jim Keadle approached with a cup of beer in one hand. "The kids over at McGee's told me what you said this morning so I thought I'd get some more practice using my new computer and printer."

"Wow," Billy said and stepped closer to the officer. "They look great."

"Nothing fancy." Keadle reached for a crab cake. "May I?"

"Sí," Pedro quickly offered. "Sí, señor."

"I'm not much of an artist. Took me all morning just to figure out how to make the letters large and bold." He belted one quick, gruff laugh. A piece of crab cake dropped from the corner of his mouth to the sand. "Scuse me." He took another bite. "Hey. This is really good, Pedro. You gotta be one of the best chefs in town."

Billy clapped Pedro on the shoulder. "That's a good sign, my friend. Officer Keadle is one of our five judges tonight."

"And I am another," Mark Walker said as he strolled up to the group now gathered at Pedro's table. He wore a brown polo shirt with the name *University of Texas Marine Science Institute* stitched into the chest.

"Hello Mark," Billy said and offered his hand.

"Great signs." Mark grabbed a plate and served himself a crab cake. "I wish I would have thought of it."

"Keadle did them up," Billy said.

"But the slogan is yours," Keadle added. "No Mayan for My Island!" He raised his voice and repeated, "No Mayan for My Island! No Mayan for My Island!"

A small group began to chant. Soon, everyone around them chimed in. The slogan rose through the crowd like a wave. Even the *Knights* picked up on it and over the microphone yelled: "Come on everybody. Let's get it up. No Mayan for My Island. No Mayan for My Island." More than fifty people joined in and the slogan became a rising roar.

And as a perfect segue, the *Knights in White Satin* began their first set of the evening singing a 60s song entitled "Signs."

> *Sign, sign everywhere a sign*
> *Blocking out the scenery breaking my mind*
> *Do this, don't do that, can't you read the sign*

The protest was on.

◻ ...

An island breeze that rushed through Janine's hair was all that she imagined it might be. The cool, warm chill, sea salt smell and gritty texture flowing across her ears and neck was a stark contrast to the moist corn mash sensations that permeated all of Kansas even on the windiest day. Unfortunately, those same corn mash memories carried the baggage of horror and sadness—of that insane day nearly a year ago. The thought of Lenny's death made it hard to completely succumb to the beauty of her new paradise.

Marcy downshifted her Jeep Wrangler as she approached Cotter Avenue. She turned right. A sparse offering of restaurants and motels changed into residential housing as they drove toward the coastline. A small, green, street sign denoted that the "South Jetty" has just ahead. An arrow on the sign pointed in the direction they now traveled.

As much as Janine had tried to erase them, she realized that *controlling* her nightmare memories' unexpected push toward consciousness was about all that she could manage. She saw Lenny's bloody face instead of the tiki hut-style home that passed on her right. A huge cargo ship moved through the channel in waning sunlight to her left but visions of the Albert-thing chasing her to the storm cellar interrupted her exasperation at the vessel's enormity. Having lived in Kansas all of her life, she'd never been so close to such a large ship, but instead of being enthralled with fascination, she temporarily wept. Crying was something she had not been able to control. Only time would cure that, at least that's what Beth Blanford had told her.

"Honey?" Marcy patted Janine's shoulder.

Janine sniffed. "Just something in my eye. Sand I think."

"The island breeze has a way of doing that to a person. Here." Marcy gave Janine a handkerchief. It was silky and black with red lace sewn at the edges. Janine wiped both eyes. "What do you think so far?"

If Janine told her what she was really thinking at that moment in time, Marcy would toss her out of the Jeep in hopes of never seeing the kooky woman from Kansas ever again. Instead she said, "It's amazing how huge that ship is."

Marcy looked toward the channel. "You never seen a cargo ship before?" Before Janine could say anything, Marcy answered her own question. "Of course you haven't." Again she patted Janine's shoulder.

"The closest I've been to the ocean was on my honeymoon," Janine said. "Michael took me to Myrtle Beach but they don't have big cargo ships nearby. Lots of fighter planes flying overhead but not a lot of ships."

"I'm guessing Michael is no longer in your life."

Marcy slowed for a walking group of people who appeared to have already started their party evening. Two of the group of six swayed into the road. Marcy lightly hit her horn. "Sorry," one of them yelled.

"He died a couple years back," Janine said.

"I'm sorry, honey. Any children?"

Janine delayed her answer. Visions of Lenny's death pounded for conscious release. She subdued the vivid imagery.

"Yes. He died as well."

"Oh…honey…I'm so sorry. Just tell me to shut up. I didn't mean to bring up bad memories."

Janine blotted a fresh tear with Marcy's handkerchief. "That's OK.

Really. I need to deal with it anyway. You didn't know."

Marcy frowned in disgust of her own rudeness. "I could beat myself for that."

"No really. I'll be fine. See. No more tears. All gone." Janine handed back Marcy's handkerchief.

"You just hold onto that," Marcy said. "You never know when sand may blow unexpectedly into your eye again." She smiled lightly. "We'll leave that behind us for tonight. The luau will help. Let's just say 'To Hell With It All' and have ourselves a great time."

"Deal," Janine replied.

"Well, let's get this party started." Marcy reached between the seats and pulled out a cassette tape that she loaded into the Jeep's console. "You like Cher?"

"Sure. I haven't heard something from her in a while."

As Cher began to belt out the lyrics to *Gypsies, Tramps and Thieves*, Janine realized for the first time how much Marcy resembled the dark-haired diva. And when Marcy began singing along with Cher while licking her top lip with the tip of her tongue, Janine was sure that a star was sitting right next to her.

❒ ...

Joel Canton watched the luau fire grow from a spark to a blaze as he prepared to launch his first cast of the evening from the south Port A jetty rocks. With the thirty dollar loan from Billy, Joel had replenished his fishing reel with new line, replaced the broken globe of his lantern, and had enough left over to buy some milk, bread, potatoes, a dozen cans of half-priced baked beans and a Milky Way candy bar. He'd stashed the remaining two dollars and change in a coffee can he kept under his cot back at his one-room, clapboard home—or as many in town referred to it: the Canton Shack. It wasn't a shack, though. He kept it pretty well. But compared to many of the high-priced homes around this summer vacation town, his was smaller than many of their garages. And he liked it that way. A small house meant little needed maintenance which meant more time to devote to the Gulf.

Joel was feeling particularly lucky tonight. The official beginning of summer was just around the corner and his "fishin' senses'" always fired on all cylinders around this time of the year. He unwrapped the top half of the candy bar, took a small bite, squeezed off a bit of the nougat between a forefinger and thumb and molded it over the fishing hook. It was his secret bait, guaranteed to pull in the biggest speckled trout that might have the misfortune to be in the vicinity of Joel Canton, master fisherman.

Though he was a good half-mile from the growing crowd on the opposite side of the pier, he heard the chant of dozens of people protesting the construction of the casino. Then the band began to play. Sometimes noise was a good thing—sometimes it wasn't. It all depended on how the fish were feeling.

He cast his line a good twenty yards into the darkening water which lapped gently against the jetty rocks. The sun had already dropped below the horizon and only a thin red glow remained beyond the dunes. Overhead, multicolored bands of blue to gray to black spread across the sky. Stars slowly twinkled into existence. The Big Dipper was the first constellation he recognized. He found the pole star by following the dipper's cup, down toward the Gulf water horizon. Lights from freighters and cargo ships twinkled in the black below the pole star.

How he longed to be out there again. He wished he were riding one of those points of light on the water looking up at the points of light in the sky, navigating by the pole star, just him and his boat and the stars. It was beyond a man's intelligence to describe just how that felt. Spiritual, was not good enough. Otherworldly, was too "Hollywood." It was like trying to describe Heaven: no one really knew but everyone had their opinion.

His fishing pole jerked and Joel let out a little line. He tugged lightly and the fish struck. He whipped the pole upward and felt the power of the fish in his fingers. Slowly he reeled it in, the combined force of the struggling fish and the Gulf current working against the strength of his forearms and wrists. All at once, the fight stopped. He'd lost the fish and that was rare. Perhaps he was not going to be so lucky this evening after all. He turned his reel to recapture his line but as the hook drew close to the jetty rocks, he saw that he had not lost the fish after all. A speckled trout the length of his forearm floated toward him. Its spasms kept it slightly submerged and as Joel pulled it up onto the rocks, its fight completely stopped. It didn't flop. It was barely alive. Joel wriggled the hook free and a small chunk of nougat and several drops of blood fell to the rocks.

Joel was not lucky. Of the last nine fish he'd caught over the last four days, eight of them had been ill or dead. He dropped the trout back into the water and watched as the fish struggled momentarily before flipping over on its side. Its motionless, floating body crashed against the rocks in shallow waves.

At that same moment, a horn caused Joel to look up and toward the shore. Over on the beach road, two jeeps, almost identical in size, headed in the direction of the pier. They were a good hundred yards from him but Joel knew who was driving both. The lead jeep had emergency lights attached to the roll cage though they were not turned on. Tall radio antennae whipped from either side of the Marine Institute vehicle. Mark Walker was driving.

The jeep behind Walker's had two people on board. He knew who was driving that jeep not so much because he could actually see her but more so because he knew of no other topless vehicle in town whose occupant's hair blew in such a long stream. It was Marcy the fortune teller, another in town whom Joel could call a friend.

The dead trout was gone, having apparently floated out of his lantern's halo of light. Joel turned off the lantern and packed his gear. There would be no good fishing tonight, luck or no luck.

And he was going to ask Walker why.

❑ ...

"When were you born?" Marcy asked as she turned down the volume on *I Got You Babe*.

"November thirty," Janine replied.

They had turned onto the beach road just a few minutes ago and were following another jeep that looked a lot like Marcy's. She'd said that the man driving was named Mark Walker. He was a marine biologist from the marine institute and she'd read his palm and flipped Tarot cards for him on a couple of occasions.

"Sagittarius." Marcy grinned. "That explains your positive outlook on life and your adventurous spirit to experience things beyond the physically familiar. Like Port Aransas."

Beyond the physically familiar, Janine thought. If Marcy only knew just how right she was.

"Yes," Janine said. "I guess you might say that. I *have* become much more adventurous in the last year or so."

"You religious," Marcy said as a statement rather than a question. She turned toward Janine, her hair flailing in twisted strands about her face.

"You mean do I believe in God?"

Marcy's grin spread into a smile. "Don't we all?"

Again, Marcy broke Janine's fortune teller stereotyping. She'd never considered that mystics could believe in God. "Well, I've met a few who don't." She thought of Albert Stine.

"I know what you mean," Marcy intervened. "People just don't want to believe." She shifted down a gear as the jeep approached the pier and a crowd that looked to be in the hundreds. "For instance, I can tell a person many things about them just from one piece of information: the day they were born."

"That's information that only God knows."

"You are religious," Marcy said. "That is good. Where we are headed needs lots of faith and a heavy dose of belief for us to survive."

Janine looked around at the small tent city, the lights, and the white foam of crashing waves in a background of watery darkness.

Marcy patted Janine's hand as she parked. "No, dear. Not the luau. Our future. Mankind's future. We are headed into the Age of Aquarius and only the faithful will survive."

Marcy exited the jeep as Janine sat there, wondering why Marcy had felt the need to tell her such things. There were dots that Marcy, apparently, wanted her to connect but she could not find the right path. Somehow, Marcy sensed in Janine the one thing that had saved her from the beast a year ago. Faith. Marcy was a fortune teller—a mystic. She told people things they wanted to hear as a gimmick and she made a living doing so. No crystal ball could tell the future and no lifeline could describe the past. It was all just gimmick. But Marcy *did* know that Janine was a religious person and that her faith had guided her to safety so far. Whatever the Age of Aquarius was, Marcy certainly believed that Janine would be a part of it.

Marcy walked to the passenger side of the jeep and grabbed Janine's hand. "You are a survivor, my dear." A chill raced along Janine's arm. Marcy had said exactly what she was thinking. She was a survivor—a survivor in paradise.

Together, they approached the tents at the gathering's top end where a band full of blonde-haired, scantily-clothed young men gyrated to *Proud Mary* atop a tractor trailer flatbed. Janine's father had driven a tractor trailer flatbed to haul construction materials when she was just a kid but she'd never seen one used as a musician's stage before.

Rollin...rollin...rollin on a river...

Marcy sang along with the band as the women made their way among the tents. The crowd was shoulder-to-shoulder as dozens of people piled chunks of food onto plates and into mouths. Around a huge bonfire closer to the water, at least a hundred people drank and danced. Teenagers ran through the dark surf behind the dancers, chasing footballs and Frisbees, though Janine wondered how in world they could see what they were throwing or catching.

"Try this," Marcy said. She handed Janine a plate of shrimp and chunks of pineapple. A light red sauce was drizzled on and around the food.

"Oh my," Janine exclaimed. "This is…Wow."

"Tasty?" the man behind the tent table asked.

"Yes. Very, very."

Marcy introduced Janine to Pedro Melindez. "He is the chef at a restaurant just down the street from me," she said. "One of the best we have in town."

"Gracias, Marcy." Pedro nodded his head with respect. "I have much more. Would you like to try my crab cake?"

Janine had never eaten crab before. In fact, up until the moment she placed the Caribbean shrimp into her mouth, she'd eaten seafood on very few occasions, one being the evening she and Michael had arrived in Myrtle Beach for their honeymoon. She'd not been too crazy about the seafood buffet that night. The shrimp had been particularly unpleasant. But what rolled across her lips and tongue now was pure delight, having only the faintest hint of the sea distributed among the wonderful flavors of pineapple, coconut, and what she thought was a peachy, appley, orangey flavor with a hint of pepper scattered throughout. She took the forkful of crab cake that the chef now offered to her. Again, her taste buds exploded with delight. Though the crab cakes had more of a seafood taste, the flavor was in stark contrast to the shrimp she'd just swallowed. The mixture of the two tastes, one right after the other, was very pleasant.

"Wow," Janine said again. Pedro smiled, proudly.

"Are you visiting our tiny island?" Pedro asked.

"Just arrived today." Janine swallowed. She realized that Marcy was not standing near her any more. A group of five men stopped at the tent and plucked shrimp and crab cakes from the serving dishes. "Hey, baby. Wanna dance?" the ugliest of the five said. They were all unshaven and looked as if they had not washed in weeks. Janine guessed they ranged in ages between forty and sixty. They smelled fishy and this turned Janine's stomach and her attention away from the food and the men.

"Beat it scalawags," Marcy said, appearing from behind Janine with two cups of beer. "Go jump in a lake…or perhaps an ocean would be better for the likes of you."

The ugliest man elbowed his nearly-as-ugly counterpart. "Hey. If it ain't the wacko gypsy. You cast a spell on us, Madame Ruminski?"

Marcy handed Janine both beers then slipped a pair of fingers into her halter top between her breasts. She pulled out a pinch of sand and tossed it at the ugliest man. "Your catch in the sea tomorrow will deny you food or funds. Now, back off before I take your boats, too."

Janine gawked at Marcy's incantation and was even more surprised when the ugliest man flinched backward, tripping over his nearly-as-ugly companion and into the arms of the three other men whose mouths hung open with shrimp sauce smeared across their lips. The men seemed to want to run but did not want to show the apparent fear that suddenly resided in them. Instead, all five quickly sauntered away, keeping an eye on Marcy until they disappeared into the crowd.

Janine's expression remained quizzical. Marcy turned to her and belted out two short laughs. "Haa…Haa!" Pedro joined in almost simultaneously. Janine sipped from her beer to wash down the remains of the crab cake and grinned but didn't laugh. Marcy took the other cup of beer but didn't drink from it until her laughter had subsided.

"Amazing what a little sand and a whole lot of superstition can do for a lady," Marcy said. "Those toads are infamous for causing trouble on the island. Don't let their rudeness turn you off to our little slice of heaven."

"Sí. They are problemas," Pedro agreed. "They cause trouble even at the Surf Side."

"Surf Side?" Janine questioned, taking another sip of beer and looking toward the crashing waves. Marcy had downed her entire cup.

"Where he works," Marcy said atop a tiny burp. "Oh, pardon me."

"Well, thank you, Pedro, for a wonderful little meal," Janine said. "And to answer your question—before we were so rudely interrupted—I am from Kansas and I am new in town. I think that I will be staying here for quite some time."

Pedro shook her hand with both of his. "We are happy to have you. I would be glad to show you mí isla. Yes?"

Janine looked puzzled. Marcy translated. "He wants to show you around his island."

"Oh, yes, thank you," Janine said, her hand still clasped between

Pedro's. Of the few Spanish words she knew, thanks was one of them. "Gracias. Gracias."

Marcy chaperoned Janine toward the bonfire, around a crowded sandy dance floor full of gyrating bodies that had found some way to dance to AC-DC's *Back in Black*, then strolled to the left toward the pier away from many of the partiers. She stopped, slipped off her sandals, and stepped ankle-deep into shallow waves. Without a word, Janine followed.

"Beautiful, isn't it?" Marcy stared at the clear, black sky. "And to think we are all a part of that wonderful vastness. Just starlight, Janine. We are all just starlight." She pointed upward toward the constellation of Gemini. "The twins are bright tonight. They always help guide us through the summer months. They helped guide you here tonight."

Janine had been following her finger, trying to understand where Marcy was pointing. "What do you mean?"

"The stars guide all that we do." Marcy lowered her gaze and looked into Janine's eyes. "We all have a destiny, Janine. It is written before we are born. The stars are our escorts on this wonderful journey. You have been through much. I can see it in your eyes and you've come to this island looking for solace, for peace, for rest." Marcy hesitated for a moment, perhaps in search of Janine's soul. "Do you believe that it was coincidence that you were dropped off at my doorstep? Do you believe that it is coincidence that you are here with me tonight at this wonderful luau? Will it be coincidence when, tomorrow, you will become entangled in the nets of this island?"

Janine had to look away from Marcy's stare. She turned her attention back toward the stars. "I don't understand," she said under her breath.

Marcy placed her hand on Janine's shoulder. "You have come to this island for solitude but this island is troubled right now. It will be tested in the days to come. It has great secrets to unveil upon the world, secrets that men should not witness."

Janine turned back toward Marcy's stare. She thought it was odd that the fortune teller talked about the island as if it were a living, breathing thing.

Before Marcy could finish her revelations, a voice from behind yelled, "Fruitcake!" It was the five ugly men. "Beware, beware, we're all going to die!" They didn't approach the women but instead continued on toward the pier. "Gypsy slut!" another yelled out.

Marcy turned back toward the water. "Men like those are the reason; men who have no understanding of what is good; men who only take but never give; men like those will be the end of us all."

Both women were silent for what seemed, to Janine, like several minutes. She became lost in the sea of brilliant starlight that reminded her of Kansas evenings just before harvest. It made her think of Michael and how he'd roll out of the fields, climb off of his John Deere and squat on the porch as the last of the heat and light fell across the western horizon. They'd sit there for minutes that seemed like hours and do nothing but stare into the heavens and sip fresh lemonade. She'd caress his shoulders and they'd kiss once or twice as the Dog Star blazed brilliantly overhead. No words were spoken. All that was heard were sounds of the light breezes brushing through cotton and corn, the occasional squeaky hinged barn door when the wind hit it from the south at just the right angle, their shallow, even breaths and the once or twice smacking together of gentle lips, and the tinkle of ice cubes in glasses of lemonade.

Marcy suddenly turned toward the pier, breaking Janine's reverent silence. Out of the gray shadows and into the bonfire haze strolled a man with a grizzly, silver beard. For a moment Janine thought it was the ugly man. He carried a fishing pole and a darkened lantern. He gazed at the beach sand as if being particularly careful not to trip over hidden obstacles.

"Joel!" Marcy yelled. "Hey Joel!"

He looked up.

"Joel. I have someone here I'd like you to meet."

Joel stopped, lowered his fishing pole's grip to the sand and stood there as if using the fishing pole as a staff. Marcy grabbed Janine's hand and led her out of the water.

"Joel Canton, meet Janine..." Marcy hesitated and looked at Janine.

"Bender," Janine added and reached out a hand to shake. "Janine Bender."

"Hello Marcy," Joel said, acknowledging Janine with a quick gaze but no handshake. "The fishing is not getting any better." His voice had the sharp edge of concern.

"I've heard," Marcy said as Janine lowered her hand. "It'll pass though. We're just going through one of those...things."

Janine could not see him very well in the limited light but what was unveiled of Joel Canton was a man who was not much cleaner in appearance than the five men who had accosted her earlier. His face, though, had a warm, gentle appeal that was ruggedly handsome. What really sparked her curiosity about the fisherman was what she saw in his eyes. There seemed to be a world of suffering attached to his pupils, as if his life had gone nowhere near as planned. The tiny, sparkled, firelight reflections added a strange, inspirational hope to the weary gaze. Like herself, this man had ended up at this moment in time, having never meant to make this particular journey. Was it coincidence that had brought her to the island? Was it coincidence that had her standing in wet sand, looking at a strangely magnetizing man whom she'd never met before? Or was it fate, like Marcy had implied?

Joel, without a particular reason, let his fishing pole drop to the sand and offered his freed hand to Janine which she took. "Joel Canton," he said. "Do I know you?"

Janine curtly smiled. "I really don't think so. I've never been to Port Aransas before."

"I see." Joel looked puzzled. "Janine, did you say?" A very small curl of a smile hinted at the right edge of his mouth.

"Uh-huh."

Joel continued shaking her hand, gently, as if it were fragile. She felt a rough sandy grip that was firm and strong, one that might easily wrestle the largest fish out of water, yet his fingers around hers offered a pleasant sensation of kindness.

"I...uh," Joel said, releasing the handshake. "I saw Walker heading in and wanted to ask him about the fish." He turned his attention to Marcy but kept peering at Janine from the corner of his right eye, as if her image would suddenly disappear if he looked away.

"Let's go together," Marcy said, smiling, and apparently happy with what she saw in Joel's expressive response. She picked up his fishing pole and Joel reached his hand forward to grab it. "I'll carry it for you and the lantern too if you wish."

They were his greatest means for life support and in every other circumstance Joel would have fought hell and high water to protect his fishing pole and lantern, but, almost hypnotically, he handed their custody over to Marcy whose smile now gleamed.

◻ ...

Joel's senses swam in a sea of memories. He tasted the salt of the water and of his own blood that ran in a swirling mixture from his forehead across his mouth. The sun was unbearably hot that day. It was the summer of 1972. The sailboat's boom had just swiveled into his head and he had not ducked in time. Bert Nookle was screaming, "Big Fuckin' Fish! Big

Fuckin' Fish!" And then Joel had passed out.

When he'd awakened, the boat was near shore and a towel was wrapped around his head. Bert was at the wheel. The shark was in tow.

Unlike in the movie, the captain of the boat did not die and the shark was only twenty feet long, but still large enough to break every record from here to Galveston Bay. Also, unlike the movie, three barrels shot into the Great White had been enough to swamp and kill it. They'd hauled the shark to the docks over by the inlet where the Corpus Christi Channel would one day be built and a hundred cheers from fellow islanders greeted them. Bert had announced, "We got the son of whore" and had clapped Joel on the shoulder with one meaty hand. "See what the bastard did to my mate."

No one except Bert and Joel's wife, Jane, had ever known the real story. It was Bert who had single-handedly captured the Great White. And the scars across Joel's stomach had indeed come from the shark but not because the killer had bitten him. He'd been careless in moving the shark out of the water and had slipped on the docks. The shark had fallen on top of him and two of its teeth had buried into his belly.

After that day, he and Bert's friendship had slowly taken a turn for the worst. Joel's shame had prevented him from revealing his own truth and Bert had used it as a strange kind of blackmail. The two had been heralded so much that Port Aransas history had written the Nookle-Canton story into the summer of 1972. Joel had gotten a new charter boat and a huge touring business out of the lie. The sudden success had prevented any revelation. The sudden success had driven him into the Gulf with his charters and his fame and his own sad false glory. It had also driven Jane away.

Bert and Jane left the island a year later. A simple note had been left on Joel's bed. It had been attached to a stapled compilation of legal papers. The note had read:

Dear Joel,

I cannot live with the lie any longer. Bert has asked me to marry him and that is that. I wish things had been different. I wish you had come home from the Gulf more often. I once loved you Joel but all you are to me now is a memory.

Please sign these papers and return to the address below. Please do not contest this. I want nothing from you. I have never wanted anything from you more than YOU.

-Jane
P.S. If the lie is to stay a lie then sign these papers quickly.

That P.S. had been the most disturbing. Joel had been convinced that Bert had written it. It was a strange kind of blackmail, one that would allow him to keep his charter company but lose his wife.

Bert died ten years later. It was 1983, the year of the Big Wind. A week before the high tides caused by Hurricane Alicia devastated Joel's charter and nearly drowned much of Port Aransas, he had gone up to Galveston to see his old friend buried. Jane had been there. She'd stood near the preacher clad in black wardrobe that covered every inch of her body. Her veil had disallowed his vision of her face. After Bert's death, she moved into her parents' home in El Paso. He'd not seen her since, leaving nothing but the memory of that black, lace veil from the funeral, a masked memory so strong that he'd forgotten her beauty and what once was their love.

Until now. Until Janine.

Joel was mesmerized by the resemblance.

❐ …

The five smelly fishermen made their way past the turnstile, past the small bait shop and souvenir stand and onto the weathered boards of the Horace Caldwell Pier. They stumbled and cursed and annoyed just about anyone who cared to notice they were there. This wasn't the first time the five men had ventured onto the pier looking for trouble, and after their confrontation with Marcy the fortune teller, their determination was more abnormal than usual.

"Hey, Baby," said the smelliest of the five, whose name was Jacque. "How 'bout a five-on-one, eh?"

The person whose long hair had instigated Jacque's rudeness turned from the pier railing; the hair rained across his thin chest. "Pardon me?" the wiry man said.

"Good God, Peter," Jacque said to one staggering buddy. "You ever seen a man with chick hair like that? What a fuckin' girl."

Peter pointed at the long-haired man. "Hey bitch. I think you need a goddamn hair cut." He pulled a gutting knife from a sheath on his belt.

The man dropped his fishing pole and ran from the pier. Peter ran after him, knife held point forward and glistening under the pier lamp light, until the man bolted through the turnstile. He sheathed the knife and turned back toward his four smelly friends.

"What about that?" he said to them snickering. "I wasn't gonna' charge him for it."

The five laughed together then continued stumbling out toward the end of the pier. The walk held slim pickins for the five. Most people were over at the luau which, from the pier, blazed brilliantly three hundred yards across the water from where they stood. They prodded a drunk who'd passed out but they were unable to awaken and harass him any further. Other than that, only two other people were on the pier. Both stood together to the right of the T that formed at the end. Both were looking back toward the luau. Both were outlined in a dim halo of red-orange light that, somehow, had reached them from the luau's bonfire across the water.

The five smelly men turned together at the T and staggered toward them. All but Jacques stopped when the larger of the two men turned to face them. The smaller of the men stayed where he was, leaning on the railing, smoking a cigarette and gazing out over the water. Before Jacques said anything, the figure leaning against the railing exhaled a lungful of smoke. "It's Jacque, isn't it?" he said without turning and looking.

Jacque took another step forward. Either out of curiosity or just plain stupidity he replied, "So who the fuck wants to know?"

"He does," the smaller shadow said as he puffed the cigarette and thumbed in the direction of the larger shadow.

Jacque looked up and for the first time realized just how large the larger shadow was. The orange-red glow was at the large shadow's back, outlining it, giving it depth and breadth and menace. Near where the eyes should have been were two circles of scarlet red that undulated and swirled and pierced Jacque's gaze until the smelly man had to look away.

"If you guys are looking for trouble," Jacque said, "look no further." He turned to see that his buddies had not moved any closer. "Come on you faggots. These guys ain't nothin' but hot air."

And then the smaller shadow flicked his cigarette into the waves below and flinched, his chin rising quickly up and down as if he'd just nodded agreement to some unspoken question.

In one swift motion that was much too fast for Jacque to challenge, the tall shadow stepped forward, snatched Jacque by the neck with one hand and lifted him off the pier. Jacque's toes were ten inches from the wooden planks when his eyes fell upon the bodyguard's hell-red stare. He uselessly wrenched at the grip on his neck with both hands. Jacque reached around and snatched a small whittling knife from his back pocket, flicked it open with his thumb, and buried it into the arm of the shadow. Jacque's four companions stood frozen as their friend dangled like a doll from the bodyguard's grip. It wasn't until Jacque stabbed the bodyguard's arm a second time and the dark shadow walked to the railing of the pier to effortlessly throw Jacque into the Gulf that all four ran.

Jacque's scream could be heard for a full two seconds before everything on the pier went silent except for the footfalls of four smelly, drunken fishermen.

☐ ...

Billy looked over Mark's shoulder and out toward the pier. He thought he'd heard something—a scream perhaps. At this distance, all that could be seen was the pier's long dark line that stretched for more than two hundred and fifty feet out and twelve feet over the Gulf.

"I doubt it's the Red Tide," Mark was saying. "I've done samples from here down to Mustang Point and no buildup of algae is present anywhere."

Billy reset his vision on Mark who sat in the sand to his left. Steph sat to his right, stroking her toes through the sand. They were a dozen feet away from the bonfire. Several empty paper plates that were slathered with a mixture of sauces and sand, and a couple of empty beer cups lay at their feet.

"Chemicals?" Steph said. It was the first thing she'd added to the discussion.

Mark looked at her, scrutinizing, the way he would have done a student who'd just suggested to his class an unexpected but quite intellectual observation. "What makes you say that?" he questioned, as he would have a student who'd made such an observation.

"Rumor mostly," Steph quickly offered. "Nothing scientific. Just…

ehh…conjecture." She'd become more relaxed after the three beers she'd had. "People talk. And inside a bank where businesses sometimes live or die by rumor, I hear the fear in many that the Big Spill has finally happened."

"I've heard that rumor," Billy said, remembering what Kale had told him earlier. "Any justification to it, Mark?"

Mark weighed his answer with more care than he had when answering Billy's suggestion of a Red Tide. The Big Spill was a rumor that had often surfaced in the five years he'd been studying the marine life around Port A and never had that great fear materialized. Everyone knew there were ample opportunities with DuPont Chemical just north of the island but never had there been documented proof.

"I don't think so," he finally said.

"But it's a possibility," Billy added.

"You know me, BJ. All answers are valid until there is proof to the contrary."

"Or no proof at all," Billy said.

"We've had this discussion before," Mark said, shifting in the sand and crossing his legs while staring out over the dark waves. "A lack of proof equates to mere theory. Without tests of the hypothesis, there can be no sound answer."

"Said just like a true doctor of marine biology." Billy looked over at Steph. "What do you think about that?" he asked her.

Before she could answer, Officer Keadle appeared behind them. He held three full cups of beer between the outstretched fingers of both hands. Each of them snatched one. The off-duty officer then squatted and slowly sipped a bottle of water he'd carried in the waist band of his shorts. Billy downed all of his beer in one gulp. Steph sipped hers, a beer buzz already roaming through her body. Mark sat his onto the sand as if waiting for Steph's answer before drinking any of it.

"I think…" she sipped some more beer. "I think that not everything has to be proven to be believed."

Billy smiled half glad and half shocked. A slight chuckle accompanied his glee when he turned to look at the astonished stare on Mark's face. "Interesting choice of words," Billy said, patting her shoulder a bit more passionately than he'd intended. "Don't you think, Mark? I mean, just because you can't prove something doesn't mean it can't be *believed*."

Mark shifted uncomfortably. "Belief is a lazy cop out. You can believe all the rumors about chemical spills that you want to, but until my test tubes collect the samples that my microscopes find to be tainted, all that the believers are doing is making themselves and anyone who will listen to them, paranoid."

"I'm not paranoid," Billy said. "But I am worried."

"You think there's a spill, Billy?" Officer Keadle asked, genuine concern apparent in his voice.

"Not if the good scientist here says there isn't." Billy reached forward and gave Mark a hearty jab with an open hand to side of the arm. Billy knew this discussion always stoked Mark's compassion with science. About proof, Billy felt pretty much the same way but he pretended not to just to drive his friend's gullibility. "I'm worried about Mark though. He's going to drive himself crazy thinking about not worrying about something he can't prove or believe in."

All three looked in silence at Billy. Then Mark smirked, then chuckled, then laughed. "I don't know what you just said but I suspect you're right. I can't argue with an intellectual equal."

"Equal?" Billy questioned, sarcastically.

Mark sipped some beer. "Why don't we check it out tomorrow then. I'll take the helo down the coast and we can pull some representative samples from several buoy locations."

"Free helicopter ride?" Billy said and whirled his index finger in the air like a rotor. "And a chance to do some experiments with the good doctor? I'm definitely in."

Keadle laughed because he knew the men's strange sense of humor. Steph laughed because everyone else laughed and because the beer had oiled her senses.

The *Knights in White Satin* returned from a break and started their second set of the night with their own version of the Moody Blues' *Knights in White Satin*. Their licks on the guitar strings nullified any of the original artist's haunting melody. It sounded more like Nirvana meets Blink 182 and raged with the teen spirit of a rock show.

The subject of Gulf pollution and the growing fish kills moved into a discussion of the impending casino vote that had been silently placed on Saturday's town agenda. Officer Keadle, though off duty, left the trio to settle a small scuffle that had broken out among some drunken dancing teens near the makeshift flatbed stage.

"No Mayan for My Island—I like that," Mark said. "I wish I'd of thought of it."

"Won't mean a hell of beans unless we can get enough people together to quash this absurd 'silent' vote," Billy countered.

"I don't remember reading anything about it in the *Jetty*."

"That is disturbing," Billy said. "I went to see Kilpatrick today but his secretary told me he was out."

"Out of his freakin' mind," Mark added, smirking. "He's got a responsibility to print in the public interest."

"That is what is so disturbing." Billy leaned forward. "What is in the public interest is what Kilpatrick says it is. If he's been lured to the dark side, he'll not jeopardize the casino and whatever kickback he's probably getting."

Mark leaned back and set his hands in the sand behind him so that his arms supported his weight. He unfolded his legs and stretched them toward the Gulf waves which were slowly crashing closer as high tide moved in. "What can we do other than hang posters and protest on the beach?" he said.

Steph let out a tiny burp. Billy and Mark grinned and looked at her simultaneously, as if another line of wisdom was about to be revealed.

"Go door-to-door," she suggested, stretched out her legs and propped herself onto her arms in much the same way that Mark had. "I can go around after work tomorrow and the rest of this week if that's what it takes."

Again, Billy looked at her as if she were the smartest person among them. Mark said that he could cover a portion of the north side of the island near the marine institute and hit the restaurants around the jetty. Billy said that his surfer buddies could pound the pavement along Alister and Avenue G. Steph offered to remind those she met at the bank and then take whatever area that was not already covered after work. Billy offered to join her and she quickly agreed.

"Not gonna work," slurred a voice from within the sound of crashing waves which were now a dozen feet away. Into the dimming bonfire glow appeared CrabMan, one of Billy's surfing friends. "Not gonna waste time. They gonna be a casino. Not gonna stop it."

"Crab," Billy said, looking up at the thin man whose red skin melded into the orange-red flickers from the fire. "You're not giving in are you Crab my man?"

"Useless, Presser." CrabMan slobbered, his spittle making his Ss sound snakelike. Rally Panini, a.k.a. Crabman, strode into the middle of the group's half-circle without looking at either Mark or Steph. His scowl was menacing, as if he were trying to pick a fight with Billy. CrabMan had never called Billy by his last name. When Billy started to stand, CrabMan pushed him back down to the sand.

"Hey!" Mark yelled and rose to a knee.

"Sit down," CrabMan growled, keeping his gaze on Billy. "You no want this."

CrabMan could not have weighed more than a hundred and thirty pounds wet. His arms were thin, his legs spindly. He'd gotten the nickname CrabMan because his skin always looked sunburned. A thin goatee made him look a lot like Shaggy from the Scooby-Doo comics except that his hair was nearly blonde-white. To Billy's knowledge, he'd never been in a fight in his life.

"You want a bunch of mobsters to come in here and take our surf away?" Billy said, trying to reason with a man who'd apparently downed too much beer, too much smoke, too many pills or a combination of the three.

"Stay out of my buzzyness," CrabMan countered.

And then, suddenly, Steph flopped forward toward CrabMan's legs. "Look out!" she yelled.

In CrabMan's hand was a short, broken piece of driftwood about four feet long. He'd had it hidden behind his back and he now brought it out and lifted it high over his head as if he was about to chop a log in two. At the end of the piece of wood was the point of a polished nail, one that had apparently been freshly driven into the wood to serve as a weapon. Steph grabbed one of CrabMan's boney ankles as the nail point glistened firelight for a fraction of a second before starting its downward motion toward Billy's head.

"No!" Steph yelled again as Billy rolled to his left.

Out of nowhere, a hand snatched the arm that held the wooden weapon and in one swift motion, wrenched it free of CrabMan's grasp. CrabMan did not scream even though his arm went backward in an inhumane twist that should have broken it. He continued staring right through Billy as his striking arm was forced into his back. Officer Keadle's thick forearm wrapped under CrabMan's chin and he held the surfer in a choke hold as he kicked the makeshift weapon into the surf.

"What the hell have you been smokin', Panini?" Keadle said. A small group of luau onlookers had gathered near the commotion. "Nothing to see here," the policeman said to the crowd. "The man's had a bit too much for one night." He lowered his voice and spoke into CrabMan's ear. "Isn't that right, Panini?"

"Screw you," CrabMan slurred.

"That's it! A night in the pokey is in your immediate future."

As Keadle escorted CrabMan away from the crowd, the angry surfer peered down at Billy. "Stay out, Presser. You need some other surf… before too late."

A strange crimson glow flickered in CrabMan's pupils, firelight reflection perhaps. This coupled with what he'd said sent Billy's mind in search of…

Lett's bodyguard—the goon at the bar yesterday.

Those had been his words, though they'd been much less slurred and much more threatening.

He'd had that same hidden rage.

He'd stared with those same crimson eyes.

❐ …

Out on the pier, the big shadow that had thrown Jacque the smelly fisherman into the Gulf watched the scuffle on the beach. The smaller shadow puffed from a cigarette and blew a perfect circle of smoke. "Keadle's gonna be trouble," he said to his bodyguard. "Take care of it."

The bodyguard scowled, loathing the need to take orders from a man such as Chancey Lett. But, for now, it was necessary.

The illusion had to be maintained for a few more days, at least until the excavation began and the beach revealed its hidden treasure.

❐ …

Joel found Mark near a tent serving fish kabobs shortly after Mark had left Billy's company. Janine and Marcy talked in low voices behind him, chitchatting about the people they'd been watching on the beach. Joel approached Mark from behind and tapped him on the shoulder.

"You sure that's safe to eat?" he said, scowling. Burgess, the cook that looked like Chef-Boy-Ardee, stepped forward before Mark answered.

"You got a beef with my fish, Joel buddy?" He pointed the two pronged cooking fork he held in his left hand at Joel's face. A piece of fish fell from one of the points and landed on the pant leg of Joel's coveralls. Joel clenched both fists and squeezed hard.

"Wasn't talkin' to you, fat boy," Joel hissed. He kicked his leg forward to throw off the fish meat.

When Mark reached out and lowered Burgess's cooking fork with his hand, Marcy intervened. "Your kabobs are burning," she said. Burgess hurriedly turned to his grill and jabbed at the kabobs with his fork. "There's nothing wrong with the fish around here," Burgess said to Joel. "Why won't people listen to me?"

Joel's clenched fists relaxed. "They don't listen because the sea keeps popping up dead fish."

"The sea does that more often than most people realize." Mark entered the conversation. He finished chewing a piece of fish and swallowed. "Doesn't mean that there is something wrong."

"You got that right," Burgess yelled over his shoulder as he tended his meat. "My fish are the best. They don't float like yours do, Canton."

Mark stepped between Joel's scowling line of sight to Burgess. "Pay no attention," he said to Joel. "But he is right. There's nothing wrong with his fish or any other sea creatures being served here tonight."

"And how do you know that?" Joel peered over Mark's shoulder at Burgess who had found one of the luau's taste judges and was now peddling what he thought were superior cooking skills.

"Let's just say that there's been no evidence to the contrary."

"Every day for the past fours days I've had evidence to the contrary."

Marcy stepped up behind Joel and placed a hand on his shoulder. "Maybe the good professor is right, Joel. He's never steered the island wrong before."

Joel glanced at Marcy and saw Janine in his periphery. He suddenly felt very embarrassed that his anger had bested him. He'd not eaten a decent meal in several days and believed that his livelihood was dying. He'd had to borrow money just to get this far and that was something that had hit his pride hard. However, the sight of Janine eased his anger and his fear of failure. Jane had been able to do that, too. Ease his anger. Ease his fears. Just the sight of her had been enough.

Mark plucked a piece of fish from Burgess's table. The cook was too embroiled in his own self efficacy to notice. He handed it to Joel who did not take it. Janine took it instead.

"Aren't you hungry?" Janine asked Joel. She took a bite out of the one inch chunk of meat. "See—nothing wrong. It actually tastes very good and I'm not much for fish food."

Joel opened his mouth as Janine brought the fish forward. It smelled like coconuts. She slipped it into his mouth and he chewed, never once taking his eyes off Janine as she smiled and licked her fingers. His stomach groaned for more.

Burgess turned to them. "Hey. I thought you hated…"

Janine cut him off. "I know one of the chef's on the island," she said purposely loud. "His name is Pedro and his food is…" she looked at Marcy who added: "el mejor de todos. Only the very best."

Janine grabbed Joel's arm and led him away from Burgess who scowled discontent before turning back to his food preparation.

At Pedro's tent, Joel spent the next ten minutes eating better than he had in many weeks. Pedro had kept the food hot and fresh and plentiful. Joel didn't say a word until he'd had his fill. Mark had not accompanied them, saying that he'd had to get back to the institute to continue monitoring the sea for contaminants "to keep the island safe" as he'd put it.

"I guess Mark was right," Joel said, belched silently and excused himself. "Nothing at all wrong with this. It must be my bad luck." He looked at Janine and measured his words. "But I think the ole' tide is turning."

Marcy nibbled on a few hunks of pineapple. "Since you guys like Pedro's cooking so much, why don't you check out his restaurant. If you think this is good, the food *there* is much more delicioso."

"Gracias," Pedro said. "It would be my pleasure."

"And my treat," Marcy said. Janine started to protest but Marcy cut her off. "I insist. Think of it as my welcome wagon gift to you as a new member of our community."

Janine nodded.

"Joel?" Marcy asked

"I usually don't eat in restaurants," he said.

"And?" Marcy prodded.

Joel looked at Janine and wrestled a small smile loose. "Will you join me for lunch tomorrow at the Surf Side?" he asked her.

Janine blushed but not so much that anyone could tell in the dim bonfire light. "Noon?" she said.

Joel nodded.

Marcy grinned, her task complete.

❏ …

It was well past one o'clock.

Steph had increased her consumption of beer after the attack by the red-skinned surfer Billy had called CrabMan. It was as close to such brutality that she'd ever been. It had messed up her adrenal glands something horrible and the only way she had to stifle the tremble was to drown it in alcohol.

You need some other surf...before too late.

Before what was too late? She'd always assumed that the surfer crowd hung together, especially when it came to issues that threatened their way of life. But the look in the skinny red man's eyes had been as far from camaraderie as anyone could get. The surfer had meant harm. If given the chance, the surfer they called CrabMan would have driven the nail as far into Billy's skull as his meager weight and strength would have allowed. CrabMan may have been high, but Steph believed he'd been driven by power, menace and hate. A killer's instinct. She'd seen it in the red swirl of evil that beamed from each eye's pupil.

The luau fire was now nothing but embers. The *Knights* had packed up thirty minutes ago and had left with the assistance of Billy's chef, Pedro, who had volunteered to drive them to their motel using Billy's VW Bus. A few stragglers wandered the beach under a night sky that was partially obscured by a moon that glowed one quarter full. The lunar surface seemed much closer through her beer-goggled vision, so close that she reached out with one sandy hand as if to caress one of its pockmarked craters.

Billy was behind her. He'd slid one leg to either side of her and his body now provided a backrest for her to lean against as they both sat in the sand, their butts wet from the licks of high tide that had rolled in an hour ago and had helped douse the luau bonfire.

"What's it like?" she said, her hand still grasping for craters that were miles above her fingers.

"Cold, I imagine," Billy said, gazing from her elbow to her hand to her outstretched fingers. Her milky, untanned skin glowed in lunar light. He wrapped his arms gently around her waist and she openly accepted his timid embrace. "Probably can't breathe very well either. But I understand that you can hit a golf ball a hell of a long way."

Steph giggled, lowered her arm, and wrapped her hand around one of Billy's at her waist. "No, silly." A tiny burped escaped. "'Scuse me," she said as Billy giggled with her. "I mean what's it like to ride a wave?"

"Well," Billy said, pausing for just the right words. "It's like this." Then he suddenly stood, drawing Steph up onto her feet as he did so. Her head spun momentarily as blood quickly rushed from head to toes. He took the arm that, moments before, had beguiled the moon with angelic grace and led her into shallow surf that licked at her calves. Lunar light revealed soupy, wave break froth at her feet. "Look out there." Billy pointed at the Big Dipper which now sat at the ocean's horizon. "Ever wonder what it would be like to grab a hold of the Big Dipper and swing from its handle?"

Traveling to the stars was a playful illusion that Steph had often considered but she'd never imagined swinging from them. Her beer buzz augmented the fantasy. She suddenly felt light on her toes. Waves slapping at her legs seemed to lift her though she was actually sinking into the receding sand.

"Here," Billy said. He ran one hand up each side of her body, gently stroking her flesh from hip to shoulder. An excited chill raced through her as he lifted both of her arms and pulled them out to her sides like wings.

"OK," she said. "I know this part. This is when the Karate Kid stands on one leg and kicks the snot out of the bad guys." She started to lift one leg and chuckled.

"If you can pull off a one-legged stand on a surfboard I'll fly you to the moon," he said and gently lowered her leg with an open hand. His warm touch on her thigh teased out goose bumps. "Now crouch down a bit."

Together they squatted. Four arms stretched in unison. Billy's chin rested on her shoulder. His cheek was so close to hers that the goose bumps racing across her flesh puckered up to kiss his. A rush of sea breeze carried splash and wind into their faces. They licked salty wetness from their lips simultaneously.

"It's like this," he whispered in her ear. "You are about as close to God as any one person has right to be. Do you hear that?"

Steph fell silent, her giggles withheld for the sounds that Billy wanted her to hear. Wind. Waves. Crashing. Splashing. And Billy's shallow breaths in her ear. She closed her eyes and imagined flying toward the Big Dipper's handle, wondering if the vastness of space smelled like salt water. When she opened her eyes she expected to see the Dipper's cup within arm's reach. She expected to grab hold and swing from its handle.

And then Billy kissed her—lightly—a peck at the corner of her mouth. She tilted her head back into his chest and moved her mouth toward his. The kiss lasted a full minute though it seemed, to her, like an eternity. She wrapped her hands around the back of his head and he wrapped his around her waist. Together they stood in sand and surf, flying through the heavens and swinging from the stars.

When Billy's lips moved from hers, her eyes blinked open, wearily, knowing that to look at him would forever end the passion of the first kiss. She expected to see Billy gazing down upon her, his face silhouetted against the moon, his eyes searching for the desire that was certainly apparent in her own stare. But he wasn't gazing affectionately at her. In fact, he wasn't looking at her at all. His attention was guided toward the ocean. He watched the waves with piercing concentration as if they were the most important thing in his life.

The serenity of the crashing sea and its gentle tug at her legs was broken when Billy quietly exclaimed, "What the hell?" She moved her head forward from the comfort of his bare, hairless, chest and followed his gaze. The waves broke four feet high and thirty feet out. She could see them clearly under the moonlight. They curled and broke unevenly which was not odd for the surf at Port A. What was odd was their color. Under the stark contrast of white hazy moon glow, the ocean appeared red, almost crimson. The top of the waves clearly reflected an iridescence similar to looking through a glass red marble. It sparkled like champagne. And when the waves folded and crashed, a red froth rolled toward the shoreline. Steph looked down at her feet. Billy had already started to bend forward.

"What is it?" Steph said, bending from the knees beside him. She ran her hand through the water, following Billy's lead. The froth in her palm was pink and bubbly. She threw it away quickly, as if it were burning through her flesh. Billy sniffed a palm full of red froth then dropped it into the surf.

"Let's get out of water," Billy said not waiting for her to answer. He tugged her arm lightly, leading her onto the wet, sandy shore. "Smells funny. Could be an algal bloom of Red Tide."

Steph sniffed the palm of her own hand. It smelled like the air around the Ingleside DuPont chemical plant; it stung her nostrils and added to the intoxication she already felt. She wobbled, taking two quick steps backward in the sand in an attempt to regain balance and tripped. Billy snatched her forearm before she hit the ground and pulled her toward him. Her eyes drooped and slowly fluttered shut. The last thing she remembered before passing out was the overwhelming desire to take a shower.

❐ ...

Billy carried Steph to his VW and gently set her upright in the passenger's seat. He swiped the hair that had fallen across her mouth and nose and pushed it behind her head. He was certain she'd passed out from the alcohol. The algae from Red Tides was only toxic if you ate the sea life that was exposed to it—at least that's what he'd heard. He'd not known anyone who directly or through word-of-mouth had died from Red Tide.

But what if it wasn't Red Tide? What if the worst had finally happened? What if the outlandish rumors were correct? What if the disaster that DuPont said could never happen—had? He looked at his feet, suddenly wondering if the flesh was still attached. It was. He looked at Steph's legs, touched them lightly as she squirmed under his fingers. No discoloration. All the flesh was intact.

He gently closed the VW's door and locked it, then leaned Steph's body toward the open window so that she would not slouch to the left and possibly into the steering wheel. When he turned around to face the ocean, he was shocked to see someone surfing. When he started to rub his eyes in disbelief, the polluted smell on his hands caused reconsideration.

Somehow, the surf had almost doubled in the time he'd walked from the water's edge to place Steph in the VW. The surfer rode atop what appeared to be an eight-foot wave. It was impossible, of course. There had rarely, if ever, been eight-foot waves along this part of the Texas coastline unless some tropical storm or hurricane had stirred up the Gulf. But there he was, too large to be a woman, silhouetted against the thumbnail moon at the horizon, riding the curl of a monster wave that did not break for what seemed like a full minute. The shadow of the surfer raced across the backdrop of the moon like a witch on a broomstick, the bloody red wave's sparkling iridescence falling to either side of the board as it sliced though the water.

Billy looked at his feet again—sniffed his hands.

Chemicals?

Hallucinations?

Too much to drink?

When he looked up again, the surfer was gone. The eight-foot waves had fallen back to three. The moon was still there, glowing near the horizon, and the waves still sparkled in crimson, but the surfer was nowhere to be seen. Billy waited several minutes without avail.

The surfer. It must have been his imagination, by intoxication.

Still, the ocean *had* turned red.

◻ ...

The bodyguard lay flat on his surfboard and pushed himself toward the pier as Billy's VW left the beach. Red laps of water splashed into his eyes, nose and mouth without effect. Once Billy was out of sight, he ditched the surfboard and swam to shore. Walking at the water's edge to the underside of the Caldwell pier, he found what he was looking for. Jacque the fisherman's body floated face down, and was tangled in a swirl of shallow water between the pier's pilings. The body's broken neck beat against one wooden piling as waves rushed in. The bodyguard hoisted the dead man onto his shoulder with less difficulty than Billy had carrying Steph to his VW, and strode to where he'd parked his black Hummer a hundred yards away. He tossed the limp baggage into the backseat and drove off toward the Port A branch of the Big Texas Bank.

PART II

DOMINION OVER THE FISH... THE BIRDS... EVERY CREEPING THING

When Steph awakened, several thoughts raced through her mind in rapid succession. The first was that she needed a shower. The second was that she was not in her bed. The third was that Billy had kissed her. She touched her lips.

She was still wearing the halter top with the dolphin prints but a towel, the color of Texas sand, was wrapped around her waist. She slowly peeled away the Velcro strap that held the towel's hem together expecting to see bare skin. She found that her red shorts were still on and still damp. She wiped her hands across the bed sheets and they were damp as well.

"I hope you don't mind," Billy said, emerging from a room to her right. "I wanted you to be comfortable but I didn't want to..." his words trailed off.

Steph shifted to the edge of the bed, swung her feet over the side and rubbed her eyes. Her halter top loosened and nearly fell off before she grabbed the knot and pulled it tighter. She caught Billy staring at her and when she looked up, he turned his attention away as if embarrassed.

"The bed is wet," she said, standing while she refastened the Velcro hem of the towel around her waist. "You didn't have to do that. I could have slept on the floor."

Billy turned his attention to her. His cheeks blushed a timid pink. "To be honest," he said, "that's where I laid you down first." He pointed to the tan, carpeted floor at Steph's feet. "But I couldn't just leave you there. You'd have woken with creeks and cricks in parts of your body you didn't know existed. I figured a hangover would be enough to cope with the workday."

"Oh shit!" Steph said, looking sporadically for a clock.

"It's just after eight," Billy said. "And don't worry about the bank. I called them a few minutes ago and said you'd be in a little late." He smiled and took a step closer. His hand reached for her shoulder and she allowed it to settle just below her earlobe. The gesture reminded her of his breath in her ear as waves slapped at her legs less than seven hours ago.

"I'll take you back to your place so that you can get ready. If you'd like, use my shower. I've got a shirt and shorts you can wear. It might make you feel better. We can stop for a quick bite downstairs."

Billy was a gentleman. There was no other way to put it. He was a kindhearted, considerate, surfer gentleman. He'd not taken advantage of her, had sacrificed his bed, had notified her workplace, had offered her his clothes and wanted to feed her breakfast before escorting her home. What man is his right mind would ever do that for a woman? Was one kiss worth all of that?

Or did Billy just want to get in her pants? Isn't that what all men wanted? That's how her two previous "relationships" had treated her. The phone calls and favors had come fast and furious until she'd given in. But *they* had been college creeps, and this was…well, not just any man. He'd not even minded that her wet body had dampened his bed sheets and mattress. He could have stripped her clothes off first but this man, who was not just any man, had more respect for her.

"And don't worry about the bed," Billy continued as if reading her mind. "It will dry. Won't take long either. This isn't the first time a body wet from the surf has slept in it." He moved his hand from her shoulder and patted his chest.

She smiled. "OK, it's a deal. As long as you let me wear what you wear when you surf."

This brought a quizzical look to Billy's face that lasted a mere second.

"Deal," he said. "But only if you go surfing with me in it tomorrow."

Quickly, before considering any other obligations, she accepted. A ride on the ocean toward the stars and the Big Dipper's handle would easily place her job on hold. Though she'd be late today, she'd still ask for tomorrow off. Or perhaps she'd just call in sick. Mitchell Bone didn't seem to give much of a shit any more. Carol was doing most of his loans and she'd been relegated to gopher: an errand girl—a job she'd not signed up for.

Billy walked to his dresser, pulled open the second drawer and snatched a pair of boardies. From the third drawer he grabbed the first shirt on the stack. He handed both to Steph then escorted her toward one of the only two other rooms in the apartment.

"Hope you don't mind the mess," he said. "Haven't had much time to clean things up."

There wasn't much of anything to mess up, Steph thought, then saw the stacks of papers strewn across the desk in his lab-office as she passed it. The office was about half the size of the front room and was packed with stuff. There was the desk with papers on it, a computer and a printer on a second smaller computer desk, a bookcase with at least a hundred or more titles orderly shelved, a stack of boxes all the same size that reached from the floor to the ceiling in one corner, and a card table about four feet squared in the opposite corner. On the table was a small chest of drawers, the kind that tinkerers and craftspeople use to store small items such as buttons or beads or small electronic components. Something that looked like a starfish sat in the middle of the table and scattered around it were tiny screws, some thin wires, and what looked like small computer chips.

Billy snapped on the bathroom light and motioned for her to enter. "There's a new bar of soap and a towel in the closet there." He pointed to a door in the wall beside the shower. "Hope you don't mind the shampoo. It's the Dollar Store brand."

"That'll be fine," Steph said, consumed by the masculinity of his bathroom. "Thank you." She closed the bathroom door.

Pedro whipped them up a quick plate of huevos rancheros which Steph downed hungrily as she watched Billy and Kale in a concerned discussion at the Surf Side bar. Billy would put a forkful of egg into his mouth then respond to Kale. In the ten minutes it took Stephanie to eat all of her eggs, Billy had managed to eat only three or four bites. She handed her empty plate to Pedro, who quickly bowed, and told him how wonderful the eggs had been. "Could I get a glass of water from you?" she asked.

"Sí señorita. Un momento, por favor." Pedro plucked a clean glass from a rack behind the front counter and filled it from the waitress island. "Did you have a good time last night?"

Steph had not considered it until now. She was wearing Billy's clothes, had come down from his apartment and was eating breakfast with him. How that must have looked to Pedro and Kale. But she did not think that Pedro would be so rude as to imply such thoughts and assumed that he was talking about the luau. In truth, she really didn't care what anyone thought.

"I had a wonderful time," she said and smiled. "You are the best cook on the island—maybe all of Texas."

"You are too kind," Pedro said. "You come to the restaurant later and I will fix you something muy especial."

"More special than last night?" Steph smiled. "That'll be hard to beat."

"Gracias," Pedro said and again lightly bowed.

Steph finished off half the glass of water as she sauntered over to the bar. Kale was saying something about dead tuna and Billy was asking why.

"Nobody knows," Kale said as Steph stepped closer.

"Hi, hon," Billy said. "Kale, meet Stephanie Drake."

They shook hands and Steph could tell that Kale's mind was not open to anything except restaurant business. He politely smiled, then turned back to Billy and the discussion.

"I'm heading out with Mark today to test for chemical spills," Billy said.

"Dear God in heaven." Kale's face turned pale. "You don't think... does Walker think...?"

"He doesn't know what to think. He's pretty sure it isn't Red Tide but then again he couldn't say yes and couldn't say no. That's why we're going out a few miles to grab some samples. I think everyone wants to know what's going on."

"Businesses are gonna drop like flies around here," Kale said, insinuating the Surf Side but not saying so. "What'll we do in the meantime? Without fish, we're..."

"Dead in the water," Billy finished. "We have enough in cold storage to get us through a couple of days."

"What we have in the freezer isn't the big worry." Kale leaned forward on the bar. It was clear that he'd not shaven in a couple of days. "I think we both know that once word gets out, no one will want to eat anywhere near the Gulf Coast."

Billy stuck a forkful of eggs in his mouth. More than half his serving remained on the plate. "Let's just continue business as usual. No 'word' has gotten anywhere further than those in the business. We'll just have to hope that it's something short term and that DuPont hasn't gone and screwed up."

"Hope and faith," Kale said. "You can't really serve that on a plate with cocktail sauce."

Billy turned to Steph. "We gotta get you home or else the bank is gonna be absent its best employee for not only tomorrow but today as well."

Kale shook his head, knowing the conversation had ended, and headed for the telephone near the waitress station.

Steph left her cottage apartment a little before ten o'clock. She'd quickly changed into her neutral bank attire—nothing too dressy but a little more than casual. She noticed as she left that someone had rented the cottage next to hers. The light inside the kitchen window was on and the "For Rent" sign had been removed from the front lawn. The cottages were not connected to each other (which was one of the features that had convinced Steph to rent here) but their separation was less than six feet; wooden fences at either end of the narrow alleys prevented passage. A small lot of front yard accompanied each unit. Parallel parking was available at the curb.

After a drive of less than five minutes, she parked in the Big Texas Bank lot in a space farthest from the front door. This was Mitchell Bone's policy. The parking spaces closest to the bank were to be left for customers.

When she entered the bank, no one said a word to her. Not even a *Hello*. Everyone seemed extraordinarily busy. Carol, sitting behind her teller window, had a line of six people waiting for her. Barbara Wallace sat at her desk near the front door and was talking with a family of five. The children were well-mannered, sitting with their hands clasped at their waists as their mother and father looked over a papered stack of account information. Chester Kalimaris had a young couple in his office, probably working on a home mortgage. Mitchell Bone's office door was closed and Steph assumed that he was not in.

She sat at her desk to see that her computer was already running. The screen was Microsoft blue. There was no sign that it had been used but she assumed that Carol had accessed it—she was the only other employee that knew the password.

She checked her email. Nothing more than a half dozen spam messages appeared. She checked her telephone voice mail. There was only one message; it was from Billy and had been recorded just moments before she'd arrived at the bank. It said:

> *Hi Steph: Sorry I forgot all about setting up a time for our surf date tomorrow. I'm assuming the water will be fine but I'll find out more on that today. I'm not concerned. But, anyway, I'll call you later on in the day. I don't have your home number so I'll try you at work. Or you can call me at the restaurant. Talk to ya soon. Ciao.*

Not concerned? That's not what she'd thought as he'd driven her home. He hadn't said much, the discussion with Kale apparently reverberating through his mind, the concern for his business and only lifeline in jeopardy. He'd given her a short peck on the lips, the kind of kiss that a son gives to his mother, not passionate at all and done more so out of absent obligation.

His message seemed like an apology for his earlier lack of attention.

Steph pulled a manila folder of paperwork from her desk and quickly noticed that it was not as thick as she'd left it yesterday. She looked over at Carol whose attention was on her own computer monitor. The owner of Island Ice Cream was at the window. Her name was Misty Percy.

Steph thumbed through the short stack of loan applications in the manila folder; she'd placed Percy's there after canceling Bone's appointment with her before leaving yesterday—she was sure of it. The paperwork was not in there. The next four people in line after Percy were each loan applicants whose names she knew from Bone's appointment book. Each owned some business or property in Port A. None of their applications were in her folder either. When Steph looked up from her search, Carol was staring straight at her. What might have been a curt grin spread from the left corner of her mouth. Steph grimaced in response. A lack of sleep and a nagging hangover, coupled with the idea that Mitchell Bone had not informed her of any change in customer relationship management—and the simple fact that she hated Carol—was more than she could handle. Even though she'd been late this morning and even if her confrontation of Carol would make for some interesting drama in front of the bank's loyal customers, she stood, slamming the manila folder shut.

Carol, as if desiring the aggressive encounter that was about to take place, walked from around the teller counter, never removing her grinning stare from Steph. Misty Percy joined her at the end of the counter and together they walked to the vault where the door was only slightly ajar.

Steph rounded her desk, took three steps toward the two, began the confrontation with "Hey…" and then fell silent. Before Carol reached for the vault, it opened. From within emerged Chancey Lett and his bodyguard. They escorted a third person whom Steph did not know. By the way he was dressed, Steph thought that he could not have been a business owner. His clothes were ragged and dirty and looked damp as they clung to his body around the shoulders and thighs. A waft of dead fish emerged from the vault with him.

"We'll see you for the vote Saturday, Jacques," Lett said. Jacques nodded and passed Steph without a word. His smell grew worse as he bumped her shoulder, then he walked out of the bank, feeling the vacant space in front of him with both hands as if he was blind. "Miss Drake." Lett turned his attention to her. "How good to see you again. Miss Percy, here, would like to check out a security box today. Could you help us help her?"

Steph wanted to ask each of them a question. To Misty Percy she wanted to know why the town's favorite ice cream shop owner was now dealing with Carol for her banking needs. Steph had always been her customer rep. She wanted to ask Carol why she'd taken documents that were not rightly hers and why she'd been nosing around on her computer. She wanted to know who had given Chancey Lett the authority to direct business at the Big Texas Bank, Port A branch, when that was Mitchell Bone's job. She also wanted to ask him just where the hell Mr. Bone was anyway. Finally, she wanted to ask the bodyguard what had given him the right to take anything off of her desk. In the breast pocket of his pinstripe blazer was her toy Patrick the Starfish, his purple, pointy-headed face peering from the cloth as if trapped and wanting escape.

"Do you mind?" she said to the bodyguard. "What gives you the right?" She pointed at Patrick not caring that the man was at least a foot taller and almost twice her width.

Lett either did not know of his bodyguard's improprieties or mocked surprise. He pointed at the toy and opened his hand. The bodyguard hesitated, his eyes roiling with what Steph imagined to be boiling blood, and reluctantly pulled Patrick from his pocket. Lett snatched it from his hand and handed it to Steph.

"My apologies," Lett said as he handed the toy over. "I just don't know what gets into him sometimes." He glared at his bodyguard as if chastising a child for improper behavior.

Misty Percy interrupted. "I'm sorry to intrude here." She looked quizzically humored but annoyed at the same time. "I have to get to my shop. Can we get this business over with?" She snatched the security box key from Carol's hand and motioned for Steph to follow her into the vault. "I am sorry, Miss Drake. I should have known that the good service I've received at this bank is because of you. This woman's got issues." She thumbed at Carol who stood right beside her.

Misty Percy was an energetic young entrepreneur that reminded Steph of Billy. Sharp, eager, and unwilling to accept bullshit when the truth was a much easier sell. Steph smiled and led Misty into the vault. Together they walked to the wall where, yesterday, she had escorted Billy. Misty's box was right above Billy's. Behind them, Lett, his bodyguard and Carol stepped into the vault. Carol pulled the door closed.

"What are you doing?" Steph said. "Our policy."

Misty removed her key but had not yet opened her box. "Do you mind?"

And then the crate behind Lett and the bodyguard started to glow. A nearly inaudible hum, an undulating energy, seemed to come from inside. It was just as she'd remembered from the day before. The crimson glow from under the vault door. The hum.

"We'd like to show you something," Lett said. "It is quite beautiful and unique. The only one of its kind."

Misty stepped closer to Lett, halving the short distance between them. "Would you mind doing this at some other time?" she said, mounting frustration apparent in the way she held her clasped arms together. She looked down at the white plastic watch on her left wrist. "You make me late and I'm taking my business elsewhere."

Lett smiled, making his tanned face come to life. His dark eyebrows and hairline scrunched a forehead that had only begun to wrinkle with age. "This will only take a second. You see, I'm building this casino and I wanted to get your opinion on a piece of art that will be displayed inside. Being the business intellectual that you are, I think that your thoughts will be most valuable."

"Do you see that?" Steph said, pointing at the crate.

Misty followed her finger. "What? What is it?" she said.

"It's glowing—the crate."

Lett intervened. "Don't be ridiculous," he said. "Nothing in there glows." He looked at his bodyguard and Carol then back at Steph who had taken the two steps necessary to stand shoulder to shoulder with Misty. "Perhaps you're still a bit...tired—from last night. You were up mighty late."

"And just how the hell would you know that?"

"A matter of logical deduction. I saw you at the luau. You called in late for work...or should I say your friend called you in late. Billy Jo Presser, isn't it?"

"And that's none of your damned business."

"Calm down, Stephanie," Lett said, holding his hands out as if to ward off an attack. "We wouldn't want to cause a commotion in front of our fine customer here. Mitchell doesn't know anything about your tardiness. We'll keep it just amongst ourselves."

"Former customer," Misty blurted out. "Former customer." She stepped to where Carol stood in front of the vault door. "The door, please."

Lett nodded and Carol stepped aside.

Misty looked over her shoulder at Lett and flipped the security box key a bit too aggressively for him to catch. It clanged when it hit the steel vault floor. "And don't count your chickens, gambling man. No one on this island has given you permission to build anything yet. Whatever is in that crate you can cram it up your ass." She exited the vault and Carol pulled the door closed.

"Now where were we?" Lett said and rubbed his hands together. "Ah, yes. The Cub…" He stopped mid-sentence. "The crate," he continued.

"I don't care what's in there," Steph said, standing her ground. "You're not building any damned casino on my island if there's anything I can do about it."

"But you can't do anything about it." Lett motioned with a hand toward the bodyguard who went around the back of the crate and pushed it toward Steph. Lett quickly stepped aside as if the wooden container carried some contagion.

The crate grew a brighter crimson revealing a glowing star etched into its surface near its top edge. The hum grew louder. Steph wondered if it was just her imagination since Misty had not apparently seen or heard any of it.

"I'll scream," Steph said.

But she didn't. Her wide eyes and her confused mind became transfixed on the wooden cube that glowed and slid closer to her as she stood motionless. Her jaw hung open and a tiny drop of saliva hit the vault floor at her feet.

"Our Father who art in Hell," Lett said.

"Hallowed be his name," Carol added.

Without knowing it, Steph added, "Thy kingdom come. Thy will be done. On earth as…"

And suddenly, she saw a bright light.

◻ …

After dropping Steph off at the bank, Billy headed for the beach road to check the surf before hooking up with Mark whom he'd arranged to meet in thirty minutes. He turned onto the beach road three miles south of the marine institute and parked. Few vacationers had yet to wander this far from the pier. A mother and her daughter walked the wet sand looking for sand dollars and shells. A fisherman stood knee deep in shallow waves casting into the surf. A small group of teens toed a large mound of sargassum weed that had yet to be removed by the town's public works.

"Whoa. Neat. Hey, finder's keepers, losers weepers," one of the male teens in the group suddenly exclaimed. He'd found something hidden beneath the sargassum. His four friends circled around as the teen lifted the nose of a surfboard from the wet sand and rotated it sideways to inspect the board's broken fin; it was nearly twice as long as the boy was tall. "Aww, man," the teen said. "The tail's broken." The only female in the group added, "And the nose is chipped, too. Lotta work ahead to get that ride back in shape." The boy nodded dejectedly, dropped the surfboard and the group moved on to inspect the next mass of weeds. In Port Aransas history, there had been many reports of small treasures found washed ashore within the sargassum. Billy suspected the teens were looking for their own small claim. The surfboard, apparently, wasn't worth their hassle.

He walked over to the broken surfboard; it reminded him of last night: a surfer on an eight foot red wave silhouetted against a nearly full moon. It reminded him of the surf's smell: almost toxic. He remembered having felt very weary, his vision blurring, much in the same way he'd felt when the hallucinations of gunshots and speeding cars had grabbed hold of him outside the restaurant and then again as he'd headed out of town to pick up the *Knights in White Satin*. He remembered the coin with the Wayeb symbol that the "corpses" had found buried in the sand. He remembered—coincidence.

Was this the board the night surfer had ridden? Was it just coincidence that, along the many miles of Mustang Island shoreline, he'd chosen to stop right here? Of course there was no way he could determine if *this* was *that* board. Hell, he couldn't even say for sure that what he'd seen had been real.

Upon closer inspection, he could not determine the manufacturer of the board. He was damn good at matching board designs with the many he'd stored in memory but this one was not in his mental catalog. The board was wooden and much too heavy for a man under two hundred pounds to handle.

He kicked at the sargassum mound expecting to find a mass of sea life now dead from the toxic red water he'd waded through the night before. All he found was a dead sea trout with one eye and two dead starfish. He stepped into the surf, cupped a handful of white, frothy water and sniffed it. Sea salt. Nothing extraordinary.

He walked several hundred yards up the coastline in the opposite direction that the teens had traveled, looking for dead fish, discolored sargassum, or red water—anything that could verify his experience after the luau. A seagull hopped on one leg across the wet sand, its single webbed foot stamping impressions, a tangle of flesh stuck to its beak. It moved toward him like a feathered Pogo Stick with eyes.

"Seen any red tides?" he asked the bird. "Anything fishy at all?" He snickered at his own weak pun. The bird hopped twice. "A simple yes or no would be fine." The bird blinked, craned its head from side-to-side, hopped once more, then opened its beak and let out a wail so loud that Billy stepped backward to ward off a possible attack.

But the bird didn't attack. Once the screech subsided, the bird toppled over on its one good leg. Its eyes and beak remained open, frozen in a last moment's gasp for life, then it fluttered once before dying.

Billy cautiously approached, toed the dead bird then knelt beside it. Surf rolled in and filled the gull's open mouth.

And then it occurred to him. He'd seen very few seagulls. He'd not really noticed since seagulls were such a part of the ocean beach tapestry as to be interwoven to the point of irrelevance. He looked up, across the beach, in both directions, and out over the surf. One or two birds flew here and there. There were no flocks.

Billy decided to take the bird with him to the marine institute but did not want to touch it. He returned to where he'd parked, grabbed the broken surfboard and a handful of sargassum, placed them in the back of the VW and drove to where the dead bird now bobbed in shallow surf. Quickly, before the ocean could steal his evidence, he grabbed a roll of paper towels, ripped off two sheets to protect his hand, ran from his VW and snatched the bird by its dead leg. When he returned to the VW, he rolled paper towels around the carcass and dropped it next to the pile of sargassum, then drove off toward the marine institute, the sun shining bright white over a birdless blue sky.

⌐ ...

Steph had recited the Lord's Prayer on many occasions as a kid. Her parents were not strict Catholics but the Lord's Prayer had been one of the uncompromising ceremonies they had always held true to. Years of Mass had engrained the Words into her soul.

She remembered the part about the valley of the shadow of death and the part about not being led into temptation, but the word "Hell" was not in there. Neither was there any allusion to the Dark Lord or the Devil.

Steph chanted, "For thine is the kingdom, and the power, and the glory, for ever and ever. Amen."

And into the light emerged Mitchell Bone.

"What's going one here?" he said, standing in the vault's doorway. "We just lost a good customer because of you knuckleheads."

The crate sat inches from Steph's hand. Her fingers tingled. She quickly stepped backward.

"Carol," Bone continued, agitated, his voice controlled so that the encounter would not create a scene. "You've got a line of busy customers waiting for you. I suggest you take care of them."

Carol looked at Lett as if needing permission, then strolled past Bone in her slow, methodical, unhurried way.

The bodyguard repositioned the crate to where it had been when Steph entered the vault.

Lett said, "Timetable has been moved up. There won't be enough unless we work through the day."

"Enough what?" Steph said. She noticed that the crate no longer glowed nor hummed. "What's in there anyway?" She pointed at the crate.

"The future Stephanie," Lett replied. "The future."

"You buying influence, Mr. Bone?" Steph asked. "You letting *him* buy the vote?"

"Relax, Stephanie," Lett said. "It's nothing like that. Tell her, Mitchell."

Bone hesitated. He looked out into the bank lobby where several people were now looking at the vault. "We'll talk about this later," he said to Steph. "Now…please...back to work. We've got a lot of new accounts today. The promotion has gone over better than we'd anticipated."

"Promotion?" Steph questioned. "I didn't hear of…"

Lett intervened. "If you'd have been to work on time then perhaps you would have."

Steph glared at Lett. Bone glared at Steph and motioned for her to leave. "Later, Miss Drake."

When Steph emerged from the vault three people were waiting in the three chairs around her desk. She replaced her angered, confused frown with a friendly, customer-service-smile. "How may I help you?" she said.

Bone, Lett and the bodyguard entered Bone's office and closed the door.

"We'd like to take advantage of the promotion," one of the customers said. "We'd like to rent a security box."

⬜ ...

The University of Texas Marine Science Institute sat on more than seventy acres of prime island beach-front real estate just below the south jetty of the Aransas Pass Shipping Channel which linked Corpus Christi Bay to the Gulf of Mexico. It was uniquely positioned among the large range of marine environments nearby—from the Gulf to the internal bays and inlets—making it a preeminent research institute for coastal zone ecosystems. Ironically, it was founded in the 1940s by a scientist who had come to the island to investigate an enormous fish kill.

Though the institute had summer programs for its marine biology degree, enrollment was down this year. Billy had no problem finding a parking spot near the main building. He grabbed the paper-toweled bird and mound of sargassum and entered the tan brick building under a marquee made of metal and painted silver. It read: UTMSI. Inside, a security guard sat behind a semi-circular desk, reading the current edition of the *South Jetty* newspaper. When he saw Billy, he folded the paper and stood.

"Mr. Presser," he said.

"Hello, Dave," Billy replied. Dave had been the institute's chief security guard for nearly twenty years.

"What'cha got there?" He pointed at Billy's hands.

"Presents for Mark."

"You guys gonna find out what's killing all the fish?" Dave was an old islander, close to sixty, and had probably started as many rumors as he'd spread in his lifetime.

The seagull had stiffened. Its open beak poked at the palm of his hand. "What have you heard?"

"DuPont, a'course. Ain't they the ones what get the crap all the time anyway? Hell, since I been here there must'a been two dozen of them make-believe chemical spills. Not a one of'em ever panned out."

"Well, if it's any consolation, we really don't know what's going on." Billy had the notion to ask Dave if he'd seen any suspicious bird behaviors then quickly decided not to chance the start of any more rumors.

"Good luck with this one," Dave said. "Sure is a mystery, ain't it? And I love a good mystery. Like this fella Chancey Lett." He pointed at the front page of the newspaper. "What a mystery man he is, eh?"

Billy did not have the time nor the desire to discuss Chancey Lett and his brute force. "Mark?" He questioned. "You know where he is?"

"Out getting measurements from the instrument room on the pier. 'Least that's what he said he'd be doing around the time you arrived." Dave sat back down and flipped open the newspaper. "You know your way, Mr. Presser. Ya'll have fun figuring out the mystery. If I was ten years younger I'd be beggin' to tag along."

Billy smiled, acknowledging the old man's desire, knowing Dave had probably never touched a research instrument in his entire life.

The UTMSI main building's central purpose was for tourism and outreach education. The corridor walls were lined with examples of Gulf sea life and each was accompanied by easily read descriptive text. Painted onto a concrete beam that supported the corridor ceiling were the words "UTMSI is your Window on the Sea." Billy turned right at the end of the corridor, went through a set of double doors that connected the main building to the central lab complex and headed for the entrance to the research pier. Mark came through the door just as Billy arrived.

"You about ready?" Mark said. He wasn't much for ritualistic greetings. "Sargassum?" he added, pointing at the sea weeds Billy held in his hand. "I did a run on that this morning."

"I figured you might have." Billy shrugged his shoulders. "But I bet you didn't find one of these." He dropped the sea weeds into a nearby trash bin and unrolled the seagull.

"Dead bird," Mark said and lightly chuckled. "I wasn't looking for any but thanks anyway."

"Something's messed up with this bird." Billy pointed at it.

"Yeah. He got a foot bitten off."

"No," Billy said, annoyed. "This sucker did something I've never seen a bird do. It let out one hell of a squaller then collapsed, right there in front of me, as if it had a heart attack or something."

"Maybe it did. Birds have heart attacks."

Billy never considered heart attacks as being deadly to any species other than human. "Hmm…well maybe," he said. "But maybe not. You wouldn't mind running a test or two on it would you—maybe after we get back from our ride? I've got a feeling about this."

"A feeling? Now that's scientific." Mark grabbed the bird by its one leg and carried it without the paper towels to a lab room on the left where he dropped it in a stainless steel sink. "But I certainly can't deny my favorite roboticist his gut feeling." He smiled, which was a rare expression coming from Mark. "Come on. Lacey's got the bird ready to go."

"Bird?" Billy thought about the dead seagull.

"Helicopter." Mark's smile faded, returning to an expressionless norm that resembled a man who was always thinking about solving some problem: a concentrated absence that pushed eyebrows together and delayed acknowledgement of others around him.

The two men walked together to the main lobby, Mark wearing his usual blue jeans and polo shirt with the institute's logo stitched into the chest, Billy wearing the same surfer's wardrobe that he'd had on the night before. They waved at Dave simultaneously, and exited. As they passed Billy's VW and turned the corner around the main building, Mark said, "You know you should really think about getting yourself a new ride. That thing looks like it came out of the 1950s."

"More like 1963," Billy said. "It's cheap on gas, easy on maintenance and a classic. Besides, you know me. A non-conformist wouldn't be seen dead driving around in a new Jeep Wrangler."

The quip on his own vehicle almost put the smile back on Mark's lips but his concentration on the helicopter a hundred yards ahead kept his mind narrowed and task-oriented. The rotors on the Long Ranger sprang to life as the men approached. A woman emerged from the copter. She stood tall and lean and her skin glowed a deep tan that had been coated in lotion that made it look slippery. Her blonde hair had a long, think braid stitched around each temple. She reminded Billy of Bo Derek, but much taller with a slight touch of Hispanic heritage molding her face.

Mark nodded. "Lacey. This is Billy Jo Presser," he said, his voice rising as the blades chopped the air above them.

Billy and Lacey shook hands. "I thought Mark knew how to fly one of these things," he yelled at Lacey.

Lacey laughed. "Are you kidding? There'd be no safe place on the island."

"Good to know you, Lacey." Her hand slid from his grasp and she ducked around the front of the copter to the pilot's seat. Mark emerged from the rear of the copter and offered the open door to Billy.

"Everything looks in order," he yelled. "Let's head out to sea."

Billy climbed in and Mark took the passenger seat in front of him. As the copter lifted off, Billy was reminded of how few birds he'd seen earlier.

Their scarcity became more pronounced as the copter gained altitude. They were in the air fewer than five minutes when Mark observed what Billy already knew. "Where in the hell are all of the birds?" he said. "No gulls, no pelicans, no anything."

"There's a couple over there," Lacey said, pointing out over the nose of the copter to a point near the pier directly below them.

Mark craned forward for a look. "What I meant to say is that there are abnormally small populations of birds flying about today." Mark frowned at Lacey who was not looking at him.

Billy also leaned forward, his knee clanging into the collection kit that held a dozen plastic jars, each resting in its own square pocket. The kit reminded Billy of the thing strapped around the neck of vendors who walked through ballparks selling cans of beer. "I'm glad it isn't just me," Billy said to Mark.

Mark turned in his seat. Sunlight flashed across his smooth cheeks, enhancing his youthful complexion. "You didn't say anything because you wanted to see if I would come to the same conclusion."

"I admit it," Billy agreed. "Looking for a little corroboration of an observation, that's all." Conversation with Mark always stimulated upper-level thinking. "And now that you've substantiated my observation, perhaps you will look at my one-legged avian offering with more curiosity."

Mark stared at Billy as if looking straight through him. Billy knew that the cogs of his left-brain dominant colleague had kicked into high gear. "Yeah," he said, absently, almost hypnotically. "Very strange indeed."

Lacey interrupted. "First bobber dead ahead," she said.

An ocean science buoy bobbed in calm water two hundred feet below the hovering copter. The number 12 was emblazoned in black on the side of its pyramidal structure.

❒ …

The man with the receding hairline dropped a copy of the *South Jetty* onto Steph's desk. It had been folded to the second page. Filling the bottom half of the page was an ad for the promotion that Steph, until now, had not heard of. In bold title lettering it read:

OWN YOUR PIECE OF THE FUTURE
ENTER FOR THE CHANCE TO WIN 10 ACRES
ON MUSTANG ISLAND

Under the title, Steph read the details of the contest. Apparently, Lett was using his huge cache of cash to sponsor a contest that tied the rental of a Port A Big Texas Bank security box to a chance at winning ten acres of land yet to be developed south of town. The value of the land was estimated to be worth more than a million dollars, according to the ad. Basically, what a person needed to do to "enter" was to rent a security box from the bank and either store collateral worth $5,000 in it or add $5,000 to an existing or new account. Inside each rented security box was an "official entry" to an "official drawing" that would be held at the end of June. The contest was a win-win situation. Pay a small monthly charge for the security box, keep your valuables safe, increase a cash investment of $5,000 with a competitive interest rate and receive a chance to win a million dollars worth of real estate that was sure to be of greater value once the Mayan was operational. Stephanie assumed that the large investment requirement of $5,000 was meant to attract only those who had the monetary means necessary to do so. The bank wanted to increase its influence on the island but it did not want lower income investors involved. Only upper class individuals were eligible.

"Miss Drake," the balding man said. "We pooled our resources and have $5,000 to open a savings account...and to, of course, rent a new security box. There are no rules in the contest against pooling money is there?"

Steph did not know. She hadn't even heard that a contest existed. If her assumption was correct, if the contest was meant to lure only the wealthiest, then she also assumed that pooling cash was prohibitive to entering the contest. To allow pooling would mean a hundred low income individuals could enter with fifty dollars each. Perhaps pooling was allowed but within limits. In any case, she did not have an answer for the balding man or either of his younger, eager male amigos.

Steph set the newspaper on her desk and started to rise. "I'll verify that for you, Mr....?"

"Rodriguez," the man said. "Manny Rodriguez."

And then Steph fell back into her chair. Everyone in the bank except Carol turned toward Mitchell Bone's voice that thundered from his office as the door opened.

"That was not a part of the deal!" he yelled. "I'm flying her in tomorrow. She owns half the interest in this venture. We'll see what she says."

Bone emerged from his office, disregarded the stares and tromped toward Steph's desk. The three investors flinched as Bone angrily told Steph that she would be going to the airport tomorrow instead of Friday as had been previously arranged. He turned away without waiting for a response then left the bank, fists clenched, his stride, aggressive.

Steph had wanted to say: *But I'm going surfing tomorrow. Dammit, Mr. Bone. I was going to call in sick and go surfing. What the hell are you doing to me?* Instead, she maintained her customer service smile even as Lett and his bodyguard strolled from Bone's office, seemingly indifferent toward Bone's response or the multitude of eyes that were on them.

"Mitchell works much too hard," Lett said to Steph directly and to her three customers indirectly. "I think he needs some time off." He smiled that perfect white-toothed smile that Steph was beginning to hate. "I'll see *you* later." He pointed at her then he and his bodyguard left the bank.

"That was fun," Manny Rodriguez said, sarcastically. "Perhaps our investment at this bank is not such a smart idea."

"We all have our bad days," Steph said, absently tapping the ad in the *South Jetty* on her desk. "If you are still interested in entering the contest, I'll verify the rules on pooling." Steph didn't believe that Mr. Rodriquez was serious about taking his business elsewhere. The chance at a million dollars was too tempting. He was playing her like any smart perspective customer would. Besides, his two male co-investors had not said a word the entire time and had actually frowned when Mr. Rodriquez had threatened to leave.

"Yes," Mr. Rodriguez said. "I suppose you're right." He dropped $5,000 in cash on the newspaper that Steph's fingers absently tapped. "Put it all on number 123."

The stack of cash was tall, mostly made up of twenty dollar bills. "Number 123?" she asked.

"We'd like to rent out security box 123." He peeled an extra twenty dollar bill from his shirt pocket and shoved it toward Steph, then turned to each of the men sitting beside him. "Right?" Each nodded without a word. Steph was beginning to wonder if either of them could even speak... or at least speak English. Mr. Rodriquez had never intended to leave. Mr. Rodriguez and his amigos were gamblers. They wanted to place their bet on the number 123 even if it meant moving someone else's items to another box. And if there were rules against pooling, they did not want those rules to get in the way of their shot at a million dollars worth of real estate. Bribery was totally appropriate.

"You hold onto this for just a minute." Steph handed all the money back to Mr. Rodriguez. "Let me verify the status of the contest and of security box number 123." Mr. Rodriguez maintained his smile but Steph knew that he was not happy. She also knew that he would sit tight, his gambler's blood roiling, until she had an answer for him.

She asked Barbara Wallace who was still busy with the same family who'd she'd been helping since Steph entered the bank. Barbara didn't have an answer. Steph asked Deli Clayton and one of the newer tellers, Francis Gerts. She had not dealt with any money pooling issues related to the contest and told her to ask Carol. Instead, Steph went to Chester Kalimaris' door and knocked. Chester asked her to come in. A man and a woman sat in padded chairs near his desk. Steph asked to be excused then asked Chester if he knew any of the details about the contest. He politely said that he didn't and referred her to Carol.

Mr. Rodriguez watched in anticipation as Steph emerged from Chester's office. The wad of money rested in his lap. Beyond him, at the teller window in the far corner nearest the vault, Carol waited on a line of five people. Standing frozen for a complete second, Steph measured the situation. So what if there was a rule against pooling? No one had told her. Her job was to satisfy the bank's customers. She could not get in trouble for that. Regardless, anything was better than having to deal with Carol, to ask any favors from that woman—even if it meant being reprimanded by Bone.

She returned to her desk and asked that Mr. Rodriquez be patient with her as she looked on her computer for a list of open security box numbers. She found that nearly half of all the boxes had been rented when, just yesterday, the number had been less than a third. The bad news was that Misty Percy had rented out box number 123. The good news was that Misty had stormed out of the bank a half an hour earlier, relinquishing her box number and a chance at one million dollars in real estate to Mr. Rodriquez and friends.

"You're in luck," she told the triumvirate. "No rules against you and number 123 is open for business."

She pulled out the necessary paperwork as Mr. Rodriquez placed the $5,000 stack and the twenty in front of SpongeBob.

❐ …

"Take her down," Mark said to Lacey, then turned to Billy. "It'll take about three hours to sample each of the buoys down the coast and do a point-source check inside the shipping lane."

"I've got three hours," Billy replied. "We want to be thorough—a no-questions-asked complete survey."

Mark nodded approval as the copter's floats settled in calm sea a dozen yards from the buoy. To Lacey he said, "We'll be here for a few minutes, Lace. You can go ahead and cut the engine." She did so and the copter blades' circular motion slowed. "Billy," Mark added. "If you'll hand me the jar labeled 12, I'll go ahead and collect the sample."

Billy looked through the carrier of jars. They were neatly arranged in numerical order from top down and left to right. He snatched the one in the lower corner and joined Mark who has already out of the copter and standing on the float. A light breeze made the direct sunlight tolerable.

"Nothing visually odd," Mark said, kneeling and pointing at the water. "No alga blooms, no chemical streaming. Smells just like the Gulf always smells." He took the jar from Billy, filled it with sea water, spun the jar lid tight, and handed it back to Billy who replaced it inside the copter. "I'm going to go ahead and check the buoy data while we're here."

"Can't you do that back at the institute? These things do have RF don't they?" Billy wondered how Mark was going to get over to the buoy. His jeans and polo shirt would make for an uncomfortable swim.

Mark stood. "Yeah," he said. "But there's nothing like getting your hands dirty." He clapped his hands together as if brushing off invisible sand. "Besides, I haven't done an inspection on this buoy in over a month. As the closest one to the institute I always think I'll get to it later. But I never do." He grinned mischievously and added, "Feel like going for a swim?" Before Billy could answer Mark turned to his pilot and asked her to throw him the tow line.

Lacey shifted in her seat to reach behind her, showing both men how beautifully proportioned she was from the rear. She caught them both staring at her as she emerged with a coil of fluorescent orange rope.

"Not bad, huh?" she said to both of them with a smile. "The water. It looks just fine."

"Fine indeed," Mark said to her and caught the rope when Lacey tossed it to him. He walked to the end of the float where Billy stood. Both men knelt.

"I know what you're thinking," Mark whispered to Billy as he looped one end of the rope through a hook in the float. "We're all business. I assure you."

Billy stripped off his shirt and dropped it on the buoy. "All work and no play?" he whispered back. "You can do better than that."

Mark gently shoved Billy who fell backward into the water. "Hey. You're right," he said. "A little play never hurt anybody." Lacey sat inside the copter with her long legs dangling outside the passenger door. She laughed.

Billy's insinuation had embarrassed Mark and Mark had retaliated. These were small victories for two men who lived their friendship through a silent competition that continually measured wits, intelligence and, occasionally, humor. He swam the short distance to the buoy then climbed onto it. The buoy nearly capsized, but Billy's knack for balance, a skill he'd honed as a surfer, righted the buoy before it toppled. Mark tossed him the rope and Billy tied it off. "All set," he shouted. Mark pulled the rope through the hook in the copter float then tied it once the buoy was close enough to step onto.

The buoy was a three-meter discus that housed an onboard computer. Four yellow, steel tubes provided pyramidal framing and rose from a circular platform a foot over Billy. Three long antennae rose several feet farther above the top of the steel frame. Within the framing, the PC was housed inside a protective, water resistant box. Mark stepped onto the buoy and pulled a key from his pocket which he used to open the PC cabinet. A pelican landed on top of the buoy and looked at the men as if expecting to be fed.

"Strange," Mark said as he punched a series of squares on the PC's touch screen. At first, Billy thought Mark was referring again to the scant bird population, but realized that Mark had not even noticed the pelican.

"What is it?" Billy said, craning his head forward to see what Mark was reading.

"Wave data here. There must be something wrong. It's impossible."

Billy looked at the graph on the computer screen. "That big spike in the curve. Does that mean what I think it means?"

"Eight feet," Mark said, confused. "We had an eight foot wave here last night."

Billy's heart pounded; it felt as if it would burst.

"But that's impossible," Mark reiterated then noticed that Billy's hand shook. He looked up to see that Billy stared, trancelike, at the coastline which was at the horizon a mile away. "What? What is it?"

"I saw this guy last night," he said without looking at Mark. "I thought maybe I'd had too much to drink or that toxic water was making me see things."

"Toxic water?" Mark followed Billy's stare toward the shore. Only a few birds were visible near the Caldwell pier. Dozens, if not hundreds, usually inundated the pier in search of kindly vacationers that tossed bread and chips and other assorted food scraps.

"Smelled funny, last night, and it was red," Billy said, almost hypnotically.

"When were you going to tell me this?"

Billy looked at Mark with distant eyes. "I thought I was hallucinating. I mean…" He hesitated. "I mean it was like the other visions I had. Unreal."

Mark patiently listened as Billy recounted his strange slips from reality the previous day, and his suspicions about the contents of the crate in the Big Texas Bank vault. When he finished, Mark said, "You got any evidence?"

"I'm working on that," Billy replied but did not reveal how he'd infiltrated the bank with his robot. He felt that Mark was trustworthy enough with the information he'd offered, but breaking and entering was an act best kept secret. At least for now.

"And what about the surfer you say you saw?" Mark asked. "You know who it was?"

"Not a clue. And I didn't stick around to find out. I had to get Steph home. Besides, like a said, I didn't think it was real."

Mark closed the computer box and locked it then stepped back onto the copter's float. Lacey still sat with her legs dangling out of the copter's passenger side door. He was unsure if she'd heard any of their conversation. "Let's get going," he told her then turned back to Billy. "Would you mind if I take a sample of your blood when we get back in? If there's some drug or toxin in your system perhaps I can detect it."

Billy stepped onto the float and Mark untied the buoy as the copter blades spun above them and the pelican took flight, nearly decapitating itself. "Yeah. No problem. Even though you aren't a medical doctor." He managed a smile.

As the men climbed into the copter and Lacey flew it into the sky, the buoy floated back to its mooring point where, nine hours earlier, Chancey Lett's bodyguard had ridden an impossible wave.

❑ …

Janine had sworn that, after Michael, she'd never love another man. She'd certainly never loved Albert. Their marriage had been a lie from the start.

So she found it a little disorienting that she'd dreamt of Joel Canton.

Joel was with her back in Kansas. He'd come to her home (which was now demolished and the land it stood on sold) and he'd strolled through the front door with a stringer of fresh fish dangling from one hand and his fishing pole in the other. This, of course, was not logical since nowhere within a fifty mile radius was there a place to fish in Pickett's Crossing, Kansas. But dreams were never logical.

He'd called her sweetheart. It was if they were married. It was as if Michael had returned to her in the body of Joel. He'd even kissed her in the dream. Her sleeping heart had recaptured that fleeting feeling of what once was love.

And that's when Albert had appeared from her storm cellar room, a dagger with a long, thin blade clasped in one hand. He'd *risen* from the cellar as if floating to the surface from Hell.

The dream had been so vivid that she smelled the fish in Joel's hand and the Jim Beam on Albert's breath. And then Albert had attacked.

That's when she had awakened in Marcy's guest room. It was a quarter past eleven.

She'd not slept for ten hours since the first night she'd stayed with Beth Blandford back in Kansas City. In fact, it was rare that she slept much at all anymore. Memories of Lenny and the thing that had looked like her son haunted recesses of subconsciousness so deeply that, not only did she have sleeping nightmares, she often found herself fully awake and catatonic, visions of the Lenny-thing, the professor and Albert flashing like a slideshow in front of her open eyes.

"Are you awake, hon?" Marcy's voice asked from behind the guest room door; it was open just a couple of inches.

"Yes. Yes, I am awake. Come in."

"You gave me a horrible fright last night." Marcy sat at the foot of the bed as Janine rose to a sitting position. "Do you often scream in your sleep?"

Janine flushed with embarrassment. "I am sorry. I used to do it a lot more."

Marcy patted one of Janine's feet. She started to say one thing then apparently changed her mind. "There's a clean towel in the bathroom if you want to freshen up before your date."

Date?

It took her a second to remember. She'd agreed to have lunch at the Surf Side with Joel.

"What time is it?" Janine asked before noticing the clock on the wall to the right of the bedroom door. The clock's face was black and had Tarot card prints positioned where the numbers should have been.

"You have about forty-five minutes," Marcy said. "I didn't want to wake you. I figured you must have had a terrible nightmare and did not sleep well." Marcy stood and handed Janine a robe made of black velvet that was trimmed in red lace. "Also," Marcy added. "Your landlord said everything is a go for you to move in tonight. Mr. Agey can be a hell of a nice guy when he puts his mind to it."

Janine slipped on the robe. It felt soft and slick on the bare skin between her bra and panties. "Thank you, again," she said. "Really… you've gone way beyond Good Samaritan. I'm a total stranger. You don't know me from a psycho killer. I cry without reason and scream in my sleep. Marcy, the fortune teller, you're something else."

Marcy smiled and placed an open hand on each of Janine's cheeks. "And the King said, 'For I was hungry and you gave me something to eat, I was thirsty and you gave me something to drink, I was a stranger and you invited me in.'" She kissed Janine's forehead.

Marcy's knowledge of Bible verse comforted her. "You are with the righteous, Marcy. Your inheritance will be grand."

"If you're talking about life after death, I can wait a while for any kind of inheritance." Though Marcy was at least a dozen years younger, she seemed quite motherly at this moment. It was contradictory to Janine for a fortune teller that looked like Cher to quote scripture. But Marcy's care went far beyond mere appearance. Humility was her greatest strength—as was her gift for prognostication. Marcy winked at her. "Forty minutes," she said.

When Janine finished her shower, she found that her guest room bed had already been made and her two sacks of life lay on top of the black and red bed sheets. All of her possessions were still in the bags. Marcy had not dumped them out nor had she, apparently, gone through them.

Janine chose her most valued blouse from inside one sack. She'd made it from scratch the day before she and Michael had gone on their Myrtle Beach honeymoon. It was made of soft white cotton and had subtle patterns of prairie grass and wheat stitched into it. She'd carried only two pairs of shorts with her in her sacks of life; one nearly matched the tanned stitching of the wheat pattern in her blouse. She slipped it on.

She descended the steps to the first floor that served as Marcy's shop. An aroma of coffee filled her nostrils.

"In here," Marcy said from a room down the hallway that paralleled the staircase.

Janine entered a small kitchen. This room, unlike most of the others in the house, was decorated in cool pastels. The sunlight from a single window over the sink provided great warmth, both visually and across her skin. Marcy handed her a cup.

"Coffee's on," she said. "I didn't know what you wanted in it but there's cream and sugar and regular milk if you prefer that. I don't have any sweetener. Never really trusted those chemical substitutes."

"Black will be just fine," Janine said and filled her cup from the pot on the kitchen counter. She sat next to Marcy in one of the four chairs around the kitchen table.

"You look wonderful," Marcy said. "Here. I've got the perfect island accessory for you." Marcy handed Janine a ponytail scrunchie the color of sand and water. "Made it myself."

Janine was thrilled. She thought it was the perfect accessory, not so much because it matched her own self-made top or the color of her gray hair but that it had been made by hand.

Marcy noticed how proudly Janine held the gift. "It's nothing really. Nothing like what you can do. Your top is beautiful. This came from a kit my daughter got for Christmas last year."

"How did you know I made this blouse?" Janine flexed the scrunchie between the fingers of both hands.

"Remember the sign outside? Marcy sees all."

"Come on…no…really."

Marcy grinned. "My mother was a seamstress. Retailers can't hold a candle to the precise subtleties of a hand-made piece of clothing."

Janine twisted the scrunchie and pulled a tail of hair through it. Her face cooled from the absence of hair at her temples.

"Looks perfect," Marcy said. "Scrunchies are a Godsend for us ladies with long hair who have to tolerate the Texas sun."

Janine sipped coffee while Marcy looked at her, adoringly, for several minutes as if she was trying to sketch every nuance of Janine's face into memory. Janine broke the silence.

"So tell me about, Joel."

Marcy's elbows were on the table and she placed her chin in her hands. "I thought you'd never ask."

Marcy told her what she knew about Joel, about his charter boat company and his wife that had both left him many years ago. She told her about the summer of the Great White and how history had placed Joel within its context. She did not know Joel's truth so her recount was much in the way most Port A islanders understood Joel today: a man who'd lost everything when he'd lost his wife, a man whom the island owed a great debt for the capture of a shark that could have easily killed lives and the livelihood of one of Texas' great vacation destinations.

"You'd better be getting over there," she said, ending her story. "It's just a couple of blocks away. I've got an appointment at noon or I'd walk you over."

"No, that's fine. Just tell me where to go."

Janine walked from Marcy's shop and stood in the exact same place where she'd exited the cab the day before. Marcy stood at the front door like a mother seeing her child off to school and waved. When Janine turned, she nearly ran straight into Mitchell Bone. "Excuse me," he said to her then walked up the steps to greet Marcy with a handshake. He stepped inside and Marcy closed the door.

◘ ...

They'd flown all the way down to South Padre Island, landing near each of the science buoys along the way. The round trip had taken more than two hours and a full set of twelve jars now held the contents of sea water from each of the locations.

The flight had held no surprises: no red seas, no alga blooms, no dead fish—nothing that sparked curiosity in Mark remotely close to the data he'd found at Buoy 12. Billy, however, had noted that the farther south they'd traveled from the Port A coastline, the more "normal" *his* observations became. The bird populations had returned. The public beaches were crowded with summer vacationers. There were sailboaters and jetskiiers, and parasailers, and surfers.

But beyond his visual observations, Billy had also *felt* different. He couldn't really explain it, but being away from Port A filled him with the sense of freedom, as if somehow, Port A had become a cage filled with unknown fears and the helicopter had freed the three of them from an invisible entrapment. Now, as the copter again approached Buoy 12, the fear-filled loneliness of a caged animal returned.

"One more stop and we'll head in," Mark shouted to Lacey. "Let's head out another mile or two along the shipping lane."

Lacey guided the copter out to sea, flying over a huge tanker headed in toward the jetty.

"It's the Energia," Mark said, turning half around in the passenger seat so Billy could hear him. "Chemical tanker out of Campeche, Mexico, headed for the DuPont plant. This thing can probably hold ten million gallons of trichloroethylene, enough of DuPont's sully solvent to mess up life along the coast for many miles and for many years."

A thousand yards past the tanker, Mark told Lacey to set down onto what Mark described as a water trail. "The tanker's empty so they've probably released their bilge already. There could be a few hundred thousand foreign aquatic tag-alongs. We've got a good opportunity to log the introduction of foreign populations into our marine ecosystem."

Lacey landed softly as she'd done twelve times already, and Mark asked Billy to hand him a metal case that sat next to the orange fluorescent tow line. Mark pulled from the case a glass jar that, Billy assumed, would more safely hold what might be found here.

"Grab the rope and join me outside," Mark said to Billy as he slipped on a pair of gloves which he'd not used while collecting the samples at the buoys. Both men stepped out onto the float. Mark unsealed the glass jar, tied the rope through the eyelets at the top of the jar, then slowly lowered the jar into the water.

Looking over his shoulder, Billy observed the defined edges of what Mark had called the "water trail." The stream was a good hundred yards wide from where the copter sat and narrowed to a point behind the Energia which had become much smaller at this distance. Multicolored bands of some surface slick twinkled on the top of the water: a prism of pollution.

"What the…!"

Billy turned his attention to Mark who was reeling in the seawater sample. As the jar emerged from the surface, a twenty-five-inch-long sea trout bobbed up from the sea with it. A huge air bubble followed. Then another fish, this time a tuna. More bubbles. More fish. By the time Mark had the glass jar in his gloved hands, the sea was bubbling up dozens of fish in a five foot circle. To Billy, it appeared that the water was boiling but no steam rose to the surface, only dead fish.

Then Billy noticed the contents within Mark's glass jar: hazy, red water, the same color as the eight foot wave he'd seen the surfer ride the night before.

Let's get out of here, Mark was saying. *Billy!*

But Billy couldn't move. He couldn't stop staring at the bubbling water that had now doubled in circumference and was not only spitting out dead fish in numbers, but had also turned a crimson red.

❒ …

The Canton Shack's plumbing was a mess. Sometimes it worked—most times it didn't. Today it was cooperating but only in thin streams as Joel tried to wash the fishy filth from his body. The shower stall barely allowed enough room to turn around in. It needed cleaning. The water was room temperature as he did not have a water heater. It had broken earlier in the spring. Still, it was very refreshing, particularly since the day would certainly break a hundred degrees and his one-room house had already reached the high eighties.

No. Joel Canton did not have much. He struggled each day of his life. Each day he was one more bad piece of luck away from becoming Port A's most beloved bum. The only things that kept him in from the streets were that he owned his house, as small as it was, and his friendships with a few key people on the island. Marcy was one of them. Billy was another. Officer Keadle also lent a hand from time to time. Keadle was a great handyman and Joel hoped that he'd have some time to look at his water heater before winter set in.

Joel dried himself, pulled the shower curtain closed, and considered cleaning the stall. What if Janine dropped by unexpectedly? It was just a hunch. He'd not invited her but she *had* hand-fed him fish. No one had touched his lips like that in over twenty years. A touch like that deserved an invitation. But his "Shack" was such a mess.

He dressed in his only pair of jeans. Coveralls were not the clothes of a man going on a date. Besides, his coveralls smelled like fish and seawater. He had one brown, collared shirt which he'd never worn and as he slipped it over his head he realized how new it still smelled. He made his bed and put his dirty clothes in a cardboard box inside his makeshift closet—these, too, were chores he rarely made time for. But he kept thinking about Janine.

Before looking at the bedside clock that Marcy had given him last Christmas, he tried to guess the time: 11:30. The clock's face featured a magician and his hands pointed out that it was 11:40. Not bad. Marcy had given him the clock because, as she'd said, in that fortune-teller way she possessed, "You may one day find that your internal timepiece has busted a spring."

He tapped his forehead with an index finger. "Still working fine," he said to the clock magician, thinking of Marcy, and grinned.

He walked the half mile to the Surf Side, thinking of the perfect seafood dish he could order for Janine. He'd never eaten there—though he'd supplied the restaurant many pounds of fish over the past year—so he was unfamiliar with the menu. The restaurant's chef, Pedro, had cooked up some fine finger food the night before and he assumed that his full course meals were just as tasty. Personally, he loved redfish, but he didn't know if Janine would like it. She'd eaten shrimp at Pedro's luau table so that was a guaranteed winner, but, perhaps she'd want to try something different. But what? He was unsure. One thing was certain though, he was thinking about it way too much.

He arrived in the parking lot of the Surf Side and to his dismay, the Black Hummer he'd seen two days ago sat in the handicap parking space nearest the front door. The Hummer's driver had reminded him of Bert Nookle and that memory was the last thing he needed on his first date since Jane.

Candice met him at the door as he entered. There were no other diners. Janine had not yet arrived.

"Joel!" Candice said, surprised to see him. "After all this time you've finally decided to visit our little slice of the sea." She looked around the dining area where tables sat in empty solitude under spotlights of sunshine that streamed through the bay windows. "Really, the food ain't bad," she added. "I don't care what the locals say; there ain't nothing wrong with the fish. But you see how rumors can bring bad business. And we ain't the only ones."

Joel nodded. "I'm meeting someone here for lunch," he said. "Could

I get a table over there." He pointed at a table for two built into the far wall away from the bay window sunlight.

"Well...let me check our reservations." She pretended to look in the book on the hostess podium. "You're in luck. No reservations. Follow me sir." She grabbed a menu and led Joel to his table. "Want to start with something to drink?"

"Not yet," he said, politely. "I'll wait for my..."

"A date, huh?" Candice lightly chuckled. "Well you ole' dog." She slapped the table in front of him. "I'll bring over a couple of glasses of water to tide you over until she gets here."

"That'll be fine," Joel said, trying his best to follow proper restaurant manners. He didn't care much for the sit-down, have a waitress, napkin in the lap, leave-a-tip etiquette of indoor dining. It just wasn't his style.

Joel studied the interior of the Surf Side and was impressed by the collection of assorted fishing artifacts that decorated the walls, particularly the large blue marlin nailed to the wall over the entrance. The thing looked to be thirteen feet across, easy.

And then, into his solitude and discomfort, someone yelled.

"Pedro don't know nothing!" The voice came from the kitchen. Joel started to rise but Candice intercepted him with two glasses of water. She tried to calm the situation.

"Everything's just fine, Joel," she said, setting the glasses on the table in front of him. "Just a little misunderstanding with a food order. Appetizer, perhaps?"

"No...no thank you," Joel said looking beyond Candice toward the blue marlin. Underneath the big fish, Janine walked in. "Here's my, eh... date now."

▢ ...

"He's concerned about fish," Pedro said to Chancey Lett. "He went to the ocean with de science man from college. But over that, Pedro don't know nothing!"

Pedro's back was to the sink. The hallway to the rear exit was to his left. He did not feel cornered until the bodyguard stepped in front of the exit. That's when his voice had risen.

"Calm down, hombre," Lett insisted. "We're just inquiring." Lett nodded for the big man to step back. "What I really came to tell you is some great news that concerns *you*."

A paring knife rested in the sink within arm's reach behind him but Pedro had not even given the weapon a thought. "Yes?" he said as a question.

"I know you've been wanting to get into the culinary academy. I know that you need U.S. clearance to do so." Lett grinned like a friend might before playing some physical prank. "Your cuisine was so wonderful last night. I'm convinced of your ability to get through such a challenging program of study. I'll push through your green card quickly and you can start school next fall."

"You can do this?" Pedro said, his nerves calming.

"The only thing we need to do is make the case that a similar position such as yours can not be filled by an American worker who is willing and able to take the job. I'll serve as witness that this is true. There might be someone willing to do a gourmet chef's job, but few are able. Once you get the card, getting into school will be a cinch." Lett still grinned.

Pedro answered, "Yes," thinking that if he said *No*, the bodyguard would not like it.

"Of course we'll need a second recommendation from a respectable source. Your boss would be a superb choice."

Pedro nodded.

"Why don't you bring Mr. Presser down to the Big Texas Bank around, oh, say, six o'clock tonight? We'll take care of all of the necessary paperwork then."

Pedro nodded again, considered the bodyguard, and wondered how he was going to ask his jefe for such a favor. "I'll see you at six."

"Excellent. And don't forget to bring boss man. We'll need him, too. You'll be enrolled at The Julienne Academy before you know it."

Kale came into the kitchen at that moment. "Hey Pedro. You seen..." he started to say.

"Excuse us," Lett said and turned. "We were just leaving." Lett was about the same height as Kale but much stockier. The bodyguard, of course, made everyone look small. Kale stepped aside as the casino men exited.

"They were looking for Billy," Pedro said, still shaky.

"Yeah," Kale answered, bewildered. "Seems like a lot of people are."

⬚ ...

They were safely on land now, but there were moments when Billy thought the sea was going to open up and swallow them, helicopter and all.

Before Lacey had gotten them airborne, the sea had begun churning so fiercely that the copter shook as if caught in a hurricane. It had bubbled up hundreds of fish and had spewed forth a large diameter of red water, a small sample of which Mark had sealed in a jar and had placed in its metal container. By the time the copter's floats had been released by the gurgling ocean, it had looked as if God had dropped a big eyedropper full of red death right there in the Gulf. The water immediately below them had turned into a bloody, thick red pool that had spread out from its center to encompass a good hundred yards. Dead fish had been everywhere, so many in fact that Billy had believed he could have walked across them. By the time the copter had risen a couple hundred feet, the outward, increasing diameter of the red death had stopped. It was as if one small circle of the Gulf had suddenly hiccupped, bringing to the surface a blood-colored substance and a whole bunch of dead sea life.

Mark had been completely silent the entire way back. He'd stared at one point through the windshield for the majority of the return flight. Billy had supposed that Mark was anxious to get to the lab and find out what it was in the Gulf that had suddenly done something Mark Walker had never seen the Gulf do. But Billy believed that Mark was also truly scared. Billy didn't have the proof but, perhaps for the first time, Mark had used belief over truth in coming to the conclusion that something was disturbingly wrong with the water around Port Aransas.

Mark thanked and dismissed Lacey then carried the metal container with the jar that held a sample of what he called the *Blood Drop* and asked Billy to grab the twelve plastic samples they'd collected near the buoys. It was the first thing he'd said to Billy since the anomaly had developed. Now, he mostly babbled to himself.

"I really don't know what it is, Billy," Mark said as if Billy had asked him a question. "It could be a vent. Yes. It must be." He led Billy from the helicopter to a side of the laboratory accessible only by the entry card he held. "Just a bunch of alga and dead fish. Why dead fish?" He shook his head and shrugged his shoulders, still talking to himself but having the presence of mind to lead Billy through the lab and to a station where, in the sink, the dead, one-legged seagull still lay. He pulled the jar from its metal container and set it next to the sink.

"You still going to take my blood?" Billy asked, trying to gain his colleague's attention.

Mark turned from the sink and stared through Billy, his eyes still wandering in the curiosity of science. "Blood," he said and blinked. "Yeah...yes...yes, of course. What do you think of this?" He pointed at the glass jar.

"You mean what's my take on all that crazy shit that just happened out there? What the hell was that, Mark?"

"Heat vent, probably." He snatched the jar full of red water and moved over to one of the lab's microscopes.

"You know that ain't right, Mark. A heat vent causes the water to heat. That water wasn't heated."

"Well...maybe not always." Mark slipped on a pair of lab gloves.

"Maybe not always what—what does that mean?"

Mark turned and pounded the air with a clenched fist. "Maybe," he said, maintaining his patience but struggling to do so. "Maybe the heat dissipated on its way to the surface. Maybe this is another kind of heat vent that isn't hot and perhaps should be called a cold vent. Maybe we've uncovered a never-before recorded event in the Earth's oceans and maybe it'll be called the Walker-Presser Gulf Event to all of those who study it afterward."

"So you *don't* know what it was."

Mark dropped his arm to the table and opened the glass jar with one gloved hand. "No," he said. "I really don't."

Mark tested the contents of the jar five times in an attempt to eliminate false negatives, to make sure that what his microscopes were telling him was the truth. The cold, boiling water had looked like blood...that's why Mark had called it the blood drop. Now, his analysis confirmed that it not only looked like blood...it was blood—at least blood mixed with seawater. The blood was aquatic, probably composed of the fluids from the fish that had bubbled up with it. Knowing this, though, did not provide any answers. Mark admitted that nothing like this had ever happened, at least not to his knowledge, and he offered an educated guess for its existence. "A violent eruption deep in the ocean could have changed the water pressure so dramatically that the blood was squeezed right out of them, just like orange juice."

"The water isn't very deep just a mile or so out."

"Yes," Mark said. "I know. But at least it's the start of a hypothesis." He grabbed Billy's wrist. "Come over here. Let's see if anything is floating around in you."

Mark took a syringe full of Billy's blood. After mixing it with other chemicals and numerous passes under the microscope, he found that it contained a slight trace of alcohol but no toxins, neither industrial nor natural.

"I guess that whatever is in the crate in the bank vault isn't narcotic after all," Billy said. "I guess I wasn't hallucinating last night. I mean, your instruments confirmed the big wave, right?"

Mark shook his head. "Well, if anything in there is narcotic, you certainly weren't affected by it, at least that's what your blood says. And, yes, the instruments recorded the wave but I have yet to eliminate the possibility of a malfunction." And then Mark's eyes glazed over. Absently, he added, "Maybe it was because of the hurricane." He pointed.

Billy followed Mark's finger toward a muted television. The Weather Channel crew offered an update on tropical storm Antiago which, just an hour ago, had been upgraded to a Category 1 hurricane. The track of the storm had moved from the northern tip of the Yucatan peninsula and into the Gulf.

"Hurricanes have produced many anomalies," Mark said, staring as if hypnotized by the hope that a hurricane could explain everything.

"If that thing hits us, *we'll* be the only anomaly," Billy said. He patted Mark's shoulder as Mark leaned toward the Weather Channel. "But it'll turn. They always do. Besides, it's much too far away to provide causation." Mark nodded, and Billy continued. "If you find any *real* reasons to explain all of this, give me a call."

Mark shook his head to disengage his attention with the Weather Channel. "The fish are all right as a whole. It's just these strange anomalies. I really don't think there is anything in the water." He grabbed the first buoy sample they'd collected at marker #12 and poured several samples into small test tubes as Billy headed for the exit.

☐ ...

Nothing could have prepared Janine for it. It was supposed to be a simple lunch with a newfound friend. She'd sipped twice from her glass of water and had thanked Joel for meeting her as the restaurant's kitchen doors swung open. Sudden shock crept up her spine and she hunkered further into the dining room shadows, as an animal might upon seeing its predator.

She'd hoped he was dead but there had never been any proof. They'd assured her that no man could have survived such a blast. But that was just it. The man who walked from the kitchen and back into her life was no man. He was a monster. He was Albert Stine.

He sniffed the air as if the hunter had just detected its prey, then followed a shorter man with slick hair out of the restaurant.

Joel was gawking at her. She didn't look at him but she knew that he must be. Her paradise had become purgatory—again.

"Are you okay?" Joel was saying, but the buzzing shock that scrambled her mind made hearing difficult. He grabbed her forearm gently, but she jerked away and gasped, startled. "You look like you seen death itself."

She now turned to him, wondering how he knew. "Death," she whispered within a sigh.

Joel patted her hand. "If it's of any account, I don't like them much either. They're trying to take over the island."

Candice returned and asked what they wanted for lunch. Joel ordered for both of them. He chose redfish for himself and a sampler platter for Janine that was not on the menu but could be created by Pedro just for her.

By the time the meal arrived, Janine had regained much of her composure. She asked Joel what he'd meant—that *they are taking over the island*.

Joel told her what he knew. When he'd finished, Janine was not surprised that Stine was part of such gambling conspiracies. What she did not understand is why God in Heaven had placed her here at the same time.

⌐ ...

Mark remained shaken up. Part of the reason for his chattering nerves was that he was actually excited about the chance at a new discovery. Having your name attached to new phenomena was every researcher's dream.

But a deeper feeling of self-doubt was what had really done the trick.

All of that blood and all of those fish had roiled and boiled to the surface in one big clump. They'd splashed life's last breath all around the helicopter floats and his feet, slapping at his ankles, nearly pulling him into the blood drop. The memory of it had simply screwed him up. How could he be afraid? He was a doctor of marine biology. Finding reasons for mass fish kills was one of the field's greatest priorities.

He finished testing the buoy #7 sample and still he'd found nothing alarming— nothing that could be argued as a reason for fish kills or blood drops.

He went to the sink to clean up and noticed the one-legged seagull that lay in the sink's right-side basin. It had rolled free from its paper-toweled enclosure. Its face was twisted in apparent surprise and shock, its eyes wide open, its beak stretched into one last scream; even the talons on the one good dead leg pointed straight out in a kind of sudden death surprise.

Maybe the bird *had* died of a sudden heart attack. He'd seen humans who'd stiffened in similar ways.

He plucked the bird from the sink and carried it to a sterile station to dissect it. He first inspected the bird for evidence of unnatural death. The bird was so stiff it felt as if it were stuffed. The talons on the one foot stretched out so widely, he wondered if it would stand by itself.

He tried it.

The bird remained upright for a half a second before falling over with a thud. Mark shrugged then began the dissection.

He was quick to find the reason for its death, and when he did, he stumbled backward. The bird had no heart—at least not anything that resembled a heart. An indistinguishable mass of flesh was all that remained. It was as if something had grabbed hold of it and had squashed it in its grip.

And then he heard the crash of breaking glass beakers and turned to find Lett's bodyguard staring at him.

❏ ...

Joel was relieved to see that the color had returned to most of Janine's face. For a few moments he'd thought she might pass out. Joel only knew of the casino men from what others had told him. Apparently, from her reaction to them, Janine knew more than he did, and more than she was willing to tell.

He was unsure if she'd liked any of the items on the seafood platter. She'd toyed with one butterfly shrimp, nibbling at its fat edges but never consuming the whole thing. She completely avoided the crab legs or anything else that required any physical strategy beyond picking it up and eating it. The icy glasses of water seemed to be her favorite; she'd consumed five of them in the time it took for him to explain the casino men and devour his meal of redfish.

"So the vote needs to pass for them to do anything," Janine said.

"From what I've heard," Joel replied. He eyed the crab legs in front of Janine. "Do you mind if I…"

Janine waved her hand. "No. Please. Go ahead. They look…" she paused as if searching for a word that was more courteous than she felt. "They look good."

"Did you like the shrimp?" he asked while snatching one of the two meaty legs and the crab shell cracker.

Her stare still wandered though Joel could see she was trying to concentrate on their conversation. "It's all good," she said, looking directly into his eyes. "I'm just not hungry. In fact, I really don't feel very well at all. Would there be any way you could help me back to my place? I've not even seen it yet."

Joel released the crab leg in mid crack. He put it and the cracker on his empty plate. "I'd be happy to," he said, and then for no other reason than pure honesty, he added, "I really like your hair tie. It's very unique."

Janine almost smiled. The left edge of her lip tweaked upward but the rest of her mouth remained motionless. "Thank you," she said. "Can we go?"

As they left, Candice told them that Marcy had already paid their bill. Pedro was behind the bar sipping from a small glass of what looked to be cola. A bottle of Southern Comfort sat near the glass.

"Thank you for a great lunch," Joel told him, while gawking at the big blue marlin nailed to the wall above his head.

Pedro looked up as if dazed, nodded once, returned to his drink.

The two walked a few blocks to Alister Street and waited for the next trolley. Janine remained quiet except for telling him where she lived. Joel wondered if her silence was because of something he'd done or said.

"This will get us close to Paradise Cottages but we'll need to walk about a half a mile or so," Joel said, sitting beside Janine on the trolley stop bench. "That place is relatively new and out beyond where the trolley goes right now."

Janine shifted on the bench to face him; her cheeks flushed all at once. "I know one of those men, or at least one of them looks a whole lot like someone I know."

Joel didn't respond. If Janine was going to tell him something, he was all ears. She'd been way too silent for too long.

"There are a lot of bad memories associated with that man," she continued. "He's one of the reasons I came to the island. Now it seems he's found me." The trolley approached before she could say any more.

They stepped onto a trolley filled with a dozen people, most of them visitors to the island. Janine did not continue her revelations amongst the strangers but her pain was apparent to Joel from what she'd already said. One of the casino men was after her. She'd not even seen her new residence and already her dreams for this island, her new home, were shattered. And for that reason, Joel did something he'd not done since losing his wife to Bert Nookle.

"Would you go fishing with me tomorrow?" he said, hoping that such an adventure would calm her nerves. A little boy no older than five who was holding his mother's hand and sitting at the back of the trolley looked up as if to say: *Come on lady. Are you kidding? He said fishing. He said fishing.*

Janine stared at Joel for the longest minute, weighing the question. She looked at the little boy who could think of no other answer and said, "Yes. That sounds like fun." The little boy smiled.

"The trolley starts at eight. Would that be too early?"

Again, the faint hint of a smile touched the left corner of her lips. "We'd want to catch the first worm, right?"

"I'll come pick you up on the first trolley over."

Janine shook her head. "How about if I meet you at your place? You've been much too kind already." She covered his hand with hers. "Where do you live?"

Regardless of his home's condition, he couldn't hide from her, and quite frankly didn't want to, especially now that he felt the need to watch after her, to protect her from the casino men.

"Well, it ain't much," he said, apologetically, feeling the dampness in the palm of her hand across his knuckles.

"I don't need much," Janine said.

Joel explained where he lived, thumbing over his shoulder with the hand that was not held by Janine in the direction of the Canton Shack. The little boy who liked to fish sat concentrating on Joel's explanation as if he was trying to understand the directions with the intent of joining them in the morning. The boy's mother had to jerk his arm to get his attention when the trolley stopped at their corner.

"Fishing," the boy said as he passed them. "Dead fishing." He waved his small hand as his mother tugged him off of the trolley.

The boy's observation reminded Joel how angry he'd become at the luau. He'd yelled at Mark and had almost duked it out with fat boy Burgess. Fish equaled food. Fish equaled cash. Dead fish meant that Joel would end up on the streets, in the soup kitchens, begging for pennies from Corpus Christi strangers. But right now, right here on this trolley, just a dozen minutes after he'd seen Janine's expression of fear from the presence of a man who apparently threatened her, Joel Canton did not care about himself, his livelihood, or fish. And this was an epiphany for him and his soul. Until this very moment, he'd not really considered loneliness, and the idea of growing old without anyone to care for or to be cared by. As he sat on the trolley with Janine's moist, warm hand over his and the air blowing waves of heat across his cheeks as Alister Street passed them by at thirty-five miles an hour, he began to realize that Joel could no longer be the most important person in his life. He began to realize that self-salvation is a useless concept when uncoupled with instances of care and consideration for others. In the end, he'd not cared about Jane, and Bert had not cared about him. It was Joel's own lack of compassion about anything other than catching the Great White of '72 and every other fishing excursion he'd taken since then, that had made him what he was today. The only one that would ever need protecting was himself. The only food that was important was what he could obtain for himself. And ever since his meager charter boat company had gone bankrupt some twenty years ago, any time Joel had gone fishing it was always by himself. He had never let anyone into that world. It was *his* world. The only thing left. The sea, and all it had to offer, was his self-salvation. The sea was his love and nothing else could ever receive whatever passion was left in the fisherman's soul.

At least not until now.

"Last stop," the driver yelled. This shook Joel from his thought trance. He smiled at Janine but not so widely that his teeth showed.

"Can I walk you home?" he asked, slowly standing.

One busy 7-11 sat on one corner and several new construction projects occupied the other three. Hammers and saws and men shouting orders punctuated the landscape. Janine peered up and down both streets at the crossroad as if looking for something specific and said, "Well. Since I don't even know where I live, most definitely yes."

Joel had not released her hand and he used it to gently guide her off of the trolley and onto the street. Together they strolled along unpaved sidewalks, like a pair of teenagers setting out for experiences unknown, like two youthful innocents who were no longer alone.

◻ ...

The last mortal vision that Albert Stine had seen took place at Pickett's Crossing, Kansas, almost a year ago. It had found him though he'd thought himself well hidden in the barn.

The last mortal emotion Albert Stine had felt was fear. It had been an odd sensation: being afraid to such an extent. Albert Stine, until then, had not been so scared in his life.

It had been *him*!

It had ripped the flesh from mortal Albert Stine's face with the strength only matched by something that was as evil as itself.

The real Albert Stine, the evil one that was in gambling debt up to his ass to a Vegas shark named Chancey Lett, the one who vociferously enjoyed his Beam shots and Coke chasers, the one who, even as a mortal, had Hellishly slapped his wife on one occasion or two, had created a cubited replica that was so horrible even Evil could not live in its presence.

The replica, the one that many on the island town of Port Aransas now referred to as Chancey Lett's bodyguard, had made quick work of the mortal (as much as he deserved the right to be called such) Albert Stine. The death had been quick and easy. But it had taken some time to devour so much human flesh.

From that day forth, the new Albert Stine had been on a quest. It had taken nearly a year for all of the pieces to come together, for it to procure the entirety of Stine's personality—to become Albert Stine. And now it was only days away from seeing the dark prize come to life.

The Cubit would change this world—this time—just as it had for eons.

He'd still not seen that former bitch of a wife Janine but he knew she would be here. All of the players would be here, like stars aligning on the

Galactic Center.

    Joel Canton.

    Chancey Lett.

    Janine Bender.

    Alixel.

    And, of course, Jean LaFitte.

    Together, they would help him rule a new age that would last 5,000 years—an age full of chaos and catastrophe: the Age of Hell.

    There had been some minor interruptions in destiny's plan. Some of the islanders were troublesome but manageable. The key right now was the vote for the casino. It would be the reason he'd need to start digging up the beach and reveal what lay underneath: the last piece. Control of the future.

    Chancey Lett was one of his biggest problems. The gambler had a kind of sixth sense, one that was not easily led, one that was manipulative, sly and heartless in its own right.

    Lett had not been cubited. Stine needed him mortal for now. The cubited dead could emulate their mortal selves in many ways but interacting convincingly with the living took time that Stine did not have. Lett would push the vote through and Stine would get his bulldozers.

    The bank promotion had really been Stine's idea but he'd consciously let Chancey have the credit. The vault provided a safe and secure environment to change the needed key people and the contest provided a reason to get them near the Cubit.

    Bone had told them in his office earlier that day that almost forty new security box accounts had already been recorded. For Chancey Lett (and Stine), that was not enough; Lett had told Bone this. They'd need additional numbers if the vote for the casino was to be guaranteed, he'd said. Bone didn't really understand how a contest would guarantee a vote, but the man was easily manipulated. Most greedy mortals were. Bone thought that the crate held some valuable artifact. In a way, he was right. What he didn't know was that it was the artifact that would guarantee the vote by changing the voters.

    Billy Jo Presser was an extreme nuisance; he'd sparked a rally that had threatened the vote's guarantee. But really, all that had done was cause Stine to make a little adjustment in plans. Those who would be cubited sooner rather than later now included a surfer, a policeman, and a publisher. Though it would have been nice to have Billy's spiritual strength on their side to expedite things, Presser would simply have to die. Pedro had told him that Billy had gone out with the "science man from the college." Other than that, Billy's chef "did not know nothing."

Stine arrived at the marine institute looking for Billy thirty minutes after Billy had left. What he did find though was Mark Walker: another nuisance that had to be eliminated.

⌐ …

It was nearly two in the afternoon when Billy pulled into Pat McGee's. Not only would Bottlenose help him find some used plywood to cover up the windows at the restaurant should the hurricane hit, he might also provide some insight into the maker of the beautifully strange surfboard Billy carried from the back of the VW through the front door of the surf shop.

"Yo, BJ." Coolie said from behind a counter that displayed board wax and sunscreen lotion. "Dude. That 'cane's a headin' in our general direction."

Billy set the nose of the surfboard on the floor and said, "Saw it on the news just a few minutes ago. Nothing to be overly worried about yet… just cautious."

"What'cha got there?" Coolie came around the counter to check out the board. "Never seen one like that before. It's a freakin tree!"

"You ever seen wood like that?"

Coolie rubbed his hand across the board's glassy surface then lifted it from Billy's grasp. His thin frame had trouble with the board's weight. "Not balsa for sure. Thing is huge on weight. Must be at least nine feet."

"You know anyone who makes these long wooden rides anymore?"

Coolie shook his head. From behind both of them, Bottlenose added, "Neither do I." His eyes were filled with wonder. He took the board from Coolie and held it in his muscular grip with much greater ease. "Christ! This baby is at least fifty pounds. Beautiful. Vintage. And the wood. Definitely not a pop-out."

Coolie continued rubbing the board's surface as Bottlenose held it. "You know what it's made of?"

"I got a guess," Bottlenose said. "Seen a similar design off the Yucatan coast in Mexico several years ago." The board had three distinct colors:

the outside edges were reddish brown, the nose and tail were dark brown, almost black, and the center stringer was a blonde tan. Bottlenose traced the edge of the board with one finger. "This could be a lot of things. Most people would guess mahogany by its color. But when you match it up with this wood," Bottlenose tapped the board's nose with his hand, "you've got to consider the board's origin. It's my guess that all of these woods came from southern Mexico. And it's my guess that these woods are all quite valuable…and rare. The nose is perhaps Chechen. The edges I'm sure are Cocobolo. The center is…hmmm." He rapped the center of the board with his knuckles. "Definitely not hollow."

Billy got to thinking about the red wave rider, the surfer's silhouette against the moon. "Who rides a board like this? None of the locals. Corpses perhaps?"

Bottlenose took the board to the back of the shop where the surfing museum still had not seen today's first visitor. Billy and Coolie followed. "A corpse with a long wood board…nah. I mean those mainland surfers wouldn't know what to do with a beauty like this." He set the surfboard face down atop a pair of sawhorses he used to demonstrate board waxing. "But I'll tell you one thing. The guy riding this board is probably huge… at least his weight is huge…and his strength…and his courage. Can you imagine what would happen to the ol' noggin if this piece of lumber came down on top of it?" Bottlenose inspected the chip in the nose of the board. A good inch wide and two inch long chunk had been busted out of the nearly black wood surface. "Amazing. Huge amazing."

"How's that?" Billy asked, leaning forward to inspect the chip.

"You can't chip a board like this…at least not with anything less than a jackhammer." He suddenly rose and studied Billy quizzically. "Just where did you get this anyway?"

Sweets, Shana Greathouse and Peter Jennings entered the shop together. They made a beeline to where the three men stood.

"Hey, man," Sweets said. "New addition to the museum?"

"Slick," Shana added. "You wanna take me for a ride on it Bottle?" Shana had never been shy about showing her desire in public for Bottlenose.

"Not mine," Bottlenose said. "Ask BJ. It's his board."

"How much did that run you?" Peter asked then saw the chip in the nose. "Aw, man. The value's already been robbed."

All four surfers gathered around the board, staring from it to Billy in silence, waiting for him to fill them in. Billy felt the need to lie, to raise his reputation by fabricating a cost and a place of purchase. Surfboards promoted status. He'd already obtained much symbolism on the island. A board like this would solidify it for years to come. However, to claim ownership would mean that he'd have to ride the monster in front of all those that would lift him to local stardom. Bottlenose was right. A board like this smashing down against his head might kill him.

"It didn't cost me anything," he admitted. The four surfers remained silent but their quizzical stares mixed with sudden disbelief. "I found it."

"Found it?" Coolie questioned, his voice rising two octaves. "Who finds a board like this? I mean, come on."

"On the beach," Billy continued. "This morning. Just a couple of miles south of the pier."

"Well, it *is* busted," Peter interjected.

"Not so much that it couldn't be fixed," Coolie added. "Right, Bottlenose?"

Bottlenose shrugged his shoulders. "Gotta be worth a grand easy. It would be worth patchin' up. It wouldn't be the same though. Hell, there'd be no way of finding any wood like this around here. The integrity would suffer. It would take a great laminator. Might serve better as a museum piece."

Billy had to agree. He wouldn't be using it. Too heavy. Too long. It would kill him for sure. And it wasn't like it cost anything. "All of your boards are in such good condition though," he said to Bottlenose. "You sure a board with a broken nose and tail fin could find a place among such mint condition pieces?"

A big question mark surfaced across Bottlenose's expressive face. "Broken fin?" He stepped to the tail of the board, brushing past Shana who beamed with pleasure. "This fin ain't broke."

But it was broken. At least it was when the teenage boy had found it on the beach. At least it was when Billy had inspected it. The last two inches of the fin had not been there. Billy was sure of it. Coolie stepped aside as Billy moved toward the fin.

"I'm tellin' ya," he said to Bottlenose. "This thing was broken this morning."

"Well it ain't broke now," Coolie said.

Billy leaned in, inspecting both sides of the fin, looking for a crack that wasn't there. What he did find shocked him more than the idea that he'd imagined it all. At the very tip of the fin etched in deep red across the dark brown, almost black, wood surface was the Wayeb symbol, the same Mayan icon that had been on the papers carried by Chancey Lett's bodyguard and had been etched on both sides of the coin the Corpus Christi visitors had found in the sand. He could not hide his surprise from the others. They were all staring at him when he rose from the board.

"You gonna faint or something?" Shana said.

Billy shook his head and absently reached into the front pocket of his shorts, the same shorts he'd worn the day before. The coin was still there. He pulled it out and let it rest in the palm of his open hand and said, "This is what those corpses dug up in the sand yesterday." He gave the coin to Bottlenose who drew it closer to his eyes for inspection. "Now look at the fin."

Bottlenose did. "Same thing," he said. "So?"

"Strange coincidence don't you think?" Billy said.

Bottlenose flipped the coin back to Billy. "Yeah, but there are a lot of those in the world aren't there? Really, I don't see anything special about it. What I'm more concerned with is you thinking the fin was broke. You sure you're okay?"

There had been a lot of shit that had happened to him in the past twenty-four hours, so much so that he wondered he if was merely dreaming, that suddenly he'd wake up in bed, his shorts still wet from an evening of surfing, a huge knot on his head from where his surfboard had crashed down causing a concussion. If anything made sense, that did. There'd been glowing vaults, strange crates, menacing bodyguards, visions of displaced time and space, and of being chased and shot at. He'd witnessed red tides and eight foot waves, blood drops and massive fish kills. Birds no longer flew on an island famous for its avian complexity. How could a person explain such things? Easy. He was dreaming.

"Yeah, I'm fine," he said. "It's just been a long couple of days. Very stressful."

"I know what you mean, bro," Bottlenose said, comforting. "You've taken on way too much, fighting those bastards from Vegas and all. Shit, your business can't be doing that hot either with all this rumor of chemical spills. And now we got a hurricane whirling up our ass."

Coolie interjected, "But that's a good thing ain't it? It'll miss us and shoot up the coast and leave eight foot waves in its wake. Talk about knarly, dudes and dudette. Like, Port A will be the greatest surf spot in the lower forty-eight."

"Always one to look on the bright side," Shana said. "Won't do us much good if that Vegas asshole gets his way. We won't even be able to walk on our own beach."

Billy stepped back from the surfboard and dropped the Wayeb coin in his pocket. "If you want it you can have it," he told Bottlenose. "I'm not much into the long board rides. And as for the rest of you. If we're gonna keep our surf and ride Coolie's eight foot swells this weekend, we're going to have to make sure the vote is on our side. The *South Jetty* ain't helping us. In fact, other than the luau last night and what we can do by pounding the pavement, lots of islanders aren't going to know the ramifications of the vote. They may not even know that a vote is going to take place."

"What can we do?" Peter Jennings said.

"Knock on doors," Billy replied. "I'm going to print up some door hangers. Can you guys help distribute them?"

Simultaneously, all the surfers shouted, "Hells yes!"

"Excellent. I'll be back around five o'clock then." Billy started out the door then turned to face Bottlenose who was still examining his new museum piece. "You still have a bunch of that used plywood out back you saved when you tore down the old board shaper's shop?"

"Yeah," Bottlenose replied, not looking up from his new museum piece.

"You got enough to where I might borrow some in case that storm breaks our way."

"Should be enough for McGee's and the Surf Side."

"Nice. I'll see you in a couple of hours then."

Coolie, Sweets, and Jennings gave him the thumbs up. Shana was too busy staring at Bottlenose's biceps.

Billy stopped at the CopyKatz on his way home. He hoped that the girl there would have no problem throwing something together for him in an hour or two. He figured a couple thousand door hangers would probably do the trick. Luckily, the copy shop was not busy and the girl was happy to oblige though she was not certain she could print and cut two thousand hangers in such a short time. But she did promise that when five o'clock came around she'd have as much done as possible. She didn't like the idea of the casino either and the pavement pounding sounded like a great idea. In fact, she offered to help which Billy gladly accepted.

When he arrived at the restaurant, Candice and Kale were sitting at the bar drinking ice water. Their expressions were as if someone had just died. As he entered, they did not look up. There were no diners.

"What gives?" Billy asked.

"Our jobs," Kale mumbled.

"And by that you mean…"

Kale swirled a finger through the ice in his glass. "You know how many people we've had in here since noon?" He lifted his hand from the glass, showing two fingers. "You know how much fish I was able to purchase today?" The two fingers curled inward to form a zero. "You know how long we can stay in business this way?" He returned his hand to the glass of water. "We can't. No one can. The Wharf and the Tarpon have already closed their doors. Now we got this damned hurricane to deal with. I've pretty much given up, Billy."

Billy moved to the bar and stood where the Vegas bodyguard had just two days before. "Where's Pedro?"

"Left about an hour ago," Kale said. "He didn't seem too happy. He said something had suddenly come up that he had to deal with. I didn't figure we'd have much business anyway."

"You're right," Billy said.

"What do you mean?"

"We can't stay in business this way. We're gonna have to close shop. At least until all of this rumor and the storm passes."

"What if it isn't rumor?" Kale sipped some water and looked into Billy's eyes for support. "If they find chemicals, Port A will be a ghost town."

"Mark's working on that. We didn't find anything today that would point a finger at DuPont." Billy told him only part of the truth. Talking about one-legged birds with heart attacks and blood spots full of dead fish would not help calm his manager's nerves.

"They denied it, you know." It was the first thing Candice had said since Billy had entered. "It was on TV earlier. That Chagnard fellow—you know the one with the crazy blue eyes—he was on the afternoon news and said that there was no reason to think DuPont would ever be so irresponsible. He reminded his audience that DuPont had had a clean record since the disaster in Galveston and that their safety program budget had swelled into the millions since then. He pretty much guaranteed the public that DuPont had nothing to do with the fish kills."

"Well there you have it," Billy said.

"You trust that weasley-faced press agent?" Candice said. "Man, I wouldn't trust him as far as I could throw him."

Just then, a couple of obese men entered the restaurant. Each of them easily weighed more than three hundred pounds. "Damned nice to see something open on this island," the one with the rosier cheeks said. "What's the special today? Got any buffets? Any all-you-can-eats? We're starved for seafood and lots of it."

Candice leaned forward and whispered. "Looks like we're two diners too late for closing. And they ain't gonna make us any money that's for certain." She mustered a smile and added, "So who's cooking?" then escorted the men to a table in the center of the dining room.

"You go ahead and do an inventory," Billy said to Kale. "See what we can store on ice and what won't last four or five days. I'll cook these guys up something. I don't think they're going to be too picky. They seem more into quantity than quality."

"We won't be able to save much," Kale said and chugged down the rest of his water. "We got the reputation of freshness. Perhaps we can cook some of it up and refrigerate it for stews and platters."

"Good thinking. And we'll need some signs about the closure."

"I'll take care of it. The sooner the better before we lose any more money." Kale nodded toward the two fat diners.

◻ ...

Carol had screamed at Steph, and everyone in the bank, all twenty-three of them, had turned toward Steph's desk.

"No fucking pooling!" she'd yelled.

At least three people in the teller lines had gasped. One of them, a mother with her young son, had covered her child's ears. That had been almost four hours ago and still Steph could not get the memory of the uncontrolled outburst out of her head.

Steph stared at Patrick the Starfish. The toy had an expression of surprise, a gasp planted on its plastic face as if SpongeBob had said something shocking or stupid, as if a twisted bank teller had just yelled in a cursive slang that was not indigenous to the bottom of the sea.

"Screwed up," she whispered to the starfish. "This has been one screwed up day." Steph signed.

Business at the bank, however, had not been screwed up. The million dollar real estate promotion had been nothing less than a major success. More than a hundred new accounts had been opened so far and there were at least twenty more prospects standing in line at the teller windows or sitting with bank reps at desks. Carol had directed most of the new business away from Steph since her outburst and she'd not allowed Steph into the vault. This had pissed Steph off. How had Carol gained so much unofficial control? Steph had been tempted on several occasions to test her, to enter the vault just to see what Carol would do, but Steph wasn't that brave. Anyone who would scream such language in a place of business with a couple dozen customers around didn't have all of their marbles. Carol's proverbial cheese had slid of the cracker and who knew what she was capable of, the least of which would certainly entail another foul-mouthed tongue lashing. It was as if Carol had become the guardian of the vault, a sentry placed conspicuously and menacingly at its door. Only Carol and customers would enter and each time she went in Steph swore she heard that low hum though no one else in the bank seemed to notice.

Patrick the Starfish's gasp lured her into an imaginary conversation. In its dopey voice the toy said:

I don't know about you, but the crate in there sure is creepy.

"I agree," Steph said in a hush so no one in the bank would notice her talking to the toy.

I wonder why that big ugly fella pushed it at you?

"I'm not sure," Steph whispered.

He sure is ugly. He's got Squidward beaten by a mile. And he stinks, too. The inside of his pocket smelled like Mr. Crab's crabby patties.

Steph considered the Mr. Crabs toy, leaning against the side of her computer monitor, who now entered the conversation.

The only thing that stinks around here is you, Patrick. My patties are the best tasting and smelling crab cakes in all of Bikini Bottom.

Apparently, you haven't tried Pedro Melindez's crab cakes, Steph thought but didn't say.

But we're not in Bikini Bottom, Patrick said. *We're in the Big Texas Bank, Port A branch, where you can get a security box and a chance to win a million bucks worth of real estate all in the same day.*

Don't you think that's a little weird, Patrick?

Yeah, Mr. Crabs, but it's workin'. The bank's pulled in at least a half a million dollars in new accounts.

Patrick, you're an idiot. The bank doesn't care about the money. They just want to get as many influential people as possible into that vault and close to that crate. You never were able to put two and two together.

Four, Patrick said and giggled. *I got an A in math.*

You're enough to make a crab pull its hair out.

But you don't have any hair, Mr. Crabs

I know that you idiot.

Hey, now. Wait a minute, Mr. Crabs. Do you hear that?

Hear what?

That hummy noise coming from the vault.

That's not a hummy noise. It's the telephone ringing. Starfish are so stupid.

Steph was shaken from her daydream daze. She had no idea how long the phone had been ringing. She snatched the receiver.

"Are you going to do any work today Miss Drake or are you just going to play with your toys?" It was Carol's voice, and when Steph looked up and over at the teller window, Carol had the phone to her ear and was glaring at her. "Mr. Bone is on line one. Would you mind picking it up?"

Steph did not reply but instead cut Carol off by pressing the blinking button on her handset.

"Yes, Mr. Bone?" she said.

"Carol tells me you allowed some customers to pool their money. Would you mind explaining yourself?

Steph wanted to respond in many ways. She wanted to tell him that Carol was insane. She wanted to tell him that the crazy bitch had screamed

"Fuck" right in front of his beloved customers. She wanted to explain that Carol had taken command of his bank and was not allowing Steph to take part in any transactions. But instead, she replied, "I'm sorry Mr. Bone but I didn't know the rules of the contest."

"If you'd gotten to work on time that would not be an issue."

Carol was grinning but not looking at her. She escorted another customer into the vault and closed the door.

"I…" Steph started to say but Bone cut her off.

"I'm counting on you to pick up our investor from the airport tomorrow. I want you to provide her with every amenity she requests. Can I trust you to do this one small thing?"

"Yes. Of course, Mr. Bone."

"Her plane arrives at two o'clock. I expect you to be there at least a half hour early in case the flight arrives early. Take your car and the bank will reimburse you for the expense. She'll be staying next door at the Treasure Trove.

"I'll take care of it," Steph said and Bone hung up.

In a way, Steph was relieved. She'd not need to go to the airport until the afternoon which would allow plenty of time to spend with Billy. However, if she called in sick, what signal would that send? How could she be sick and escort this woman all in the same day? How could she explain herself? The short answer was: she couldn't. She had to make a choice. Surfing and Billy weren't as important as her job, were they? She was only three years outside of adolescence and the irresponsible tingle associated with immaturity still pulsed vibrantly within her. For responsible, mature adults, there was no choice. But recently, her responsibility had been shanghaied by a crazy woman named Carol. Was she still Bone's executive secretary? Did her job no longer require her to keep tabs on Bone's daily schedule? Had she been relegated to nothing more than a chauffer? Would she still have a job by week's end?

The hum from the vault and shrill ringing of the telephone engaged her senses simultaneously. She picked up the receiver expecting Mr. Bone, but it was Billy. He wanted to know when would be a good time to start their door-to-door protest campaign, something Steph had forgotten all about. She suggested five-thirty and Billy said he'd pick her up at her apartment.

As she hung up the phone, Carol emerged from the vault. Professor Nelson followed. The professor looked dazed, as if bright headlights had just blinded him. When he walked past Steph, she said to him, "Hey Professor Nelson. How are you today?"

The man continued past without acknowledgement, seemingly catatonic, as if only one thought occupied all of consciousness. She wondered if he was thinking about the Lord's Prayer, or at least the version that Carol and friends had come up with. She wondered if he'd touched the crate. She wondered if *she'd* touched the crate. She looked at her hand then down at Patrick.

There's something creepy going on, the toy said. *And you are right in the middle of it.*

⬓ ...

It took the two men an hour and a half to eat what Billy had termed "The Super Platter." None existed on the menu but it was what the men wanted and it was one of the easiest things to make. No special sauces. No extravagant presentation. Just pounds of shrimp, scallops, and redfish and almost a gallon of seafood gumbo that Pedro had simmering in a large crock pot. Kale had placed signs on the entry door and in one bay window an hour ago.

Along with the Super Platter, Billy cooked up much of the fresh seafood remaining in the refrigerator freezer. There really wasn't a whole lot left; Kale had not been able to purchase much this week. Billy stored everything in plastic containers and filled the shelves of the refrigerator. By the time he'd finished cooking and cleaning up, the two men had paid their fifteen dollars each and had left a measly tip for Candice which she'd been quite angry about. He had called Steph and had arranged to pick her up at five-thirty, and he'd also tried to call the marine institute several times but had gotten no answer, not even from Dave, the security guard. Billy knew Mark well enough to believe that his colleague had simply gotten so involved in his blood drop research that every other outside intrusion had been blocked by his concentration. But Dave not answering—that was a different story. It was part of Dave's responsibility, especially in the summer months when activity at the institute slowed. Billy made a mental note to stop by and check the place out while distributing the protest door hangers later that evening.

He closed and locked the door of the restaurant. Kale and Candice had left ten minutes ago. It was nearly five o'clock. He stood outside the restaurant reading the sign that Kale had created:

The Surf Side will be closed until further notice. Please keep our island in your prayers.

Sufficiently vague with a bit of helplessness mixed in. Was it the rumor of bad fish or the threat of a hurricane that had caused this restaurant to lock up? In either case, the Surf Side had closed for reasons beyond its own control. When would it reopen? Only God knew the answer.

Billy slid behind the wheel of his VW Bus and headed for the CopyKatz.

❏ ...

It was like an itch that she couldn't scratch: the feeling, the intuition, that she would not have a job by the end of the week. The feeling was that Carol had somehow taken over her position and Mitchell Bone had let her freely ride with the opportunity. He was never around the bank anymore; he'd been in his office a total of four hours since Monday. There had been no scheduled meetings beyond those with Chancey Lett. Mr. Bone just wasn't himself. Granted, he'd never been what you might call "kind" but recently he'd become "unkindly." This whole thing with the casino and the money power that came with it had turned the greedy man's head into opportunistic mush. His bank had brought in more than a half million dollars worth of business. There should be celebration. There should be pats on the backs of all the employees. There should be bonuses and time off for excellent work. But he seemed not to care. And the only one taking advantage of the situation was Carol.

So Steph made the decision at five minutes to five that she would not come in for work tomorrow. And the investor she was supposed to chauffer back to the island? Screw her. Screw Bone, screw Carol, screw this whole damned thing. She could find another job. Perhaps Billy could help. She'd waitressed herself through college; she could waitress herself until something better came about. One thing was certain though: she was not going to be pushed around any more. She was going to scratch that itch with insubordination. She'd leave the investor hanging at the airport just out of spite.

Few people remained in the bank. Stealthily, Steph dropped her three cartoon toys in a grocery store plastic bag. She added to the sack, her favorite pen, a diet book entitled *Skinny Bitch* that Misty Percy had let her borrow a month ago, and a print out of all the people who had taken out security boxes and had gained an entry into the million dollar real estate contest during the day. She thought the list might come in handy though she did not, at this time, know how. It served as a log of all those who had been in close contact with the crate in the vault and might prove to be valuable as the vote on Saturday approached.

She stood to exit, following Chester Kalimaris who drug his feet as if he'd just pulled a sixteen-hour shift, and made it to the bank's double doors before Carol spoke out from behind her. The voice was close, not more than a few feet away.

"Miss Drake," Carol groaned. Steph did not immediately turn around. She snuggled her plastic bag full of evidence closer to her side. "Miss Drake!" Steph slowly turned only partially around to the right, leaving her left side and the plastic bag unexposed.

"What is it now?" she stammered with apparent indignation.

"What's in the bag?" Carol's eyes boiled red, as if she hadn't slept in years. She pointed.

Steph's nerves kicked up several notches. "My toys," she said. "You apparently don't like them so I'm getting them out of your face."

"Give them to me." Carol took a step closer.

"I will not!" Steph took a step backward. She felt the need to run.

"I think you're a liar."

"Back off, bitch." But these were not Steph's words, though she wanted to say them. These words came from behind her. Chester came around and stood between Carol and Steph. "You've been riding Miss Drake all day long," he continued. "I don't know what's gotten into you but," he turned to acknowledge Steph, "WE don't like it. Bone's going to hear all about it, I guarantee you that."

"You're fired," Carol said to Chester.

"On what authority?" Steph had never seen Chester this angry. "You're just a simple teller."

"I'll make it happen," Carol countered.

"Well you had better bring an army because that's what it's going to take."

And just like that, Carol shut up. She smiled very widely, which was quite disturbing, but she shut up. She turned around and walked back toward the vault as Steph and Chester exited.

"Thank you," Steph said, stepping off the sidewalk and onto the asphalt parking lot.

"I don't know what's gotten into that woman," Chester replied. "Hell, I don't know what's gotten into this entire bank. Everything has gone… crazy."

"My thoughts exactly." Steph could have continued a conversation on the subject but she really didn't know Chester that well. At least she knew she wasn't the only one in the bank that was annoyed by the sudden changes.

"We'll take care of it tomorrow," Chester said and gently patted Steph's shoulder. "And for the record, I really like SpongeBob. I watch it with my kids just about every day."

Steph smiled. "Again, thanks."

Chester turned toward his car which was parked at the opposite end of the lot as Steph climbed into her Chevy Cavalier. Chester's small addition of noble fortitude had made the end of the day somehow palatable. And thank goodness for that. Had Carol gotten a hold of her bag, Steph could have been arrested for stealing confidential records.

Chester exited the parking lot ahead of her and as Steph followed his Mercedes' taillights, she saw Pedro Melindez out of the corner of her eye. He walked across the parking lot toward the front of the bank. She thought about turning around but considered the papers she'd taken from the bank and decided that giving Carol another chance was not smart. Instead, she continued on toward her Paradise Cottage apartment and an evening date with Billy Jo Presser.

❒ …

The clerk at the CopyKatz, whose name was Rachel, said she wouldn't mind distributing a hundred door hangers to the residents around the copy shop. She'd managed to print and cut 1,411 hangers which was, as she'd said, "a production record for me this summer." Billy thought that her enthusiasm to work so diligently toward the cause was based as much in her attraction toward him as it was in her passion to save the beach, perhaps more. She'd not stopped smiling from the moment he'd entered her shop.

At Pat McGee's, Bottlenose had already made a place in the surfboard museum for what he had named "The Yucatan." He'd not yet set the board on display, wanting first to polish it and create its history. Each board in the museum had some kind of history to it. Most were factual; many were based loosely on fact. The Yucatan would most likely have a plausible but totally fictitious history created for it that did not include surfing at night on red waves.

Billy had kept 311 door hangers and had distributed the rest, giving each surfer a designated island area to cover. Shana had said that she would double-up with Bottlenose but Bottlenose had reminded her that he'd have to manage the store until closing. Billy had chosen the area around the marine institute for himself and Steph.

At a little past five-thirty, Billy turned into Paradise Cottages and parked behind Steph's Cavalier in front of the cottage next to hers. Steph greeted him at the doorstep, grabbed his hand, and guided him toward his VW. Billy got the impression that she did not want him to see inside her cottage. Perhaps she'd not had the time to straighten up. Women were funny that way.

Before driving off, he saw Steph's neighbor through that cottage's front window. The woman sat at her kitchen table, her head down and resting across folded arms. She was crying.

Billy parked at the marine institute. Two other vehicles were in the lot near the front door: Mark's Jeep Wrangler and Dave's old Buick Cutlass. He left the door hangers in the VW and he and Steph entered the building. Dave was not at the front desk. Though this was not necessarily unusual (Dave could be making the rounds) his chair was flipped over and several papers, including the edition of the *South Jetty* he'd shown Billy earlier, were strewn in a mess on the desk; a few sheets of paper lay next to the toppled chair.

"Dave?" Billy shouted out. "Hey!" His voice traveled down corridors to the left and right leaving a hallow echo behind.

"What is it?" Steph asked. "Who's Dave?"

"The security guard."

Billy collected the messy papers into a pile and set the chair upright. He led Steph down the corridor to the right, trying not to alarm her though he felt alarm was of optimum concern. Through double doors and down another corridor toward the research pier, he found the wet lab door open.

"Mark?" he said to the open doorway. "Hey Mark. You in there?"

Inside the lab, Billy's feet crunched across broken glass before he found the one-legged seagull opened at the chest and pinned back to allow for examination. He knew enough about avian anatomy to understand that all of the bird's organs were not in place. Mark had apparently removed its heart.

At a second station, Billy found Mark's toxicology report on the buoy samples and reviewed each. Only minor pollutants had been recorded; nothing out of the ordinary. At the bottom of the last page, Mark had hand-written: *The Water is Safe*.

Steph stood wild-eyed beside him. "He must have left in hurry," she offered.

Billy considered this but even in haste, he could not believe that Mark would have left the lab in such disarray. "Perhaps," he said. He pointed at the reports. "Toxin tests are negative. The water is safe as far as Mark was able to find."

"That's good news," Steph said. She managed a smile though her pressed eyebrows bared concern. "Maybe he's gone to the paper."

Billy turned to her again surprised at how easily she deduced what seemed to be quite obvious. He nodded. "That makes sense. He's probably at the *South Jetty* right now. We'll stop in there as we pass out the hangers."

Billy and Steph walked at a comfortable pace; the weather was too muggy for anything expedient. Near the institute were several residential apartment complexes and some of the richer homes on this side of the island. It would take them a good hour to cover the ten square blocks. They'd unload half of the door hangers in this area alone.

Billy took one side of the street and Steph took the other. On some occasions, the occupant of the home or apartment met them at the door. Seldom, had any of those people even heard about the impending vote and its ramifications.

For forty-five minutes, they pounded the pavement, lobbied to those who would listen and slipped their cardstock hangers on doorknobs. What they didn't notice was that CrabMan, who'd gotten out of jail that morning, was following them. He lurked in whatever shadows the bright sunny day offered, emerging only after Billy and Steph moved on to the next block. His sole purpose was to remove every door hanger the two had delivered. Once in awhile, he got caught by the occupant or a neighbor and, for the most part, he'd just ignored them. But that was not the case with the owner of the house on 25 Cotter Avenue. That man got all bent out of shape and

CrabMan had to put him down. Crab's strength had grown immensely in the past twenty-four hours; he'd not really tried to break the guy's jaw but it had been so easy. One right cross and the owner had fallen backward into his home. Crab had simply pushed his legs inside and had closed the door. He'd be long gone by the time the man woke up and called the police. But even the police would not stop him. Not any more. In fact, the police were busy on the other end of town doing the very same thing behind Billy's surfer buddies though there had been no occasion when any occupant of any resident had needed to be silenced as Mr. 25 Cotter Avenue had. People trusted the police, right? No one would question an officer's intent to remove "garbage" from doorknobs.

With about a hundred hangers remaining, Billy and Steph came across the *South Jetty* building. Kilpatrick was not there and the rude receptionist told them that she didn't even know who Mark Walker was.

"I don't believe her," Billy said as they left and walked toward the next section of residences.

Steph stopped suddenly and pointed. "Hey. Isn't that Crab…what's his name?" Billy followed her finger. "He just ducked behind the newspaper building."

"Are you talking about CrabMan?" Billy clarified.

"Yeah. The guy who tried to stab you last night. He was right there."

Billy handed his short stack of door hangers to Steph and told her to stay where she was. The idea of being followed unnerved him, especially if the follower was someone who had tried to slash him with the point of a nail.

Slowly, he walked thirty yards to the front side of the *South Jetty* building and stealthily craned his head around the back corner. He found nothing more than a few broken wooden pallets sitting within an overgrowth of seagrass and weeds. He looked back in the direction where Steph still stood and raised his arms in confusion. At that moment the *South Jetty* receptionist appeared, seemingly out of nowhere. She stood between his line of vision with Steph, hands behind her back, her black, thick horned-rimmed glasses slightly askew.

"What the hell do you want anyway?" she hissed. "I told you. No one is here. If you keep poking around, I'm gonna have to break your arm."

Billy shook his head but not because he intended it as any kind of acknowledgement. It was purely involuntary; a shake of disbelief. Had she really just said that? Didn't she really mean to say that she was going to call the cops? She stood five-foot-nothing and probably couldn't break the lead in the point of a pencil if she tried. But break his arm?

Steph was yelling something at him.

Cat?

Hat?

She's got a hat?

No. What Steph was trying to tell him was that this crazy woman had a *bat*, which she now produced from behind her back: a 35-ounce aluminum Louisville Slugger. Before Billy could say a word, she swung for his forearm, missed, and landed the head of the bat against the brick face of the *South Jetty*. The force was so great that a spray of brick chips and dust peppered Billy's bare legs and arms. She'd made a fist-sized divot in the wall and dented the bat.

"Jesus…" Billy moaned and quickly stammered backward.

"Even He ain't gonna help you now, Presser," the tiny receptionist snarled and swung the bat again, missing his head this time by only a few inches. Wind whirred by at incredible bat speed.

And just as suddenly as the receptionist had appeared from the building, Steph was there with a two-by-four. She swung the lumber hard and fast as the receptionist lifted the bat high above her head in an axe-chopping motion. The bat flew from her hands and ricocheted off the wall. A clear, sharp cracking noise accompanied the lumber's impact with the woman's swing. Either the board had broken or the receptionist's arm had. Steph dropped the two-by-four as Billy grabbed her hand and both of them ran from the building and the receptionist whose arm had already swelled with a deep purple bruise. When they reached the spot where Steph had dropped the door hangers, both turned in unison. The receptionist was gone. Gulf breeze had scattered several of the hangers and she and Billy collected them. "What in God's name is going on around here?" she said, gasping slightly from the exertion of the run.

"It's not just me then." Billy brushed the sand from his door hangers.

"What do you mean?" Steph, again, looked toward the *South Jetty* newspaper building before following Billy toward the next block of residences.

"I've lived on this island for more than two years now and I've seen some crazy shit." He hesitated, hoping that Steph did not mind his choice of words. "Like last year when the Spring Breakers went bonkers on the beach, flipped a couple of cars over and set them on fire. They had to bring the riot police in for that. The next day they pulled a car from the channel with four teenagers in it. Witnesses said that beer cans were floating all around their dead faces. We even had an axe-murderer living here up until the end of last fall. The loon had chopped up his family in Vermont then had decided to take a permanent vacation on our island. He would have never been caught had the murderer not videotaped the entire slaughter. And then of course there's the occasional drug runner that gets nabbed offshore and a whale or two that have beached themselves on the south end of the island." Billy noticed the concerned frown on Steph's face and continued. "But you've got to understand. A place like Port Aransas is meant for those who want to get away from it all. Civilization as they've found it just doesn't cut it anymore. They come to the island for its peace and tranquility, for its wonderful Texas hospitality, to dream, to get away from the doldrums of life and the despicable people they've found in it. Unfortunately, a place to escape from rote living also attracts wayward transients. Port A is perfect for those that want to hide from their pasts, be they good or bad."

"Is that why you came to the island?"

"Yeah."

"And what were you escaping from?"

Billy stopped. He looked directly into Steph's eyes and said, "I'm not a bad person. I just couldn't live in a city that rewards achievements in intellectual theft and bribery."

Steph smiled. "I know that…I mean, I know you're a good person. It's in your eyes."

Billy returned the smile then continued walking. "But ever since that Chancey Lett fellow came to this island, everything seems…you know… off."

"I've gotten that same feeling," Steph said. "That receptionist back there. She reminded me a lot of Carol. Just kind of whacked out. Like someone took away their true personalities and replaced them with…" Billy stared in anticipation. "I don't know. Like something programmed. Like they've been replaced by robots. And there's more."

"More?"

Steph looked at the door hangers in her hand. "Come on," she said. "We're never going to get these things done. I'll try to explain as we finish up."

Steph recounted her day at the bank in small chunks. It seemed to Billy that she could not find all the right words in one long explanation and needed the breaks supplied by their distribution of door hangers to each side of the street. Each time they'd covered a block and came back together, Steph would add more to her story until, finally, when all the door hangers had been distributed and they had returned to the marine institute, she'd told him everything. From her encounter with Lett, Carol and the bodyguard inside the vault to Carol's cursed outburst, to the hypnotic way each new account holder exited the vault after Carol had taken them inside, to her decision to surf instead of work, she tried to explain what she meant by "controlled" and "robotic."

"I don't blame you for not wanting to return to such a situation," Billy said, wiping fresh sweat from his forehead. "Now I've got a bit of a confession to make to you."

But before he could tell her about Shoe and how he was using the starfish to record evidence which would substantiate Steph's claims, security guard Dave's Buick Cutlass suddenly roared to life. The two of them stood at the entrance to the marine institute's parking lot as the car sped past, bottoming out as it exited the lot and turned onto the street. Dave was driving but ignored them, instead staring straight ahead as if every motion was programmed, as if he too had become what Steph had termed "robotic."

◻ …

Billy decided to take the beach road back to her place. Coincidentally, it was at about this same time yesterday that they were on this same stretch of sand but had been driving in the opposite direction toward the luau.

What a difference a day made.

She'd been so excited just twenty-four hours ago. She'd had a job. She'd had growing friendships with people to whom Billy had introduced her. She'd felt the spark of romance and of desire that she'd not experienced since leaving college. She'd ridden imaginary waves to imaginary stars and had felt on top of a world that she could control.

But control was the last word she'd use to describe her emotions now. Nothing, really, made much sense. Hell, she'd carried on a conversation with a bunch of children's toys—how much more absurd could you get?

A woman trying to use Billy's head for baseball practice?

And how about Carol? If you wanted a definition for absurd, you could stop right there. And wasn't it absurd that she, Stephanie Drake, a woman who'd graduated in the top ten percent of her college class and had been voted most likely to succeed, had even contemplated ditching work for pleasure let alone had decided to go through with it? Work had become absurd. The people she worked for had become absurd. Residents of the island had become absurd. Really, the only sane thing left was Billy. Thank God for Billy.

Shortly after Dave the security guard had nearly run them over, they'd gone back inside the institute, again looking for Mark. Dave's desk had been as they'd left it, but the broken glass had been cleaned up from the lab and all of Mark's toxicology results had been missing. Even the one-legged bird that had been dissected (and had turned Steph's stomach upon seeing it) had been removed. Billy had assumed that Mark had returned to the lab and guessed that he'd probably taken off for Corpus where the media was more influential.

Rays of waning sunlight peppered her legs as she absently gazed at the only thing that currently made sense to her. Billy's silhouette filled her with protective comfort, as if he were the eye of the storm, a harbor in the tempest. He did not smile. His furled eyebrows denoted a man whose mind moved in calculated complexity, as if he was trying to answer some unwieldy equation or solve a complex mystery.

"I've infiltrated the bank," he said after a long stretch of silence.

Steph shifted in the seat toward him. "What do you mean?"

"Well, you know how much I trust that Vegas fellow and Mitchell Bone."

"Like, zero?"

"Yeah, even lower." He mustered a quick grin. "I figured that if I could get some evidence, any evidence, that would undermine their attempts to destroy our beaches and bring in the sloth of people a casino would attract, it would be worth the chance of being caught. Hell, if the casino comes in, the island will change and I'd lose everything anyway. Instead of the peaceful tranquility I talked about earlier, this island would become the place that people would want to leave, myself included."

"So you broke into the bank?"

"Not exactly. I am…or was before I left MIT…a roboticist—a creator of mechanical toys if you will."

Steph remembered the table in Billy's apartment and the tiny parts that rested on it.

"I used you," Billy said and lightly blushed. "And I apologize. But your desk is right in the middle of everything. It provided great camouflage. And it was the best vantage point for Shoe."

"Shoe?" Steph's mind raced with visions of robotic sneakers.

"My starfish robot. He's attached to the side of your desk. I got him in via the drive-through tubes. He's equipped with audio and video capture devices. Any suspicious thing Bone does within Shoe's perimeter, Shoe will record."

Steph tried to remember everything she'd said and done in the past few days. Had Shoe recorded her, too? She suddenly felt embarrassed and intruded upon. A small hint of anger that began to unease her mind was quashed when Billy added, "There's something wrong about that bank. That crate in the vault. Whatever it is, it is not what Lett or Bone or anyone else claims it to be."

"I thought I was loosing my mind," Steph said. "I've felt its…"

"Power," Billy finished.

Steph thought about that for a moment. Power. The power to attract and repel at the same time. The power to invade the subconscious. The power to turn people into controlled, robotic drones. But that was ridiculous, wasn't it?

"How?" Steph said. "Why?"

"I don't know. At first I thought perhaps Lett was running narcotics and using the bank as a distribution channel. I thought that I'd been affected by whatever drugs were in the crate—yesterday when I came to see you, to check out the security box." He paused for a moment then confirmed exactly what Steph was thinking. "And yes, that was just a ploy to get into the vault. Again, my apologies."

"So what do we do now?"

"Shoe has limited energy life so I've been a bit selective in turning him on, but given all of the information you told me earlier, I'm certain that tonight should be a good opportunity to move him closer to the vault, to get a better angle of the crate. Perhaps I'll get lucky and there will be some after-hours activity worth recording as well."

"I wish you could get the robot into the vault. That's where the real action is taking place."

"A starfish would look a little out of place in such a sterile environment, even if the vault door was left open over night. Luckily, much of the bank has the Sea Life theme running through it. Shoe mixes in quite well. I'm thinking the teller window closest to the vault should give me a good angle once the vault is opened tomorrow."

"That's Carol's window. That'll be perfect." Steph thought of all the juicy tidbits the robot could record from that vantage. "Can you fill me in tomorrow?"

"Mix business with pleasure?"

"If you get what you—what *we* hope to get, business will be pleasure."

Billy turned from the beach road onto Paradise Lane, drove past several new construction projects and parked in front of Steph's paradise cottage. He walked Steph to her front door. "I'll pick you up around, say eight-thirty-ish?" Billy said.

Steph nodded and kissed him on the cheek. She peered deeply into his brown eyes. "We're going to get through this. We'll figure it out. And the island will return to some kind of sanity."

"*We* will," Billy said and left.

Before Steph entered her cottage, she noticed that her new neighbor had poked her head outside her front door. The woman looked to be in her mid-fifties. Her face was emotionally twisted in what Steph thought was a combination of sadness and fear, the ashen cheeks wet as if she'd been crying for hours.

"Hello…" Steph said but the woman quickly ducked back inside and closed her door.

◻ …

Billy felt apprehensive about how much information he'd given up to Steph. Really, how well did he know her? Was it so wise to admit a felonious crime, especially a crime committed at her place of employment? She was the bank manager's personal secretary. She was *that* close to someone who could put him away for life, if not longer.

She'd revealed herself. Her revelations had threads within his own disbeliefs. They shared a common crazy enigma. But could he believe her? Did he believe her? Did he have a choice? The proof was in the pudding, as the old saying went. And he was going to prove something one way or another.

His VW sat in the very same parking spot he'd parked in three nights before. It was nine o'clock. The Treasure Trove lot was nearly empty, providing no inconspicuous cover, but the bank was not vacant. A black Hummer, a grey Mercedes and a white Ford Ranger dotted with lots of rust were parked in the handicap spots nearest the front door. He knew the owners of all three vehicles and questioned whether he'd be able to accomplish his primary goal: to stealthily move Shoe from Steph's desk to the teller window closest to the vault. The night, however, would certainly not be a total loss, not with Lett, Bone and the woman whom Steph hated named Carol inside. Shoe could certainly steal some valuable info from them.

When Billy snapped on the computer console, ten seconds elapsed before the RF transmitter connected to Shoe's receiver. Five seconds later, the first video image scribbled black and white across one of the station's two monitors.

Again, a horizon of perception appeared. Closest to Steph's desk, the top two-thirds of two empty chairs was visible. Beyond the chairs, most of the last two teller windows, all of the vault door and a truncation of Bone's and Kalimaris' office doors were shown in panoramic pixels.

Black and white scan lines temporarily blurred the video images as a block of RF interference suddenly passed between Shoe and Billy. When the blur reassembled, Billy saw Lett, his bodyguard, Bone and Carol. Their knees came into view first and as they neared the vault he saw each clearly. He snapped on the console's audio system.

"...can't keep using the bank like this," Bone was saying. "This is my bank, dammit! Our deal did not include such indiscretion." Billy turned up the volume.

"A half a million dollars, Mitch," Lett replied. "I made you half a mill."

"What about Alixel?" Bone said. "She's as big a part of this. You seem to have forgotten her. I've certain promises...to you...to her."

Carol intervened. "It's time you made a choice, Mitch. Are you with us or against us?"

"She'll be here tomorrow," Bone continued as the four of them entered the vault. The door remained open though Billy could not see them or the crate inside. Voices became mumbled, incomprehensible.

And then one, sharp exclamation erupted.

"NO!"

The shriek was squeaky high, the sound of a woman's scream from a man's throat.

Almost simultaneously, a gray aura of pixels spread from the right side of the screen. Billy knew that later, when he reviewed the recorded video on the color monitor at home, the gray glow would reveal its real crimson color.

Lett's bodyguard appeared in the vault's doorway from the left, disappeared to the right then reappeared, pushing the glowing crate toward the left.

Another girly burly scream erupted, this time causing the speakers in Billy's computer console to crackle.

"SHIT!"

About thirty seconds elapsed in silence. Only the gray, pixilated, undulating glow was visible. To Billy, it was like watching an Alfred Hitchcock film interspersed with an intentional director's pause to build tension. And he felt himself fortunate and unfortunate all at the same time. Having a color monitor would have made what he saw next horrifically realistic.

He clearly remembered how gruesome the black blood running from Janet Leigh's body to the shower drain had appeared. He'd been only twelve when he saw *Psycho* for the first time. Even in black and white (or more appropriately, because it *was* in black and white) the violence of the shower scene had been, up until that time in his young life, the most disturbing thing he'd ever witnessed.

But this was different. What he now saw was real. The black drool that leaked across the floor into the vault's doorway from the left was, without question, blood. It flowed slowly, its thick viscosity, clumpy. And the grey glow that most certainly emanated from the crate within, spread outward, seemingly magnified by the increasing blood flow.

And then Mitchell Bone's head rolled into view. Everything scary from the pubescent memory of Janet Leigh and Anthony Perkins was forever dashed. When a hand appeared in the doorway from the left, snatched the head as if it were a deformed basketball and crushed it, Billy fell off of his stool wondering about his own sanity. Something was terribly wrong with Shoe, he thought. Its video eyeball was malfunctioning. What he just saw could not be real. Something had intercepted the RF signal and was feeding him cinematic Hitchcock propaganda.

He rolled onto his knees, never taking an eye from the monitor, flooded with self-denial.

That's when the bodyguard's face filled the monitor. The video started to shake as Shoe was plucked from the side of Steph's desk.

"You're next," the bodyguard said.

Then the monitor went black.

His mind raced. Visions spun. He was certain he was, again, hallucinating. Memories of false images from yesterday raced forward. Gunshots. Someone telling him to "Shut the fuck up." He was nauseous.

He was puking. And then there was the red tide, incredible waves, and a surfer who rode a board made from the rarest of woods. Birds with one leg screeched in sudden death—*but that had been real, hadn't it*? Fish boiled in blood bubbled to the Gulf surface at his feet—*but that had not been imagination, right*?

Then there was CrabMan. And that crazy bitch from the *South Jetty* who'd tried to take his head off. That *had* been real. The bat had missed his head by inches and if it hadn't been for Officer Keadle, CrabMan's crude nail weapon certainly would have planted deep into his flesh.

Was he going mad?

And then there came a knocking. He grabbed his head between both hands.

But the knocking only grew louder.

He wanted to scream but could hardly breathe.

Knocking. Between his hands. Within his head.

"Anyone in there?"

Billy quickly removed his hands from his head, looking at his palms as if they'd just spoken.

"Hey!"

The driver's side door of the VW deflected inward as three more short, pounding knocks assaulted exterior metal. The door handle was yanked but he'd locked it. It was Officer Keadle.

Billy slipped belly flat to the floor and snugged up against the shadows behind the passenger seat. A flashlight beam wandered through the windshield, probed the inside like a stage spotlight looking for an actor. The monitor above him was still on but it now only revealed blackness. The light beam disappeared; silence took its place. Then the crunch of shoe on gravel moved toward him.

Bang! Bang! Bang! came Keadle's fist again, this time right beside him. Billy almost yelped.

"Presser! Hey, Presser!"

The flashlight beam reappeared, probed near his feet, crawled across the floor toward his head, stopped momentarily then went out. The passenger side door handle was tried but he'd locked it too. He'd locked all the doors, including the rear hatch which was now handled without success. A full minute later, Billy heard Keadle open and close a car door. An engine revved. Tires crunched gravel. Headlights passed through the windshield, briefly lighting the VW's interior before exiting the Treasure Trove parking lot.

Slowly, Billy rose from the floor, peered beyond the passenger seat and through the windshield. The Big Texas Bank and three cars were in the distance, their shadowy outlines visible under two street lamps and the quarter moon. Keadle was gone.

He decided to wait a few more minutes, just in case the VW was being watched. So he sat in the driver's seat, keys in the ignition, waiting for heartbeats pounding against his ears to subside, waiting for his intuition to signal it was safe, waiting for fear to dissipate.

But none of that ever happened. In fact, his heart now nearly exploded, his fear culminating toward a plateau that would be hard to step down from. Everything was not okay nor would it ever be again.

From inside the bank a dull crimson glow emanated through two sets of windows. Red halos around the panes were interrupted by several short blasts of bright white, as if someone was shooting photographs with a gigantic flash bulb.

And then the bodyguard suddenly appeared in the window to the right, his tall, wide silhouette outlined by the crimson glow behind him. Billy couldn't see his eyes from this distance but he knew the man stared straight at him.

You're next, he'd said.

Maybe not, Billy thought. Maybe I have all the evidence I need. Bone had been murdered and Shoe had sent the recorded signals to his computer. Billy was afraid, but he was also confident. The mixture made him nauseous.

He shot the bodyguard his middle finger then drove off with fear and courage fighting for control of his stomach…and soul.

☐ …

Janine's nightmares had become reality. They had followed her from Kansas to Texas. And she'd been crying ever since Joel had left her more than eight hours ago. Her new cottage apartment had been a blur. Thankfully, the former tenant had left a full roll of toilet paper in the bathroom. More than half of it was now gone. Matted wads lay on the bed beside her; several others were scattered on the carpeted floor. Still more were on the kitchen table where she'd done most of her crying.

The medical doctors and psychiatrists had told her that none of it had been real, except for the part about the barn exploding. Dynamite had not been stored properly, they'd said. The explosion had taken the life of the man she'd claimed to have had a "magic dagger." That man had been an imposter. The real Professor Cower had been found murdered in his upstate New York home; he'd been stabbed repeatedly through the heart.

The dynamite had also taken the life of her son. No one had eaten anyone. The psychiatrists had been particularly concerned about this part of her psychosis. They'd been incapable of actually visualizing such a gruesome scene let alone considering that it had been real. People just didn't eat people, they'd told her. People just didn't eat themselves. How could they? It didn't make sense. It wasn't logical, and if it wasn't logical, how could it have been real? At least that's the argument they'd made.

As for Albert Stine and the thing she called a Cubit, they'd found no trace of him or the box in the rubble. The doctors had reasoned that they'd simply been evaporated. Anything too close to an explosion that large would disintegrate, they'd said.

But those logical, well-reasoned, highly educated men and women had been wrong. They'd kept her in the hospital under "close observation" for three months before releasing her to friend Beth Blandford. And for what? To convince her that her reality was all in her mind, that she was living in a nightmare from which she could not wake up? Damn those people. Damn their accusations. Damn them for making her partially accept their own false reasoning. She'd started to believe that, just perhaps, it had all been her mind's way of explaining the loss of those closest to her. She'd haphazardly stored the dynamite and her carelessness had caused their deaths, they'd said. It had been all her fault but her mind had denied it with such an elaborate story as to make her appear insane. Once she'd accepted the diagnosis, basically admitting that she'd inadvertently caused the deaths of three people, they'd let her go. She would not be arrested. There would be no trial. That was part of the deal. Sixth months of probation in the care of Beth Blandford had been her penalty. There hadn't been a court in the country that would have convicted her of anything based on the lack of evidence but she could no longer sustain a life in bed under doctors' microscopes. So she'd signed the paper.

They'd been wrong, of course. The snot wads around her were evidence.

She was afraid to go to sleep and now wished that she'd had enough courage to ask Joel to stay with her. A Christian woman didn't do such things though. But God made concessions for frightened Christian women, didn't he? If God had again placed Stine in her path then he must have also provided for her protection.

Marcy?

Joel?

Her eyes now red and swollen with misery fluttered. Fear kept them open. Fatigue closed them. Bare bedroom walls and the mirror that sat on the furnished bedroom dresser flashed on and off until fatigue finally won.

It didn't take long for the real nightmares to return. Albert and the Cubit sat atop a huge pile of sand. Behind them, clouds blacker than oil whirled in anger. Bolts of lighting skittered and clashed. Around Albert, sprawled out in the hundreds at the foot of the sand pile were dead people. She knew one of them, Marcy. And half way up the sand pile, lying dead on his back with a stiff hand reaching for Albert's leg was Joel. His skin was charred as if struck by lightening.

"Rise," the Albert thing said. "Rise and join me my dear, sweet wife."

The Cubit began to glow. Crimson light flooded the star at the top edge of its wooden surface. Slowly, its lid lifted on hinges that weren't there. A bolt of lighting careened into the opening as if the Cubit had pulled it, unwanting, inside. Dark, bloody crimson grew in a giant halo and from within it rose a figure dressed in a black wedding gown, its face turned away toward the ocean. The black lace was shredded at the hem. Patches had been ripped from the arms and neckline. Something red drooled haphazardly, as if an artist had flicked brushes full of paint across the gown's surface. When the figure stepped from the Cubit it turned. Janine's own face stared back at her, the cheeks sunken, the teeth gone. And the Cubit slammed shut.

This brought her out of the nightmare screaming. Someone was pounding on her cottage door. She jammed the bed sheet in her mouth to stifle her cries.

"Hey!" the door-pounder yelled.

It was the Albert thing. It had come to take her away. It had come to make her part of its dead world. It had come to make her its wife. She bit down hard on the bed sheet. Blood sprouted from her lip.

"You all right in there?" the pounder yelled.

She wanted to hide but there was no place that the Albert thing could not find her: in Kansas, in Texas, under her bed, it didn't matter.

And then the door opened. She'd forgotten to lock it. Why had she forgotten to lock it? Dear God!

"Ma'am," the voice said from beyond the open bedroom door. "You in there?"

The shadows of the approaching visitor, stretched into the bedroom's doorway. A board creaked. It was all she could do to keep the scream down.

But it wasn't the Albert thing. It wasn't even a man. Had she not been so panicked, had she not just awakened, screaming from another nightmare, she would have heard the soft voice of a concerned woman. It was her neighbor. It was the woman who'd waved at her earlier in the day.

But the revelation was too much for the scattered remnants of logic to comprehend. Reality and nightmare were one in the same.

And she fainted.

□ ...

Just after midnight, they massed a hundred strong within the bank. The Cubit had been efficiently busy. Each of the contest entrants, those that had entered the vault with Carol during the day and had been introduced to the seamless, wooden crate inside, now stood in cubited glory—like drones. Like robots. Each understood its task. Just as the cubited Mitchell Bone had "recycled" the real Mitchell Bone, so too would each of these new Port Aransas residents. By the time Saturday rolled around, the cubits would act pretty much like their human counterparts, except of course, when it came time to vote. All cubits would vote one way.

That's how Albert Stine had planned it. The influential would vote for the casino. The influential would influence others to vote for the casino. The vote would pass and the bulldozers and backhoes would get busy. The ancient treasure would be uncovered. The final piece would be in his grasp. The beginning of the end of the world was only days away.

The crimson glow from the Cubit faded as Professor Nelson crawled from its depths. He was the last for this evening and like all those that had emerged before him, he looked and acted as if he'd risen from the dead—which was not far from the truth. He assembled in ragged disarray, stumbling over one of Stephanie Drake's customer chairs, as he moved toward the front of the bank.

Without a word, Stine opened the bank's double doors and the walking dead spilled out into the parking lot. Some stumbled and fell, a comical sight for Chancey Lett who, after all, was the only human in the bunch and therefore was the only one with a sense of humor.

In the distance, Stine saw four cubits enter Officer Keadle's cruiser which sped off toward the south end of town. Noel Kilpatrick also arrived with a van that held fifteen cubits. His receptionist was with him. A half a dozen got into Stine's black Hummer, seven stumbled into the bed of Carol's Ford Ranger, but none got into Bone's Mercedes. The cubited Bone could not drive yet. Such a complicated skill, like so many others, would be acquired over the next day or so.

The rest of the cubits lurched and staggered into the dark shadows around street corners en route to recycle their human counterparts. Within twenty minutes, only Lett and Bone remained. They reentered the bank; the cubits had left quite a mess, especially in the vault where its sterile interior remained splattered by the cubited bank manager's feeding on bone and flesh.

PART II

A DAY AT THE BEACH

At 3:35 a.m. Thursday morning, the NOAA upgraded Hurricane Antiago to Category 3. Antiago had left the Yucatán coastline off of Merida and had entered the Gulf shortly after two o'clock. A Category 3 hurricane in the Gulf during June was not unusual. What was odd, which Jim Cantore reiterated during the early morning Weather Channel broadcasts, was that in less than thirty minutes the storm's sustained winds had gone from a hundred to a hundred and thirty miles per hour, a rarity unmatched in the history of the tropics, especially since the hurricane's diameter was less than fifty miles across. Stranger still was that Antiago had made an abrupt turn of nearly ninety degrees, a dogleg to the west that set it on course for the southern Texas coastline. Cantore made the comment that it was as if Antiago had suddenly connected with some invisible Texas magnet. And because everything in Texas was big, he joked that a magnet from the Lone Star state might just be large enough to have caused such a sudden shift.

For the fishing industries around Port Aransas the idea of a hurricane slamming into them was far from funny. The industry had already suffered from a massive fish kill that was yet to be explained. A hurricane would certainly decimate what was left. But the wrath of Mother Nature was nothing compared to the terrible evil that was slowly transforming the people of Port A. Reports of screams had come into the police dispatcher throughout the night. There had been at least twenty calls and Officer Keadle had been sent to respond to each.

After sunrise, another twenty or so witnesses stopped by the *South Jetty* with stories ranging from worrisome, to outlandish, to horrific. The newspaper receptionist recorded each with a smile and told each storyteller that publisher Kilpatrick would review their accounts for possible publication as soon as he returned. "Look for your story in Monday's edition," she lied to each resident.

Around the same time that Billy Jo Presser's alarm sounded Thursday morning, a flatbed tractor-trailer rolled onto the beach close to where the *Knights in White Satin* had entertained luau guests two nights before. The red lettering on the Kenworth cab read: *Reed's Excavation*. Chained to the lowboy was a Caterpillar backhoe.

Billy dressed and headed out the door. Minutes later he stopped next to the trailerless Kenworth on Alister Street a mile from Paradise Cottages. The lettering on the cab's door made him think of the impending vote Saturday. He glared at the Kenworth driver as if the driver was the sole reason for the mayhem that had turned a wonderful island getaway into a trap from which everyone could not get away from fast enough. Billy had not meant to scowl, but he did; it was a menacing scowl, a threatening scowl, one that tested the Kenworth driver's patience. When the light changed, the driver flipped off Billy then spun eight of the Kenworth's ten tires which bolted the cab from the light.

Car horns blared behind him while Billy continued staring at the space emptied by the screeching truck cab, but he paid them no attention. He couldn't. His mind was too engaged with visions of *his* beach, with hills of excavated sand and scooped-out holes. Huge machines surrounded him with metal teeth and ribbed feet, and at the center of the mayhem was the bodyguard. He stood directing the destruction, his hands to the sky, a black storm boiling behind him.

"Asshole!" a passing driver yelled. This shook Billy from trance. When he looked up the light had already changed back to red. A black Hummer pulled up beside him but he couldn't see beyond its tinted windows. Again, the light turned green and again the car horns blared from behind. The Hummer's window slowly lowered.

"Hi cutie," the girl in the passenger seat said. "You want to join us?" the driver added. Both girls giggled then the Hummer peeled away.

It was as if he was back in Cambridge taking a test or engaged in research. Once his mind locked it was hard to disengage. Like a computer stuck within an exponential equation, his brain could not stop its processes until some answer was complete. But these thoughts had no solutions, at least none that would enable him to keep his head.

Billy blinked and shook his head then finally set the VW in motion.

❒ …

When Billy pulled up to the curb outside her cottage apartment, Steph was rubbing Janine's temples. The two women stood together on the narrow lawn.

"How can I ever thank you enough?" Janine repeated. Steph had stayed with her until she had fallen asleep just four hours ago. Circles of exhaustion rang both of the women's eyes. Steph pushed stray gray strands away from Janine's forehead.

"You go on now and get ready," Steph said, smiling. "You and Joel are going to have a great time." She turned toward the VW and waved at Billy. "Are you sure you don't want a ride? Billy won't mind."

Janine grabbed one of Steph's hands and gently massaged it. "You've done enough," she said. "Besides, a morning trolley ride into town might just be what the doctor ordered."

Steph, who was a couple of inches taller than Janine, bent forward and kissed her forehead, turned without another word, walked briskly to Billy's VW and got in. She waved from the window as Billy drove off.

Janine had found a third friend, but more importantly, her neighbor had found her—screaming in the night, paralyzed with fear. She'd found her and they'd talked, and she'd stayed there until Janine had finally fallen asleep.

Janine had said nothing about seeing Albert. How could she? A stranger could never understand. So, instead of telling her neighbor that a dead man—who ate people and had killed her son—was in Port Aransas and would soon kill her too, and instead of telling her that Albert would probably kill anyone even obscurely close to her, all she'd said was that she'd had a really bad dream. And she had. She'd become the demon's wife.

Miss Drake (Steph, she preferred to be called) must have wondered how any nightmare could make a person shake so intensely or why nearly a full roll of toilet paper lay in scattered wads throughout the kitchen and bedroom, but she'd asked no such thing. Steph had brought her a glass of water, had combed Janine's hair and had placed a damp washcloth on her forehead, and had repeated, "Everything is going to be okay. Everything is going to be okay." Steph was cut from the same good people stuff that Marcy was, the same Paradise Island hospitality. The same care. And Janine felt fortunate that God had chosen her new friends so purposefully.

The thought of Marcy reminded her that she'd left her "sacks of life" in the fortune teller's guest bedroom. She'd been so frazzled after seeing Albert that she'd not even considered them on the trolley home with Joel. The same clothes that she'd worn to the Surf Side were now heavily wrinkled and damp with tears (particularly in the cleavage hem of her blouse). She'd need to stop at Marcy's on her way in to town.

Janine slipped Marcy's scrunchie on her head, brushed what wrinkles she could from her blouse and shorts, and pulled her cottage apartment door closed. She twisted the knob to check that it was locked. The smell of Volkswagen exhaust still lingered as she set out for the trolley stop at the end of the road.

It was a quarter past eight when she boarded Thursday's first trolley run.

"Welcome back aboard," the driver said, though Janine did not remember him from the previous day. When she offered him the dollar fare, the driver waved his hand. He was a small man with a small face. His age appeared close to hers. "You can get a monthly pass that will save you at least fifteen bucks."

Janine looked at the bill, turned it over in her hand to see if something like snot or tears was awash on its surface. She noticed a curious look from the passenger sitting three rows behind the driver. "Okay," Janine said. "But the fair today is one dollar. That's all I have."

The driver suddenly blushed with embarrassment. "No, no," he said, now waving both hands. "I don't mean to be a salesman. I just thought, ya know, being new to the island and all, you just didn't know."

Janine smiled, her wall of suspicion crumbling.

"Carl," the woman three rows back exclaimed. "Can we get going already? You know I have to be at the docks by eight-thirty. Hands on the wheel please." The twenty-something woman scowled at Janine.

Janine handed the bill to Carl. "Thank you," she said. "I'll take your advice when I get to town." She walked past the dock lady without looking at her and sat in the very rear of the trolley. A young boy, no more than ten years old, sat unescorted two rows up to the left. His attention was connected to the white iPod earplugs stuck into both ears. His head bobbed to the digital, pre-teen beats.

She stepped from the trolley ten minutes later, and stood a block from Marcy's shop. The boy with the iPod exited the trolley with her, paying little attention to anything except the beat between his ears. Janine walked the short distance and when she stopped and turned to climb the three-step rise to the shop's front door, the iPod kid ran right into her, nearly knocking her down.

"Hey!" she exclaimed, rubbing her shoulder. The iPod kid did not look up but instead continued staring at the sidewalk, his head bopping, a tiny bead of Texas sun sweat trickling across his forehead. "Pay attention to where you're going."

The iPod kid took two more steps and his head stopped bopping. He stood there, motionless, as if his feeble brain could not continue without the accompaniment of digital juice. She was less than a dozen feet from him when he looked up with a bewildered expression, one often found on the face of habitual sleepwalkers who've awakened in places far away from the bedroom. He turned toward Janine.

She gasped, took a shuffled step backward, tripped on Marcy's first step and fell into a sitting position onto the third. Something swirled within the iPod kid's eyes. Pools of crimson and silver sparkles, filled with stupidity and intelligence—repelling and attracting all in the same instant. They were Albert's eyes in the face of a ten-year-old boy. The morning's warmth did nothing to prevent the vertebrae-freezing chill that raced to the back of Janine's head.

The iPod kid stared as if he didn't comprehend, like a little boy who'd seen a toad for the first time, had found a sudden attraction for such a little boy thing, and was considering what to do about his newfound discovery. Then, like an automaton, the iPod kid resumed his position on the sidewalk, not looking at Janine but instead again at the sidewalk. She heard the beat of a new song throbbing from the earplugs. The iPod kid's head resumed its beat-throbbing movement and he continued along the sidewalk, not stopping at the next intersection where a car patiently waited for him to cross, then turned in the direction of the beach.

Of course she'd imagined it.

Right?

A lingering aftereffect of last night's dream.

Right?

Something that the doctors in the psycho ward would have called residual dementia.

How could a person eat themselves, one of the doctors had said. That's just not logical. And if it isn't logical it didn't happen.

How could the iPod kid have the Albert-thing's eyes? It wasn't logical.

So, it didn't happen.

She slowly rose, rubbed the soreness in her shoulder and butt cheeks, turned to the front door and knocked. Knocked again. And again. She desperately wanted to change. Beyond presenting herself to Joel as unkept, the clothes she wore were battered memories of last night's fight against logic.

She twisted the knob and found it locked. Moving around to the back of the shop, she approached the back door while looking around to see if others were watching. She remembered that this door opened into the kitchen and that Marcy had said she usually kept it unlocked. It was.

"Hello," she whispered then raised her voice. "Hello?"

When no one answered she entered the kitchen then climbed the steps toward the guest bedroom, found her two sacks of life where she'd left them on the bed, opened one, and spilled its contents. Folded blouses, shirts, and shorts unraveled into a pile on the bed. She shook the sack to release a book which dropped on top of the clothes. Etched into its red, back cover was the image of the magic dagger.

The book was all that she'd salvaged from the piles of her former life. After being released from the psycho ward, she'd convinced Beth Blandford to take her back to Pickett's Crossing just one more time. The doctors had demanded that Beth do no such thing. They'd said that if Janine ever returned to the cause of her dementia they'd have no choice but to try her on manslaughter charges for the death of her son. They wanted to protect her, they'd said. But what they hadn't said was their real, illogical reason: They didn't want such an experience to tip her psychopathic scales in the direction of murder. And Beth would be her first victim.

Among the heaping piles of weed-overgrown barn, cars, house, dirt, and corn, Janine had found the book jammed into the vacant hole of a tree she'd dynamited near the barn years ago. Investigators had never recovered the book; it had been hidden two feet deep. So what had led her to it? What had made her stick her arm into a space that no human had a right to do so? Perhaps it was because within five minutes of exiting Beth's car, she'd tripped and had landed within a foot of the hole and had *heard* it—a nearly inaudible hum.

But that was illogical. Books didn't hum.

And then the depths of the hole had begun to glow, taunting her residual dementia, testing the reasoning of logical doctors. *And if it was illogical, it did not happen.*

Beth had seen nothing, of course. And when Janine had stuck her arm in and had pulled out the book, Beth had asked her why she'd stashed it there. *It's my personal diary*, she'd lied. Something so sacred as a widow's diary could never be questioned. And Beth hadn't.

Janine massaged the book's leathery surface; she touched the point of the dagger with care and reflection, remembering its power to heal. She'd never been able to read the book's entire contents since all of the pages were stuck together except for the center spread. But it was on these two pages that the book's magic was revealed. She flipped it open.

The left page was completely drawn in what appeared to be pencil. Pictured were temples that were not Egyptian pyramids, but resembled them in structure. There were strange animal/human hybrid creatures written along the page edges. Some had bodies of mammals, birds and reptiles sporting human heads. Some images were completely glyphic and indiscernible. But her favorite image was the magical one—the one on the right side. It was that page's single entry: a bird with wings of fire. It swooped majestically from the center binding at the top of the page, a trail of dust or wind following close behind. It seemed to dance on the page and to Janine appeared to be smiling. But her fascination with the drawing's beauty was unmatched by the magic of its existence. It had not been there when she'd recovered the book from the stump hole. The Bird of Fire had drawn itself into the page over the last six months.

But that was illogical, and if it was illogical, it did not happen—it did not exist.

But it did! And as she stared at the drawing, another minute stroke of the heavenly pencil added one more tip to one more flame that engulfed the bird's wing.

She wiped the pads of her fingers across the delicate paper surface and closed her eyes, to see, again, the face of Professor Cower whose anguish from the bullet planted in his chest would quickly fade when Janine stuck the thin blade of the dagger into the entry wound. Professor Cower, who had brought the book and the dagger into her life. Professor Cower, who, according to detectives, also did not exist.

She closed the book and dropped it back into the linen sack. She snatched a pair of shorts, a green t-shirt that read "John Deere," and went to the guest bathroom to freshen up and change. When she switched on the light she found a Post-it note stuck to the bathroom mirror. It read:

Janine: Went to see a man about a loan. Make yourself at home. I'll catch up with you when I get back.

>   -   *Love,*

Marcy

"Ok, Marcy," Janine said to the note. "We'll catch up when you get back."

And boy do I have an illogical story to tell you.

She removed the note and began washing the wrinkles from her face.

❐ ...

Joel stared at the magician's hands and tapped two fingers against the paint-peeled metal railing that constituted the foot of his bed. The clock, Marcy had given him. The mustached man on the clock's face pointed out that it was nearly eight-thirty. A black top hat with two little rabbit ears poking out of its brim was painted on the clock face near the six o'clock position. The magician's long minute hand closed in on the top hat, inching closer to the six as if the mechanical magician was about to perform one fantastic illusion but was taking forever to pull it off.

Joel had never wasted so much time staring at a device that ticked so much time away. And this clock wasn't one that slowly eased through sixty minute cycles either. The clock that Marcy had given him was an antique. Its minute hand actually jerked forward for each minute that passed with an audible click. With each forward jerk-click movement, Joel's fingers strummed the bed frame metal faster.

Janine was supposed to be here by now. The trolley would have picked her up by eight. The ride was no more than ten minutes.

Jerk-click!

Had she decided against it? Had she decided that Joel was the bum that everyone had said he was? Had she decided that there was no future with a man who lived in a one-room shack, a man who had no job and little means of support?

Jerk-click!

And after all the hard work he'd put into cleaning up the place last night. He'd scrubbed the mold from the shower stall. He'd scraped the rust from the bed railings where his fingers rapidly tapped. He'd washed his clothes and the linens, had hung them to dry overnight, and had gotten up early to fold the clothes and dress the springy, oblong bed mattress.

Jerk-click!

He'd expended a great deal of time thinking about how this day might unfold. What fishing lessons he'd teach her. How he would teach them. If he'd get any closer to her both physically and mentally.

Jerk-click!

He wondered if she'd free her mind and trust in his confidence. Why had she come to the island? What was in her past? Why was she running? Who was chasing her and for what reason?

Jerk-click!

The magician's minute hand jerk-clicked onto the top hat when Joel realized, again, that all he'd been thinking about was himself. Poor Joel. He'd cleaned his shower and washed his clothes. Poor Joel. He'd spent time thinking about teaching someone something new. Poor Joel. Janine was not yet here because Poor Joel was… poor.

But what if he was wrong? What if none of this had anything to do with Poor Joel? What if her tardiness had everything to do with the casino men? What if one of them had found her on the trolley? She'd acted so frightened at the restaurant. What if the casino men had harmed her? What if it was because of them and not Poor Joel that Janine was not here? Or worse, what if he, Poor Joel, the man who'd sworn against a life of solitude less than twelve hours ago found that the woman who could have saved himself from himself had been taken from him by these men?

Jerk-click!

The magician's hand revealed no secrets and provided no answers as the clock clicked to 8:31. Joel's hand stopped drumming and started trembling. He tried to look away from the magician but he couldn't.

"Please let her be all right," he said to the clock.

"Joel," the clock seemed to say. "Hello, Joel?"

He sat upright on the bed, glaring curiously at the magician whose mustache revealed no lips.

"Joel Canton?"

But the voice, he realized, was not coming from the clock; it was coming from beyond his screen door. He turned to see Janine as she walked along the pebble-dirt sidewalk toward him. When she reached the screen door, she repeated his name. "Joel. There you are. Are you okay?"

He smiled, relieved, and almost leapt from his bed spring.

"Welcome," he said exasperated. "I…eh…" He pushed the screen door open. "Come in." He shot a quick scowl at the magician, at the clock. Janine followed his glare.

"Sorry," she said. "Are we too late?"

Joel's immediate urge was to swipe the clock from its place on the wooden milk crate. Instead, he grabbed the circular metal timekeeper and offered it to Janine.

"Clocks are so overrated," he said. "But this one is more a keepsake than anything else." Janine gave the clock a curious stare but did not take it from his hand. "Marcy gave it to me," he continued. "She said that my old fisherman's intuition might some day leave me. This ole thing is supposed to, you know, help me keep track of time."

"The rabbit is out of the hat," Janine said, smiling.

Joel looked at the clock face. He'd never given the clock enough of his time to realize that some mechanism inside pushed a rabbit out of the magician's hat at thirty-five minutes past each hour.

"Uh, yeah," he lied. "That's what I've been waiting for. The magic trick."

Janine continued smiling, her eyes filled with a childlike wonderment. "I don't think I've ever seen anything like it."

It was an awkward moment, Joel holding the clock in the palm of his hand not knowing of its mechanical magic, Janine staring at it having moved no more than a foot into his home, Joel trying to avoid the assumption that he'd been patiently waiting, using the clock as a guide that had summoned all kinds of false conclusions.

Janine grabbed the clock and reset it on the wooden crate end table. "That Marcy is one special lady," she said then grabbed Joel's open hand and added, "so what are we fishing for today?"

Her hand felt like melted butter in his rough, wrinkled grip. "Whatever the sea offers." He led her farther into the Canton Shack and together they sat on his bed which squeaked in stress from the unknown added weight. "How have you been? You look tired."

She released his grip and lightly tapped his knuckles. "I've never been able to sleep well in a new bed."

Joel suddenly stood. "Is it the casino men? Are they bothering you?"

Janine stood beside him. "No. Really, it's the bed." She looked at Joel's mattress. "Shouldn't we get going? I'm really excited to learn sea fishing."

His ex-wife Jane had always wanted to learn how to fish in the Gulf but for many reasons, every time the idea had surfaced, she or Joel had always been busy with some other more important task. For Joel, the charter fishing boat company had overridden any leisure time the two could have spent together. From the day that "Jaws" had been captured, the charter had been his number one priority. But it hadn't lasted. The charter had slowly gone bankrupt, giving Joel plenty of time for leisure and for sea-fishing lessons to anyone who asked. But by then it had been too late. Jane had already separated from Joel, though not legally but certainly in mind and spirit. Bert Nookle had stolen her away. She'd left Joel a Dear John and had moved to Galveston. He'd not taught anyone to fish since.

"Yes," he said to Janine, again relishing her striking resemblance to Jane. "Yes, I'll get the gear."

Joel disappeared into an adjoining room he'd created using a shower rod and bed sheets, the space in his small home that served as his bathroom and closet, and returned with his fishing rod. In the corner at the foot of the bed next to the wooden crate end table and the magician clock was a small, dorm-room-sized refrigerator which sat atop an empty wooden spool, the kind used to store coils of telephone and electric pole wiring. From within the dingy white door, he pulled out the remainder of a Milky Way candy bar and slipped it into his coveralls. "Special recipe bait," he said in response to Janine's curious stare. "Bet you didn't know fish had a sweet tooth?"

Janine shook her head.

"Well then, let's get started."

"Where's the tackle box and the stringer?" Janine asked.

Joel giggled. It was the first time he'd done so in a long time. "We won't be needing any of that commercial mumbo jumbo. All that's really needed is a pole, some strong line, and just the right bait."

"You sound like Huck Finn," Janine said, smiling.

"Ah, yes. Of the Mississippi Finns. Clever boy that one. Don't know how he ever got them kids to whitewash his fence."

"You mean Tom Sawyer," Janine corrected.

Joel's eyebrows furled for a moment. "Sawyers. Yeah. Dammit if I don't get them kids confused. Ornery rascals, both of them. If it weren't for Becky, they'd both of ended up in the pen."

Janine grabbed Joel's free arm and locked her elbow around his. "And *they* kept *her* out harm's way," she said.

Joel understood. He would protect *her* and she would keep *him* out of trouble. Just like Becky and Tom. Just like Samuel Clemens might have imagined his young characters as senior citizens. "Shall we, Miss Thatcher?" Joel said, snuggling her elbow within his own.

"Lead the way, Mr. Sawyer."

It had all of the purity and innocence of the first American love story. Two people, young at heart, newly acquainted, strolling arm-in-arm, without the cares of the complicated world they lived in, under a perfect sun, with only scant white fluffs of marshmallow-cotton clouds breaking the heat in spurts that carried light, salty breezes into the faces, noses and lungs of the youngsters. Their outer skins belied their inner youths. They were giddy. They talked about nothing important which was the most important conversation any newly coupled humans could engage in, the kind of conversation that rarely happens more than once, a conversation of probing, one without political, economic or social underpinnings. Babbling some would call it, nonsense others might say, but it was this very collection of babbling, nonsensical talk that connected men and women like glue. Nothing material ever came of talk like this. It could not be labeled. No price tags were attached. Its channel was spiritual, and for every couple it was always different since the only understanding that could be deciphered was done by the human soul.

That's how it was for Janine and Joel, alias Becky Thatcher and Tom Sawyer, as they strode across dunes that protected Port A from the ocean surges of the Gulf.

Janine coddled Joel's arm as if it were a valuable piece of Venetian sculpture. His coveralls smelled of Tide detergent. A couple of stains were visible across the chest and lap. She had the overwhelming urge to slip her free right hand into the coverall's right breast pocket. In fact, as she and Joel crested the final dune to the visual and auditory beauty of the crashing beachhead waves, Janine fantasized about jumping into the coverall pocket. She would be safe there. Albert would never find her. In the security of Joel's pocket, the nightmares could not reach her. She'd have Joel's heartbeat to comfort her and the Milky Way candy bar would prevent starvation.

"And that cloud looks like a bunny," Joel was saying as she stared at his pocket. She looked into the sky. To her, the cloud looked more like a dog with really long ears but she didn't say this. Instead, she continued their nonsensical conversation by referring to another cloud, closer to the horizon where the south jetty stretched its long rocky finger into the Gulf.

"A mushroom," she said and quickly wished that she hadn't. It broke the mood. The connotation of a mushroom cloud brought the real world smashing back down upon her. The unimportant conversation that came only once in a lifetime had ended.

And to make matters worse, at the bottom of the last dune where the beach road stretched north and south a hundred yards away from the water break line stood the iPod kid. Nothing much had changed about him since he'd cornered her back at Marcy's front porch. His wavy blonde hair jumped to the seemingly pneumatic drive of his head as it beat like a piston back and forth, chin to chest. The white iPod ear plug wires drooped and tangled around his left arm which carried the digital music box. A white pickup nearly hit the iPod kid as he stumbled hypnotically, his head down and thumping, across the beach road toward Joel and Janine.

"Ted Lavender," Joel said of the boy. "Is that Ted Lavender?" Janine shrugged her shoulders. She, of course, knew very few people on the island, but she realized the question was not meant for her.

At the base of the last dune, the iPod kid and Janine and Joel stopped and stared at each other. The iPod kid looked up from the sand, his head still thrusting to beats in his ears. He looked quizzically at Janine and quickly dismissed her. They were a good ten feet apart but Janine could still sense the crimson sparkle that reminded her of Albert. Again, she felt the urge to jump into Joel's coverall breast pocket.

"Is that you, Teddy?" Joel said. "You okay, kid?"

The boy who was apparently Ted Lavender did not seem to know his own name, but to Janine it appeared that he recognized Joel. Little Teddy's head stopped beating though the music still thumped in muffled volume from the iPod earplugs.

"G-G-G..." little Teddy's lips began to pronounce. "G-G-Gee..."

"Joel," Joel said. "Remember me, kid?"

"G-J-J-Joel?" Teddy's eyebrows curled inward with an expression of concentrated study. "F-f-fish," he continued. "We... caught...a...fish... Joel."

Joel took a step toward Teddy. "Son? You look tired."

Teddy pointed at Joel's fishing pole. "F-fish," he muttered. "Fish... are...dead. Teddy...are...dead."

Janine didn't know if Joel saw it but at that very moment the crimson and silver swirls and sparkles that occupied the center of Teddy's black eyes suddenly brightened and twisted in a moiré of chaos. Then, without reason, Teddy belted out a scream so viciously loud the white pickup truck that almost hit him moments before stopped abruptly on the beach road and the driver looked back through the cab's window. Teddy threw both hands in the air and ran between Joel and Janine, brushing both with both of his shoulders. He raced up the dune, screaming.

In his sudden maniacal rush, Teddy had dropped his iPod and it now rested at Joel's feet. He picked it up and dropped it into the breast pocket where Janine had imagined roosting. "I'll get it back to him the next time I see him," he said with the same quizzical stare that Janine imagined was sketched across her own face. "Lord knows I wouldn't know what to do with the thing."

They walked on toward the south jetty within the Nueces County State Park without another shared word.

◻ ...

At about the same moment that Janine stepped onto the jetty rocks for the first time in her life, Steph stepped onto a surfboard for the first time in her own.

"You can swim can't you?" Billy said grinning but totally serious. "I mean, you look as though you can handle the surf."

Steph had chosen her two-piece, baby blue bikini on purpose. It revealed the fine lines of her abdomen and the sleek curves of her legs and buttocks. She had always been very athletic, a self-indulgence that only once included team play in high school where she was named All-State as a setter for the volleyball team. She'd been offered an athletic scholarship to Texas A&M but had opted for an academic scholarship only. Succeeding in business meant, to her, a devotion to studies that did not afford much time for practice and play.

They were a couple of miles south of the jetty. No one was on the beach except the two of them. Billy grabbed her waist with a gentle but instructional force and told her to kneel. They were not yet in the water. Her first lesson was what Billy called a "dry start." A nine-foot Malibu surfboard rested in the sand a dozen yards from the breaking, foamy surf. Billy had dug a small divot in the sand so the board's fin could lie safely during the lesson. She stood on its waxy surface about a third of the way up the board from the tail.

"I swim like a fish," Steph said, squirming silently with delight between Billy's soft hands; his grip of her flesh reminded her of their luau date—and flying to the moon.

"Good." Billy guided her down onto the board, his hands still clasped just above her hips. "You never know when the surf might test you."

The board's waxy surface grabbed her navel and the very faint hairs that surrounded it as Billy continued his instruction.

"This is the most important maneuver. You can surf all day with your belly to the board but that ain't surfin'. You need to stand. It's called the pop-up."

Her face was against the board. Billy's legs straddled each side of her waist. It was hard to concentrate.

"Once you paddle into the wave, you need to pop-up onto the board in one smooth motion. This entails pushing on the rails while swinging your knees inward and planting your feet in a crouched position. Use your knees as shock-absorbers, kinda like you would if you were water-skiing."

Steph turned her face from the board and into the sun. Billy's head silhouetted the blazing orange circle in the sky. "I've never water-skied," she said.

Billy was smiling at her, his long arms draped toward each side of her body. "Ever slid across a patch of ice in your sneaks?"

Steph remembered that, as a kid, she had. "Yeah. About ten years ago."

"You remember falling?"

Steph *had* fallen. It had been in Colorado while visiting her uncle who worked at Wal-mart. She remembered how much it had hurt her tailbone. She nodded while looking up at him.

"So the next time you tried to slide, your balance was controlled by your knees. The knees kept you from falling on your ass."

Steph knew that Billy was serious about his surf instructions, but at the same time he was so cute and timid and caring. It was hard not to giggle. Funny thing was, what he said was accurate. After she'd fallen and had busted her tailbone, after the tremor of pain had fizzled out of her spine, after she'd wiped the cold tear from a cheek that was rosy with embarrassment, she'd stood, that competitive, athletic attitude roiling within her young soul and had tried again. This time she'd not fallen. This time she'd controlled her balance. And only now did she remember how she'd done it. Her knees had kept her from falling on her ass.

"Yeah," she said in revelation. "Okay…I get it. Balance. One foot in front of the other. Knees bent. I can do that."

Billy leaned forward to within inches of her upturned lips and said, "Let's see it." He pulled upward on her waist, his hands firmly entrenched on her hip bones, and, naturally, as if she'd done it a million times over, her knees came forward, her feet swung inward, and she popped-up. Her feet planted incorrectly as one straddled each rail but she quickly shifted them, her right foot moving forward, her left moving backward just as if she was back in Colorado sliding across the icy Wal-Mart parking lot.

"Goofy-footed," Billy said a little surprised. His hands moved off her waist. "You sure that feels comfortable?"

"It's how I safely slid across the ice. Doing it the other way made me fall."

"Let's see it again."

Steph dropped onto her belly and quickly popped-up, this time planting her goofy-footed stance with near perfection.

"To hell with that lesson," Billy said. "You sure you've never done this before?"

"Never."

"Ever done any kind of water sport?"

"None."

Billy's mouth hung open. Then, like a true stereotypical surf dude he said, "Whoa! Too totally cool. You are one righteous babe. Whatta'ya say we catch one?"

Steph gleamed with pride. She really had never done any type of water sport beyond swimming laps in a public pool. And up until now, she'd never really had the desire. But Billy filled her with such positive reinforcement; she felt she could ride the Hawaiian pipeline.

Twenty minutes later she realized that duplicating in the water what she'd done on land was much more difficult. Riding the surf was in no way analogous to sliding on ice. They were only thirty yards out and the surf was less than three feet on average but she had yet to successfully pop up. She'd ridden several waves belly-to-board but that wasn't surfing. Still, Billy provided encouragement.

"Remember to keep the knees bent. It's one fluid motion. If need be, pop to your knees then stand." Billy sat on his board, legs draped over the rails and pointed. "Here comes a good one. Now start paddling."

Steph started stroking the rising water just as Billy had directed her a dozen times already. Her arms moved faster as the board lifted onto the growing wave. This one looked to rise higher than any she'd attempted so far. Billy yelled out.

"Whooo...Yah-yaa! Hang it baby! That's one knarly wave!"

She sped forward. Wind and spray pelted her cheeks, cooling the heat supplied by the sun's water surface reflection. The wave began to crest and she maneuvered into the curl. She quickly pressed against the rails, pulled her legs inward and planted her knees onto the board's waxy surface. Billy would tell her later that the whole event lasted less than five seconds but to her it was a lifetime. Her speed increased and she fought the water's attempt to throw her off. Seemingly far away she heard Billy yell, "Do it!"

And she did.

In one swift motion, she released the rails and popped up from her knees to the same goofy-footed stance she had perfected in the sand. For a fraction of a second she was surfing. For a fraction of a second she was flying. For a fraction of a second she felt as if the Big Dipper was within mortal reach and she now understood the freedom from reality that Billy had described as they'd waded in the surf at the luau. It only lasted a fraction of a second but the memory of it etched deeply into her subconscious. It *was* possible to tame Mother Nature if only to be humbled within a fraction of a second.

When she fell, she dumped forward into the curl, a picturesque wipe-out. She felt the ankle strap tug and stretch as the board fought the wave's attack on its buoyancy. She gasped in a mouthful of water only because she was smiling so widely in victory as her face hit the wave. When she surfaced she coughed, laughed, and screamed.

"Yah-yaa!" She pumped her fist then grabbed the surfboard.

Billy, sitting on his board twenty yards out, pumped his fists in response. "Yah-yaa!" he answered.

Her success had released some locked energy. She paddled effortlessly toward Billy over surf that, minutes before, had denied her the right to stand against the ocean. These juvenile three-foot waves were miniscule. She could surf these, she thought. She could stand atop them and ride them to the shore. She had conquered a curl twice their size. Yah-yaa!

As she neared the spot where Billy sat waiting, she pushed the nose of the board forward, swung her thighs across each rail and planted her butt, straddling the board.

"What do you think about that?" she gleamed.

The tail of her board touched the tail of Billy's. Her right knee stroked the surface of his thigh. Billy's exuberant expression allied with the tranquility she felt streaming through her body.

◻ ...

His mind swirled with a mouth-opened, astonished wonderment that Steph had ridden the elusive, rare, five-foot Port A wave. There was jealousy in the thought, one reserved only for Port A surfers who rarely saw such surf let alone was afforded a chance to ride one. She'd stolen what was reserved for veterans.

But she was *His* girl.

Right?

His girl had ridden the five-footer.

And he, the veteran, had been paramount in her success.

He'd ridden the wave with her. His mind's energy had helped her pop up. His muscles had involuntarily gone through the motions with her. Pushing, curling inward, fighting for balance, standing, looking around, feeling proud, conquering Mother Nature. If only for a fraction of a second. If only for a fleeting moment.

He'd fallen head first with her. He'd swallowed salt with her. He'd yelled *YahYaa* with her. And now, her body and board were connected to him by something greater than physical restraint. It was, metaphysically, cosmic.

❏ …

There was a stream near Pickett's Crossing. Michael had taken her there one week after they'd met. It was about an hour east of "the crossing" over in the lowlands in a valley near the Missouri River. In stark contrast to the flat brown landscape of agricultural Kansas, the Salt Creek River was nestled amongst evergreens, oaks and maples, and smelled not of the dry dust but of cool wetness, of wildlife that slithered and swam, of mist on tree leaves and branches.

He'd brought a lunch; they'd been the best peanut butter and banana sandwiches she'd ever eaten.

"Those shoes won't work out here," Joel said.

Even now, as she slipped off her sandals and stepped onto the Port A south jetty rocks, the taste of peanuts and bananas lingered between her taste buds. The wet spray of aquatic life engulfed her nostrils.

Michael had said pretty much the same thing twenty-two years ago. Her future husband had held her hand, had guided her across smooth, wet boulders—some round like bowling balls, some flat like concrete steps— toward a very large rock that sat in the middle of the stream. Her feet had grasped the wet surface; cool water had cascaded through her toes. She'd lost her balance only once but Michael's reflexes and strength had saved her.

"You seem to have done this before," Joel said as he tried to maintain his grasp of her hand. She released it and moved quickly forward. The jetty rocks were ten times larger than those she'd crossed in Kansas but none matched the size of the big "picnic" rock where she and Michael had sat for hours, soaking up the sun and eating peanut butter and banana sandwiches.

"Janine. Hold up."

It was Joel's voice just a dozen feet behind her.

"Janine?"

The long stretch of rocks that narrowed to a point several hundred feet in the distance locked her attention. She thought that if she stood on the very last rock at the very point of the jetty it would be like walking on water, as she'd done in Kansas, as she would now do in the Gulf. She imagined Michael standing at the point of the jetty, his arms held out, a picnic basket draped around one forearm. The smell of salt water and peanut butter and bananas teased her forward.

"Janine!"

The jetty rocks were fifty feet wide at the beachhead but only five feet wide at the point. Waves crashed at the base of the jetty near the beach but the jetty rocks were totally awash at the point.

Janine was already a third of the way out. The jetty rocks had already narrowed by ten feet. Though there was a flat path intentionally created on top of the jetty for visitors and fishermen to easily traverse, Janine chose to walk the rocks about midway down from the path to the water.

"Janine! You can't go past that sign!"

Janine looked up and to her left. She read:

No trespassing beyond this point.
By order of the Nueces County Sheriff's Department

But she kept on going. Michael was out there waiting for her. He'd taught her how to walk the rocks. She wasn't scared.

"Janine! Please stop! Fishing won't be no good out there!"

Fishing? Who said anything about fishing? She and Michael were going to have a picnic. Then she and Michael were going to be married and have a son and a farm with cows and chickens and corn and a barn perhaps—and a pickup truck. And they were going to live happily ever after.

Janine's heart started racing and she picked up her pace. Michael was waiting. A chance to start all over. Out at the point. Out on the Salt Creek River picnic rock where they'd first made love. Where Lenny was conceived.

The jetty had narrowed to twenty feet. The pedestrian path had ended at the sign. More rocks were Gulf water wet. A splash or two pelted her calves. She slipped and reached for Michael who still waited another two hundred feet ahead, but without the strength of his hand, she toppled backward.

For a second she thought that she'd find her balance as she moved her right foot backward but when her bare toes found nothing but the space between two boulders, she fell, her body angling for the rocks and water below, a collision that would certainly bash body and bones.

And then Michael was there, grabbing her hand, prohibiting what would have placed her back in the hospital under the microscopes of logical, intellectual idiots. Her right arm flailed sporadically as her left arm tugged in the opposite direction.

"Are you crazy?" Joel said, wrapping an arm around Janine's waist, his fishing pole dropped and forgotten behind him. He balanced her on the slick rock that challenged their combined weight. "I mean… It's dangerous out here. That's why the sheriff put up that sign."

Janine turned to him. She smiled and cozied into his grasp. "Michael. Thank you, Michael." She looked up. Somehow, Michael looked like… "Joel," she cried. "Oh my God! Oh my God! I…I…"

Joel coddled her tightly then, and together they sat. Gulf water froth lapped their legs and feet, leaving brown rivulets as bubbles popped and drooled onto the rock. Her tears dropped into his overall's breast pocket, moistening Teddy Lavender's iPod. They remained like this for a good five minutes. When Janine stopped crying, she lifted her head and looked out toward the point of the jetty. Michael, of course, was not there.

"The Gulf can play some funny tricks on a person," Joel said, his arm draped over her shoulder. "I've seen things."

Janine wondered how he could read her mind. "Really?" she said, still looking out at the point. "Me too." She wiped away what was left of the salty tears moments before her face was again moistened by salt water spray. "What did you see?"

"Loved ones."

She turned to him.

"My wife, particularly. She'd visit me right here on these rocks."

"Did she die?" Janine asked, wondering if the deceased and the jetty had some ghostly connection.

"To tell you the truth, I don't know. I haven't heard from her in many, many years." He released her shoulder and brought both arms forward to rest on his lap.

"I saw Michael," she said. "He was my husband. He died in a farming accident years ago." She, again, looked out at the point. On the horizon appeared the small dark outline of a ship. She guessed correctly that it was headed for the jetty though it would be hours before it reached them.

Joel followed her gaze. "Why are you here?" he said without looking at her. "Do those men from the restaurant have anything to do with it?"

Janine looked directly at the side of his face. Fluffs of grey hair that were longer and thicker than most men his age stuck to the Gulf moisture on his cheek. His eyes remained on the horizon.

"Does your husband's death have anything to do with it?"

Janine's mouth hung open. She imagined that Joel could hear her thumping heartbeats which had not yet calmed, beating out an alien language of fear and anxiety.

"Are you running?" He now turned and their eyes locked.

She needed to tell someone. Keeping it all inside had become unbearable. It tore through her emotions as if they were made of papier-mâché. But could she trust him…this stranger…with the darkness locked up inside?

"I don't know how he found me," she finally said.

"The men from the restaurant," Joel concluded.

Janine shifted on the rock to turn more comfortably toward him. In her periphery she saw his fishing pole where he'd dropped it on the jetty. In the distance she saw few people on the beach which her mind absently recorded as something strange. "The big man," she said. "He used to be…I mean, you could say we're divorced."

Joel's eyebrows rose. "Your ex is chasing you?"

She needed someone to trust her, to listen to her revelations, to help her release some penned-in misery. But telling Joel, or anyone, a dead monster that ate people was a part of her reality would certainly end any chance for friendship.

"Yes," she said. "Yes. He must be."

Joel's stare did not leave her even as a seagull suddenly crashed into the jetty rocks a dozen yards away, its body flapping momentarily before dying and rolling into the water. "Why?" he asked.

Truthfully, Janine wasn't really sure. "He killed my son and now I think he wants me gone, too. Clean up any evidence."

"What!?" Joel's grey eyebrows lifted into his forehead. The stray hairs that stuck to his cheeks fell from skin that suddenly filled with wrinkled shock. "We should go to the police. Keadle will help us." Joel licked his lips. "He killed your son?"

Janine patted his hand. "Shhh." She placed a finger to her lips. "That won't do. The police don't believe me. They think I'm…" she paused for the right word. *Crazy* wasn't it nor was *Insane*. "They think it's all in my head—that I imagined it."

"You saw him do it…kill your son?"

"Yes. Almost a year ago—a very long year ago."

"So if you saw it, how could you have imagined it?"

It was bound to happen. No matter how the conversation would have started, and no matter how hard she tried to control the information, sooner or later what she saw would become the principal question. A dead man… eating flesh…a thing straight from hell itself, chasing her, wanting her dead, Joel dead, the world dead.

"There was an explosion," she revealed. "Debris knocked me out. The doctors said it was a head injury. I was in therapy for several months but…"

"But it wasn't your imagination."

Janine cried. "He chopped Lenny up." Her head fell to his chest again. Tears welled into fresh pools on the pocketed iPod. "He's an animal from Hell."

Joel patted her head. "Shhh," he soothed. "He's not here now but I am."

She looked up and he stroked her forehead, one rough fingertip following shallow wrinkles. She tried to smile—a dim glimpse of hope— but couldn't. Joel was a brave man but only human and no match for Albert Stine.

"Besides," Joel continued, "I've got a cure that heals all wounds… Fishing."

At the end of the jetty where the ghost of Michael Bender had lured his wife into the Gulf, another seagull dropped suddenly from the sky, its wings lifeless and stiff, and plopped into the water.

❏ …

They sat on their boards beyond the break for what seemed like hours though it had only been twenty minutes or so since Steph had conquered the surf. The silence was nearly absolute. Save for one or two gulls Billy saw fall awkwardly from the sky, no beach life was present. He'd seen no fish surface and none had bumped his submerged, dangling feet. Though they were surfing far from where most visitors chose to enjoy the Port A beaches, mid-June always promoted some kind of activity for miles down the Mustang Island coastline. It seemed odd that no one was walking, playing, or sunbathing for as far as he could see in either direction. Apparently, the fish kill supposition had made it into public knowledge with such negative grace that even the locals were not taking chances. Apparently, Mark had either not contacted the media with the lab results from the samples they'd collected yesterday, or the media had not listened. There were no contaminants in the waters along Mustang Island. Though he'd not yet seen any fish today, he also had not seen any dead fish. And no crimson waters. And no blood spots. But newspapers sold better when the news was negative.

In such complete silence, with nothing but the intoxicating splashing, lapping water surges slapping past he and Steph, it was hard not to think about the bloody end to the life of Mitchell Bone. He stared out at the horizon where a ship slowly grew in size as it crept closer inland and wondered: he'd not seen it first hand; they were video clips transmitted by Shoe; they could have been manipulated; someone could have jacked into the frequency and could have fed him any lies they wished. Chancy Lett and the bodyguard came to mind. But why would they have him believe such a thing—that Bone was dead, that Bone had been murdered, that he'd had his head ripped from his body?

Of course, the images could have been real. The ramifications of such reality were still beyond his comprehension, as was so much that had gone on in the past few days. All he'd intended was to collect evidence that could have been used against the construction of the Mayan casino. What he'd uncovered was...

"Did you move Shoe?"

He looked at Steph, curiously, as if she'd been wandering through his thoughts.

"You said you were going to move your robot to a position where it could see better into the vault."

Billy drove his surfboard closer to her. "I did," he almost whispered. Steph looked around. "At least I tried."

"What do you mean?" She emulated his whisper.

"Shoe never made it to the teller window."

"Did it break down or something?" Steph's disappointment became concern. "What will happen when they find it in the middle of the floor?"

"It's not in the middle of the floor." Billy looked back toward the horizon. "Quite frankly, I don't know where Shoe is. I lost his signal."

"Well that sucks...doesn't it?"

Without looking at her, Billy said, "I saw something. Shoe saw something."

"The crate? What? Can we use it against them? Can we use it to take down Bone?"

"He was murdered," he said bluntly.

"What!?" she pushed her board against his. "Who? Who was murdered?"

He looked into her eyes, hoping that truth and not dementia would shine through. "Your boss. Mitchell Bone. That big fella took his head off."

Steph stared at the churning water as if it were some crystal ball that enabled her to see what Billy was describing.

"I saw the head," he continued. "It rolled right into to vault's doorway. There was a tremendous amount of blood."

"How do you know it was Bone?" Steph said.

"I saw it!" He'd not meant to sound so harsh and Steph flinched. "Sorry." He touched the rail of her board just behind where her left thigh straddled its surface. "Lett's bodyguard did it. One minute Bone was arguing something about indiscretions, the next minute he was directed into the vault along with the bodyguard, Lett and Carol. Then there were screams. The head just rolled into the doorway; the bodyguard picked it up and crushed it. He grabbed it like a bowling ball through the eyes and mouth and just squeezed."

"We have to report this?" Steph grabbed his arm. "Did you report it? You have the evidence?"

"Yes, I have the evidence. It should be stored on the computer back home, though..." he took a deep breath, "...though I'm not in a hurry to look at the footage just yet."

"Give it to the authorities."

Billy grabbed her hand and gently petted it. "Do you think that would be such a wise idea? Breaking and entering a financial institution will certainly draw me five-to-ten in the state pen."

A fish suddenly darted between their boards. It was the first one he'd seen all day and it startled him. He released Steph's hand.

"I was thinking more in the line of the press," he continued. "I might be able to get certain protections through them. Besides, all I have is the video. There's been no body found yet. No crime has been committed until the victim is found."

Steph shook her head. "Well, we'll have the evidence when the body does show up and that will be the end of that for the Mayan." She swirled her legs through the water, contemplating. "You think the body is in the vault?"

Billy flinched a short grin. "That would be my guess. But how could we know? Are you going back to work there?"

"I decided yesterday that you were more important."

Billy's grin turned up a notch but he was not yet able to smile. Though he didn't agree with her decision he was flattered. "You quit your job to go surfing." He shook his head. "I know a lot of guys around here that have made that choice a dozen times."

Steph blushed. "Not to change the subject but I will be needing a job."

"Waitress?"

"You're good at reading minds."

"Maybe. Some equations are just easier to complete than others." Another fish, or perhaps the same fish, darted between their boards, this time brushing aggressively against Billy's calf. "I think I can find something for you, that is, once all of this fish kill frenzy subsides and business gets back up to speed again."

"Thank you. Now that's one problem solved. What about Bone? Can you get Shoe running again?"

Billy recalled the face of the bodyguard on the video display in his van. "I doubt it. I think the bodyguard may have…terminated him."

"Then we're stuck. If the body is in the bank vault, it won't be there for long. For all we know it's already been moved."

"I was thinking of tipping off Officer Keadle but I'm not really sure how to go about it without making myself suspect."

They floated for several minutes, each contemplating their next move. Billy had the evidence to rid the island of the future malaise a casino would certainly bring. Now all he needed was a headless body. Shoe was certainly of no use any more. The bodyguard had taken care of that. He wondered now if he could talk Keadle into opening up a security box. Perhaps Keadle would see something suspicious inside the vault. Perhaps his suspicion would cause him to demand that the wooden crate be opened. There he would find, among other incriminating evidence, Bone's body. All Billy would then need to do is hand over the video and Chancey Lett would be nothing more than a bad memory.

Steph suddenly grabbed his board and swung it toward her. "I think I have a possible answer. Not sure it will work. I don't even know her. But it's worth a shot."

At that same moment, the fish that had been swimming between them surfaced, flipped onto its side, and floated. Billy thought he saw a strange crimson light swirl within the fish's eye just before it blackened into a cold stare.

◻ …

He could not remember the last time someone cried on his shoulder. It was certainly before he'd met his wife. By the time he and Jane were married his rugged, sea-faring, fisherman persona would not have permitted such displays of caring and emotion. His shoulders were meant to handle the laborious task of pulling in the day's catch. They held the weight of responsibility, of being the man of the house, of bringing home the bread. If you wanted to cry in front of him, he'd lend you his hanky, a fishy-smelling accessory he kept in his back coveralls pocket, but you could not have his shoulder. Besides, nothing good every came from crying. It was a weakness, with the sole purpose to make others sad and depressed. It was a waste of energy that was better channeled into something productive and worthwhile like making a living for your family so that they had a roof over their heads and food on the table.

At least that's the way he used to think.

Years without Jane and hours with Janine had changed all that. He now questioned the sensibility in it all. How many years had he wasted? How many opportunities? Certainly "love" had taken a backseat. Realistically, though, had he ever known what the term "love" really meant? He loved an orange sunset as much as he loved watching grey-black thunderheads roll in under the same orange horizon. There had been a time when liquor and leisure had been loves…the feeling of knuckles to jaws…a pool stick used as a weapon. And then there was fishing, the Gulf, the vastness of the unknown. What measure could one give to such things? He loved them all. But he'd never really "loved" Jane—at least not in any way he could understand. Jane had never soaked his breast pocket with more salt than the average flipping, flailing redfish that had slipped the hook before the net. No woman had ever cried on him. What value was there in it?

Crying.

Tears.

Janine released her fear and depression onto his coveralls. A pool of salt as large as the palm of his hand encircled the right breast pocket. He gently grabbed her shoulder and set her up straight. As much as some internal desire wanted him to, he could not find the courage to wipe away the remaining stray tears on her cheek.

"Sit here," he told her. "I gotta get my fishing rod." He questioned her ability to hold herself upright. "Good with that?"

Janine managed a flickered smile. She placed her hands onto the rocks for balance.

"You settle," Joel said. "I'll be right back and then we'll get us the big one. A fish that could feed the whole island."

Janine nodded as he rose to his feet. He stole glances back across his shoulder as he moved away, fearing that she might suddenly leap forward and into the surf. But for the entire two minutes that it took him to retrieve the fishing pole and return to her side, Janine did not move. Her arms remained rigid, her hands clasped to the rocks as if any relaxation would cause her demise. He reached into the salty, tear-stained breast pocket and fished around Ted Lavender's iPod for the chunk of Milky Way.

"A fish with a sweet tooth," he said to her. "Quite funny if you think about it."

He could not deter her attention from whatever locked her thoughts.

"Fish cavities," he tried.

Nothing.

"How many fish does it take to make a full set of teeth?"

No response.

"Thirty-two." He laughed but she didn't.

A minute of silence followed.

"I never caught him," he said, abruptly, not really knowing why. "It's all a lie."

Janine looked up and over.

"My life is a lie."

She stared at the Milky Way wrapper that covered half a bar.

"I don't know how he did it but Nookle pulled that son-of-a-bitch in without my help. I was knocked out of it the whole time. And then a couple years later the big movie came out. We were the heroes but I had nothing to do with it. I used the public's ignorance for gain. Hell, *Jaws* was the talk of the country. And Bert and I were the real-life counterparts. But I had nothing to do with it. I only wish…" He hesitated. Janine still stared at the wrapper of the half of candy bar which Joel now opened. "I only wish it never would have happened." He grabbed the fishing hook and baited it with a round ball of Milky Way that he'd rolled between thumb and forefinger. He licked his fingers and offered the rod to Janine.

She quizzically stared at it as if it were a precious form of art, but said nothing.

"I'm running, too," he said. His grin was slight and concerned—reinforcing. "We're all running from something: people, our hearts—" He swallowed. "Death."

"Joel?" It was the first thing she'd said since drowning his breast pocket. "Do you...?"

The fishing rod, offered within Joel's knurled hands, a sticky ball of candy wrapped around its lined hook, waited for her to take it.

She continued, "Do you trust me?"

The question seemed impossible for him to answer, but he was quick to understand that her question was directed in response to his own revelation, information that was meant only for those that people trust. Janine, a woman he'd known for little more than two days, was the only person to whom he'd ever confessed the history of "Jaws"—and the confession of love—though Joel still struggled with that concept.

❒ ...

"I wish I knew what the hell was causing all of this," Billy said, kicking at the dead fish with his naked heel. "It's so frustrating."

"And where are all of the birds?" Steph added. She'd seen only one or two in the few hours they'd been surfing.

"I know. Weird. One thing's for sure, whatever it is ain't in the water. At least not in any water around this island."

Steph watched the fish bob out of sight then said, "I think that if we can run Lett out of town, everything will return to normal. Everything seems to have started going badly when he arrived Monday."

"With the crate," Billy added.

Steph considered this. She remembered the strange power it had emitted when she'd been accosted by Lett, Carol and the bodyguard as they'd recited their own dark version of the Lord's Prayer. The strange glow. The nearly inaudible hum. Every time Carol had taken another customer inside the vault to set up a new security box, the person had changed, had become almost robotic.

"So what was your idea?" Billy said. "How can we get into that vault?"

"I suspect that with Bone out of the picture, Lett and his cronies will take charge of the bank, at least until we can uncover evidence."

"With them in control, that seems pretty impossible. I could ask Officer Keadle for some help."

"What if they've gotten to him?" Her question seemed to throw a wrench into Billy's reasoning. Apparently, by the way his eyebrows suddenly squashed inward with an expression of befuddlement, he'd not considered that possibility. Steph had grown use to his expressions. It was easy to determine just by looking at his face when he was deeply calculating, when his thoughts were, to him, well-reasoned, and when, like now, his well-reasoned thoughts had suddenly met with some cognitive obstacle. "My idea concerns this investor from Sedona, the one I'm supposed to pick up today at the airport."

Billy's expression suddenly turned into that "deep calculation" mode. "Bone said something about that last night. Alixel, I believe is her name. But how can she help? And besides, I thought you said you didn't work for the bank anymore."

"Alixel won't know that."

"But what if she's in on it? What if talking to her would be no better than talking to Lett?"

"Not sure yet. We'll have to feel it out. Perhaps she's an innocent investor being manipulated just like Bone was. Maybe her head is meant to roll at some point in time as well." Steph's feet were suddenly tickled by a tiny mass of bubbles that rose from beneath her and moved between her toes. The little bubbles popped at the water's surface. She shivered.

Billy looked up at the sun that bore heat down from its apex onto his face and shrugged. "When are we supposed to pick her up?"

"We?"

"Of course. We're in this together now. It's up to us to stop him. It's more than just the casino. It's murder."

She was glad to hear him say that. It made her decision to quit the bank comforting. It made her decision to come to Port Aransas worthwhile. She'd left some friends back in College Station but few were those that she had truly bonded with. That's how it was when you were a valedictorian in your college class. A closed-minded attitude toward anything but educational success tended to alienate many who were only in college for the social party ride into adulthood. Now, she had Billy Jo Presser, an intellect in his own right but a real beach "dude" to boot. *They* were going to figure all of this out. *They* were going to put Chancey Lett in his place. *They* were going to the airport. A few more bubbles running through her toes added to the tingly sensation streaming through her emotions.

And then someone screamed.

Simultaneously, both of them turned to the shriek near the shoreline. Steph's board collided with Billy's and she dumped into the water. Her board shot out from under her but her ankle strap kept it from slamming into Billy's head. Her board fell into the water upside-down and Billy helped her right it. She draped both arms over the board, her legs kicking in the water for balance, and floated as she saw someone crest the top of the nearest dune and run down its slope toward the surf, tripping once in the sand and leaping back up in a brisk jackrabbit motion. A second person topped the dune a moment later. Something flashed in this person's hand, a metallic glint of bouncing sunrays. The words in the screams of the person being chased became clearer as the figure neared the water.

"Billy!"

They floated a good thirty yards out and the crashing, splashing water made the words sound muffled, but Steph was sure that they were:

"Billy, help me!"

Steph knew this person. It was the chef from the luau. It was Billy's chef, Pedro.

"Pedro?" Billy yelled out. "Pedro, is that you?"

Pedro stopped at the surf perpendicular to where Billy and Steph floated out beyond the breakers. He turned and pointed at the figure chasing him who had now halved the distance as Pedro stood there.

"Sí," he yelled. At least to Steph that's what it sounded like. Perhaps it was "oui" but she didn't think he spoke French. But as he yelled the same word repeatedly, it became clear.

"Me!"

And that didn't make any sense either.

"Me! Help, Billy! Me!"

Pedro took off, running along the shoreline for another fifty yards before heading back up into the dunes. Right on his heels was…

Steph blinked. The sun glinting off the metal object that the assailant held temporarily blinded her. Billy started paddling in toward the shoreline as bubbles began racing between her toes and thighs, and across her breasts. These were big bubbles, at least ten times the size of the small tickly ones that had teased her moments ago. And these bubbles were red.

"Billy!" she screamed. "Billy, help me!"

□ ...

What Billy saw on the shoreline was impossible. Pedro was yelling. "Mí jefe" is what it sounded like. Pedro said that a lot. But that's not what he was saying. "Me!" he was screaming. And for good reason. Pedro was being chased by...

Himself.

Billy blinked. He thought he was hallucinating again. The sun—it was playing mind games with him.

"Me!" the first Pedro yelled again, then ran into the dunes.

And then from behind him...

"Billy, help me!"

He turned to see Steph immersed in the same phenomenon that had mesmerized him and Mark the day before. She roiled in an expanding blood spot. Dead fish popped to the surface around her. Some were as long as her small feet which now flailed against the water's surface. Some were half the size of her surfboard which, to Billy's horror, freed itself from Steph's grasp leaving her alone in the middle of the boiling mess. Somehow, the board's ankle strap had slipped free.

He quickly paddled to the middle of the blood spot, grabbed one of Steph's arms at the elbow and paddled with his free arm away from the bubbling surface. He stroked and pulled and yanked as the blood spot expanded, seemingly wanting to take both of them down into its crimson depths. Steph's body bounced repeatedly against the red death that floated in mass around her. His one-armed strokes became labored and he released her, guided her hands to his legs where she clamped on tightly, and paddled with both arms, towing her free from the blood spot.

She gasped and choked and spit. Her hair was red and she submerged to wash the color from it. Horror and shock coupled in a singular expression that told Billy that he'd have to get her to shore immediately. He pulled her body up onto his surfboard where she lay draped over the nose.

"Everything will be fine," he consoled but she said nothing. Drool clung to her lower lip and stretched down to the surfboard in a slight, wind-blown arc.

He began paddling toward the shoreline but stopped after two strokes. The second Pedro was just now disappearing over the same dune where the first Pedro had gone. But it wasn't the Pedros that caused him sudden distress. It was the bodyguard.

He stood just beyond the waterline, the surf rolling to within inches of his sparkling, polished black boots but never touching them, as if the water was afraid, as if the black boots were poison. He wore a three-piece black suit that must have felt extremely uncomfortable under the hot Texas sun. In his hand was a starfish. Billy assumed correctly that it was Shoe. The bodyguard raised the tiny robot over his head and squeezed in much the same way as he'd done Mitchell Bone's head. Then in one aggressive thrust, he slammed Shoe into the beach sand and crushed it with the heel of one boot.

From beyond the dunes, a gut-rattling shriek echoed out in agony. "AGHHH!" Some Spanish gibberish followed. Then complete silence. The bodyguard smiled which was creepy in its own right.

"You're next," he said, not yelling, but just loud enough for Billy to hear.

Steph started gasping and coughing again. "Billy," she said. "Yes. I'll be okay. You can't go in—not with him there. He'll kill us both."

Billy eyed Steph's surfboard still floating in the mass of bloody water and floating fish. The blood spot had stopped bubbling, still, he really didn't want to swim into that mess. "We'll wait for your board to clear then paddle up the coast toward the pier. He's not going to touch us if there are witnesses."

"Yes," Steph coughed. "*We* can do that."

❒ ...

So they both were liars. The only difference in them, as far as Janine could tell, was that Joel had, moments ago, revealed a part of his soul that had been eating at him for many years. Shame, jealousy, loneliness—he'd pretended to love but had never really known how to love. His encounter with the great white shark had changed his life and, for a brief moment and perhaps for the first time ever, he'd felt comfortable enough to open up to someone who just happened to be, for all accounts and purposes, a complete stranger. His heart lay on his sleeve, vulnerable to whatever

Janine decided to do with it.

She, on the other hand, had continued her lie. Her heart remained hidden behind memories that were much fresher than "Jaws." While Joel bargained for truth by bartering his own disgrace, Janine had nothing to offer in return. It was a matter of belief and sanity. How could he believe her? Professor Cower. The magic dagger. Albert and the Albert-thing. People eating people. Lenny! He would think her insane. He would call in the white coats. She'd be returned to the sterile environment where logical men made illogical decisions. Unless...

Unless she trusted him. Unless he trusted her.

"Let's see if you can get this hook in the water without snagging me," Joel said.

Janine took the pole from his hands. A courteous smile remained on his lips though she could tell he'd tensed by the concern revealed by his thick, salty eyebrows. Nobody touched Joel's pole. Nobody. But he trusted *her*.

She had no idea what she was doing. She'd never fished in her life. As she started to swing the pole forward in a motion she'd seen portrayed in movies and television, Joel gently, but with authority, grabbed her shoulders.

"You and my..." he started. "You and the pole are both headin' into the surf if you cast like that. You gotta find your balance. Why don't we try to find a flatter spot?"

"I can do it," Janine said, not fighting the strength of Joel's vise on her shoulders.

"You've never done this before," Joel said, understanding the truth. He released one shoulder and grabbed her left thigh directly above the knee. This sent sensations into her bones that she'd forgotten existed. "Move your leg forward and bend it a little." He guided her leg then lightly karate-chopped the back of her knee. "Yes. Like that. Now move your other leg behind you a bit. You want to get your weight behind the cast so the hook finds a spot beyond the breakers or else all you'll be doing is playing cast and reel with the surf."

"Can you show me first?" Janine felt uncomfortable. The weight of the pole, which was at least two feet longer than she was in height, had suddenly gained fifty pounds in her hands.

"I trust you, Jane." Joel's eyes bugged. "I mean..."

"I know what you mean." Somehow, his slip gave her confidence. She was as important to him as Jane had been, perhaps even more so.

Her first cast was lame at best. The hook traveled farther in the air than it did into the water. The line slapped the water and Joel helped her reel it in. The Milky Way nougat ball was gone.

"I got enough for about five more casts like that," he said and baited the hook with fresh candy. "Go out to the side a bit. Not so much over the head. You should be able to feel the Milky Way."

"Feel the Milky Way?"

"Yes." He moved behind her and grabbed her arms, then rocked them back and forth while remaining attentive to where the hook was at all times as it swayed behind them. "I can feel it. Can you?"

What she was feeling was certainly not what Joel was referring to. He was, basically, hugging her. His strength felt protective. Her spine shivered. They moved on the jetty rocks in some strange, stationary slow dance to the music of the Gulf. She closed her eyes.

"Can you?" he repeated.

"Yes," she said, trying not to swoon.

"You feel the hook?"

"Yes," she crooned.

"Okay…ready?"

"Yes," she repeated, drowning in emotion.

"Excellent!"

She opened her eyes as he released her arms and stepped onto a rock behind her. There she stood, the fishing pole in her hands, her weight evenly distributed by her bent-knee stance on the jetty rocks, the line from the pole strung out in front of her that disappeared well beyond the crashing surf some hundred feet away.

"Now take your finger and press the line against the pole," Joel directed.

She did so.

"You'll be able to tell if you get a bite when the line tugs on your finger."

"It's tugging now," she said, excited. "It's tugging now!"

Joel giggled. It was quick and nearly silent against the crash of the waves but Janine definitely heard it. "That's the wind you feel," he said. "Catching the wind is pretty easy. Feeling the fish…well, I think you'll know the difference when it happens."

She'd not remembered any of it, her first official fishing task, which was depressing and not so at the same time. Somehow, her mind and body had not connected. She wanted both experiences repeated. His touch. Her cast.

The sound of a distant horn, from the ship that had only been a speck on the horizon almost an hour ago, displaced the experience. It was like being on the Mississippi: wet spray in the face, the paddle-boat whistle, fishing in the "mud", Tom Sawyer her educator, warning her of dangers while reinforcing her actions. She was Becky Thatcher, and Tom would keep her safe. No monsters could get to her, not on the Mississippi, not with Tom's strong hands wrapped around her. No monsters had ever penetrated Trust between two people. Evil was undefined.

"I have something to tell you, Joel, and I hope that you can trust me," she whispered, not knowing if Joel had even heard her. "I am not insane."

Joel stepped forward but did not touch her. "Look!" he shouted, pointing. "You got one!"

◻ ...

"I saw him last night," Steph said.

"Saw who?" Billy continued paddling ahead. They were near the Caldwell Pier. The bodyguard kept pace along the shoreline. Only two people occupied the pier—not enough, Billy suspected, to deter any harm that the bodyguard might have in store for them.

"Pedro." Steph looked tired, haggard. She had the body of an athlete but Billy supposed that most of her athletic maturity was not attained in the water. "He was headed into the bank. When I was leaving, I saw him."

Billy stopped paddling and pulled up to a sitting position on his board. Steph did the same. The bodyguard stood and stared at them. The pier was less than fifty feet away. The two people on the pier, an elderly couple, looked down and waved. Steph stared as if dumbfounded. Billy returned the wave but did not think about the action; instead, he wondered why Pedro would have gone to the Port A branch of the Big Texas Bank. He wondered if Bone's death had anything to do with it. He wondered if the bodyguard had anything to do with it. He wondered if the wooden crate in the vault had anything to do with it. He wondered if two Pedros, one chasing the other, had anything to do with it.

"Do you know why he was at the bank?" Billy said, absently, still waving at the elderly couple on the pier who had stopped waving at him and had turned their backs.

"No." Steph stared at the bodyguard. Her breaths were shallow. "He might have wanted to enter the contest."

As their boards carried them under the pier and to the other side, Billy considered this. "Do you remember ever seeing Dave come into the bank?" he asked.

"Dave?"

"The security guard from the marine institute. The one who almost ran us over yesterday."

"No," Steph said. "I didn't see him but then I wasn't in the bank all afternoon. I did take a short break for lunch."

"And that crazy bitch from the newspaper office. You ever see her in the bank?"

"Nope." Steph paused. "What are you getting at?"

"It's got to be in that crate," Billy said, not looking at her but only at the nose of his surfboard. "I think we both agree that whenever someone goes into that vault, they come out somehow...different. You called it 'robotic'."

"Not everyone," Steph said. "You went in and came out okay. I've been in several times and came out okay."

"But you said that when you went in with Carol, and the fellas from the casino they pushed the crate at you. Did you ever touch it?"

"I don't think so."

"Are you sure?"

Steph stared in silent contemplation. "I don't know," she said. "Why?" Her eyes welled with sudden concern. Billy pulled her board closer to him and patted her hand.

"Nothing, really. I mean, you feel just fine, right? You don't seem 'robotic' to me."

Steph jerked her hand from Billy's grasp and examined it as if it were infested with some invisible disease. "You think the crate has some kind of contagion?" she said. "You think I contracted it?"

"No," Billy said. "—I mean, yes."

She stared at him as if he were crazy and purposely let her board drift away from his.

"No, I don't think you are infected," he clarified. "And yes, I think there may be a contagion, something distributed by touch. Nothing airborne." He paddled to her and pulled her close. And before the surprise left her face, he kissed her, lightly, quickly. "And if you are, then we both are."

And then there was laughing, deep and guttural, emanating from the shore.

"Sweet," the bodyguard growled. "Sweet. Sweet. Sweet." His voice was two octaves below baritone. He stepped into the water and started toward them. Ten feet in, the breakers hit him in the chest and face but his body broke through as if the water had no force at all.

"Holy shit," Steph said as the bodyguard took his first stroke into the water and began swimming.

"Time to paddle out of here," Billy suggested and laid belly to board. Steph got into the same position and both of them started paddling farther out and in the direction of the jetty.

The bodyguard kept pace, his black boots beating the water behind him, his black suit a mass of soaked weight that promoted the image of a hungry shark moving in for the kill. Billy's arms tired and he suspected that Steph's were reaching exhaustion.

Still, the beach remained vacant of sunbathers. No witnesses. Out beyond the jetty, a ship cruised inland, its horn sounding the approach, but it was still too far away to provide witness. Billy believed they had no other choice but to head for the shore and take their chances on land. Certainly they could run faster than they could paddle.

"I can't go on much more," Steph said, her voice hushed and choking on splashes of seawater.

"Let's head in," Billy said. "We'll have to run."

"I can't," Steph said. "I can't make it." She started falling back as the boot-driven shark closed the distance. "Billy!"

◻ . . .

"Hold on," Joel said. "Feed a bit of line." He showed her how to do so.

Janine had felt the unusual pressure across the pad of her finger but she'd not reacted. She'd been thinking about telling him everything.

"That's it," Joel said, excited. "Can you tell? You hooked a big one, now let's reel the sucker in."

Again, his arms were around her waist, his hands on her forearms.

"Crank it slowly. Don't want to rip out the fella's lips."

She did so, still contemplating insane revelations.

"Now slow down a bit. This one's a fighter. My God, Janine. First time out and you bested the best."

She cranked on the reel as Joel directed but her mind still wandered. *I am not insane*, she continued to think. *Trust me, Joel, I am not insane.*

"That's it," Joel teased. "Yes. That's it."

And then, Janine whipped the fishing pole in an upward arch; her elbows knocked Joel backward. She had tired of the fight. She had something to say…something important. It was much more important than fishing.

When the hook came out of the water, no fish was attached. The fishing line vaulted high, much in the same way as it had when she'd tried to cast the line the first time, only now the hook was moving in the opposite direction. The sun glinted off the tiny piece of metal just before Janine ducked.

"Agghh!"

She turned to see Joel with a hand clasped to his left ear. A tiny spot of blood drooled through his middle and fore fingers. Joel stared as if in disbelief but instead of scolding her, he said, "Well, there's a first time for everything. Never been hooked in the ear before."

Janine released the fishing pole as if it were diseased. It dropped to the jetty rocks and settled between the cracks. "Oh…Oh…I…"

"Well you hooked one, my dear, and a big one too."

"I…"

"And I just love Milky Way."

Janine reached out to coddle his bleeding ear. The hook had fully penetrated the lobe.

"No worry. You just settle." Joel reached into the back pocket of his coveralls and pulled out a knife which he used to cut the fishing line. Then, with gentle strokes, he used the knife to slowly saw the barbed end of the hook which dangled just below his earlobe. In seconds, the metal was severed and he removed the hook. He now held the two pieces of fishing hook in one hand and the knife in the other.

Janine blinked.

It couldn't be!

"I just love this thing," Joel said. "Sharp as Hell. Can cut through anything."

"What…Where…" Her face turned ashen.

Cupped in Joel's right hand was an exact duplicate of something the doctors had told her didn't exist. In Joel's hand was the magic dagger, the one that had removed the bullet from the professor who had never visited her on a night that never happened.

No, she wasn't insane.

"How?" she said to Joel. "How could you have that?"

Joel turned the dagger in his hand. It had the same impossibly thin blade, the same jeweled handle. But at the same time it was different in a way that went beyond the build up of red rust on its surface. He dropped the severed fishing hook, and the two pieces disappeared between jetty rocks.

"I found it," he said, giving the dagger a sudden reverence that was dictated by Janine's awe.

"May I?" Janine held out her hand. Joel passed the dagger with much less thought that he had his fishing pole. She quickly studied it, traced the haft's edges with her fingers and drew the rusty artifact closer for inspection. A red jewel occupied one point of a star. But something was different. It nagged her. Something about the jewel. Something that told her this dagger was in every way the same dagger that had entered her farm house a year ago except for the red jewels. This was that dagger…but it wasn't.

"Proof," she said. "This proves that I am not insane."

"My knife?" Joel said, surprised.

"A magic dagger," Janine corrected.

Joel smiled. He held his earlobe to stop the blood flow and just stood there, his eyes searching hers as if measuring her truth.

"I only told you part of the story, Joel," she began. "Now it's time to tell it all. I am not insane and you can trust me on that account."

They sat on the jetty rocks and Janine recounted everything—withheld nothing. She explained every gruesome detail. She told a story that could rival the fiction of Stephen King. Joel remained silent and only nodded a few times throughout her explanation. When she came to the end she said, "Unbelievable, isn't it?"

"I, uh…" Joel said, again looking into her eyes as if looking for her soul. "I don't know what to say."

The dagger, which Janine had set on a rock in front of them suddenly twitched. A metal-to-rock scraping sound accompanied the dagger's shuttering. It was as if the dagger was cold and shivering…

…and alive.

The jewel in the haft began to glow, creating a red halo around the trembling artifact.

"Help!" someone yelled, and together Joel and Janine looked out into the surf to see two surfboards heading toward them, and the black, splashing outline of a swimmer in close pursuit.

◻ …

The shark closed to within ten feet by the time Billy reached Steph. Three more strokes and the bodyguard would have her—would have them. Without warning, Billy grabbed the nose of Steph's board and flipped it over. Steph went into the water at the same moment that the bodyguard's hand grabbed her ankle. She tried to scream but water filled her mouth. No strength to fight remained in her exhausted arms. She quickly went under.

Billy lifted the nose of Steph's surfboard. Then, in one forward thrust, he hurled the back of the board at the bodyguard. The board's fin missed Steph's struggling, submerged head by fractions of an inch and struck the bodyguard in the face, ripping open the flesh of one cheek and causing the black shark's grip to release its hold on human prey. Billy grabbed Steph's flailing hand and pulled her torso to him; the added weight almost toppled him. Steph coughed up seawater as she struggled to hold tight to Billy's surfboard while Billy began back-pedaling. In a disturbing display of rage, the bodyguard did not simply push Steph's surfboard aside as most angry humans in pursuit of homicide might, but instead, proceeded like a shark, attacking the surfboard with all of its energy, beating the fiberglass into small pieces as if the surfboard was the appetizer to the object of its aggression.

Though Billy distanced himself and Steph by more than a dozen yards while the bodyguard destroyed the surfboard, he knew that it would not be enough. The jetty rocks were another thirty yards away, the shore, forty. The bodyguard's powerful strokes would certainly have them in his grasp before they could escape.

"Billy!"

The shout came from behind him.

"Over here. Swim hard!"

Billy had already stroked for almost two miles. As fit to the water as his muscles were, the combination of time, distance and, now, weight, sucked any hope from his determination. The voice of imperative direction, which he quickly determined was that of Joel, served only to exacerbate the dilemma. Steph barely hung to the end of the surfboard. His arms felt like thick glue.

The bodyguard had satisfied himself with the destruction of the board and now resumed his efforts toward them, his boots pounding the waves like fins, his black menace swiftly engaging them like a predatory torpedo.

Billy stopped paddling, his hope swallowed by the reality of his physical limitations. He, sitting on the surfboard, and Steph, draped across its nose, drifted with the rise and fall of the current while the bodyguard closed the distance, an eerie, wide grin of incisors predominant under the fresh red tear that pulsed across the flesh in his right cheek. The image of Mitchell Bone's decapitated head reemerged in his mind. He glared, hypnotized, at the bodyguard's hands and each hand's powerful stroke; he imagined how easy either appendage could snatch his noggin from his shoulders, an index and forefinger through his eye sockets, a thumb stuck in his mouth—just like a bowling ball. It would be a matter of seconds before he and Steph met the same fate as Bone. The bodyguard had them.

And then…he didn't.

And then, as if some spiritual entity snapped its mystical fingers, the entire scenario changed. A force field developed though Billy knew such a thing did not exist.

The bodyguard drew back. The final swim stroke that would have landed on Steph's flesh was averted by…

Billy looked over his shoulder. On the jetty, an aura of crimson light that engulfed a twenty-foot circle glowed and grew. The halo of red light raced across the water and, seemingly, attacked the bodyguard. It produced a reaction of nauseating madness from the black-skinned shark. The bodyguard writhed and retreated, swimming with equal aggression as he'd used in his assault. As the crimson halo expanded, the bodyguard swam faster, keeping just beyond the halo's outer rim until, at the edge of the pier, a good hundred yards away, the halo disappeared and the bodyguard returned to the shore.

❒ …

Janine grabbed the dagger, her right hand's grip swallowing the glowing, crimson jewel. The weapon buzzed her entire arm, inducing reverberated chills that raced past her elbow and into the back of her neck and down her spine. Crimson colors peeked between her fingers. Five red rays escaped, looking much like thin laser beams. Without knowing why, she lifted the dagger over her head and yelled as loud as she could, directing her bellow at Albert who was little more than a speck of inhumanity crawling to the shore near the pier.

"Back to hell, you son of a bitch!!"

The glow from the jewel faded as Janine lowered her arm, opened her fist and, again without realizing it, spun the dagger atop the palm of her open hand in two complete circles before grasping the haft with the blade pointing down and at her side.

"Mother of God!" Joel whispered, more to himself than to Janine. "What in the name of..."

"...everything Holy," Janine finished. "Well he's not. He is a demon."

Joel looked perplexed. "Who?" he asked. "And where did you learn to handle a knife like that?"

"Dagger," Janine corrected. "A magic dagger." She lifted the dagger from her side as if praising it. "A magic dagger that performs surgery and wards off demons."

Billy and Steph floated on one surfboard near where Janine had dropped her fishing cast just moments ago. "Joel," Billy yelled out. The crashing waves against the jetty rocks made the word sound hallow. "What the hell was that?"

"A demon," Janine repeated under her breath.

"Come on in here," Joel said to the surfers, waving his hand as if reeling in a fish.

A few minutes later, the four of them sat together. The dagger lay behind Janine, its magic seemingly gone from the moment that had encapsulated her. Each person occupied one rock. Jetty spray splashed around them. The cargo ship that had been on the horizon at the start of the day now entered the jetty behind them. Its horn shrieked as if sounding the beginning of some great change which the four would later refer to as the "moment of great enlightening."

Janine, naturally, went first. She knew about those things which had brought them together: the dagger and Albert. She told them everything she'd told Joel. She opened up her soul to the possible ridicule of more strangers. Evil came from the Cubit, she explained. Albert came from the Cubit. He'd murdered her son. He'd destroyed her life.

Janine's was a crazy story of insanity—but it was only slightly worse than the delusion of Billy's revelations who now told the group all that he had discussed with Steph: what he'd seen in the vault, the day on the coast with Mark, blood spots and dead seagulls and the creepy secretary of a missing newspaper publisher.

Steph added her facts about robotic security box recipients and the crazy bitch known as Carol, the bank teller.

Joel added the connection to Steph's word "robotic" with the mannerisms of little Teddy Lavender.

"Anyone seen Pedro?" Billy said after Joel had finished. He looked at Steph. Both Joel and Janine shook their heads. "Well we have. In fact there are two of them." He turned toward Janine. "Didn't you say that while you were in Kansas, you saw…eh…." Steph frowned in disgust in much the same way as she had when Janine had told the story moments before. "Didn't you say you saw your son eat himself?"

"Yes—but that's one part of my memory that I still question. People just don't eat themselves." She hesitated. "Do they?"

"Following the logical path of reason, the answer is absolutely: No!" Janine frowned and Billy took her hand. "But nothing around here is logical anymore. I've—" He gently stroked her flesh with his thumb. "*We've* seen too many things that cannot make sense to logic."

"Zombies!" Joel suddenly added to the discussion. "The walkin' dead."

Billy glared, a compiled expression of *Are you crazy?* and *You have something there!* all mixed into a confused frown. "I just don't know, Joel, but I wouldn't use the word zombie."

Steph leaned forward. "Billy and I have a plan."

Billy looked quizzically at her.

"There is another player in all of this and she has yet to make her appearance." She told Joel and Janine of the investor from Arizona and the plan to meet her at the airport. "Maybe Alixel can shed some light. In the meantime, I don't think any of us should be left alone."

"I agree," Janine said quickly.

Joel covered Billy's hand which still rested on Janine's. Steph solidified the pact by topping their hands with hers.

"I'm scared," Janine said while reaching with her free hand for the dagger.

"With that," Joel said, nodding at the weapon, "I don't think you have anything to worry about."

PART II

REVELATION

The dunes now held no innocent magic. That morning, as Janine and Joel had walked toward the Gulf, the scattered, uneven heaps of sand had posed as obstacles to anticipated beauty. The water, the surf and the melding of their naive souls had shadowed all of the troubles that the "real world" dictated. Cresting one dune only to be confronted by another had increased the anticipation. She'd seen the ocean only once before. She'd never gone fishing. She had been Becky Thatcher and Joel had been her Tom.

But as they headed back in from shore—from the madness and revelations that had shattered what could have been Janine's final break from her year of insanity—all she could think about was death, demons, and the demise of *her* Paradise. The dunes no longer stood in the way of beauty; they now protected her from the ugliness of certainty. Insanity had been an unwanted but convenient excuse to forget her past, but the south jetty of the Corpus Christi shipping channel had provided the setting for a reality that, in a few abrupt moments, had made her past inconveniently true and more complex.

As she and Joel traversed the sand away from the heat and the confusion of the morning, Janine questioned her belief in choice. Perhaps, in the end, no human being had such luxury. The decisions of every soul were preordained. God was the director. Her decision to arrive in this Paradise was not hers. Her decision to break from the past was really the most insane idea she'd ever held. You couldn't run from destiny. You couldn't choose to stand on the sidelines while Evil played out the antagonist's role. She was *meant* to be here. She and Joel, Becky and Tom, and the roles *they* would play in the days that followed were already written into destiny's script. What she had to do was accept it. What she had to do was believe. But to help her mortal ineptitude, and to help forward God's plan for her, she would have to understand the mysteries that had been revealed.

"Careful," Joel said as they crossed the final dune between them and the asphalt surface of Cotter Avenue. "That little ball next to your foot will grab hold if you aren't careful."

Janine looked down. An inch from her open-toed sandal was a tiny, unassuming, egg-shaped cactus that had no roots. It sat atop the sand like a prickly grenade.

"That sucker can smell human flesh and will snag you in a way that makes fishing hooks feel good." He touched his ear.

Janine casually avoided the tiny cactus, her attention more on the curiosity of Joel's dagger which she still held in her hand.

"This is in so many ways the dagger I used to pull the bullet out of the professor's chest," she said, raising the thin blade toward the sun's glinting, midday heat. "But it isn't. And even if it was *that* dagger, how in God's name could you have it?"

Joel only shrugged his shoulders, sensing that her questions were not meant for him to answer. He twiddled his fishing pole, nervously, between the fingers of his left hand.

"Which can only mean that there's more than one of them. Where did you get it? And please don't tell me Kansas."

"On the beach," he said. "Or more appropriately, in the beach."

"In it?"

Joel hesitated as if embarrassed by what he would say. "A few years ago I went on this…craze, I guess you might call it. I went treasure hunting. You see, I've always had this fascination with pirates." He paused for some expressive response from her, but Janine said nothing as she avoided another tiny, human foot-hungry cactus. There seemed to be many more of the spiked plants than she'd remembered on their way out to the jetty. "In particular, I've always had this thing for Jean LaFitte. A fascinating character if there ever was one. He made the Gulf his home during the early part of the nineteenth century. Some say he wasn't even a pirate. Some say he was more a profiteer in a day when Spain and America were at odds and slave-trading was a way of life."

"The dagger," Janine said, a bit too impatiently. The history of Jean LaFitte was not one of the mysteries she was interested in solving. Her impatience surprised Joel.

"Yes…well. LaFitte, it is said, had a huge treasure which he took with him when he was forced out of Galveston in 1820. Some say he took it to the Yucatán where he used the wealth to build a new life. Others say he lost it in a massive hurricane that nearly destroyed his ship. Then there's the myth that his treasure is buried right here on Mustang Island. I went digging around for almost a full year back in '95 in search of the myth. The only thing I ever found was that knife…eh…dagger."

"Where?" Janine stopped and looked back toward where the ocean was now hidden beyond the dunes.

"By the pier," Joel said, pointing. "Pretty much near the spot where I met you two days ago at the luau."

"How far down was it?"

"You mean how much did I have to dig to find it?"

Janine nodded.

"Couple of feet was all. Digging too far that close to the pier would have brought the badges out."

"Didn't Billy say that the casino was supposed to be built in that area?"

Joel nodded.

"And Albert's one of them," she said more to herself than to Joel.

"What was that?" Joel asked.

"It's just that Albert is playing bodyguard for the man in charge of bringing the casino to Port Aransas."

"Okay."

"And they are planning to build it where you found the dagger."

"Yeah."

Janine saw the confusion in his stare. She smiled.

"Oh, I don't know. Just running some of the facts through my head. It's just that everything seems so 'convenient' if you know what I mean."

"Convenient?" Joel said. "You mean as in how convenient it was that your dagger came to life just when that…what did you call him…ah, yes—I think it was demon. Just when that demon nearly killed Billy and Steph?"

She raised the dagger at arms length. "Strange. There are so many mysteries. But we're going to figure them out. Aren't we? As long as we stay alive that is."

"I wouldn't worry about that zombie if that's what you're referring to. You have the ultimate in zombie radar devices right there in your hand."

"I suspect that he is not the only *zombie* around here. From what Steph was saying, there may be hundreds more."

"Now that's an idea a person could lose sleep over." Joel covered her hand with his and she released the dagger into his grip.

"We'll pick up some rust remover," Janine said. "It's quite beautiful once it's all shined up."

They walked in silence the rest of the way to Joel's Canton Shack. Janine kept a weary eye out for anyone who looked suspicious though she wasn't quite sure what "suspicious" really looked like. The iPod kid came to mind—little Teddy Lavender. He'd certainly acted inhuman, or as Joel had put it, zombie-ish. What continued to trouble her, though, was that there might be "zombies" out there that didn't act zombie-ish. And worse—what if the dagger did not warn them? Just because it had gone nuts when Albert had gotten too close didn't mean that it would protect them from what could be hundreds of these things. If they looked human and acted human and nothing could tell her or Joel any different then they had little chance of surviving. And being torn apart and eaten—the way poor Lenny had been—was a horrific thought. She'd not come this far to die like that. It just wasn't in God's plan. It could not—must not—be her destiny. She had to believe.

But believing was hard, especially when she and Joel turned onto the pebbled path that led to the Canton Shack and found the screen door ripped from its top hinge and flailing askew on its single, twisted bottom hinge. The screen mesh had been ripped as if sliced by a knife. Joel immediately pushed Janine behind him, lifted the dagger in a defensive posture, and dropped his fishing pole. The dagger's haft did not glow but Janine was unsure if this was a good thing.

Cautiously, Joel stepped into his home. The first thing his toe touched was the clock that Marcy had given him for Christmas. The glass face was broken and in shards on the floor. The magician's hands were bent at odd angles. It did not work.

"Stay here," Joel said to Janine.

"No," she insisted. "We're in this together."

They entered what looked to be the aftermath of a tornadic storm. Joel did not have much, but whatever material belongings he owned were in mass disarray. All of his clothes and linen were scattered everywhere. His mattress had been flung from the bed spring, torn open and disemboweled— pieces of foam and fluff sat like brown snow on the floor, the bed spring, the window sill, his makeshift bookshelves and tabletop spool, his tiny refrigerator which had been turned upside down, its meager contents emptied and mixed in with the mattress stuffing. The curtain that had served as a divider to his bathroom-closet lay in a balled mass on the shower stall floor. His fishing lamp was busted and lay in ruin around the balled curtain, as if someone had thrown it against the shower stall wall.

"They're looking for this," Joel immediately concluded, referring to the dagger. "I don't have anything else of value. And from what I've heard and seen, this must be worth a fortune."

"Maybe," Janine agreed. "But whoever *they* is might also be looking for something else. We have to get to Marcy's."

◘ ...

The foursome had made an arrangement to meet back at Paradise Cottages later that evening. The hope was that Billy and Steph would gain additional knowledge from the woman whom all of them knew only as Alixel. Meanwhile, Janine said that she and Joel would make their way back to Janine's cottage.

Billy and Steph had a long walk ahead of them. Traversing two miles in the surf had not seemed so exhausting—at least not up until the time that Albert had entered the water and had chased them from the pier to the jetty. The water had provided relief from the unrelenting heat of the Texas sun. And the joy that had been shared by both he and Steph, the innocent moments together in the surf and Steph's victory over the five-foot wave, had made time slip away. But now, as they trudged barefoot along the wet sand at the Gulf's perimeter, minutes seemed like hours and the hot sun stripped them of energy. Worse, though, was the concern for the wide and deep footprints that paralleled them. Albert's, no doubt. His destination was certainly theirs: Billy's VW.

"Do you believe her?" Steph said. "I mean really."

Billy walked a good thirty paces before he answered. His mind's logic fought the apparent reality that Janine's revelations had conjured. But the facts spoke for themselves. And no matter how hard he tried to reason away the events of the past two days, no matter how hard he tried to calculate an explanation using what had always been the reliable scientific methodologies solidified through academic study, the truth seemed apparent.

"It sounds absurd," he said, finally. "But until we find out what's in that crate, whether it be Janine's Cubit or something more realistically sane, I can't ignore the possibility."

"Even if that means there are dead people walking amongst us?" Steph absently kicked a broken seashell into the surf.

"Yeah. Even if it means that. Even if it means that the Pedro we saw running and the Pedro we saw chasing and the scream we heard from across the dunes when the one had caught up with the other means that the real Pedro is now dead. Even if it means that we have to consider, based on Janine's storied past, that the one Pedro ate the other. Even if it means that we could go crazy thinking about what all of this means. We have to consider the possibility."

"So we have to find Pedro."

Billy nodded. "And we have to find out more about what's in that bank vault."

"Until then we have to assume that anyone could be something they are not."

Billy stopped walking as did Steph. He turned to face her. "That could lead to paranoia."

"I'm already paranoid," she said, looking back toward the pier which, in the distance, was no more than a shadowy line atop the surface of the water. "I'm already thinking about what I'd do if I saw myself holding a knife. I'm already wondering if I could outrun…me. And if I couldn't escape, then what would it be like to be eaten alive?" A tear welled in her left eye. "This can't be real, can it? I want you to tell me that it can't be real." Her lips twitched as the tear fell onto one breast.

Billy pulled her to him; her chin rested on his naked shoulder. Wet streams of salt trickled down his spine. She sighed, trembled. "I wish I had an answer," he said.

Billy's back was to the distant pier. Up ahead, along the shoreline and still a good thousand yards away, he saw the vague outline of his VW. He also saw what he believed was Albert though at this distance the figure could have been anyone. The bodyguard would be at—and certainly be in—his vehicle within minutes. Albert would destroy it, Billy was certain, the way he'd destroyed Steph's surfboard.

Steph suddenly yelled out.

"Look!"

Billy turned around to see that a vehicle was approaching along the beach road, a Chevy van, circa 1979, that had a medieval retro-paint job slathered across the body's copper-colored surface. He recognized it immediately. It was the *Knights in White Satin*.

As the van slowed to a crawl beside them, the driver leaned out the window. His bleach-blonde hair was knotted in a ponytail. "What's up with all the lame activity around here dude and dudette?" It was Richard, the band's vocalist and leader.

Billy avoided the formalities. "Can you give us a lift to my v-dub?" He pointed toward the gray outline which now appeared to merge with the bodyguard's.

"No problemo. Hey, you saved our butts. Right? Right…"

Billy led Steph to the opposite side of the van where one of the painted knights on the van's metal split in half as the band's drummer opened the sliding door and offered his hand. "Enter, me lady," the drummer said, his white mustache and beard manicured in a way that reminded Billy of the face on the cover of a pack of ZigZags. "Let us escort thee to thine own divine providence." The drummer's smile was one that could easily be contagious under other circumstances.

"Please hurry," Billy said as he sat on a bench seat next to Steph. The drummer sat behind them with the group's guitarist. Behind the guitarist were two cases shaped like the musical instruments he played.

"Gunnin' it now my friend," Richard said. "Like what's up with this island, man? I thought this place would be the bomb but it's nothing more than one giant crater of boredom."

Billy saw that Albert had now reached his VW and was attacking the driver's door.

"Whoa, Bill," Richard said. "That dude's fuckin' up your ride."

"Faster," Billy replied.

"On it my man." Richard looked over at the bass player sitting in the passenger seat. "You still got that punk bat, Dillon?"

Dillon leaned forward and pulled a short wooden bat, the kind you might get as a baseball game souvenir, from under the seat. Billy saw the word *Mud Hens* emblazoned in the grain. "Holy crap," Dillon exclaimed, his voice as deep as the chords he played for the band. "That motha' punched right through the window." He looked at the small bat, as if suddenly questioning the success of its intended use.

Albert had beat several dents into the driver's side door of Billy's VW, and was reaching through the window he'd busted when the *Knights'* van diverted his attention. He stepped away from the vehicle, his wrinkled black shirt, pants and boots riddled with streaks of dried sand, and clenched both fists.

"Hit him," Billy said. Steph looked at him with a shocked but confederate stare.

"What?" Dillon replied, smacking the fat head of the small bat in the palm of his hand.

"That tiny toothpick ain't gonna help us one bit," Billy said. "Believe me. He'll rip us all a new asshole."

Richard glanced over his shoulder at Billy. A short, quick grin spread from the corner of his lip then was gone. He whipped his head back around and his white-blonde ponytail followed in an arc that Billy seemed to see only in slow motion. In fact, the next few minutes all came at him in slow motion. "Bon...zai..." Richard wailed, though his words came out as if they'd been recorded and were being played back at half speed. "You... muth...a...fuck...ah..."

The *Knights'* van jumped as Richard hammered the gas pedal but to

Billy the jump was more like a tiptoe. He felt the additional g-force that pressed him into the van's seat and he saw Steph's head jolt backward in unison with his own, but the moment seemed to last forever, the way a momentary dream seems to endure for hours, the way he'd felt when he'd left the Surf Side on Tuesday and then when he'd pulled over in the breakdown lane of Route 361 on his way to rescue the *Knights* that evening before the luau. His mind had blurred into slow motion then as he'd somehow been transported to that other dimension where he was being chased and shot at, where someone was telling him to "Shut the fuck up!", and where he'd puked into the shattered pebbles of windshield glass.

A dream that seemed more like a memory.

Richard's hands yanked the van's steering wheel to the left, but the motion seemed incredibly slow. "Come…here…you…muth…a…," he snarled. Through the windshield, Billy saw that the distance between them and Albert was less than twenty yards. He noticed that the speedometer read fifty-five. But time seemed to stand still. It came at him in still-framed succession.

Snap!

Richard clamped down on the steering wheel, his knuckles showing white.

Snap!

The bass player named Dillon dropped the bat and grabbed the dashboard.

Snap!

Someone screamed, though he was unsure if it was him, Steph, or one of the band members behind them.

Snap!

Albert stood to the left of the van's hood. Impact was a nanosecond away. He did not flinch. He did not try to avoid the van. He just stood there, grinning, his eyes filled with the crimson swirls of dark insanity that Billy remembered from the Surf Side bar.

Snap!

And then, suddenly, the slow motion stopped and the reality of the impact sprang catastrophically alive. When the van hit Albert it seemed as if the Chevy had actually hit a wall. Richard fought for control of the steering wheel as the van fishtailed to the right, its rear bumper missing Billy's VW by inches. Dillon's head lurched into the windshield and made a sickening thud! He grabbed his nose which was now bloody. Both Billy and Steph plowed shoulder first into the headrests of the front bucket seats and the drummer behind them flew up and over their seat and landed behind them, his ZigZag beard planting in the small of Steph's back. The van spun 180 degrees before coming to a complete stop. A cloud of sand enveloped them and rained in through the open windows. Everyone coughed for clean air.

"Holy shit!" Dillon said. Billy didn't know if his exclamation referred more to the impact with Albert or the blood in his hand.

"Are you all right?" Billy asked Steph whose spine looked uncomfortably arched with the drummers head behind her.

"Oww," she moaned. The drummer shifted and pulled himself up and back into the seat behind them. She rubbed the place where his beard had scratched her skin then stretched the muscles.

"Some divine providence," the drummer said. "Weren't nothin' divine about that. What the hell did you hit?"

The sand in the van trickled down—brown sparkles under a Texas sun—and as the cloud dissipated, all six of them stared out the windshield with anticipation.

"That big mutha fucka," Richard said, shaking the disorientation from his head. "Didn't I? Or was it a fuckin' freight train?"

Buried in the sand just a few feet away from Billy's VW was the outline of Albert. The body was pressed into the sand face first. His black clothing made it appear as if someone had poured a shadow into the beach. Albert did not move.

"Is he dead?" Dillon said.

Billy and Steph stared at each other, knowing the truth.

"You ran right over him." It was the first thing the guitarist said since Billy and Steph had entered the van.

Richard stepped out of the van. Dillon exited and slid open the van's side door with one hand while he pinched his nose with his right and tilted his head back. The blood flow slowed, trickling in thin rivulets across his cheeks toward both ears. Outside, Billy moved around to the front of the van where Richard stood, gawking at the dent and smashed left headlight.

"Shit," Richard said. "I thought for sure he'd jump out of the way." He turned toward the shadow planted in the sand. "I killed him. Holy shit. I killed him." He looked at Dillon and the drummer and guitarist who stood behind him, then gazed out across the dunes, up and down the beach road and out into the surf. The reality of what he'd done was gaining self-importance. "We gotta get outta here."

Billy grabbed Richard's shoulder, feeling the soreness in his own as he did so. "Just get back into your van and drive away. You probably saved all of our lives not to mention the v-dub. I'll call the authorities as soon as I get into town." Billy looked over Richard's shoulder at Albert. "To tell you the truth, I don't think you killed him."

"Holy shit," Richard repeated. "Of course I did."

"No you didn't," Dillon confirmed. "Look!"

One of Albert's boots suddenly shifted in the sand. The heel turned downward and the pointed tip turned up, which looked physically impossible.

"Broken leg," Richard said. "I broke his leg."

The other boot followed the motion of the first, heel turning down, toe twisting up. Now both feet were pointing in the wrong direction, looking much like two shark fins in the sand.

Billy pushed Richard toward the Chevy. "Get out of here," he urged. "You didn't kill him, but you probably pissed him off something horrible."

Richard's expression was one that reminded him of how Steph had looked as they sat on the jetty rocks listening to the impossible stories told by Janine. He apparently did not believe what was occurring but could not question its reality.

"Man," the drummer said. "We gotta move, bro. If we didn't kill him already, we ain't gonna get another chance."

One of Albert's arms lifted from the sand, then the other, and the shadow which was no longer a shadow did a push-up. Albert's face turned upward toward them. His eyes boiled in crimson red and emitted a glow that developed a faint, crimson halo around his head.

Everyone scattered at that instant.

The *Knights in White Satin* almost tripped over each other as they raced for the open van doors. Billy and Steph bolted for the VW.

Albert rose to his knees making the pointed toes of his boots, still turned in the wrong direction, seem even more anatomically incorrect.

It took four turns of the ignition key to get the *Knights'* van started and with each unsuccessful turn, Billy saw through his own windshield how much more concerned both Richard and Dillon became. They watched Albert, who now rose onto his backward pointing feet, reach down, grab his left leg just below the knee and twist it in a clockwise motion. Impossible as it may have been, and as sickening as it was to watch, the lower leg turned 180 degrees under a knee which could not have possibly supported such a motion. He applied the same technique to the right leg then stood up straight, his eyes beaming hatred at them.

The Chevy tires spun, causing the van to fishtail. For a moment, Billy thought that Richard was going to drive it right into the surf but a second later, control was regained and the van sped away down the firm, wet sand at the surf's edge.

Billy had a similar problem getting his VW to start. He turned the key twice before it came to life. By that time, Albert was three steps from the back of the vehicle. The crimson glow from his eyes filled the VW's interior as he grabbed the rear bumper. Billy stomped the accelerator to the floor and for split-second, he thought that Albert had them, that his strength was too much for the meager vintage horsepower of the four-decade-old vehicle. The VW spun in place, not moving an inch and Steph screamed.

"Go! Go! GOOO!"

The VW suddenly broke free causing Billy to struggle with the steering wheel for control. As they sped away, both looked back, almost knocking heads between the bucket seats. Albert stood in the center of the calamity, shards of broken windshield, headlight and van reflector scattered at his feet. He held Billy's rear bumper in one hand.

❐ …

Marcy was not home but her back door was still unlocked. Janine and Joel entered into the kitchen and Janine led the way upstairs to where she'd left her sacks of life. Nothing appeared out of place but to Janine that meant nothing. She thought that those that had devastated Joel's place could have found what they were looking for at Marcy's without destroying property.

When she entered the guest bedroom, she was still unconvinced that her sacks, and the book that rested within one of them, would still be there. She knew that the book held dire significance. Pages just didn't write themselves. But her sacks *were* there, untouched, just like she'd left them. She grabbed the bottom of the sack closest to her, felt the impression of the book inside, opened it, dropped in the dagger, then pulled the sack closed and draped its pull-string around her hand. Joel grabbed the other sack and slung it over his shoulder.

"You want me to carry that for you?" he asked. She said nothing, only shaking her head instead.

She headed down the stairs and Joel followed. "What is it?" he said. "Your face looks…" She turned to him as her foot hit the last step at the bottom of staircase and scowled unintentionally. "…twisted," he concluded.

Janine paused, one foot on the landing, one foot on the last step, the sack and its contents weighting her left arm with what she now believed was salvation. She stepped to the landing, looked up at Joel who towered three steps above her, and was suddenly stricken by memory. Of Kansas. Of Michael. Of Lenny. Of her own special room that doubled as a storm cellar against tornadoes. Of Spirituality and God and Paradise.

Then, for reasons she could not understand beyond divine intervention, Janine thought about *The 23rd Psalm*. She stared straight through Joel and back into time, to that place, in her home, and at the framed page of scripture mounted on her "Paradise" wall. She read aloud:

"The Lord is my Shepherd; I shall not want.
He maketh me to lie down in green pastures:
He leadeth me beside the still waters.
He restoreth my soul:
He leadeth me in the paths of righteousness for His
name' sake.

Yea, though I walk through the valley of the shadow of
death,
I will fear no evil: For thou art with me;
Thy rod and thy staff, they comfort me.
Thou preparest a table before me in the presence of
mine enemies;
Thou annointest my head with oil; My cup runneth over.

Surely goodness and mercy shall follow me all the
days of my life, and I will dwell in the House of the Lord
forever."

Joel stood frozen for a full minute. "Christian woman," he finally said. "That could come in handy." Then he joined her at the bottom of the stairs.

The storm cellar wall faded from memory and was replaced by Joel's concern. "We need to go to the Surf Side," she said not looking up. "The shadow of death. We'll find it there."

"Shadow of death?" Joel questioned.

"Yes."

Janine headed into the kitchen and out the back door before Joel could say anything further. He followed.

They found that the Surf Side had been broken into. The glass from the side entry door was in pebbled shards; webbed, sharp edges still clung to the aluminum frame. Joel swept Janine backward with a gentle but forceful stroke of his left arm. He dropped his sack to the pavement and it crunched atop the broken glass pebbles.

Shadow of Death.

Janine's words kept nagging him. He'd met many *Shadows of Death* in life but none that even closely resembled those that had been suggested to him in the past hour. People didn't eat people...sharks did. But as the Psalm that Janine read revealed, he—Joel—was with her. His rod and staff would comfort her. In fact, his rod and staff would beat the crap out of anyone that laid a finger on Janine. Janine should fear no Evil as long as Joel walked with her through the Valley of the Shadow of Death.

"Stand back," he said, now reinforced with a will reserved for protectors and guardians and saviors, and stepped into the shadows. The hostess podium had been toppled but none of the tables in the dining room ahead had been touched. The bar immediately to the left, however, was in shambles. Liquor, and the bottles that had housed it, lay scattered on the floor in a pooled Technicolor mess one-inch deep. Wine glasses and shot glasses and beer mugs and the mirror behind the bar had been swept to the floor, adding to the glistening reflections of moisture and crystal. The only two items that had not been destroyed sat atop the bar: a full bottle of Jim Beam less one shot that sat within a jigger next to the bottle. Joel dismissed it but when Janine entered behind him, she gasped.

"He's been here," she said.

Joel knew. "Albert?"

"He used to drink that fire juice and then hit..." Janine quickly looked away.

"He hit you?"

"He tried to kill me." She still had the sack hanging from her left hand and it looked as if the weight was taking its toll on the muscles of that arm.

"Why don't you put that down? Or I could carry it for you."

"NO!" she yelled, then placed a finger to her lips. "Shhh…he might be here," she said to herself.

She turned toward the kitchen and Joel rushed in front of her, again using his gentle strength to force her back. He eased through the swinging double doors to find a kitchen so dimly lit that it was almost impossible to see. He searched for the light switch and flipped it up with a forefinger. Nothing happened. The only illumination into the room came from the open swinging doors and this was so dim, Joel's shadow was quickly eaten by the darkness beyond six feet. An intruder could easily be hidden.

Joel grabbed a broom which leaned against the door frame to the left and took a step forward.

"If it's Albert," Janine said from behind, "that broom will be of no use."

Joel looked at the wooden handle then quickly slammed it against one raised leg. It snapped almost completely in two and Joel had to wrestle with the rounded end to separate it. What remained would serve as a spear, the edges of the splintered wood shaped into a jagged point.

"Still," Janine warned.

Joel stepped forward and disappeared into the shadows just as a loud THUD! echoed above them from Billy's apartment.

◻ …

They traveled the length of the island on Route 361 in silence. Off to the left, Steph noticed that, for the first time in two weeks, clouds were rolling inland and it looked as if the island would finally get some welcome wet relief. It was fitting, she thought. The dark days were on the horizon.

Billy's blonde hair whipped in disarray as wind swirled into the now-shattered driver's side window. Since they'd left the beach in such a panic, they'd had to stop at Steph's apartment to get some decent clothing before heading to the airport. She'd given Billy a yellow T-shirt with the words *Mary Kay* stamped on the chest; it was the only clean shirt she had that fit him.

Steph, still trembled from the experience on the beach; she clenched her jittery hands and sucked in one deep breath. Dried tears of fear rested on both cheeks. "What in the name of God…"

Billy gently grabbed her hands and stroked the knuckles. "Not God," he said.

For a moment, she almost yanked free of his grasp. Somehow, his touch no longer excited her. Gone was the simple innocence of their first kiss at the luau. Gone was their shared victory over the five-foot wave. Funny, how the walking dead did that to a person, how the threat of death ripped desire from the soul. It was a fleeting moment...his hand, ugly, menacing, as if it were made of the same dead flesh that had decimated her surfboard, had punched through the VW window, had withstood a direct hit from a speeding Chevy van, and had ripped bolted metal from the back of the VW as easily as one might peel a banana. His hand was Albert's hand and it would kill her! For a fraction of time that almost sent her over the edge, she almost jerked away and screamed, "Stop this fucking car!" She almost screamed and then she almost puked.

And then the moment subsided. Billy was Billy again. His touch, though not full of anticipated desire, was reassuring. She glared at him knowing her face had turned green; her lips trembled and the tears rushed uncontrollably.

"I'll pull over," he offered.

She moved her hands over his, sniffed and mustered a smile. "No," she said and patted his hand. "I'm fine...really. We can't be late."

"We have plenty of time."

She shook her head. "What if they get to her first?"

Billy's eyebrows raised, again in that calculator-that's-lost-a-transistor expression of confusion, but he said nothing.

When they arrived at the corner of 361 and South Padre Drive where Billy would turn right toward Corpus Christi, Janine noticed him staring into his rearview mirror. His gaze remained even after the traffic light turned green. Vehicles zipped by them, the drivers blaring horns and shouting obscenities. He continued staring, oblivious, through a complete traffic light cycle. What was most troublesome to Steph, though, was the way his face shifted with expressions that ranged from curiosity to fright, as if the mirror contained some projected suspense movie that glued him to its screen. When the light, again, turned green she gave his shoulder a gentle but forceful shove.

"Green means go," she said.

❒ ...

The kid was no older than an average college graduate. His hair was dark and straight with no wave to it whatsoever; it almost touched his shoulders but not quite. His twin looked *almost* like him, except the twin's eyes were red, its hair a molted tangle and it smelled so bad a word for the stench was not in the English language.

Billy watched the smelly twin eat its primary through the looking glass of his VW's rearview mirror. He knew that the dead and the dying were both Lenny Bender, the son of the woman who had revealed this small piece of an insane story back on the jetty rocks. And Billy realized that his previous visions, Tuesday—the one outside of the Surf Side when he'd been transported into a chase scene with police and gunshots and someone named "professor", and the one that had caused him to pull over and puke on Route 361 while en route to pick up the stranded Knights in White Satin—were all pieces of Janine's story. A woman he'd never met...a story that could not be true...a vision of the past revealed to him in the future.

The mystic part of his reasoning that he'd always cloaked in a veil of scientific denial leaked into his consciousness, and as he'd always, habitually, done, he tried to push it aside; he tried to ignore it; he tried to reason it away. But this time it wasn't going to work. He knew it, and that's what made his rearview mirror, now a wide screen of projected magic, so much harder to resist. He looked into the past. He saw someone eat themselves.

No, Janine. You're not insane, he thought. *The world is.*

And then the vision blew apart, scattering across the rearview mirror surface like shards of glass. Twisting. Twinkling. Bouncing against the edges of the mirror then reforming into another image that occupied its center. A book. And an image of Janine's magic dagger embossed into its red surface.

Steph shook his arm. Someone else yelled, "Asshole! Get off the damn road!" He looked away from the mirror.

A passenger on the back of a Harley Davidson, a woman in black chaps and tattoos, flipped him off as the motorcycle passed on the left then sharply turned right onto South Padre Drive in an aggressive move that nearly clipped the VW's front bumper. A police cruiser quickly crossed the median from the opposite direction and its lights swirled into action, following the motorcyclist into the Go-Mart parking lot at the corner of the intersection.

Billy peeked back into the rearview mirror, slyly, the way children do from under the covers when they know monsters are chasing them. And that's exactly what he saw.

He'd not realized it, and had no idea how long they'd been following behind, but there they were: Officer Keadle and Crabman, sitting in the front seat of a brown Chevy Impala, one of Port A's unmarked state trooper cruisers.

"You're right," he said to Steph. "Looks like others are interested in the airport arrival." He grabbed her arm. "Don't turn!"

They traveled across the causeway to the mainland with Keadle and Crabman two cars behind them. It wasn't until they reached the traffic light at the intersection which led to the airport terminals that the Impala pulled up beside them on the left. Crabman, in the passenger seat, turned toward Billy, his head twisting on a neck that seemed disconnected, a skull with no spine, like a child's toy doll with a head that spins a full 360 degrees with little more than the twist of a hand. Crabman's eyes were huge, doll-like, the whites completely encircling the center crimson color Billy now associated with those who had been changed. And the thing that used to be Crabman, which looked in almost every way just like the real Rally Panini, grinned. Its lips curled up into its cheeks impossibly deep and a set of bright white incisors appeared. The big, round eyes atop a half moon of teeth that were etched into a face painted onto a spineless skull reminded Billy of John Carpenter's *They Live*. It was as if Billy had that special pair of sunglasses through which he could see the beasts that had taken over the Earth's population.

And then, just as Keadle stomped the accelerator to race toward the terminal ahead of them, Crabman's teeth parted to reveal a cavernous, black pit—no tongue, no gums, no throat, just emptiness—and he bellowed forth the sound of diseased laughter. It was of such a piercing high pitch that Steph covered her ears. Even as the cruiser raced out of sight, the maniacal craziness remained, as if it were trapped inside the VW, a foul entity that could drive a person insane.

❑ . . .

Billy's apartment door stood wide open; bed sheets fluttered across the threshold. Inside, the mattress had been toppled and, like Joel's mattress, had been gutted with a knife. Chunks of foam that had been ripped in handfuls were scattered everywhere, including the wooden porch where

Janine and Joel now stood.

Something fell to the floor inside and shattered. Joel crept into the open doorway; he held the makeshift broom-handle-spear defensively in front of him. The porch boards creaked as he stepped from them, alerting the intruder.

And then he saw him—Pedro. The Surf Side cook poked his head from the recesses of Billy's makeshift lab-office.

"Pedro!" Joel immediately said, while lowering the broom-handled weapon in confidence. "Who the Hell did this?"

But it took Joel only a fraction of a second to answer his own question. This was not Pedro. It looked like him, but it was not him. It was the other one. The *dead Pedro*, as Billy had called him; the one that had eaten the real Pedro. Joel raised the point of his spear.

"Back, you zombie," he warned. "Now you just back on into the bathroom where I'm gonna lock you up until the authorities get here."

The cubited Pedro stared for a moment, animal-like, its eyes roiling in crimson and silver. It looked past Joel to Janine who stood in the doorway, her sack of life in one hand, the dagger which she'd pulled from it in the other. The haft of the dagger glowed a dull red but nothing with the magnitude it had when Albert had approached the south jetty in pursuit of Billy and Steph. Pedro rushed the door, zeroing in on the dagger as if the weapon was what it had been looking for. It paid no attention to Joel who plunged the point of the broken broom handle into its lower back, piercing one kidney. The cubited Pedro wailed in agony but did not stop its forward assault toward Janine. When it reached her, Janine twirled the dagger in the palm of her hand in one complete circle then slashed out at Pedro's throat. She opened a small slit just under the chin which immediately gushed a stream of blood that was much darker than normal human blood. The cubited Pedro flailed past Janine, grabbing its throat and the wooden spear which still protruded from its kidney, and hit the deck railing with all of its forward momentum. Through the railing it went and plummeted twenty feet to the hard, sandy ground below. Joel ran to Janine, checked that she was uninjured, then looked out over the deck to see the Pedro cubit rise to its feet, one broken arm dangling, the broom handle now pushed completely through its body and protruding from its stomach, a mess of black blood coating the skin, then limp run in the direction of the beach.

"I cut myself," Janine said.

When Joel turned, he saw that Janine was holding her wrist; blood leaked between her fingers. "I guess I'm not as good with that thing as I thought I was."

"Ah, Jesus," Joel moaned then snatched one of the bed sheets from the open doorway and quickly tied a tourniquet around her forearm.

"That's not the man who fed me Caribbean shrimp two nights ago." Janine swooned as she grabbed one end of the bed sheet, covered the bloody wrist slit and mopped up stray rivulets of red that flowed on her skin along the same lines as the blue veins underneath.

"He's one of them," Joel said. "An Albert. A cubit. Just like BJ said, the Pedro that served you shrimp has become his own dinner."

Janine dropped to the wooden deck. Her blood continued its relentless escape from her wrist, drooling down her fingertips and dropping through the divisions between the six-inch deck boards. "Joel," she said in a weeping squeak that usually accompanied throats without moisture. "Why?" She blinked. Red drops as large as dimes fell from between her forefinger and thumb. Joel clasped her wrist between both of his sea-beaten hands but the blood flow continued, leaking over and through his grasp, his strength useless against Janine's heart which pumped the life from her across flesh and wood and the sandy hard ground that lay beneath.

Joel crouched over her, wondering: *What if she bleeds to death right here in front of me? What if I lose her like I lost Jane? What if...*

And at that same moment, as Joel considered the consequences of a life without Janine, the blood flow stopped. In fact—and Joel would forever remember it—the blood that had escaped down both his and her forearms and the blood that freshly pooled atop Billy Jo Presser's porch suddenly reversed like a rewinding video. Janine's blood hungrily returned to her wrist. Streams and drools flowed back through Joel's fingers and disappeared under his palm which had not loosened its clasp of her right hand. She blinked and then her eyes flapped wide open. Crusty remnants of crimson adhered Joel's hand to her wrist and when he peeled it free—a Saran Wrap crunchiness accompanying the movement—the wrist slit was in the process of closing. The red mouth of open skin and veins actually stitched themselves together right then, in a matter of seconds that should have taken days, the skin folding, a plump hill of flesh protruding, the final remnants of blood deterred by the closing mouth.

And then it was done. There was no scar. It was as if the flesh had never been severed. The only evidence that remained stained the porch wood, the sandy ground below, and Billy's bed sheet.

"Why?" she repeated, her voice nearly a whisper. Joel hugged her body to his chest. The wrist may have miraculously healed but her body remained as limp as any bled animal. "The shadow of death…I see it."

"Nonsense," Joel countered.

"The valley. I'm going there, Joel. Oh…it's so beautiful."

Her breathing slowed and she gasped. At that same moment, a gush of wind exited the apartment through the open door as if the place was belching forth some unwanted gas. It knocked Joel to his knees and he tottered at the edge of the porch, Janine against his chest, the rail splintered from where Pedro had slammed through it. Had a second blast followed, he and Janine surely would have fallen. Janine rolled from his grasp and reached for the apartment's open doorway, her eyes drooping, her strength depleted. Through the doorway floated two pieces of paper. They curled and twisted like feathers before landing on the porch where Janine's blood stained the wood. They were the copies of the snapshots Billy's robot had taken of Chancey Lett's satchel. On the top of one printout someone had written the word "Lafitte." The Mayan symbol known as "Wayeb" was at the top of the other. Janine pointed at the symbol and said, "The valley of the shadow of death."

◻ …

She and Billy stood in the terminal, reading the list of arrivals. Steph could not remember if Mitchell Bone had ever told her the flight number nor which airline Alixel was to be flying in on, however, she knew the plane would be coming from Arizona, most likely Phoenix, around two o'clock. Unfortunately, there were three flights due to arrive from Arizona around that time but none precisely at two. All of the flights were on Southwest Airlines; the one closest to the top of the hour was scheduled to arrive at 1:55. The flight number was 33. She and Billy headed for Gate 15 with an hour to spare.

The fear she'd experienced while walking the shoreline—the idea that anyone at any time could easily be one of the living dead—now resurfaced, but she didn't cry this time. Her acceptance of the nightmare had grown to exclude tears but it was impossible to subdue the adrenal rush, the anticipation that at any moment any one of the hundreds of travelers might suddenly turn on her.

A man bumped her shoulder and she wondered if he was one. A trio of flight attendants simultaneously turned and stared at her and she wondered if they had touched the Cubit. So many people…so many chances…so much adrenaline.

And then there was the idea that she, herself, a Steph-cubit, might appear at any moment. Had she touched it? Had Albert and Chancey and Carol initiated her? What would happen if that were true? If she saw herself, she would surely go mad.

Inadvertently, she latched onto Billy's arm and hugged it close to her hip. He smiled reassurance, a gesture she knew he realized she needed.

Near Gate 10, a large group of at least thirty people had assembled around The Pecos Bar. None of them were eating or drinking—they were just standing there, looking into the bar's dining area.

"…has grown in strength to a Category 5…," Jim Cantore was saying, "…and has taken an unprecedented turn while picking up speed. I have never in my twenty-five years seen such a meteorological event."

Bustling talk ensued among the onlookers as a graphic appeared on a large, flat screen television mounted on the bar's dining room wall. *Hurricane Antiago*, was written above a satellite image of a storm that was not very wide but had a clearly defined center. A solid red line traced the storm's path from a town called Merida in the Mexican Yucatán. In only two days, Antiago had traveled more than five hundred miles and was set to make landfall in southern Texas by Friday morning, if not sooner. A shaded triangle depicted the storm's possible collision with the coast; it spread for hundreds of miles and included all of Texas and parts of Mexico and Louisiana. The most probable landfall, depicted by the red line, was drawn straight to Corpus Christi.

"We now have the latest from the hurricane center in Miami," Cantore continued, "and you're not going to believe this. Sustained winds of 175 miles per hour. The pressure at the center of the storm has fallen to 890 millibars. That's a drop of twenty millibars since the last reading just an hour ago.

"The mayors of dozens of coastal cities have ordered immediate evacuations but there is a concern that many could be stranded in the storm's path if this very unusual and sudden shift in speed and direction continues."

As Steph and Billy stood within the growing crowd, they did not notice that Keadle and Crabman were seated near Gate 15 and were staring straight at them.

◻ ...

Janine stowed the dagger and the two pieces of paper in her sack before she and Joel boarded the trolley. She remained physically weak, but the strength of her faith had returned, having been in hiatus since the doctors had convinced her that she was crazy. And she knew that it would take more than faith and more than the dagger to save herself from the likes of Albert. The dagger had apparently been unable to detect Pedro as it had done Albert and, therefore, she could no longer trust it as a "warning beacon" as Joel had suggested.

They sat in the same two seats they'd occupied the day before. Five people sat in front of them. Joel immediately snatched Janine's right hand and gently, as if it were made of fine crystal, cupped it between both of his. "Look!" he exclaimed, pointing. "It's Marcy."

Janine followed his finger to the front of Marcy's home. Marcy walked along the sidewalk in front of her shop then slowly climbed the three concrete steps to her front door. Her movements were stoic, straight and without freedom, without personality, without individualism—robotic. The fortune teller had so much grace in her gait; it was a quality that Janine admired (along with her old Cher tapes and her brutally honest way of making sexist men squirm). But her grace was absent and Janine considered the obvious reason.

When Marcy entered and closed the door, Joel said, "I hope not." He knew what she was thinking and was probably thinking the same thing himself. "Do you want to stop and tell her you retrieved your bags?"

Janine's denial was unwavering. If Marcy had been cubited, she didn't want to know. "No!" she replied with more volume than was necessary. Three of the five riders turned with expressions of anger.

Five minutes later, the three angry trolley riders exited. The two remaining passengers still had not revealed themselves. They sat on opposite sides of the same row, three back from the front. The one on the left had short, dark hair with a neck and ears that were either very tan or were Hispanic. This person wore a white baseball cap and seemed to be male though it was hard for Janine to tell. The one on the right was certainly a woman. She wore a blue bonnet over a head of curly silver hair. Her sun dress, which flowed over the left edge of her seat and into the aisle, was light blue with white flower prints that were trimmed in red and orange. Someone's grandmother perhaps…a little old lady returning home from a day of shopping. The two remained seated, neither moving an inch (and Janine knew it because she kept staring at the backs of their heads) even after Joel reached up and pressed the *Stop* button.

Janine hesitated, waiting for the two riders to exit. This was the last trolley stop but neither moved.

"We're here," Joel said rising, Janine's hand still held within his. He led her forward, passing the strangers who paid him no attention. But as Janine passed, both turned to her simultaneously.

Skulls. Janine expected them. Fleshless jaws parting, cackling out some belligerent rants, telling her it was a ridiculous waste of energy to believe that they could be stopped, that she or her lying God could change the course of fate, which of course was the end of the world.

But that's not what happened. Both looked up and both smiled. The tan male was a teenage Hispanic and the old lady in the bonnet was surely someone's kind grandmother; you could tell by the geniality conveyed by her cheery face. Nothing dead could ever smile with such absolute kindness. Janine returned the smile; she couldn't help it.

"Be careful, Janine," the grandmother warned. "They are everywhere."

The Hispanic boy nodded in agreement.

Janine stood mesmerized. The two strangers knew her? That couldn't be.

Janine.

She blinked.

Janine.

She looked to the front of the trolley.

"What is it?" Joel said while tugging her arm.

She turned back toward the two passengers. Neither made any expression of recognition. Both stared at the seats in front of them as if Janine and Joel were invisible. Janine shook her head and followed Joel without looking where she was going. When she passed the trolley driver, he reached out and grabbed her arm. It was the same driver who had given her ticket fare information that morning.

But it wasn't. His eyes told her so.

"You fuckin' bitch," Carl, the driver snarled, sounding strangely like Albert. "When I get my hands on you death will be a blessing."

Joel punched Carl's forearm ten times before the driver released her. Both quickly jumped from the trolley.

"Your boyfriend will suffer greatly and I promise to show you every fuckin' minute of it," the cubited Carl howled before making a u-turn back toward the center of town.

Standing at the corner of Route 361 and Paradise Lane, Janine and Joel waited for more than five minutes. And though they were both thinking about Carl's rants, the big reason why they could not move was because of the steady flow of traffic that streamed in one long line, a flow of traffic that was escaping the town of Port A.

□ ...

From the periphery, Billy saw them first. While he stood there calculating how much time it would take for the hurricane to hit the island given Cantore's meteorological data, he almost turned all the way around but caught himself. He whispered to Steph without moving closer to her. "Do you remember the gate number for the two-ten flight?"

She continued staring at the television. "That flight is from Tucson. She wouldn't be on that one."

"The gate number," Billy insisted. "What was it?"

"Thirteen." She now turned to him.

"Don't turn! Keep looking at the TV." She did so. "Keadle and Crabman are near the ticket counter at Gate 15. We are going to pass them as if they aren't there and head down to Gate 13."

"But what if..."

Billy interrupted. "Gate 13. We'll talk then."

Billy watched from the corner of his eye as they walked past Gate 15; Keadle's and Crabman's heads turned in unison but they didn't rise. Billy doubted they would. Alixel was their target. Had they wanted Billy and Steph, they could have taken them during the drive from Port A. Billy additionally hoped that both men—who were, of course, no longer men—would believe that he and Steph were at the wrong gate and would consider them a non-threat to their goal. How he and Steph would steal Alixel away from them, he had yet to determine.

Billy settled for a seat that faced the terminal aisle and away from Gate 15. Steph sat to his left, Billy's body hiding hers from the stares of the two cubits. Billy asked, "What do we have—about thirty minutes?"

"Yeah. The airport clock is over there." Steph pointed toward the clock but realized that she was also pointing toward Gate 15 and quickly lowered her arm. "Sorry. I'm not use to this Sherlock Holmes meets Stephen King shit."

"Agreed. So how do you figure we distract them long enough to sweep Alixel away?"

Steph looked at him as if the question was the dumbest thing he'd ever said. "I don't even know what she looks like."

"Too much chance," Billy mumbled. "Not enough facts. This is going to be tough but we've been going by the seat of our pants since this morning. Maybe that's our new strategy. Maybe the most logical is the illogical: wait and see what the hell happens next." He grinned, uncomfortable with the idea of inaccuracy.

And then a curious thought occurred. What if she didn't arrive at all? What if there was no Alixel? What if they were left to deal with this "crisis" all by themselves? If there had been an evacuation ordered, planes may not be allowed to land. Apparently, the idea had not been a concern of Keadle and Crabman. They believed that Flight 33 from Phoenix would arrive as scheduled and that Alixel would be on board. But they were dead…what could they know?

Billy looked out the terminal's tall windows. Planes were landing. He could see them taxiing in from the runway. He could see passengers disembarking several gates away. The flow of traffic at Corpus Christi International Airport was a vibrant tussle. Many of those that had just arrived joined the growing arc of people that stood outside The Pecos Bar and now blocked half of the terminal aisle. Most of those people had expressions of surprise, shock and fear from the Weather Channel's revelations. Two men, who had just arrived moments before, turned immediately and ran back toward their gate, their business suits fluttering as they fled with what appeared to be panic.

The airport's public address system announced:

> *Southwest Flight 33 from Phoenix now arriving at Gate 15.*
> *Southwest Flight 33 from Phoenix now arriving at Gate 15.*

And then after a short pause, continued with:

Due to the evacuation declaration of Mayor John Richardson,
all inbound flights will be diverted from Corpus Christi
International Airport beginning at four p.m. central time.
Please see your carrier's flight information desk concerning
diverted arrivals.

The evacuation announcement repeated and when it finished, for the smallest fraction of time, the entire airport went silent, which to Billy seemed impossible. Everyone stopped talking, walking, working, and waiting. At that very moment, time switched onto a path of an alternate thread. Life would never be the same for every person that heard that announcement. And then, in a sudden rush, half of those who stood outside The Pecos Bar rushed away. There was tripping and falling and cursing. One man punched another. A child cried. Billy noticed that Keadle and Crabman watched with delight. Their dead faces brightened with pale glee for the melee.

"What do we do now?" Steph asked.

"We wait."

One-by-one, passengers entered the terminal through Gate 15. None looked like Alixel, or at least none looked like the person Billy had already pictured in his mind as Alixel.

"That her?" Steph pointed.

"No," Billy said. The woman was too thin, and her hair was blonde though she did have a nice tan. Billy thought Alixel would be an extravagant specimen of womanhood, with a walk that spoke of riches and a body sculpted by the money she possessed. Alixel would not have blonde hair, he thought. Red hair seemed inappropriate as well. Alixel's hair would be dark. Her skin would be dark. But no one who exited Gate 15 looked like that. In fact, once the door was closed Keadle and Crabman stood there studying the passengers for Alixel who, apparently, was not on the flight.

Chatter among the airport's new arrivals increased. Most had been told of the impending hurricane and the conversations Billy could hear now centered on how possessions could be saved: homes, cars, computers, little Johnnie's brand new tree house. The chatter and confusion was so intense that neither Billy nor Keadle and Crabman noticed that Flight 20 from Tucson had arrived and was now disembarking through Gate 13 behind them. Steph grabbed Billy's sleeve, turned him around and said, "How about her?"

Alixel did not look exactly as Billy had imagined but her appearance was close, and though he had no proof that it was her, his instincts told him the truth. Her figure did appear as if it had been sculpted by wealth and she did wear some extravagant clothing that flowed with Southwest colors and prints, but her hair was much longer than the Alixel drawn in his head. Two orange-red streaks traced along the temples through hair as black as night. The streaks flowed back above the ears, down her neck and ended an inch short of the full length of her mane which stopped at the waist. Her skin was very dark and Billy guessed accurately that she was, indeed, of Native American descent. She wore no make-up which surprised Billy, but her natural skin tones did not need it. High cheekbones, a small rounded nose and lips that were full in the middle but thin on the ends highlighted her beauty. She stood with hands on hips just inside the gate's doorway, a small bag that was not a purse hanging from one forearm, and blocked other passengers who maneuvered around a woman apparently upset that no one was there to greet her.

Quickly, Billy and Steph moved in her direction. The two men that had started fighting shortly after the public address warning were now back at it and, this time, the fight went out of control. People gathered around the two men. There was blood. There was screaming. Two security officers appeared. Billy did not plan it; all he'd had to do was wait. Fighting was never logical, but it now provided the perfect opportunity.

"We're here to escort you to your hotel," Billy said to Alixel, thinking that he should bow but not knowing the reason why. He'd forgotten that both he and Steph were still wearing beach clothes.

"What are you!" Alixel demanded. "Certainly not my chauffer."

"You are Alixel?" Steph questioned. "You've come to Port A because of the casino?"

The woman paused, scanned Steph from head to toe, then added, "And what are you? Of course I'm Alixel, but what are you? And Port A?"

"Port Aransas," Steph grunted. "Where the casino will never be built."

"Where is my chauffer?" Alixel demanded.

"We are they," Steph countered. "And if you'll follow us, we'll get you to our lovely island A.S.A.P."

Both security officers were now engaged in the scuffle between the two men.

"Please," Billy said in an urgent but consolatory voice. "We need to go—Now!"

Alixel measured him, his clothes, his woman and his statement. "Yes," she said. "These heathens are not to be trusted." Billy thought that she looked directly at Keadle and Crabman but there was so much commotion, her stare could have been directed anywhere.

Together, they scurried into the terminal aisle. Keadle saw them. Crabman turned as well, his red, not-sunburned skin a bit paler, his lithe body a bit lither. Both advanced, pushing through the crowd, dodging the melee caused by the two men, their sole, combined purpose aligned. Keadle threw a woman and her child to the floor. Crabman rammed a man whose glasses flew from his face and landed in the makeshift ring of the wrestling combatants. A baby in a stroller whose mother had been distracted by the fighting lay between the hunters and the hunted but this did nothing to divert them.

Three Corpus Christi police officers entered the confusion. One grabbed Keadle. "Jim!" he said. "What's this about?" Keadle brushed aside the officer's hand with such force that the officer's shoulder dislocated; the officer screamed. Crabman rammed the baby carriage with his thigh and as the carriage toppled and the baby screamed, a second of the three police officers righted it, coddling the basket with both arms and smiling at the screaming infant. The third officer, a heavyset man three times the size of Rally Panini, tackled him at the waist and both went down.

Billy, Steph and Alixel quickly walked away. Down the escalator they went, briskly, not running, past the security checkpoint and baggage claim areas, and exited the airport through swooshing electronic double doors. They stood for a moment on the sidewalk under the concourse before turning toward the parking lot.

"My bags," Alixel exclaimed.

"Our associates will get them," Billy answered without thinking. He looked over his shoulder. No one followed.

Steph sat on the floor of Billy's VW as the trio raced above the speed limit toward Port A. The evacuation was apparent. Many vehicles moved in a concentrated line in the opposite direction. Several flashed their headlights.

"Please roll up your window," Alixel said to Billy.

"Not an option." His candor was emotionless.

"Why?"

"Broken."

"Why didn't you get my bags?"

Steph broke in. "Listen. We've gone through a whole lot of hell just to get you this far." She saw Billy shaking his head. "Billy told you that we've taken care of your luggage. All we ask is that you bear with us. As you can tell, our island is not in the best of ways right now."

Alixel turned in the seat, her long hair whipping in the wind that rushed through Billy's window. She scowled. "Who are you people? You aren't my designated drivers. Lett and Bone are not such fools."

"Actually," Billy said before Steph's increasing aggravation became unmanageable. "Steph was told to pick you up."

Alixel turned to him. "In clothes such as these? How ignorant. You don't know who I am do you?"

"Alixel. From Sedona," Steph said. "An investor who wants to help ruin Port Aransas."

"I really don't think any of us has much to say on that issue." Alixel nodded toward the evacuating cars and campers and trailers and trucks.

Steph leaned against the computer console which had been closed and locked since the night Mitchell Bone was murdered. "Hurricane Antiago or Hurricane Alixel. Either way, the island is doomed."

Alixel scowled. "The wealth a casino would bring to this island is immeasurable."

"And wealth to you no doubt. Wealth to you and Lett and Bone..." Billy was shaking his head again. His eyes, peering through the rearview mirror, told her to behave. Alixel picked up on this.

"Let her speak her mind. I've heard worse I'm sure. The lack of knowledge always manifests in ignorant behavior."

"How well do you know Chancey Lett?" Steph said, holding back the aggression that boiled like a knot in her stomach.

"Well enough to know that he knows how to manage casinos and make them profitable."

"And Mitchell Bone?"

"Don't know him other than through phone conversation."

Billy now shook his head with greater urgency.

"He's dead," Steph said. "Murdered by Chancel Lett's bodyguard."

Alixel's expression, which had remained smug and dictatorial, like royalty in the presence of pagans, changed for the first time. She could not hide her surprise and concern which molded her face into something truly compassionate. "When?"

"Last night," Billy said, still uneasy with the release of such knowledge to a total stranger whom they had no reason to trust.

"Why wasn't I told sooner?"

Steph crossed her legs. Her feet pressed against the opposite side of the VW's interior. "Murderers don't reveal themselves," she said.

"I mean the police." Alixel scowled again at Steph.

"The police are in on it," Steph said, apparently pleased that her *ignorant behavior* pressed Alixel's buttons.

"Take me back to the airport."

Billy said, "You'll not get a flight out. The city is being evacuated. Please, please give us a chance. There's a lot more going on in Port A than the murder of one man."

"Yeah—hundreds," Steph mumbled.

"Steph," Billy pleaded, looking in the rearview mirror. "Not now." He smiled at Alixel. "Where are your reservations?"

"The Treasure Trove," Alixel replied through a mouthful of hair that had blown across her lips. She pulled it free and brushed it behind her with long fingers.

"Figures," Steph grumbled. "Right next to the bank."

Billy and the Treasure Trove's manager, Nigel Felino, had created a wonderful working relationship from the first day that Billy had opened the Surf Side. Billy supplied professional catering and reasonable prices. Nigel provided group meals as part of business conferences. But beyond the business side of their relationship, they just liked each other. They shared many common interests, including surfing. Nigel had never surfed before he'd met Billy. Now the hotelier could not get enough of the sport.

As chance would have it, the Treasure Trove also served as one of three hurricane shelters on the island. The first floor and an underground basement were strengthened by reinforced concrete and steel that engineers claimed could withstand, minimally, a Category 4 hurricane. Though evacuations were always the first line of defense against casualty, the hurricane shelters had been established after several lives were lost when Hurricane Andrew had decimated southern Florida. No one wanted the same thing happening in Port Aransas.

Few cars were in the parking lot when Billy's VW stopped under the canopy at the hotel's front door. As he stepped onto the asphalt and looked over at The Big Texas Bank, a sudden rush of fear snatched his heart. A black Hummer and a white Ford Ranger were parked near the bank's entrance. There were no other vehicles. In fact, since the bank and hotel were neighbors, the combined empty spaces between them magnified the sense of impending calamity. The thickening gray clouds overhead only added to this depression. Though he saw no activity through the bank windows, he felt someone was watching and rushed around the front of the VW to help Alixel out of the vehicle. She may have acted the prude but Billy still remembered *his* manners. He held her hand as she stepped down, then helped guide Steph around the stick shift and passenger seat. He hurriedly urged both of them toward the hotel's door. A bellboy met them inside.

"I'm sorry, sir, but we are not taking any guests at this time. There has been an evacuation ordered."

Billy did not know the kid who, most certainly, was not a resident of the island. "Yes. I know. Where is Nigel...eh, I mean Mr. Felino?"

"Doing a room check upstairs." The bellboy pointed at the ceiling.

"I have a very important person here I'd like him to meet. She will be staying at the Trove and I want to make sure her accommodations are the best."

"Can I tell him who's asking?"

"Billy Jo Presser. We're friends." Billy reached into his pocket. "And please hurry," he added while handing the kid what change he had. One of the coins fell from his hand to the floor as the bellboy turned to fulfill his request. It rolled on edge and fell flat next to Alixel's brown leather shoe. She picked it up. Her jaw immediately dropped, then instantly settled back into her stoically painted face. Steph did not see the sudden expression, but Billy did. "What?" he said to her.

She offered the coin in the palm of her hand. "Interesting piece. Where did you get it?"

It was the coin with the Mayan mask pressed into it. "Found it on the beach. Oddly enough, I found it where you and your investors will be digging footers for the casino."

"You know what this is, don't you?"

Billy plucked it from her hand. "Mayan symbol called Wayeb."

Alixel appeared shocked at his knowledge. "You know what it means?"

"Bad times are coming."

"Yes, but that's not what I'm referring to. It means you found..."

"Billy!" Nigel appeared from within an elevator on the opposite side of the lobby. His accent was thickly Italian as was his moustache. "What brings you to my Trove under such stormy conditions?"

It means I found what? he wanted to say but minded his manners.

"Alixel. This is Nigel Felino, owner and operator of this hotel." She gave the coin to Billy and held out her hand, palm down, as royalty might do when hands are expected to be kissed. Nigel happily engaged the knuckles with his lips.

"It is my honor. I have a wonderful premiere suite ready for you; unfortunately Antiago seems intent on ruining our evening. But you know hurricanes. Most can never make up their minds where they'll end up until the last moment. You are welcome to stay in the penthouse but if Antiago does decide to visit our island, we'll need to get you into the shelter." Nigel had been so enamored by Alixel's presence that he did not release her hand until now. He bowed and she smiled, something that neither Billy nor Steph had seen her do. "Your bags?"

Alixel turned to Billy. "They're on the way," he said, knowing that the airline would hold them until Nigel called.

Nigel escorted them to the front desk where the bellboy stood at attention. "Would you please hand me the card key to 322?"

"I'd like a different room," Alixel said. Nigel appeared upset but for only a second. Steph huffed and shook her head. Billy shrugged his shoulders.

"Room 322 is our best suite," Nigel said with a smile.

Alixel replied with silence.

"Steven." The bellboy turned to Nigel. "Please see that 321 is ready for Miss…Alixel." Steven quickly scuttled to the elevator and disappeared. "While Steven is preparing your suite, please join me for a cup of coffee. My family shipped some wonderful flavors from Sicily that are still very fresh."

The Treasure Trove restaurant was small but enchanting. It became apparent to Billy that most of Nigel's staff had already left the island as Nigel handled the brewing of the coffee himself. He poured four cups and set them on the square table in front of each of them. He poured a quick stream of cream into his own cup and said, "So, tell me something, Billy."

Of all the things Billy could have said, his mind still remained wrapped around Alixel's comment about the Wayeb coin.

It means you found…

He pulled the coin out of his pocket and dropped it on the table. Alixel, who'd been looking at the front glass doors of the hotel and had not touched her coffee, turned her attention to the clinking metal.

"You ever seen anything like this before?" Billy said to Nigel who snatched the coin and turned it over in one hand while he sipped from the coffee cup with the other.

"Never. Looks like play money."

"I found it on the beach where the casino is supposed to be built." All three of them flashed a glance at Alixel. "Alixel tells me that I found…what was it you were saying?"

Steph glared at Alixel who did not give her the pleasure of acknowledgement.

"Wayeb," Alixel replied. "Like you said, Billy Jo Presser, you found a coin with a Mayan mask on it."

Billy shook his head. "But *you* said there was…"

"Bad days are coming," Alixel interrupted, frowning, her hand with its long fingers tapping the table to the right of the coffee cup saucer.

Nigel smiled to break the sudden tension. "So let me get this straight. You found a coin on the beach with markings that stand for bad luck. Now, that's what I call coincidence."

"Not bad luck," Alixel insisted. "The symbol is one that demarks the five bad days at the end of the year. Unlucky days. Evil days."

Nigel's smile wavered. He paused to find a grin then added, "Whew, glad we're in the middle of June." Nigel tried to hide what Billy could see was growing uneasiness. Alixel was good at propagating such a response from people. "But I guess you can't get more unlucky than a Category 5 hurricane hitting you square in the face, can you?"

Steven walked into the restaurant. "Room 321 is ready, Mr. Felino."

Nigel stood a bit too quickly. His thigh hit the edge of the table and coffee spilled onto the table from all four directions. "My apologies," he said and quickly turned to escort them to the elevator. Billy knew that he'd had enough of them. His urgency betrayed his good manners.

Room 321 was the size of an efficiency apartment. The bedroom was sectioned off and could be made private by closing its door. The living area highlighted the suite. It was larger than Billy's entire apartment. Its cool blue, aqua and green colors were in stark contrast to the southwest warmth that Alixel was adorned in.

"So now what do I do?" Alixel said, sitting on the loveseat. Billy and Steph sat across from her in a pair of cushioned, high-backed chairs. "I invited you two in so that you could help me work this out."

"The bank is right over there," Steph said, thumbing in the correct direction. Her dislike for Alixel had not diminished a bit. "Why don't you go see for yourself? I hear they have a great deal on security deposit boxes."

Billy peered angrily. "Steph. Remember that we need her help." He looked at Alixel. "As you've probably already surmised, the investment you planned to make is pretty much in the can. Bone is dead, Lett is a murderer and there's one hell of a storm headed this way that will surely put an end to any hopes of a casino, no vote needed. But there is more." Steph opened her mouth but Billy's look backed her down. "First, I need to know something." He took a breath. "Tell me what it is about the coin that disturbed you so much."

"You won't believe me." Alixel sat rigid in her seat. For some reason, she kept staring at the front door and spoke without turning away from it. "That coin is part of a great treasure. If you found the coin, you found the treasure."

Steph couldn't help herself. "What!?" she said, slapping her head and leaning forward. "Treasure? There's no treasure. It's some lame excuse to tear up the beach. To hell with the casino, there's a treasure to be uncovered."

"LaFitte," Billy said and grabbed Steph's hand, which had moved from her head and was now pointing at Alixel.

Alixel turned away from the front door. "You know a lot, Mr. Presser."

"Billy," he interjected.

"What else do you know?"

"About LaFitte?"

"About LaFitte." Alixel leaned forward and a string of jeweled turquoise slipped from her cleavage and onto her blouse's patched brown and tan prints. Something silver glistened within the strand but Billy couldn't quite make it out.

"He was a trader who amassed a large amount of valuables—gold, silver, jewels—and buried them somewhere along the shorelines of the Gulf Coast...or so the story goes."

"A good story," Alixel said. "One that is quite true. What else do you know about him?"

"From my research, I found that some regarded him as a pirate and some believed him to be a patriot. He helped in the War of 1812 but also dealt in slave trade. I understand he became quite rich and influential, so much so that President Monroe had to, I guess for a lack of better words, do away with him. Research suggests that he fled to the Yucatán where he used his great wealth to support a luxurious way of life. Mythologies talk about him burying his treasure then disappearing without a trace."

"Research?" Alixel sat up straight. The turquoise necklace flopped against her firm breasts. "So you are a scientist?"

"Roboticist," Steph corrected.

Alixel shunned Steph's addition to the conversation. "Do you believe in God?" she asked Billy as if it were a completely normal question for one stranger to ask another.

"You mean in a Christian God?"

"What's the difference? Either you believe in the *mythology* of a spiritual higher-being or you do not."

"I don't understand."

"Of course you don't. You're a scientist through-and-through. I've known many scientists. They are the ones who would destroy the sacred lands of the great Southwest. They do not follow faith. Facts are the only things that mean anything to them. I take it from your research that you found enough facts to support your belief that LaFitte found a life in the Yucatán?"

"Not really. No one knows what happened. There are only theories." Billy squinted, trying to make out what looked like a cross hanging from Alixel's neck. "I have faith. Believe me. In the last few days, it has been greatly tested."

"Then you are one of the fortunate." Alixel grabbed the silvery pendant that dangled on a string of turquoise and gently stroked it. "LaFitte's treasure is buried on this island and from your discovery, I'd say it's buried quite close to where you found that coin. By the way, the coin is perhaps fifteen hundred years old and worth more than this entire hotel."

Billy patted his pocket to make sure the coin was still there. "So you're telling me that Chancey Lett never intended to build a casino. All he wanted was the treasure."

Alixel nodded.

"He needed a reason to dig up the beach."

Alixel nodded.

"And you were going to help him do it?"

She shook her head this time. "Not for the same reason."

"Then why?"

Alixel suddenly looked at the front door, her face contorting into an expression of grave concern. She moved her hand from her necklace to her waist. Incredibly, her belly began to glow. Billy shook his head and rubbed his eyes but that did not diminish the fact that between Alixel's fingers, a dull red hue—much like what he'd seen coming from the hand of Janine on the south jetty rocks—grew in magnitude.

A knock echoed outside and down the hall. The knock became louder, insistent. Then someone kicked in a door, splintering wood.

Alixel stood, still holding her belly. "We have to go...Now!"

Alixel led them out of the room and to the stairwell which was, thankfully, the next door down from suite 321. Steph followed Alixel and Billy took up the rear. He looked back down the hall one last time before closing the stairwell door. The room that had been invaded was 322. Albert stepped from it into the hallway as the stairwell doorknob silently clicked.

❒ ...

Mark Walker followed Joel and Janine from the trolley stop to Paradise Cottages. Their appearance, for Walker, was an unfortunate result of bad-timing. He'd been sent to search both Steph's and Janine's cottage apartments. He'd expected them to be vacant. However, as Albert had ordered, if Janine *was* home, killing her would not be an option, at least not by anyone other than Albert himself. He could do as he liked to Steph, Albert had said, but Janine was to be left alone. Of course in Mark's cubited mind, not much made a whole lot of sense. Since killing his twin the day before, the development of Mark Walker's physical and mental attributes had been a slow process. For some reason, the word "bloodspot" kept revolving through his thoughts like a programmed glitch stuck in an endless loop.

Mark maintained a distance that would not attract their attention and when the couple entered Janine's cottage, he jimmied the lock on Steph's door and entered undetected. "Whada hewl is da blow spoot," he mumbled incoherently, the vocal chords still unable to mimic Mark Walker. "Whada is dat?" He closed Steph's door with visions of helicopters and one-legged birds rolling aimlessly in his dark mind.

❒ ...

"I thought you said he was dead." Steph pointed out the glass window of the VW's rear hatch. They'd made it successfully down the staircase and to Billy's vehicle but the ignition of its engine had apparently alerted the hunters. From out of the hotel ran Carol, Albert Stine and Mitchell Bone.

"He is," Billy yelled, adrenaline pumping into his throat and head, making his temples throb. "That man isn't Bone." He sped from the parking lot as the hunters ran toward the bank.

"Where are you taking me?" Alixel demanded.

"Quiet!" Steph countered. "We don't have time for this."

"I have something to show you and some friends for you to meet," Billy said. "Then I have one hell of story to tell, one that I think you already know about."

"What about them?" Steph said, thumbing back in the direction of the bank.

"No worries. Alixel will protect us."

Alixel sat on the floor, legs crossed, in a position that reminded Billy of a Native American ceremonial gathering. "I don't know what you are talking about."

"Of course you do." Billy glanced over his shoulder as he drove down Alister Street away from his restaurant. Much of Port Aransas had already evacuated. He dodged what traffic remained by turning down side streets. His intention was to double-back in hopes of losing any pursuit. "Somehow, you knew to avoid your original room assignment. Plus, you have one of the daggers."

"Daggers? You are insane. You are both insane."

"The only things insane around here are all the dead people walking about."

Wind-whirl whipped through the broken window; the VW's clickety-clack engine revved with increased RPMs.

"I thought you were a scientist," Alixel said.

"Yeah. Me too. But you don't go through our last seventy-two hours without seriously questioning everything you know." Billy turned onto Avenue G and continued toward the beach.

"Then you do believe in a God."

"Really. I don't see what my spiritual preference has to do with…"

"It has everything to do with it!" Alixel almost screamed, then just as quickly calmed down, her voice evening out into one of monotonic reflection. "We will not survive this unless you understand that."

Steph turned all the way around to face Alixel. "You know what's going on here! You know!"

"Of course I know," Alixel confessed. "Why else would I be here?"

"So your deal with Mitchell Bone…"

"I don't care about that weasel. All I'm concerned with is the treasure." Alixel's legs remained crossed, her voice even and matter-of-fact. "You told me, Billy, about Wayeb. How did you…" She hesitated. "Why would you even care about such a thing?"

"Because Lett cared."

"I don't understand."

Steph took the cue. "You! Don't understand?"

"Steph!" Billy urged. "To make a long story short," he said to Alixel, "I took some pictures at the bank. One of them was of a document that Lett was carrying. The document had that symbol, the one on the coin, written at the top."

Alixel unfolded her legs. "You must show me this." Her voice peaked with a hint of excitement.

"That's where we're headed. I got something else to show you too, something I haven't even looked at yet, something I'm not too sure I want to relive."

"And that is?"

Billy stared out the window at the growing thundercloud darkness that suffocated the horizon. The wind had kicked up since he'd turned onto the beach road and back toward the Surf Side, and the VW shook sporadically with each gust. "Mitchell Bone's death," he finally said.

"Shoe got that?" Steph added.

"I'm thinking, yeah, and if so, it might give us some more clues about the Cubit."

Alixel curled up onto her knees and crawled forward. It was an action that took both Billy and Steph by surprise. It was an action that drew her down to their level. Those of power and wealth did not crawl on hands and knees. "The Cubit?" she said, her mouth agape with surprise. "How do you know?"

"Janine," Billy said. "One of our friends whom you will soon meet."

Billy raced past a backhoe, a bulldozer and two yellow dump trucks that were parked near the pier. He turned on Beach Street and a block from the Surf Side, it became evident that the building had been vandalized. The glass door to the restaurant lay in shattered disarray on the sidewalk and parking lot, allowing wind gusts to invade the interior. Some of the window blinds rapped against glass; stray papers whirled inside. Behind the restaurant, the wood railing around his apartment porch deck was missing half the horizontal boards and the door to his apartment stood open; a bed sheet fluttered from it. Billy parked the VW behind the restaurant so as not to be easily seen. All three of the occupants exited simultaneously and when Billy came around to the passenger side of the VW, he could not help but to look at Alixel's stomach. Her blouse sagged at the belly and could easily hide the haft of a weapon. He looked at the restaurant then back at her stomach.

"No," Alixel said. "They are not here." Billy looked up, embarrassed. "Besides," she continued, "the glow does not promise nor preclude Evil. Caution will always be the best course of action."

"Stay with her," he said to Steph. "I'm going to check the restaurant." Five minutes later he returned, shaking his head without a word. He led them to the back of the restaurant where they encountered a large, irregular, brownish-red stain and several smaller brownish-red circles in the sandy dirt under the porch.

"Blood," Alixel said.

In the dirt near the steps was the imprint of a human body. Broken wooden boards lay scattered in all directions. Billy quickly ran up to the deck and stopped above Steph and Alixel who were peering up at him through the deck board spacing. There was dried blood on the ground below but none was on the deck itself. His attention turned to the sound of breaking glass from within the apartment. The bed sheet that was stuck in the doorway suddenly took flight, fluttered quickly into his body and wrapped around him. He screamed quietly and quickly. Alixel and Steph bolted up the steps to his side and Steph pulled the sheet free, releasing it to the Gulf wind. It flew from the deck, over the edge where the horizontal boards were now missing, and onto the ground, covering the imprint of the missing body.

Alixel entered the apartment first; one hand rested against her stomach. She tip-toed through torn mattress foam, busted pieces of furniture, and shards of table lamp glass. Billy quickly followed, disregarded the mess and went straight for his lab-office. Paperwork lay everywhere. All of the parts to all of his robotic endeavors had been swiped from the table and were mixed into a stew of destruction. His computer monitor had tumbled from the table face-first; he stepped over broken pebbles of its display screen. The computer itself appeared unharmed but the disks that held the data from the bank were missing as were the printouts he'd intended to show Alixel. He plowed through the paper heap but could not find either of them.

"How could they know?" he said, kneeling, with wads of invoices and cancelled checks in both hands.

"Whoever did this was not looking for evidence of a murder," Alixel said. "They are looking for one of these." She lifted the fold in her blouse with one thumb to reveal what looked like a belt buckle and pulled from a hidden sheath exactly what Billy had expected to see: a dagger that looked just like Janine's. The blade was long and thin and Billy wondered how it could have been so comfortably nestled against the curvature of her waist. "Did you have one of these?"

"No," Billy said. "But I know who does."

□ …

Janine was embarrassed. Balled toilet paper knots of dried snot lay on the kitchen table. Several created white, dotted trails from the front door to the bedroom and bathroom. She kicked the few at the door's threshold, then dropped her sack against the wall just inside the door. Joel set the one he carried next to it.

"Nice place," he said, smiling. "Much nicer than mine or Billy's."

"I didn't get a chance to tidy it up. If I'd have known you were coming…"

"Nonsense. I'm honored that you invited me in. Been a long time since a lady has done that to Joel Canton."

Janine smiled then. Most people only knew his rough exterior but to Janine, Joel was perhaps one of the kindest men she'd ever met—next to Michael. She knelt to pick up the tissues on the floor and had grasped a half a dozen before Joel grabbed her arm by the bicep.

"Really," he said. "The place is fine. Don't trouble yourself. You've had too rough a day to worry about a used roll of toilet paper. Come over here and sit with me. Relax. I imagine we'll be having company in short order. This would be a good time to recharge the batteries."

Having company? She wondered if he meant Steph and Billy and Alixel, or if he meant *bad* company. She wondered if he thought they were in danger. *She* certainly thought they were. Two apartments had been destroyed by dead, desperate crooks. Yes—bad company was on the way and it would arrive in short order.

She followed him to the couch and together they sat on two of the three cushions. She dropped the collected wads of stiff tissue on the third cushion and Joel immediately grasped the empty hand. He stroked it with each of his ten rugged fingertips, turned it over to look at the wrist and the scar that was not there. "How?" he said. "I've cut my hand with that thing before. Sharp bastard, it is. But I healed up just like any regular human." His gaze into her eyes that were suddenly filled with apology.

"I don't know how, Joel, but I can assure you that I am human and that whatever that dagger is, is beyond human."

"We can certainly agree on that." He traced the invisible cut with one finger. Janine saw that he was fighting with the decision to ask his next question. "Your blood. It flowed backward. The cut sucked it right back in. You know...I thought you were going to die right then and there. I thought for sure I was about to lose you."

Janine's eyes fluttered with fatigue. "Nonsense. I am honored that you saved my life. It's been a long time since someone has done that to Janine Bender." She thought of Michael as she said it.

Joel pulled her close. A kiss was the next step. Janine had fought that desire since walking toward the beach hand-in-hand, he as Tom Sawyer and she as Becky Thatcher. Michael was the only man she'd ever kissed, at least passionately. She wondered if Michael was looking down upon them at that very moment. She wondered if it was okay. And then her mind, in its need for rest, wondered if Becky had ever kissed Tom. She wondered if Becky had ever loved another man. She wondered if Becky and Michael would have ever made it as husband and wife. But, of course, that notion was crazy. It was just about as crazy as Janine kissing Joel.

Unfortunately, the chance or the choice never came. From outside her cottage apartment bellowed a scream so loud it shook her bones to the marrow. "The dagger," she cried and pointed to the sacks by the door. Joel stood, took one step forward, and then froze as the unlocked front door swung slowly open. Mark Walker stood in the frame and he looked quite mad.

"Whey is nit?" Mark slurred. "Whey is na dugger?"

"Mark!" Joel said, a welcome and friendly tone to his voice. "What did you find out about the water? Is it poisoned?"

Mark stepped into the room. Both sacks lay by his feet to his left but he did not notice them. "Fuc na wader!" Clouds had thickened outside, hiding the waning Texas sun but what little light remained glistened off the butcher knife that Mark held in one hand. He lifted it and shook it at Joel. "Na dugger! I won nit."

Joel stepped between Mark and Janine and looked at the sacks. Mark's red, silver swirling orbs followed.

"Na dugger!" he said and cackled. He turned completely around and reached for the first sack as Joel leapt for the butcher knife. Joel's weight carried both bodies through the open door and out onto the sidewalk.

"Joel!" Janine screamed. She bolted for the sack that held the dagger but as she reached it, Joel came flying backward through the door and crashed into her shoulder which sent both spinning and sprawling onto the carpet. Before either of them could recover, Mark snatched one sack and emptied its contents on the floor. The book flopped onto a pile of clothes, opening to the center spread where the invisible pencil had made its notes. The cubited Mark stared at the book, seemed to marvel at the drawings for only a second, before grabbing the second sack; he emptied its contents over the book. The dagger dropped onto the pile and rolled off toward Joel. The two printouts from the bank fluttered in a sudden rush of air and floated, twisting and turning, out the front door. Joel and Mark reached the dagger at the same moment as Mark slashed at Joel's face with the butcher knife. The sharp edge cut across his neck and blood immediately pulsed from the wound.

Janine's torso lay sprawled on the carpeted floor, her legs on the kitchen linoleum, her feet touching one kitchen table leg. When she saw the butcher knife open Joel's skin, she kicked outward in an attempt to quickly rise to her feet. The action sent the table skittering across the linoleum; used tissues from the top of the table rained down around her. She swept the white rags aside, curled to her knees and held out her arms as Joel collapsed into them. Blood rained across her bare arms. She covered his hand which covered the wound but the combined pressure was not enough to slow the bleeding.

"Agghh!!!" Mark screamed. "Na dugger is mine!" He held it in one hand above him, a victorious acquisition, a prize of great sacrifice, a tool for torture and for killing. He glared down upon them, a master to slaves.

Joel's body seemed to pump into Janine's hand as much blood as she'd dropped onto Billy's deck boards. Joel's blood, however, did not know reverse. It drooled from their clasped hands down both forearms, dripped from both elbows and onto the carpet and kitchen linoleum where it remained without hope for restoration.

"You, fitherman. You cwap uv da iwand. Die, fitherman, die!"

Death stood in her doorway just as it had done more than a year ago. It wailed crazy, nonsensical rants and threatened her with ideas that went beyond human knowledge. This cubit would chase her as the Albert-thing had, ultimately placing her back in an insane asylum where she would never have the chance to convince anyone that she had ever been sane. This thing, an abomination to all that was Holy suffocated her front door with its presence; storm clouds roiled behind it; Gulf winds whipped through its matted clothes. It screamed again, some wail of hideous victory, then coiled forward and slashed down with the dagger.

And Mark, who was no longer Mark, suddenly froze. The bump of flesh surrounding his Adam's apple opened to reveal a shiny point of metal. The dead man gurgled and the dagger dropped from his hand, bounced across Janine's head and settled on the blood-stained carpet.

Its eyes melted.

Its face disappeared.

The body collapsed, morphing into fleshless bone right before her eyes.

Behind the dissolving cubit stood a woman with long, dark hair that was pinstriped in red along the temples. Janine thought for moment that it was Marcy but this woman was too short and looked nothing like Cher except for the long, dark hair.

"Janine!" Billy yelled and stepped through the doorway. Steph followed.

The stranger swiped the dagger—which she had just driven through Mark's neck—across one thigh before slipping it into its sheath at her waist. What remained of Mark's body looked as if it had been dead for twenty years. The boney toe of the corpse's foot rested on Janine's leg and she kicked it away in disgust. Joel gurgled.

"He's lost a lot of blood," Janine said to Billy.

"Where is it?" the stranger asked, ignoring Joel's plight. The dagger rested on the carpet just beyond the spread of Joel's blood. When the stranger bent to pick it up, Janine kicked it farther away.

"Billy," Janine begged. "Don't let her have it."

Billy bent over them. "This is Alixel. She is friend not foe." His gaze went to the blood covered hands clasped against Joel's neck. "Joel. Can you hear me? Joel?" Joel's eyes fluttered, battling consciousness. "It'll be all right. You're going to be fine." He turned to Alixel who had grabbed Joel's dagger and was studying its haft. "He is isn't he?"

"Creation of man," Alixel said to the dagger. "At last I have found you."

"Joel," Billy urged. "Can you help him?"

Alixel knelt over Joel who remained cradled and now unconscious within Janine's arms. Janine was hesitant. She wanted no one touching Joel, especially a complete stranger. But her resistance faded as soon as Alixel grasped her hand and smiled.

"Please," Alixel said, in a pleasant, motherly tone. "Or else he's going to die."

Alixel's touch sent chills into her blood-coated arm. A tremor raced into her neck and she swooned as if she'd just been touched by God. Her hand was peeled away for her; she had no control of those muscles. She shook her head, trancelike, denying Alixel's intent.

"Please," Alixel repeated.

When Janine released her grip, Joel's hands fell from his throat, flopping one to each side of his body, and the blood bubbled from the diagonal cut below his chin. Janine reached forward but Alixel intercepted the hand, caressed it, nodded, smiled. She brought forth the dagger and angled it down, as if she was going to make Joel's wound even deeper. Though it frightened her, Janine allowed her to continue without protest.

The haft of the dagger began to glow. Janine's concentration on it at this point was microscopic. She remembered how one of the red points had glowed incredibly loud when she'd performed a similar ceremony for Professor Cower. She'd stuck the blade of the dagger into the professor's chest. She'd performed surgery with it. She'd pulled a bullet from him.

Alixel brought the dagger across Joel's neck and set it there, pressing the blade into the wound. The bubbling blood immediately stopped its flow. Stray, crimson rivulets wrapped and rolled, twisting around the thin blade, hungry for its shiny surface. And then, in one swift motion, as if again slicing open Joel's throat, she swiped the dagger away. All of them watched the miracle of healing. Joel coughed. He gurgled as if trying to breathe water. He spat up a small drop of blood and his breathing regained a regular, deep rhythm. His eyes fluttered. The slit in his neck folded, stitched, closed and became scar tissue in a matter of seconds. A sticky mass of blood remained and when Janine wiped it away, the wound was gone. Alixel stepped away.

Lightning raged in Port Aransas for the first time in more than a month. Its singular white disturbance illuminated the open door to Janine's Paradise Cottage apartment. The flash was so bright that it blocked out what remained of the day. Thunder quickly followed, a boisterous revelation of things to come, a malevolent screech that introduced the first day of summer and, seemingly, the rebirth of Joel Canton. The sight and sound echoed through the room and in the foreground, silhouetted by the flash of light, Janine saw the tears racing down Alixel's cheeks.

Joel had awakened and Janine stroked his temples as she watched Alixel stumble to the couch and collapse onto the tissues she'd left on the cushion. "I'm okay," Joel said. "*She* needs your help."

Janine left him with Billy who knelt to take her place, holding Joel's head as the fisherman slowly rose to a sitting position. A light rain began to fall and Steph closed the door and toggled the light switch which illuminated a small lamp on an end table in the corner opposite the couch where Janine now sat next to Alixel. Alixel's head lay limp against the backrest. Joel's dagger, which she'd used to save his life, rested on the cushion between them. The tears had stopped flowing but remnants remained stained on her cheeks. Janine gently dabbed them with one of the tissues she'd used to wipe away her own tears.

"Why are you crying?" Janine said. "You saved his life."

Alixel rolled her head toward Janine. "So many have been lost and I'm so tired." Alixel looked to be half Janine's age but her eyes expressed an epoch of existence. "We don't have much time. I can feel them coming."

"Who?" Janine said.

"I think you know who."

"No. I mean, who are they? What are they? Why are they here? What is the cubit? What are…?

Alixel extended her index finger to Janine's lips. "Shhh," she hushed. "It may be better that you do not know. Bad things happen to those who know."

That tingly sensation from Alixel's touch again raced into Janine's body. "Bad things have already happened to me," she said when Alixel removed her finger. Janine looked at Billy, at Steph, at Joel, who had all inched closer to their conversation. "Bad things have already happened to all of us because, like you said, we know. We just don't know why."

"The why is…" Alixel smiled the kind of smile that a mother expresses just before sending her first born off to war: a smile to comfort, to reassure, to provide hope, to exonerate what future sins her child must perform for the sake of all that is good. "The why is the end of world." Another fresh tear sprouted and dropped onto the pendant hanging from her turquoise necklace. To Janine, the pendant looked like Christ's cross but this one had four parallel cross members instead of just one.

Since the day that Professor Cower had entered her life Janine's world
had become a nightmare that she could not wake from. She'd questioned
her memories, her sanity, her faith, and her reality. Now she would find
out why. Alixel was about to tell her—tell them—how painfully real a
nightmare could be.

Once Janine had finished with the introduction of her friends, Alixel
sat up straight, took a deep breath and like a teacher to her students asked
them a question.

"How many of you have read the Bible?"

Janine's hand quickly rose. Billy's followed. Steph and Joel's hands
rose to about shoulder high.

"And so you know of the Book of Revelation?" All four nodded.
"It is a prophecy of the end times, of the rising of the Antichrist, of the
consumption of the world by fire. Only the purest of men and women
will survive such catastrophe. Those who have not prepared themselves
spiritually will suffer in ways unknown to human existence."

"The Apocalypse," Janine said.

"Not really," Billy interjected. "It all depends on how one reads the
term. *That* connotation is more a recent definition supported by evangelical
nutcases trying to sell fear for salvation and a heaping mound of cash on
the collection plate."

Alixel smiled, her tears aborted, her brown eyes suddenly alive as if
the teacher had just found her "A" student.

Billy continued, "But quite literally it means something like: the
revealing to selected individuals of sacred information kept hidden from
the masses, or perhaps, more specifically, the unveiling of God. So the
Book of Revelation is the Apocalypse according to John: the unveiling
of information about the milestones that precede the return of God.
To Christians, of course, God is usually manifest in the body of Jesus
Christ."

"It's all in the interpretation," Janine said. "I interpret it as the end of
the world."

Alixel patted her hand. "There are no wrong interpretations as much
as there are no right interpretations. That's the true power of faith. However,
no sacred text reveals everything. The Qur'an, the Torah, the I Ching, even
my people's sacred texts do not tell the whole story, because, as Billy has

alluded to already, some information is not meant for humankind."

"Your people?" Janine asked.

"I am Hopi by ancestry."

"So...Alixel...that name is Hopi?"

"Yes. It means Princess."

Steph chimed in, "And what are you the princess of?"

"For now, let's just say that I am the Princess of Rebirth. But that is another story."

Billy got the discussion back on track. "So the information not meant for mankind...you're going to tell us it has to do with this thing called the Cubit."

"Everything in this world has an opposite and opposing force," Alixel explained. "One cannot exist without the other. How could a person know the splendor of birth without knowing the heartbreak of death? It is a universal constant. There's no good without bad, no cosmos without chaos, no yang without yin. Alpha has its omega—the beginning always has an end. Throughout Earth's history, humans have ad infinitum found ways for speaking to their spiritual plateau—their God. They built alters, and temples, and complete religions around this one obscure need. They do this because they lack information and therefore, no matter how hard they try, all constructions for portals to Gods are inherently human and riddled with error. The only way of connecting with God is by the use of something created by God. Your soul is one good immaterial example, but too few in history have ever mastered this knowledge. They are known as prophets.

"There does exist several material objects that have served as portals. The Arc of the Covenant, for one. Though the Bible alludes to its creation by the hand of Man, this is only an interpretation. The Arc was created by that which it has a connection with: God. As Dr. Belloq from the Indiana Jones movie so eloquently put it, 'It is a radio for talking to God.' But, as I said, everything in this world has an opposite and opposing force."

"The Cubit," Billy guessed. "A radio for talking to the Devil."

"The Devil, again, is a Christian construct. Let's just say that the Arc is to Good as the Cubit is to Evil."

"And what emerges from the Cubit is Evil in its purest sense," Janine said, confident by experience.

"Yes. One touch and from it emerges the anti-you, a construction of all the Evil that resides within your human vessel."

"Albert Stine," Janine moaned. "He is the Devil himself."

Alixel still had a hold of Janine's hand and again gave it a light patting. "You might be more right than you imagine. Stine has his sights set on visions of grandeur. His desire is to be the Antichrist.

"You mean from Revelation?"

"The references in the Bible are not of the Antichrist, Janine. That is the interpretation. As is the interpretation that there have been other Antichrists in the past. Nero nor Napoleon nor Hitler were Antichrists. The only thing those men had in common was the possession of the Cubit. There can be only one Antichrist and there can be only one time in history that he or she can be born."

"*Can be* born," Billy questioned. "Does that mean we have a chance?"

"There's always hope, Billy, just as there is despair."

"So all that Nostradamus crap is just…crap?" Billy said.

"Not necessarily."

"So he was a prophet?"

"No. Definitely not a prophet. I think you misunderstand my use of that word."

Complete silence ensued for several seconds which gave the lightning and thunder a chance to showcase its anger outside. Joel, still weak from the attack, leaned back against the couch at Janine's feet and she stroked his thin hair with her free hand.

"No one person is a prophet," Alixel said. "At least no one mortal is a prophet. That would be an oxymoron. *People* are prophets. Groups of people, entire subcultures in an era of existence are prophets. These are the groups that frighten men. These are the groups that men destroy. These are the lost cultures, those that are now extinct or are very close to becoming that way. A prophecy is created by the collective. Some are false prophets. We call these religions. False prophets are fearful of the true prophets and, with great hypocrisy, slaughter those who present a danger to them."

"Were the Jews prophets?" Janine said. "After all, six million died at the hands of the powerful Aryan dictator."

"Perhaps," Alixel said. "They did reveal knowledge of the Arc in the Old Testament. How that knowledge was gained will always be one of the great mysteries."

"Unless it's all just mythological story-making," Billy said and immediately regretted doing so.

"After all you've seen," Janine said. Her hand stopped stroking Joel's head. Joel's eyes, which had been slowing closing, fluttered open then closed again. "You're not just dreaming as I was not dreaming the night my son died."

"That's okay," Alixel intervened. "The scientific way can lead to many false prophecies. Closed minds lead to closed intelligence."

Billy cleared his throat. "I deserved that. It's hard to agree on unproven truths."

"But you have proof," Alixel said.

"No one would believe me."

"I can think of many who would."

"The Jews," Billy quipped.

"Not all. And not all Hopis and not all Mayans, and not all within the Roman, Greek, Egyptian or Chinese empires."

Steph moaned and rubbed her stomach. She'd been kneeling while listening intently but now dropped back onto her buttocks and scooted over to the far wall next to the pile of clothes that had been dumped from Janine's two sacks.

"You okay?" Billy said.

"I don't know. Maybe just hunger, but something alive seems to be boiling inside my stomach."

"I've not had a chance to do any shopping," Janine said.

"No worries. I'll be fine. Just exhausted and hungry."

"So what's the deal with these?" Janine said, returning her attention to Alixel as she pointed at Joel's dagger lying between them.

"Creation Daggers," Alixel said. "They can save us."

"It's the only way to kill those things?" Billy said.

"It's the only way to make sure they are gone and don't come back. One strike with a Creation Dagger to the base of the skull and lights go out for good."

"So throwing them in a meat grinder won't do the trick."

"The Cubit can make more."

"Christ. I hope I never touch the damn thing."

Steph moaned again then suddenly rose and ran to the bathroom. A minute later she returned. "Sorry. My stomach just ain't feeling right. Perhaps I should lie down."

"Please," Janine said. "Use my bed. You might have to clear away a few wads of toilet tissue."

Steph disappeared into the bedroom but did not close the door.

Janine grabbed Joel's dagger from the cushion and traced the star pattern on the haft with a finger. "Quite beautiful," she said. "The red jewel glows just like yours." She nodded toward Alixel's waist.

"Jade," Alixel said. "A very rare red jade." She pulled her own dagger from its sheath.

"Created by the hand of God, no doubt," Billy added.

"As a matter of fact…" Alixel did not finish the testimony but instead continued with the description. "There are five points on the star, one for each Creation. Each dagger and each jaded point represents one of these creations." She pointed at the red jade in the star's left arm in Joel's dagger. "The Creation of Man." She pointed to the red jade in her own dagger. "The Creation of Religion. The top of the star represents the Creation of Good and Evil." To everyone's surprise, Alixel reached to her waist and pulled another dagger from a second hidden sheath, displayed it, and pointed to the jade in the top of the star. "The star represents the story of the Fifth Age."

"Fifth Age?" Billy said.

"The last of the Mayan's great 26,000-year cycle. In it there has been or will be the Creation of Good and Evil, the Creation of Man, the Creation of Religion, the Creation of the Antichrist and the Creation of the End. The five points of the star. The first three have already happened. The last two will take place in the future at nearly simultaneous points in time."

"Wait a minute. I've heard of this: Mayan prophecies of destruction, galactic alignment, the end date. A bit like Revelation don't you think?"

"John's revelation is not prophetic; it is a warning."

"And the Mayans were prophetic." The condescension in Billy's voice again raised its ugly head. "So you're telling me that on December 21, 2012, the world will come to an end."

Janine's face melted into an expression of panic.

"That is an interpretation," Alixel said. "The Mayans mark the end of the Fifth Age as the beginning of the next great cycle. The Alpha of the Omega. It doesn't have to mean that it is the destruction of the world."

"There you go again." Billy quickly raised and lowered his hands. "Talking in riddles. First, it's that the Antichrist *can* be born, not will be born. And now you're saying that there may or may not be an end to the world. So which is it? I get that there can be no thing in existence without its opposing opposite, but when you're talking about prophecy, the truth will eventually present itself. Either we're all going to die or we aren't. Both ideals cannot exist simultaneously. You might think that to be more of my scientific closed-mindedness, but come on."

"Billy. I think we have finally found agreement." Alixel grinned, the thin corners of her lips rising into her rounds cheeks, making the center of her lips plump outward. "And it is up to people like us to direct the outcome." She twirled her daggers majestically in the palms of her hands. "What we need are these."

"So there are five of them," Janine interjected.

"There are," Alixel said.

"Then that explains it."

"Explains what?"

"The dagger that Professor Cower brought into my house. The one I used to save his life. If I'm not mistaken, the red jade in that one occupied the left leg of the star."

"Professor Cower!?" Alixel's smile quickly morphed into an expression of surprise. Her eyes lit up. "How do you know *him*?"

"He brought the Cubit to my home a year ago. He's the reason I'm here."

"That man's name sends shivers down my spine."

"He's dead," Janine said. "He dynamited the Cubit and blew himself up."

"And now Albert has the dagger and the Cubit." Alixel almost whispered this to herself while shaking her head.

"That's four of them," Billy said. "So where's the fifth?" He paused, then quickly added, "No—wait a minute. In the ground. By the pier. Where all the heavy machinery is. LaFitte's treasure. That's the reason you're here."

"Cower is the reason I'm here as well," Alixel said. "He took the Cubit from us and I have to recover it."

Harsh winds kicked at the kitchen windows. Lightning continued in short spurts but the loud cracks of thunder had subsided somewhat. Joel had fallen asleep and began to snore quietly.

"Cower was an anthropologist from one of the state universities in New York," Alixel continued. "His interests were Hopi mythology and the Mayan classical and post-classical eras. And so, about five years ago, while exploring some of the underground dwellings at Chichen Itza, Cower found the dagger he brought into your home."

"So how do you fit in?" Billy said.

Alixel shifted on the couch uncomfortably. "I trusted Chris. He came to Sedona a few years before his Chichen Itza expedition to help us keep the Red Rock Anasazi ruins safe from private development. An anthropologist's claim that there was a historical importance to the land and the Anasazi who once lived there was much more convincing than a bunch of protesting Indians. He provided evidence that kept commercial interests out. Unfortunately, he also uncovered wall etchings that would eventually bring him back to Sedona, an etching that matched what he would find at Chichen Itza."

"The dagger—the creations," Janine said.

Alixel nodded. "He brought the dagger to me and started asking questions that I could not answer so he went looking for the answers himself. That's when he found the Cubit."

"Your people knew of the Cubit?" Janine said.

"Yes. We are its guardian."

"You are a prophet then."

"I am not. My people were chosen."

"To protect information not meant for the mass of humanity."

"And not a very good job of it. Cower took the Cubit."

Billy said, "I thought you couldn't touch it, you know, without becoming one of those things."

"That is true. And what your next question should be is 'if the Cubit makes an Evil duplicate of you, why aren't there two Cowers running around, or two Alberts, or two of anyone who touches it?'"

"Because they eat the original," Janine said.

"And take the place of that person in the world," Alixel continued, "complete with all their personality traits and memories and intelligence. The fortunate thing is that they are easy to spot early on in the transformation. It takes time for a cubited human to mature into its previous self. Their personalities will be awkward, they may have trouble speaking and their memories may be scrambled."

"And Professor Cower?"

"There is only one way to survive a cubited duplicate. You have to kill it with one of the five daggers, to the base of the skull, just like I did with that." She pointed at the remnants of Mark Walker. "If you are fortunate enough to have a dagger and know how to use it, you become immune to the effects of the Cubit."

"So Cower had the dagger," Billy said, "but how did he know what to use it for or even how to use it correctly?"

"That I'm not sure. There would have been no knowledge of such use within the Anasazi sacred grounds."

"Perhaps he found it in the book," Janine said.

Alixel's eyes widened. "Book?"

□ ...

Billy remembered the visions he'd seen in the VW's rearview mirror. "Are you talking about a book that has one of your daggers etched on its surface?"

Janine looked surprised. "How could you know that? No one has seen it since the day my farm blew up."

"I can't explain it. I had these visions—like dreams, almost. There were bullets, and screeching tires and that book with the dagger on it." He also remembered that the person driving the car in his vision was probably Professor Cower though he did not tell them this. He was trying to piece it together himself. He was trying to piece all of this together. His calculator brain was smoking with too much information, puzzle pieces placed by the hand of mythology and not reason; faith and belief were two of the largest pieces that he just couldn't find space for quite yet. He knew that once he allowed belief to take the place of reason, all that he'd ever known, everything he'd been taught, all the science, would no longer make sense. The door to Illogic was open; he had one foot inside already. Denial kept his other foot safely in the land of Reason.

And as if reading his mind, Alixel said, "You're slowly coming over to our side. Now you're having visions. Pretty soon you just might become part of the prophecies yourself. Is it so hard to accept?"

"Would you like to see it?" Janine said.

Billy's mind twisted at that very moment. If Janine had in her possession what he'd denied in his visions then—the land of Reason suddenly felt very far away.

"Oh my," Alixel moaned. "Oh great father. You have the Codex? You have the lost Book of the Djed?"

Billy thought that she had said "Dead" and immediately skepticism roared back to life, but when Janine pulled it from the pile of clothes by the front door and he saw the dagger blazoned on its back cover, he knew that he could no longer base his decisions solely on scientific methods. Science had no explanations for those who "saw things" but here was proof, an irony really. He'd found proof that illogic actually existed.

Alixel could hardly control herself. She quickly stood and met Janine halfway to the couch although the distance was less than four feet. "May I?" she said, sheathing her two daggers and holding out both hands. When Janine gave the book to her, she held it as if it were made of wet rice paper.

Her eyes were so large she could have doubled for an anime cartoon at that very moment. She shifted the book to one hand and stroked the gold embossing with a forefinger, starting from the haft of the dagger and moving slowly down to its point near the bottom of the book's back cover.

"What is it?" Janine said. "Is it valuable?"

"It has no value," Alixel said.

Billy knew it before he said it; he was beginning to believe. "A work of God."

Alixel nodded. "In a way. The message is Holy but most of the writing was done by the hand of man."

"Like the Ten Commandments," Janine said.

"Like the Ten Commandments," Alixel agreed. "But not Hebrew—Mayan."

"I've looked at the center pages but I was unable to open any other parts," Janine said. "I think the pages have been glued together."

Alixel simply patted her arm then sat on the floor and placed the book on the carpet. Janine sat to her left and Billy sat to her right. Joel snored behind them. Lightning flashed in the panes of the kitchen window. There was no thunder.

◻ …

To Janine's surprise, Alixel easily opened the book to its first page. "They were stuck together. How…" Alixel simply shook her head, reminding Janine how futile reason had become.

The first page was blank. Its edges, and those of all the pages in the Book of the Djed, were parchment brown. Alixel lifted then turned the page slowly, carefully, as if it would disintegrate between her fingers even though it had a crisp, heavy texture that prevented it from bending. She would handle each page the same way. On each page she would reveal a colorful mass of symbols that she said was an alphanumeric language few people understood. The hieroglyphs on each page would be clustered around that page's central theme, usually a drawing that told a story which Alixel, from the beginning, now revealed.

"This is the story of the Fifth Age," she said, pointing to a pair of drawings that looked remarkably like the Cubit and the Arc of the Covenant. "It begins with the Creation of Good and Evil. The Fifth Age is the only one of all five that contains both. In fact, our current 26,000-year Great Cycle is the only one in which an Age contained both. The four that came before were either good or bad, paradise or chaos. It is said that the extinction of the dinosaurs began an Age of chaos. The Ice Age was an Age of chaos. There were also Great Cycles of Eden, or Heaven as the Bible would call it, when the tranquility of life ruled."

"So why now?" Billy said. "Why is *this* Age different?"

Alixel turned the page. The answer was evident. "The Creation of Man," she said. The theme across this spread of pages depicted men's faces in ceremonial masks, of men hunting, of men fighting. One of the drawings was of what looked like men hanging from trees by their necks. At the bottom of the right hand page was the scene of what must have been a massacre: human body parts were graphically revealed in red.

Alixel turned the page and Janine gasped. On the left side of this spread, among the mass of hieroglyphic encryptions, were the drawings of a tree, a snake, and of a naked man and woman. "Did the Mayans know the Bible?" Janine asked.

"No. They did not," Alixel replied.

"Then how…"

"Some things are not meant for us to know," Alixel reminded her.

On the right, the same man and woman were now clothed and there were two children at their feet.

"The Mayans must have had access to the Bible," Billy said, again questioning the factual and mystic connotations.

"The Spanish did not invade the Yucatán until the early 1500s. It would have been impossible." Alixel countered.

Janine interrupted by grabbing Alixel's hand. She guided it to the edge of the page, urging her to move forward. From that point on to the center of the book, each of the next six pages depicted man's struggle between Good and Evil. There were pages where supreme beauty was the central theme and there were pages that were graphically horrific. There were symbols depicting fire, and water, and earth, and wind and rays of light that Alixel told them stood for a fifth element, man's psyche which, she said, was the source of the this Age's great confusion. "Those were the stories of the third creation: Religion," Alixel said of the pages she flipped through.

"We don't have a chance," Billy said and leaned back against the wall with his hands over his head.

"How can you say that when there's so much love in the world?" Alixel said. "Remember that this is the Age of both good things and bad things and given those odds we'll always have a chance. The second half of the Book of the Djed should reveal this."

She turned to the center spread which was drawn in a way unlike any of the other pages. The language appeared Mayan but the symbols were recently drawn with what looked like pencil.

"This is a diary," Janine said. "Don't you think? It looks like the professor was archiving the discoveries he'd made."

"Cower didn't do this," Alixel said. "The center is saved for the hand of only one."

"No!" Billy grumbled, throwing his arms up against the wall. Joel stirred but did not awaken. "That's going just a bit too far."

"It's the truth," Alixel said. "These are the words of God, and he's telling us how to save the world."

"Yeah? Well he left off one big chunk of information." Billy pointed at the right hand page which was mostly blank. "Is that the part we're not meant to know? I mean, come on, how are we supposed to save mankind if God doesn't tell us everything?"

"He will, in time, as 2012 draws near."

"She's right," Janine said. "The last time I looked, these weren't here." She pointed at three numerals that were stenciled in under the Bird of Fire; the numerals were no larger than those written in an average textbook. The first two were well-defined but the last one looked as if it was still being created. The numerals were 666.

"The mark of the beast," Janine said, her mouth remaining agape.

"An interpretation," Alixel reminded her. "Not necessarily true."

"So what *does* it mean?"

"We won't know until the message is complete. Then we can use the key to decipher the exact time and place of the raising of the Djed on December 21. These two pages and the key will also reveal instructions for the ceremony that must take place if the next Great Cycle is to usher in 26,000 years of paradise, rid us of Evil and destroy the Cubit."

"The key," Billy huffed. "And I suppose we have to go looking for that as well?"

"Actually, no," Alixel said. "You remember that printout you told me about? The coin you showed me? The symbol of the Wayab is a part of the key and it is right here." She turned a page. Then turned another. Her gentle caress of the pages turned into an aggressive pursuit for something she could not find. She flipped back to the center and again turned the page. She brought the book up to her face so that her nose was an inch from the binding then lowered it. "It's gone. It's been ripped out."

"It must have somehow torn free in the explosion," Janine offered as explanation.

"Which means that Albert not only has the Cubit and Cower's Creation Dagger..." Alixel began.

"...he also has the key," Billy added. "That's what he was carrying to the bank along with what must have been the location of LaFitte's treasure..."

"...and the fifth dagger," Janine concluded.

"He'll try to kill us to obtain our daggers," Alixel said with sudden revelation. "This has been his plan all along. With everything in his possession, he will lead the next Great Cycle into pure chaos."

A blinding flash of lightening stabbed through the kitchen window and thunder crashed immediately overhead. The lights in the apartment went out.

◻ ...

"FEMA is going to be all over this place in the morning." Chancey Lett growled at Albert. "We've got to get it going now!"

Albert drove the black Hummer toward the beach, loathing Lett more and more with each street he passed. He would have killed him already if only he'd known how to operate a backhoe; somehow that knowledge had been lost in his transition. All Lett could think about was greed and the power from money it gave to individuals. What the casino boss didn't understand was that the real power was not in the riches one held in their hands but the soul they possessed inside. Once you had the soul, you had the power. An individual's life force was invaluable. Fortunately for Albert and all of the demons that had ever existed, either real or conjured, nearly all humans were oblivious to that one Truth—as Albert had been before the Cubit.

The new, improved Albert had recovered the Cubit and Cower's dagger once he'd awakened after the explosion on the Benders' farm, and had taken the artifacts to the casino boss who had forgiven him his gambling debts. Albert had used Lett's greed to manipulate everything that had happened since then. The promise of LaFitte's treasure had been the lure. The priceless dagger had been the bait.

Now everything was set. He had the key, he had the Cubit, and the Book of the Djed and all five daggers were in the same place at the same time, an occurrence that had not happened since the beginning of the current Age. After a year of waiting, he was merely moments away from killing Lett, taking the dagger which Lett kept strapped in a sheath above his ankle, and using it on the rest of those who would unknowingly secure his destiny. Albert would take his rightful place as this Age's fourth creation and would direct the outcome of its fifth.

❒ ...

No one else was in the bank when it happened.

The birth of death began as it always did: the top of the Cubit cracked open—a lid on a crate. Deep crimson fired from within, splattering the interior of the bank vault like blood in a massacre. Slowly the lid rose on hinges that weren't there. A hand pushed the lid upwards, and an arm slowly rose from the depths of the Cubit, making short, jerky motions as if what was inside was ascending a staircase. A crown of light hair, which was less blonde than bloody, appeared. The head was bent forward and the long strands of hair hid the face. As was the case with all cubited humans, this one was reborn as an exact duplicate of its living counterpart at the moment the Cubit was touched, and so the pantsuit on it looked awkward, giving it the clean look of a new corpse freshly prepared for burial.

It stepped from the Cubit and looked briefly around, confused, then stumbled as it took its first few steps. Its previous mortal memory guided it out of the vault and to a desk where, in life, it had spent much of its daylight, and it sat in a chair to gaze across the barren wooden desktop. Something was missing, it thought. Something that, at one time, had made it laugh.

"Pat-twick," the cubit slurred. "Pat-twick the stawfish."

❒ ...

State trooper Andy Collar had never been as busy as he was the night that Hurricane Antiago sat on the doorstep of Corpus Christi. Weather reports said that the hurricane had sped toward Texas "at a rate impossible to meteorological science" and might hit any time in the next two hours; however, even that number was a "guesstimate" since every calculated movement of Antiago so far had been inaccurate. Its path through the Gulf, its lateral speed toward the coastline, its tight circumference, its internal wind speeds—all had teased forecasters into believing they actually knew what they were talking about. Even the shape of the storm was irregular, with the front end of the storm producing only tropical storm strength winds while the back of the storm raged with the intensity beyond a Category 5.

There had been so few troopers and so many terrified people that Andy and his partner had split up, each taking a cruiser in an opposite direction. Andy had been charged with organizing the officials of Port Aransas in hopes of moving whoever remained to safety; word was that there were still a couple of hundred people on the island. Andy had grown up in Port A for a short time, mostly before he'd turned thirteen not a dozen years ago, so he knew many of the people and, so his lieutenant's theory went, would have a better chance at organizing them. But theories went out the window when panic was in question. Regardless of his associations, getting two hundred people to agree in the few hours remaining before the hurricane hit would be difficult.

As he neared Port Aransas from Route 361, he did not notice the new construction just beyond the 7-Eleven to his right. If he had looked in that direction and if the lightning would have flashed at just the right moment, he might have seen a large number of people organizing near an apartment complex a few blocks away.

Instead, he continued into town, passing under the blinking yellow traffic light at the corner of Avenue G. Pat McGee's looked abandoned. He remembered that, in his youth, the owner of surf shop had placed a small prefabricated storm shelter in the lot behind his store; it was one of those newfangled shelters that doubled as a room addition. He briefly wondered if anyone was in McGee's shelter and made a mental note to check it after going through town.

Alister Street seemed deserted. The street lights still functioned but few homes appeared occupied. Where these so-called couple of hundred people might be, Andy could only guess. He cruised by the Surf Side Restaurant but it was too dark for him to see that it had been broken into. He cruised by the University of Texas Marine Science Institute and found one car, an old Buick Cutlass in the parking lot. He turned back toward town and cruised by the ferry station. Both ferries were moored. No one was in the control tower.

He decided to cruise along the beachfront and headed toward the south jetty back along Cotter Avenue and, again, passed the marine institute. There, stumbling along the side of the road was a young woman in a business suit. He rolled to a stop and lowered the passenger window with the automatic switch.

"Ma'am," he said. "Excuse me, ma'am." The woman took three more steps before turning to his voice. Her hair and clothes whipped violently in a gust of wind that shook the trooper's cruiser. "Can I ask what you are doing out here?"

"Pawadize cottagey," she mumbled and pointed toward the south side of town. "I am at pawadize cottagey."

Andy thought the woman was drunk. "Would you mind getting in? It's much too dangerous out here."

"Pawadize cottagey," she repeated.

The woman looked as if she'd been in a horrible fight. There were clots of blood in her hair and her face was streaked in crimson and dirt. Her lips were purple as were the circles around her eyes. He leaned across the seat and opened the door. "Get in, please."

The woman stumbled into the seat but Andy had to lean across her to close the door. She smelled as bad as she looked and Andy kept the window down to keep from gagging.

A minute later, he turned onto the beach road at the jetty and headed south. Lightning and thunder flashed and roared with increasing frequency. The winds knocked the cruiser sideways on its springs. It was raining but, oddly, not in unison with the storm's other hammering elements.

"Who wibs in pine-papples unner da sea?" the woman said. Her neck muscles were unable to withstand the wind that slapped against her face; the back of her head beat against the seat's headrest.

"Excuse me, ma'am?" Andy said. "Who what?"

The woman turned toward him and her eyes blazed blood red. Tiny silver irises sparkled with each lightning strike. "A pine-papple unner da sea. You know."

"I'm sorry, but I don't understand…"

She started humming a strange verse that somehow seemed familiar to Andy. Her head found the muscles necessary to make it sway to the sound. Her hands lifted in front of her and she tapped the dashboard with dissonant rhythm. "Who wibs in a pine-papple unner da sea?" She repeated the question while tapping and humming.

"Ma'am? I think you've had a bit too much to drink. Where is your home?"

It was then that Andy passed the Caldwell Pier to find several pieces of heavy machinery and a black Hummer parked a hundred yards from the shoreline. A backhoe started up as he came to a stop. He switched on his flood light and aimed it at a large man who was approaching the car. "Not a very good evening to be moving around machinery," Andy said to the man.

"Agreed," the man said from ten feet away. He wore a black cowboy hat and black boots. In fact, his entire wardrobe was black. A fresh cut was etched into his face near a scar that looked like it had been there awhile. "If you don't mind, could you turn that thing off?"

Andy flashed the flood light toward the backhoe but the driver was hard to see. He appeared to be wearing a business suit which, to Andy, seemed odd: a man in a business suit atop a Caterpillar?

"That's my boss," the man said. "Wants to get his machines farther inland before that 'cane hits.'"

"Spund Bob!" Andy's passenger suddenly yelled, giggling. "Spund Bob Sparepanths!"

To Andy, the woman seemed to be more of a priority than these men. Besides, how far could they take such large machines even if they were thieves? The hurricane would stop them cold.

"You guys taking shelter?" Andy yelled over a boisterous clap of thunder.

"Treasure Trove," the man said. "We're staying at the Treasure Trove."

"Spund Bob Sparepanths; Spund Bob Sparepanths; Spund Bawwwb... Spare-panths!"

"Yeah. Good. Be careful." Andy switched off the floodlight and slowly pulled away. The woman next to him was driving him crazy. He said to her, "Where did you say you lived?"

"That way," the woman pointed. "To my pine-papple unner da sea."

Andy doubted that he'd ever find her home.

⬜ ...

The lights went out the moment Steph woke up. She'd been having a horrible nightmare and the clap of thunder that now brought her out of bed had been part of it. She was on the beach. Albert was there with her. So was the Cubit. Just Albert, herself and the Cubit. As if these three things were all that remained in the entire world.

Albert stood against fierce winds and driving rain. In his hands were five daggers. He screamed something at the black clouds above but thunder drowned out the meaning. Then the Cubit opened and something emerged. Lightning flashed and she thought she saw…BANG!

Steph squealed as she sat straight up in Janine's bed. Her hands shook and she clasped them together, hoping the tremors would subside. She swung both legs to the floor and felt her way through the darkness. Blasts of lightning helped her find the door.

When she peaked from the bedroom toward the kitchen she, at first, did not understand what she was seeing. Her mind remained scattered from the nightmare. She still felt nauseas. Perhaps she was still asleep. Perhaps what she now saw was more of the dream, one in which you wake up only to enter into another nightmare.

There were faces looking in at her; a dozen of them were pressed up against the kitchen window. When the lightning flashed, she could see them plain as day: Professor Nelson, Chester Kalimaris, Jacques the smelly fisherman, Dave the security guard, and Misty Percy. Misty had been with her the day that Chancey and Albert and Carol had cornered her in the vault. Misty had been determined to take her business elsewhere.

Steph stepped from the bedroom and into the short hallway that quickly opened into the adjoining living space. The eyeballs of the window faces followed her; lips were squashed against the glass; cheeks were bloated. Lightning revealed Misty Percy's sparkling white incisors as the woman started chewing at the glass, creating a squeaking screech not unlike fingernails against chalkboards.

Thunder clasped.

Squeaky-squeaky.

Joel, Billy, Janine and Alixel were all sitting in the dark on the floor next to the couch.

Squeaky-squeaky.

Alixel drew two daggers from her waist. Janine had one dagger which she rolled between the fingers of one hand.

Squeaky-squeaky.

They stared at the window that Misty Percy was chewing at. Suddenly, the front door blew inward at the same moment that the combined face weight collapsed the kitchen window.

❐ …

Several dozen people loafed on the lawns outside Paradise Cottages. Andy stopped short of the mass. "Is this it?" he asked, feeling a bit fortunate that the drunk had led him to many of the people he had been ordered to help find shelter. "Is this your home?"

"Who wibs in a pine-papple unner da sea?" the woman repeated for the hundredth time.

"I DON'T KNOW!" Andy yelled. He'd been listening to the jibber-jabber for much too long.

"Too bad," the woman said, then reached over and grabbed Andy's neck with one hand. Her strength was overwhelming; the fingertips dug into flesh. Andy released his holster snap, drew the revolver, pointed it at the woman's head.

"Stop!" he gurgled. "Stop or I'll shoot."

And then he did. But the bullet simply sped through her forehead without effect. The woman knocked the gun from his hand with her free hand then squeezed harder. Blood squirted everywhere, darkening the windshield and pooling on the dashboard. A moment later, the woman ripped Andy's esophagus and carotid arteries from his neck. His head lolled on torn muscles and flopped against the driver's side window.

"Spund Bob," the woman said and exited the cruiser.

❐ …

Mitchell Bone came through the doorway first. Janine was to be left unharmed, he'd been told, so his assault was directed at Joel who had not completely recovered and was therefore easily knocked backward from Bone's momentum. A sharp point of metal severed Bone's Adam's apple and Bone's strength quickly vanished. Janine yanked the long blade of her Creation Dagger from the back of Bone's head and kicked the disintegrating corpse onto the carpet now marked by Joel's sticky-dry blood.

More of the living dead rushed into the room and clambered into the kitchen across fragments of glass and mushy, rain-soaked wads of toilet tissue. Billy kicked a young woman with big incisors in the stomach with no effect. Joel, still lying on his back, flung a leg out at the same woman, collapsed her knee, quickly got to his feet as the woman fell. Several other intruders stumbled over the woman in a heap.

"To the bedroom!" Janine yelled. "Hurry!"

Billy snatched the Book of the Djed and shoved it into the waistband of his shorts. He grabbed Steph who stood there comatose, led the group into Janine's bedroom and slammed the door shut. Janine immediately threw a table lamp against the bedroom window and both shattered on impact. Billy locked the bedroom door and slid the end table in front of it.

Wood split in the bedroom door frame. The interior wall surrounding the door looked as if it would implode at any moment. Plaster cracked. Something snarled.

One by one, Billy helped his comrades out the bedroom window. He pushed Steph through last, hurriedly grabbed the bricked window opening, sliced open the palms of both hands on jutting glass and pulled himself up as the bedroom door caved in. Like roaches freed from a dark crevasse, the cubits rushed into the room, lunged at Billy's flailing feet and screeched in unison at their prey's escape.

❒ …

As she passed her own bedroom window, Steph almost lost consciousness. What she saw was simply too much for the mind to comprehend. Her legs went limp and she would have fallen had Billy not been there to snatch her up by the armpits.

"Come on," he encouraged her. "We have to get out of here."

"I—I—," she pointed at the window. Billy looked but the face was no longer there. "I saw me. Oh, my God!"

"You're here, Steph. You're with me."

"I'm dead," she said, not hearing him. "Please, Billy. Don't let her eat me."

There were four cottage apartments per building. Steph's was one from the end. A wooden, tall fence blocked any escape other than beyond that last vacant apartment. Behind them, the mass of cubited townspeople flooded into the narrow passage from the opposite direction. Misty Percy led them, snarling her white incisor sneer while limping and lunging on the knee that Joel had kicked in.

Ten feet from their escape in the opposite direction, Carol, the bank teller, blocked their passage. Alixel, however, made quick work of her, brandishing both of her daggers with a whip-whirl motion between her fingers that brought both blades forward, piercing each of the dead woman's eyes. Carol scratched at her face, stumbled backward, and toppled sideways which opened the kill shot to the back of her head that Alixel engaged immediately.

Out from the back of the cottages the five of them ran, rain pelting their faces, wind knocking them back, lightning flashing like light bulbs over the main event. Steph suddenly screamed, the terrifying memory of her own face looking back at her, the thought of her as a cubit overwhelming, the dire need to get as far away from her own apartment overriding the safety provided by those with the weapons that could save her life. She jerked free of Billy's grasp and ran to the front of the building where three dozen dead citizens loafed for something to do until they saw her. Simultaneously, they turned. Steph's Cavalier and Billy's VW Bus were parked beyond them. A police cruiser sat idling in the middle of the street. To get the hell out here she'd have to go through the blockade. Fortunately, she hesitated long enough for Alixel and Janine to catch up. Billy and Joel were a few yards behind.

"You'll not make it," Alixel warned. "Their strength will rip you to shreds. Stand behind me."

Steph stepped backward as Janine joined Alixel to form a three-daggered offensive front and like a wedge through the front lines, they met the mass of cubits head on.

Alixel's prowess with the daggers was understandable but what really amazed Steph was the way Janine expertly dispatched four cubits with four quick strokes. Jacques the smelly fisherman who smelled a lot worse now, lunged at Steph but Janine buried the blade of her dagger to the top of his head. The fisherman's grasp locked onto Steph's T-shirt and as the body fell, it ripped the shirt and bathing suit top from her shoulders. She stood naked from the waist up. And that was just too much for her to take. She bolted from the protection of Janine's fight, slipped Billy's grasp who tried to stop her, screamed because she thought that one of the dead men had tried to grab her bare breasts, dodged several lunging attempts to take her down, and leapt over the hood of her Cavalier like a cop chasing a speedy drug dealer. Her athletic fortitude had helped salvage her life but when she opened her car door, none of that really mattered. She could not scream fast enough. Her cubit snatched her arm and yanked her into the car; her forehead cracked against the roof of the car and her neck snapped from the force.

□ …

Billy heard her scream but he knew it wasn't really Stephanie Drake. This scream was one of pleasure, of victory, not one of absolute horror. Steph's body disappeared into her car as if she were the victim of some giant, maniacal vacuum cleaner. Her body was then propelled from the car and when she hit the asphalt, her body convulsed several times before it was pounced on by her cubit. The feeding that ensued was something Billy wished he'd not seen. He tried to look away, and he eventually did, but the few seconds that it took to understand what was really going on was enough to engrain the memory of disembodiment forever. He stood, stupefied, until his bicep was almost torn by the grip of a large Hispanic man.

"Drop!" Alixel screamed, and Billy's feet obeyed. He dropped to the ground as Alixel lashed out with both daggers. One severed the Hispanic cubit's hand at the wrist and it remained clamped to Billy's bicep until he rolled on the wet grass and swatted it away. Alixel's other dagger sliced open face flesh then with two more slashes, she dropped the cubit to the ground beside him.

Alixel really was amazing. There must have been thirty or forty of those things surrounding her and her daggers moved faster than the lightning flashing above her. Rarely did a cubit actually touch her. While kneeling on the wet grass, Billy witnessed the fury of the blades, fingers flew in the air, an ear launched skyward, some thing's limb flopped onto the asphalt without a body. In one instant, he thought Alixel was done for, a group of cubits surrounding her in a mob that he couldn't see through. A moment later, tracers from lighting reflected on steel arced through the darkness, a blur of movement that Billy's eyes could not adjust to, the death strikes of two daggers dropping the mob in a matter of seconds.

Janine held her own as well. With one dagger, she was able to fend off at least a dozen cubits. The weapon twirled in her hand and between fingers like a baton and she knew exactly when and where to strike with it.

By the time Billy got to his feet, most of the living dead that had surrounded them lay on the ground; many were dismembered. The few that remained were inside Billy's VW, apparently hiding to avoid Alixel's blades.

"Come on," Alixel said. "Now!" She quickly peered inside Steph's Cavalier then ran to the police cruiser which was already idling. Billy took a step in that direction and froze. Steph was there, right in front of him, wearing the pantsuit that made her look so professional. Her hair was a bloody mess; her lips dripped with carnage.

"BJ." she gurgled. "My wittle BJ. Let's go thurfing and maybe I give you thumb. I know you wan me."

He should have lost his mind at that very moment. Everything started moving in slow motion just as it had back on the beach right before the *Knights* had slammed into Albert Stine. Steph reached out for his neck. She pursed her lips. She grinned so wide, the piece of flesh hanging from the corner of her lip fell onto her breasts.

"I know you wan me," she repeated.

Her hands never made it to his throat and he would have let them, too. He would have done nothing to stop the kiss the Steph cubit had planned for him. She would have grabbed his neck and placed her lips against his and he would have simply melted into insanity. But Janine made sure that didn't happen. In fact, the thing that finally made everything in his mind move at normal speed once again was the blade that suddenly emerged from the Steph cubit's mouth. Billy quickly backed away while yelping a short, girlish cry and the cubit fell at his feet. Janine twirled the dagger in a circle before bringing it down to one side. She grabbed Billy's arm and raced with him toward the police cruiser. She tossed him in the back then turned around.

"Joel!" she yelled.

❐ ...

A lot of what was now happening reminded him of the summer of the great white back in 1972, and as Joel stood leaning against the cottage apartment building, watching the struggle that unfolded before him, those thoughts overwhelmed him. He was afraid, an emotion that he'd never been able to admit.

Just as he'd not admitted to what he'd actually done to capture the beast—which was nothing. He'd been knocked out cold from the sailing mast.

Just as he'd not admitted that his false assurance made possible by his false heroism was the reason that his marriage had broken and the reason why he'd sworn to never love again.

Just as he'd not admitted that no real man could live off of lies and that pretense would someday come back to bite you in the ass.

Just as he'd never admitted that he'd stripped himself of his own manhood and that was the reason why Joel Canton took to living and hiding and being scared in the confines of his tiny shack near the shore.

He'd known Mark Walker so well and when he'd attacked him, Joel had been afraid. When they'd scrambled to the bedroom, Joel had been the first one out the window. When he saw Steph looking out at him through her own bedroom window at the same moment Steph was running with him to escape—well—that's when the cowardice really took control. But the final stroke had been Janine. He had convinced himself that love was, again, possible. And to love a woman meant to protect a woman. He would become her hero and save her from the beast she was running from. No one would harm the woman he loved. No one would be her great white shark, not while Joel Canton was around. He was her Biblical staff and rod!

But it wasn't he who would be the hero and it was hard for him to admit that. As he leaned against the wall, watching her prowess with the weapon he'd found on the beach, knowing that she could have single-handedly killed the great white terror of '72, whatever mental and physical strength remained in him drained, leaving behind a coward.

Janine stood by the police cruiser yelling his name but he couldn't run to her. He was ashamed of himself. What a joke he was. Joel the Joke they would call him. The great pretender.

As several cubits emerged from Billy's VW Bus, Joel turned toward the back of the apartments and ran there to hide.

◻ ...

Blood covered the front seat but Alixel did not seem to care. Janine, however, felt queasy and her stomach churned further when Alixel switched on the police cruiser's windshield wipers. The swooping motion of wipers over blood reminded her of what she'd just done.

"It was necessary," Alixel said. "They were already dead."

"You were something else," Billy added from the back seat.

"What about Joel?" Janine said to Alixel. "We just left him there."

"He ran from us and we don't have the time."

"I could have…"

"I need you," Alixel demanded. "*We* need you."

It became evident as the trio sped toward the beach that Hurricane Antiago was close to making landfall. Alixel wrestled the steering wheel as whips of wind attempted to throw the cruiser sideways. When she turned onto the beach road, the handling difficulties intensified. The rain had increased in density and speed. Some wind gusts practically shoved the police cruiser onto two wheels. In the distance, a single light blazed near the Caldwell Pier.

"We don't have time," Alixel repeated more to herself than to the car's occupants. "Hold on." She gunned the accelerator and took the police cruiser to a speed that was just under her loss of its control.

Nearer to the pier it became evident that Lett was operating the backhoe and Albert was directing the dig. Albert stood atop a tall pile of sand, lighting striking wrinkles into the sky behind him, wind ripping at his black clothing, his cowboy hat somehow remaining tacked to the top of his head, and Janine was reminded of her nightmare in which she had become his cubited bride. As they approached, Albert turned, his silhouette acknowledging their presence; he then shuffled out of sight down the back side of the sand mound. The light on the backhoe went out.

Alixel switched off the cruiser's headlights as she parked the car near the hole that had been created. Lightning provided short snapshots of the depth of the hole. What was at the bottom could not be seen from within the car. Beyond the hole sat the backhoe. Its digging arm was frozen, the bucket flexed, its metal teeth stretching toward the hole. Alixel switched on the cruiser's flood light.

Lett, still wearing his business suit, sat slumped within the cab of the backhoe. Blood covered the white shirt and tie. His face was buried in his chest. Behind him, also in the cab, stood Albert. He held a dagger in his hand that began to glow. The two daggers in Alixel's belt sheath and the one in Janine's hand began to glow at the same time that a red halo grew from the depths of the hole. Alixel doused the floodlight then both women exited the cruiser, leaving Billy inside.

"Protect the book," Alixel said to him then closed the door.

The women scaled the sand pile and stood at its apex; sand skittered into the hole from the weight of their feet which struggled to counteract the soft ground and mighty wind; the daggers hummed a gentle rhythm that was nearly inaudible.

At the bottom of the excavation, LaFitte's treasure lay scattered from the haphazard digging by the backhoe's operator. Wooden chests had been splintered open and small silver coins, much like the one Billy had found, littered the sand pit's floor. Gold, silver, ivory and copper statues from ancient civilizations poked their bodies up from deeper in the sand. Faces of Maya, faces of Egypt, faces of China were all present and looking up at the women as if pleading to be set free. Sticking straight up in the sand, apparently lodged into something that remained covered beneath it, was the fifth dagger. The red jade that symbolized the Creation of the End glowed with the same brilliance as the other four.

"Janine, my wife. You've finally returned to your loving husband," Albert said in a soothing tone that served only to raise Janine's alarm further. He remained partially hidden within the backhoe cab. Even the lightning was afraid to reveal his face. "And Alixel—princess of hope, guardian of despair—great fucking job you've done. I've got to admit, though, that without you none of this would have been possible. Your faults have been my gains. I was once just a simple country fuck with no money and a bad Jim Beam habit. And look at me now. I have the Cubit and the key and soon I'll have all the daggers and the recipe book which will tell me how to secure myself at the top of the sand pile." He laughed and the thunder acknowledged his pleasure with a pounding barrage.

"Three against one," Alixel yelled and pointed her daggers in his direction. Janine followed her lead, lifting her dagger to create three halos of red-jade light.

"Seriously?" Albert said and threw Lett's body from the backhoe cab as easily as one might toss an apple. He sat behind the controls. His face became visible above the glow of his own dagger. "You don't think I'd come to a fight empty-handed do you?"

At first, Janine thought that what she saw was an after-image created by the glowing daggers. She'd stared at them too long and now three red circles occupied her eyesight. It made the surf, which had moved inland more than fifty yards since they'd arrived, appear spotted. But when the fourth, fifth and sixth spots formed in the surf, she realized that it was something totally different. The spots in the surf did not glow. Under the rampant flashing thunderstorm, the spots looked like blood. Each bubbled as if boiling. The blood spots grew wider and the crimson turned darker. From each emerged a dozen cubited residents of Port Aransas. They rose heads-first and in unison, as if the sand were lifting them as a singular unit. When they'd risen to waist height, each walked forward, rigid, unwavering, even though the surf bashed their backsides. When they came to shore, Alixel turned to Janine.

"You ready?" Alixel said. "We'll have to do this together. You know what's at stake."

The world, Janine thought. Alixel never said it but she knew. *God's destiny for her was to save the world.*

She gripped the dagger with a strength that made it glow brighter and stepped forward just as the bucket of the backhoe passed within inches of her face and swatted Alixel into the bottom of the sand pit.

"Now that's better odds," Albert cackled wildly.

❏ ...

The cubits from Billy's VW had followed Joel behind the apartment building and were now hovering outside Janine's bedroom window, unable to figure out how to pull their new bodies up and in. Joel cowered on Janine's bed, hugging her pillow. He stared at the broken window, listened to the grunts and shrieks and guttural breaths of his pursuers. He could do nothing except wait. Sooner or later, the cubits would understand that going through the window to get him was not their best approach. Pretty soon, they would be rushing through the door. And they'd rip him apart. God help him, they'd rip him apart more ruthlessly than would any shark of any size.

Glass crunched underfoot outside the splintered bedroom doorway.

Crunch!

Joel hugged the pillow closer, as if he could hide his entire body behind it.

Crunch-crunch!

He started crying and moaning his former wife's name. "Jane..." he bawled. "Oh, dear, Jane."

Crunch-crunch-crunch!

Snot and saliva and tears drooled over the pillow and onto his coveralls.

And the crunching stopped.

And Joel stopped.

The cubits outside the window still bustled with discontent. He sniffed and stared and mopped his eyes with the soaked pillow then blinked.

"Joel," a hushed voice said from beyond the wall. "Joel. Is that you?"

Joel nodded but did not answer.

Her hand appeared first, curling into the doorway across the broken frame, the nails painted black as they always were. "Joel. We've got to get out of here."

Marcy shuffled quietly into the room. Her attention was on everything at once. She looked back to the hallway, then in at the window, then over to Joel. She stepped to the edge of the bed.

"Take my hand," she said. "Quickly!"

Joel reached out to her, dropped the pillow, and allowed her strength to pull him from the bed. She tiptoed through the bedroom doorway and Joel followed, tiptoeing the best way he knew how. She rushed to the open front door, wind kicking her in the face, thunder raging overhead and Joel did not release her grip. She paused at the front door's threshold then released Joel's hand and ran as fast as she could to Billy's VW.

"Come on!" she urged.

Her strength had left him and Joel found that he could move no farther.

"Joel!" Marcy yelled louder.

He stared at his legs wondering why they wouldn't move. His pounding heart made his entire body shake.

"They're coming—Hurry!"

To his left, emerging from the side of the apartment building, scuttled no less than eight cubits. One of them was little Teddy Lavender. "Dead fish," Teddy said, his hands out and grasping at nothing. "Joel, take me dead fishing." The taller, older cubits ran past little Teddy but Joel paid them no attention; he couldn't take his eyes off the boy.

"Dammit Joel!" Marcy's hand was again pulling him forward; she'd run back to get him. "We...are going...to die!"

Jacques the smelly fisherman, missed ripping Joel's arm off by a fraction of an inch as Marcy yanked him from the doorstep. She pulled Joel with her, the cubits at their heels, toward the VW. She entered through the passenger's door, yanked Joel inside, reached over and slammed the door against Jacques' hand, gasped as two fingers fell to the floor board, and pulled the door closed. The cubits attacked the VW as Marcy started the engine and pulled away. Teddy Lavender's tiny hand reached through the busted driver's side window and grabbed Marcy's throat. She couldn't breath. She beat the tiny arm but it would not loosen its grip. The VW rode in a circle as Marcy tried to gain control of the steering wheel. Her face turned purple. A drop of blood sprang from a tiny finger that ripped at the flesh under her chin.

"Jo–aghhh!" she moaned.

At that moment Joel's cowardice disappeared completely. Another of his friends was about to die and he just couldn't let that happen anymore. The urge to run became the fortitude to fight. He reached across Marcy and, with every ounce of energy his proud fisherman's body could muster, slammed his fist against the tiny arm which broke at the elbow. He pried the fingers from Marcy's throat and tossed the limp limb out the window.

"Go!" he yelled.

They drove no more than two miles before the VW's engine abruptly quit though the gas gauge read a quarter full. They'd made it to the beach road and could see the glowing commotion near the pier in the distance.

"What the..." Joel said and jumped out. He walked to the back of the VW and lifted the engine cover. Something had been drug underneath the VW and pieces of it had lodged in the engine. Body parts, it looked like: tiny, thin body parts.

"What is it?" Marcy said.

"Nothing." Joel dropped the engine cover before Marcy looked inside. "We'll have to hoof it. You much of a running woman?"

Marcy smiled. "Anything you can do, Joel."

◻ ...

Alixel lay motionless atop LaFitte's treasure. Both of her Creation Daggers were now mixed in with the mass of coins that pictured the Wayeb symbol. Sand fell into the pit and covered her feet.

"You know," Albert said to Janine. "The neat thing about having this Antichrist job is how quickly you pick up on things. You pull a lever and you bury a princess." The backhoe arm swooped across the mound of sand and Janine leapt from it as the bucket pushed more into the pit. The cubits that had emerged from the surf formed a circle around the excavation.

Janine could have escaped but, for her, that was not an option. Revenge and rescue had taken control. She ran at the backhoe, ducked under Albert's attempt to swat her with the machine's metal arm and jumped up onto the side of the cab. Albert kicked her in the face and she flopped backward and onto the sand at the feet of one of the cubits. The cubit kicked the dagger from her hand.

"I've been meaning to tell you something, my love—something I've waited an entire year to say." Albert, standing in the cab, loomed above her. "I used to be a pretty decent guy. Never could control that Beam addiction though. That's what Mikey used to say. 'That Albert Stine wouldn't be such a bastard if he'd just let loose of the bottle.' But you see, as much as ole' Mikey was my friend, he always had something that I never would... you know, because of the drink and all." Albert stepped down off of the backhoe. He pointed his dagger at her. "So I took what I could not have." He laughed. "Mikey didn't die in no combine accident. You've always known that haven't you, hon? Of course I killed him. How else was I going to get the farm? How else was I going to get you? I just wanted you to know that he suffered immensely before he died. Bleeding to death without legs and arms is a hard way to go. As you will shortly find out."

Rain pelted Janine's face so hard she could not see Albert clearly as he knelt down, the dagger in his hand. She scrambled backward, searching for her own weapon that the cubit had kicked out of her reach. Albert's dagger came down, the point angling for one of her sand-thrashing legs.

☐ ...

It wasn't until the backhoe arm knocked Alixel into the hole that Billy reacted. He'd been sitting there hugging the Book of the Djed to his chest, thinking about the slaughter in front of the cottage apartment building and how easy it was going to be for the two women to rid the world of the two men who had done so much harm. The women didn't need his help; the women could take care of business; Good would prevail over Evil.

But then the blood spots appeared, and the cubits emerged from within, and they walked as if on top of the water to the shore, and they surrounded the women and the hole and the police cruiser.

And when Alixel was gone, all that was left to save them was Janine.

And himself.

Several cubits stood near the cruiser but none attacked it. It was as if they were waiting for orders to commence with the killing. Billy was going to use the lull in their activity to his advantage and run to the aide of Alixel, but when he tried to open the car door, Antiago winds pressed it back upon him. The rain came down so hard that he could not see outside the car's windows. Albert not only controlled the dead, but apparently the hurricane as well.

He crawled over the back seat and sat down in Andy Collar's drying blood. The cruiser's engine was still running and he flipped on the wipers but the rain fell too fast for the wipers to catch up. He knew it was probably a hopeless effort but he tried the cruiser's radio.

"Hello," he said into the handset. "Can anyone hear me? I'm in a state trooper's car at the Caldwell Pier and we need backup. A murder is in progress." He waited to the sound of static. "Hello. Anyone there?" He dialed through numerous channels only to receive the same static response to his requests for help. Then he turned on the public address system.

"Stop!" he shouted. "This is the police!"

⬚ ...

Two things happened almost simultaneously and together they saved Janine's life. The pounding rain pelted her ear holes, making Albert's voice sound hollow, but Billy's voice was sharp and much too loud for any human's vocal cords: "Stop!" Billy yelled. This distracted Albert long enough for the second action that saved her life. Out of nowhere, someone rushed Albert, planted their shoulder in Albert's rib cage just below his dagger-wielding arm, and took him to the ground. Janine wiped rain from her eyes, kicked with her heels, rolled, and her hand came down on a dagger which she assumed was hers but was Albert's. A scuffle ensued on the ground in front of her; wet sand fishtailed into the air. One of the fighters was propelled backward and fell at Janine's feet, crumpled and broken. She toed the body face up.

Joel!

She tried to scream his name.

Joel!

He gasped for breath. His neck was bent at an odd angle.

Joel!

She knelt down to push the rain water away from his nose and mouth.

"Ja…ja…Janine," he moaned. "Janine…I love you."

And then he said nothing else.

"JOEL!" she suddenly screamed, releasing an energy that had been roiling inside her for an entire year. "You son-of-a-bitch!"

Albert laughed as loudly as Janine screamed. He stood above them, his eyes blazing crimson. Silver streaks in his pupils danced with delight. And then, suddenly, his expression changed to one of great concern. The dagger Janine held began spreading its bright iridescence in a halo around her. She found her own dagger and snatched it from the sand; its glowing haft added to her confidence and her rage.

And then she held nothing back.

She lunged from a crouched position, a cat toward its prey, the daggers held forward like tiny bayonets. Albert backpedaled into the sand pile and tried to climb it backward, his arms in the air as Janine slashed at them with both daggers.

"That's for Joel," she screamed and sliced off Albert's left hand.

Albert scaled the sand pile in retreat.

"And that's for Lenny!" she wailed while planting another blade into Albert's forehead. Janine released the dagger and the haft, glowing brightly, remained between his eyes. He topped the sand pile and fell to his knees, grasping in vain at the dagger with his handless left arm.

"And this is for Michael!"

With one wide, swooping motion, she stabbed Albert in the back of the neck right below the skull. The silver in Albert's pupils spun erratically. The red irises bulged. The red jades in both daggers became so bright that life seemingly jumped from them. Albert's head began to shake. His teeth broke and flew from his mouth.

And then he exploded inside a bright flash of red light. The top half of the sand pile blew apart.

Marcy, who had sprained her ankle as she'd ran with Joel, was sitting a half mile from the explosion. She would later explain that something had split the dark clouds and had sucked the red ball of light into the heavens.

When the ball of light was gone, so were Albert and Janine.

☐ …

Billy had managed to exit the police cruiser and join Alixel at the bottom of the excavation just before the explosion. When he reached her, she was already alert and had recaptured her two daggers. She nodded in the direction of the third dagger which still remained planted in the ground.

"It's not over," she said.

Billy grabbed the glowing dagger and it released freely into his hand like Excalibur to Arthur. When he looked up, Janine and Albert were no longer there but the cubits had formed a circle at the perimeter of the hole and were looking down at them. One of the cubits suddenly jumped and Alixel quickly stuck him in the back of the head as he landed beside her; the former owner of the Mustang Ranch withered at Billy's feet. Another jumped and Alixel made quick work of him as well. By the time the tenth cubit jumped into the hole, Billy realized what was happening. They weren't jumping in, they were being pushed. The wrath of Hurricane Antiago dropped them in one by one as if helping Alixel remove them from existence.

Slowly Billy and Alixel rose from the hole on the accumulating bodies of former Port Aransas residents. Billy had not used his dagger once. When they reached the top, a single cubit remained. It was Bottlenose, the owner of Pat McGee's and Billy's closest friend. The Bottlenose cubit stood between them. Alixel stepped away.

"You have to do it, Billy," she said to him.

"But he's my friend." Billy remembered how he had almost let the Steph cubit take his life. He'd almost kissed it. How was he going to kill his best friend?

"It's not over," she said again. "There will be others that you'll have a harder time with." Alixel scaled the partially leveled sand pile and stood where Janine had destroyed Albert. "The future is in your hands."

Bottlenose attacked. Billy was thrown sideways by the storm's winds and he swung the dagger, haphazardly, not really wanting to stab anything. Bottlenose turned and lunged, and, again, Billy was aided by the hurricane which knocked Bottlenose down at his feet.

Billy looked up at Alixel and stood there mesmerized as Bottlenose, writhing in the sand, grabbed his foot. He could almost see through her. He could almost see the backhoe's frozen arm behind her. He blinked and she faded further.

"You have to do it," she said, lifting both arms and both daggers into the torrent of rain and wind. "For all of us."

Billy brought the dagger down, the blade slicing into the back of his best friend's neck. Bottlenose's hand went limp atop his foot, then the body withered like a prune and lay motionless at his feet.

Billy looked back to the top of the sand pile in time to see the bright light where Alixel once stood. He covered his eyes and crouched to the sand. The hurricane's wind and rain raged around him with such force that he thought it would suck him into the sky.

Then it was over.

Alixel was gone. The hurricane was gone. The bodies of the cubits were gone. LaFitte's treasure was gone. All but one of the daggers was gone. Dark clouds remained overhead but the wind and rain had stopped. He'd been clutching the dagger so hard that when he now released it, the mark of the star from its haft remained embossed into the palm of his hand. And lying on the sand next to his hand was a page ripped from the Book of the Djed. Wayeb sat atop a myriad of symbols that were too ancient for Billy to comprehend.

"Billy!" someone yelled.

He grabbed the key and looked around. The backhoe was there as was the police cruiser. In the distance he saw Marcy waving at him. Her limp made her collapse to the sand a hundred yards away. Billy jumped into the police cruiser and drove to her rescue.

PART III

A NEW BEGINNING

Friday morning, Billy handed the keys to the Surf Side over to Kale Jurgensen. He'd made a deal with the young man: take care of the business while he was gone and he'd make him a partner when he returned.

He'd never found his VW Bus and figured that the hurricane had taken it; other cars had been swept from the island. One of the ferry boats had even sunk. Most of the buildings, however, had survived. The only property that had been completely destroyed was the Port Aransas branch of the Big Texas Bank.

The Cubit was gone.

By Friday afternoon, local authorities in Port Aransas reported that more than two hundred people had lost their lives. Tiny pieces had been found that were later identified as belonging to half a dozen residents but the rest had simply disappeared. Speculation was rampant. Evangelical leaders set on scrutinizing the casino that had never been built said that the sinners had been swallowed by the hand of God. Meteorologists had suggested a more scientific explanation. The bodies had been sucked up by a cyclonic funnel from the "hurricane of the century" and had been deposited somewhere in the depths of the Gulf. The Coast Guard had been dispatched and a search grid had been created but few believed it was worthwhile. Billy *knew* they were wasteful efforts. He knew what happened to all of those people. But no one would ever believe him.

It's not over, he remembered Alixel saying.

But she'd said so many wise things which had made her seem so real. Had she been? Perhaps he would never know for sure. He had no proof and that was good because he had his belief to guide him. She existed, if not only in his mind and memory. She had saved him from himself and had put the world back on track for 2012. He now felt obligated to continue the effort. Her people, the Hopis, would help. It was, after all, his destiny.

You have to do it for all of us.

He sheathed the Creation of the End dagger, opened the Book of the Djed and replaced the key where it had been ripped free, and noticed that the center spread now fully revealed all three sixes and had begun auto-writing the next clue that would help humanity survive the End Time.

He slid behind the wheel of Steph's Cavalier, gave the book to Marcy and was quickly consumed by tears that blurred his vision. The car smelled like Steph, but more saddening was that SpongeBob sat on the dashboard and smiled his porous, carefree smile. Marcy rubbed his shoulder.

The drive out of town was slow. Debris, the media, and emergency vehicles were everywhere. But no one stopped them as they continued along Mustang Island toward Sedona.

☐ ...

The border patrolman at Brownsville Crossing #22 suspected nothing. Why would he? Pedro Melindez was a Mexican national who lived just north of Chiapas and he had the papers to prove it. Besides, the vintage VW Bus looked a lot like the one the patrolman's father had owned.

Their conversation was in the native language. Pedro had only recently begun talking with any kind of clarity. Spanish had been easier than English. The border patrolman asked him *Where are you going?*

"Mí hogar," Pedro said.

And where is your home?

"Está en Chiapas."

That is a long drive and it is very hot today.

"Sí. Pero tengo agua."

You have water. Good. What else are you bringing to our country?

Pedro glanced into the rearview mirror while rubbing the arm that was now healed from his fall off of Billy's deck. The Cubit rested against his suitcase. He had not transformed enough to worry about looking suspicious. He had, however, become aware that smiling was a very effective way of communicating with humans and Pedro had one of the best smiles around. He used it now. "Apenas yo y mis ropas," he said.

The border patrolman returned his papers but not his smile. *Be careful or the sun will make the end to your destination.*

The end, Pedro thought. It wouldn't be much longer.

Before rolling up his window and driving into Mexico, the cubited Pedro thanked the border patrolman and with a wide grin said:

"El extremo está más cercano que usted piensa."

THE END IS CLOSER THAN YOU THINK.

On
December 21, 2009
The Trilogy Continues

THE DJED
THE 2012 TRILOGY II